CHRISTOPHER CHARLES MORLEY

CHRISSER TALES

First published in paperback by
Michael Terence Publishing in 2024.
www.mtp.agency

Copyright © 2024 Christopher Charles Morley

Christopher Charles Morley has asserted the right to be identified as
the author of this work in accordance with the
Copyright, Designs and Patents Act 1988

ISBN 9781800948679

No part of this publication may be reproduced, stored
in a retrieval system, or transmitted, in any form or
by any means, electronic, mechanical, photocopying,
recording or otherwise, without the prior
permission of the publisher

Cover image
courtesy of Christopher Charles Morley

Michael Terence
Publishing

Airgunners	1
Allotment	8
Anthony	17
Big Top	24
Bleddy Boggers	30
Bobbing and Jobbing	39
Bombs Away!	47
Bournville Boy	55
Breaking the Ice	62
Cock-Dancing in the Park	69
Darfield Road	74
David	80
Dead Dog Pond	87
Dolls' Hospital	94
Frog in the Sky	99
Frogmore Street	106
Fun Fairies	115
Galley Slaves	122
Gypsy Woman	128
Hemlock Stone	140
Kodiak	150

Lemonade Lads	157
No Smoke Without	163
Not So Smarties	169
O'd King Wenceslas	176
Old Valvone	185
Panther Boys	192
Parkside Incident	201
Pelmet by Moonlight	210
Philately	215
Picnic on Snakey Woods	223
Protect and Survive	231
Richard the Conkerer	238
Saving the Eagles	247
Snow Snow Quick Quick Snow	256
Springing Mickey	263
Tanks for the Memory	275
The Treasurists	283
Tom	293
Wall of Death	301
Warrior's Way	305

Airgunners

'Richard's gorra gun!'

On the face of it that would seem quite normal. We all had guns then. I had several. Richard had just two, the one that was his and the one that he had inherited from his older brother Alan. Both these guns were identical in design. They differed only in colour. Richard's was glossy green and Alan's was glossy red. The paint job was amateur. These guns were made of two pressed metal silhouettes which were tabbed together. They would have been more convincing had they been painted dull black. Obviously, from Terry's exclamation, there was something more.

'What sort of gun?'

I had just wandered down the close and met Terry by the street lamp.

'It's 'is brother's. It's an air rifle.'

Alan was about six years older than Richard. He was at secondary school doing exams. He didn't play out on the street.

I followed Terry up the path to Richard's back door. He was sat on the doorstep clutching the weapon. His eyes gleamed when he saw us at the gate.

'Ay a look at this.'

We moved up closer as he lifted the air-rifle to his shoulder. He was pointing it down the back garden to where the dustbin stood by the privet hedge. On top of the dustbin was an empty tin baring small dents. There was a phlut followed by a ping and the tin plunged off the bin. Eagerly Terry reset the tin.

'That was me last slug,' he said standing up, 'Gonna get some more, come on.'

He turned and went in the back door. Richard had the run of the house during the day when his parents and brother were out. We followed him through the kitchen and living room and up the stairs. His Council house was more or less the same plan as my own. Richard went into the front bedroom. It wasn't as I had expected. His parents did not have that room. It was shared by Richard and Alan. Between the two single beds was a cabinet. Waiting for take-off were six Airfix aeroplanes. I was amazed by the paint finish. I had tried to build a

Spitfire and a Stuka but was not satisfied with my level of skill. I particularly admired the American Corsair carrier plane in dark blue.

'Alan meks 'em. Don't touch, or 'e'll kill me. Look in 'ere.'

Richard opened the door to the tiny cupboard space over the stairs. In my house it was crammed with my Mother's clothes. This cupboard had a chair and shelves and a table lamp. It was a space dedicated to model making. Pictures of aircraft were pinned to the edge of the shelves. The main shelf was cluttered with paint, brushes, a craft knife and glue.

Richard picked up the polystyrene glue, 'He 'as to keep the door open when 'e's gluin' or 'e might get 'igh.' Richard could see that he had an audience so he continued gleefully, 'The glue can do yer brain in. Some kids squeeze it aht into a paper bag and then sniff it. It's like drinkin' booze.'

Terry did his impression of a drunken clown and I nodded wisely. Richard opened the top drawer to a small set of drawers on the main shelf. Inside were two card boxes. He took them both out. One contained hundreds of grey metal pellets and the other held just twelve little darts with colourful feathery tails. They put me in mind of the plumes that sprouted from the helmets of my toy knights.

'The fancy uns are for target shooting. The slugs are for 'avin' fun.'

He took a handful of the pellets and stuffed them in his pocket. I picked up a couple of the fancy ones to look at and admire.

'C'mon let's go.'

I returned my hand to the box but released only one dart. He didn't notice. I kept the red plumed dart safe in my fist. The dart was transferred to my pocket on the stairs.

I thought that Richard would continue shooting at the tin can. But he announced that we should take our fun *over tins*. Richard was well aware of adults' attitude to guns in the street, so he pushed the slender barrel down inside the waistband of his short flannel trousers and concealed the butt beneath his jacket.

Once *over tins* and away from prying eyes the gun was drawn and loaded. To load, it was necessary to 'break' the gun into a ninety degree position. This allowed the slug to be positioned, and also compressed the air. Terry rummaged along the bank of the stream for targets. He set up a couple of cans, three bottles and a headless plastic doll. Richard blazed away. I desperately wanted to try it, but was cautious of asking.

'Your turn, Tez.' He handed the gun to the beaming Terry.

Terry inserted the first pellet and took aim. His aim was good. The doll flicked over backwards again. His second shot wasn't as good. One tin can only slightly wobbled.

'Yo' nah, Chrisser.'

I took the two pellets and the gun. Suddenly I became nervous of making a fool of myself by missing the targets. Whilst I loaded the airgun, Terry reset the targets on the opposite bank. I put the gun to my shoulder and squinted along the barrel. The targets seemed a long way away. I squeezed the trigger. There wasn't any tumbling target.

'Missed.'

'Try again, Chrisser.'

I tried again. I was sure I had the target lined up.

'Hard luck, giz the gun.'

As I returned the weapon to Richard a figure appeared out of the bushes on the target side of the stream. I recognised him.

'Well if it in't o'd Adrian,' exclaimed Richard with a hint of derision.

Adrian lived on our estate. He went to our school. I was in the A stream with odd number classes, Richard and Terry were in the B stream with even number classes. Adrian was in neither stream, he was in the special class, Class 9. He was not a play mate. He was wearing the sort of cowboy hat and waistcoat that came in a dressing-up set.

'I'm looking after the cows,' he said quite seriously pointing at five or six black and white beasts in the field beyond. 'The farmer says I can. I'm a cowboy.'

Terry sniggered.

Richard said, 'Is 'e payin' you owt?'

Adrian looked puzzled, 'No.'

'What y'a doin' it for then?'

'Because I want to, and the farmer wants me to look after 'em.'

'Cahs don't need no lookin' after in a field.'

Terry kicked a stone into the water. Adrian looked puzzled again.

His face brightened, 'What are you doing?'

'Shootin',' answered Richard. He swung the barrel up to point at Adrian. Adrian looked quite worried. Richard laughed and swung the gun to one side with one hand. 'But not cowboys. Not cowboys today. We're shootin' dicky birds.'

Richard lifted the gun to his shoulder and aimed up into the trees along the bank. Phlut. A startled blackbird fluttered to a safer perch. Richard reloaded. I looked at Terry. He didn't seem bothered, but I was. Shooting tin cans was one thing, but shooting birds was something I hadn't reckoned on. I didn't like this turn of events. Whilst I was trying to think of something to say, Adrian beat me to the draw.

'That's naughty. You mustn't do it.'

Richard fired again. More birds fluttered. Adrian moved. He came across the stream using the stepping stones of broken slabs. Richard snapped the gun back together. He looked in amused disbelief at Adrian. Terry looked gleeful. I thought Richard was going to shoot Adrian, but he aimed high.

'You mustn't,' repeated Adrian. He lifted his hand to the end of the barrel.

Phlut. 'Ow!' Adrian spun away clutching the middle finger of his right hand.

'You shot 'im,' said Terry who was generally quick with the obvious.

'No I di'n't. He done it his sen. He put 'is finger on the bleddy end. The silly sod.' He reloaded.

Adrian was now alternately wagging his finger and sucking it. He was also making pained noises. I wanted it not to have happened and to be well away home.

'C'm'ere, let's 'ave a look.'

Richard waved the gun at Terry, who took, it whilst he examined the whimpering Adrian's finger.

'S'all right, s'not bleedin'. Just a lickle bruise. You'll live.'

The tip of his finger was dark purple. The pellet must have skimmed it.

Richard turned toward Terry, 'Right, let's get on with shootin' birds.'

Terry didn't move. He didn't hand the gun over.

'Giz the gun, Tez.'

'It's wrong to shoot birds.'

I could hardly believe what Terry was saying. He rarely made a complete sentence. He usually did whatever Richard wanted. He was not known for his care for animal life either. Terry was now a hero. He was the second hero today. I had not said or done anything.

'He's right. Adrian's right. It's wrong to shoot birds for no reason.' My cheeks were burning. I was ready for the torrent of abuse and maybe the fists. Richard glared at the opposition.

'They're only bleddy birds, bleddy lickle dicky bird,' he said sarcastically. He snatched the gun from Terry. 'Saint Terence of Lenton Abbey. You'll be goin' to chu'ch next.'

Terry had gone pale, having realised what he had just done. Richard moved things along though.

'Oright if we ain't gonna shoot no birds, we better go 'ome.' He made it sound like he was doing us a big favour.

'What about Adrian?' I asked.

We turned to Adrian. He had stopped groaning, but was still sucking his finger. He took his finger out of his mouth and said, 'I'm goin' 'ome.' He turned and re-crossed the stream. He could walk diagonally across the field and climb the fence into his back garden.

We turned towards the *tins*. As we approached the pile of garden rubbish, which made climbing back easy, Richard made to conceal the weapon. He pushed the muzzle inside his waistband. Phlut. 'Ow! Ow!' He staggered into Terry. It looked like he was trying to pull his sock up. He continued squealing. He sat down clumsily pulling the gun out of his trousers. A bright red bead appeared on his left calf.

'He's shot his sen,' Terry said with the voice of disbelief.

Richard was now rolling about, moaning and cursing and clutching his leg. The red bead had smeared across his calf. He sat up with his cheek pressed to his knees. Tears rolled freely across his contorted face.

Terry picked up the gun, 'He musta forgot it was loaded.'

'Friggin 'ell,' gasped Richard, 'I can't go 'ome like this. Ow. Alan'll kill me. Me dad'll give me a belting.'

I looked at Terry. He made a small shrug.

'We'll get an ambulance,' I began, but Richard cut me off.

'No, they'll find out. I can feel it just under the skin. It's got to come out.'

He looked up at me. His eyes looked like he had been peeling onions all morning.

'Chrisser, go an' get some tweezers, an' a plaster,' and then to Terry he said, 'Tek the gun 'ome. Put it in the wardrobe. Here's the key.' He took the back door key from round his neck.

I gave Richard my handkerchief. Terry never had one, he used his sleeve.

We left him sitting in the grass whimpering. Terry looked apprehensively at the gun. He must have realised that it was no longer loaded, so he stuffed it down his trousers. At the point where Terry would turn off I said, 'Meet you back here in five minutes. Get Alan's hobby knife.'

I walked up the close trying to be calm. Washing had been hung out and Mother was standing talking to a neighbour over the back. I quietly slipped inside. *One of our guys was left on the ground in enemy territory. They might be closing in for the kill. This was a rescue mission.* I opened the left hand door of the sideboard and pulled out the second drawer. This was where the medical things lived. I pulled the lid from the tin box that bore a red cross on a white disc which Father had painted. I lifted the shiny tweezers, two large *Elastoplasts* and a small bottle of TCP. As an after-thought, I tore off some cotton wool from the roll. She was still talking when I slipped away.

Terry was ready with the knife. It had a hard plastic guard over the sharp bit. We galloped back to Richard. He was sat in the grass hugging his knees. I showed him the things that had been collected. He nodded.

'Tez, yo've got to get it out.'

Terry looked mortified. 'I can't.' He looked at me. 'Chrisser can do it.'

'Please,' Richard moaned.

'Lay down on your tummy,' I said, wondering who was talking.

He rolled over. I started to tremble. Terry was breathing hard. Richard's calf was smeared with blood. All those scenes in cowboy films crowded my mind. It wasn't a Sioux arrow.

I tore up the lump of cotton wool. One piece was dowsed in TCP. I began to wipe away the blood. Richard groaned and twitched. I nodded to Terry. He got the message and knelt down to hold the leg. I could see where the pellet had gone in. There was a one inch maroon line under the skin. At the end of it was a raised lump. The pellet had not penetrated deeply, but had travelled just under the surface. I looked at Terry. He looked ill.

'I can't pull it out with the tweezers. It's gone too far. I'll have to cut it out.'

Richard moaned again. Terry looked frightened. I picked up Alan's modelling knife and removed the plastic guard. 'Hold him tight.' Terry sat across Richard's back. I put my knee onto his ankle. I took three deep breaths.

The knife was very sharp. It wasn't necessary to cut much at all. The pellet was exposed easily. I exchanged the 'scalpel' for the tweezers. Richard gasped as the pellet was lifted. I sloshed TCP onto the area.

'It's aht,' said Terry. The colour was coming back to his face.

I wiped away the TCP and the blood. Terry had come alive, and had a plaster ready. I jammed it over the wound quickly.

Richard sat up and examined his leg. He patted the plaster.
'That plaster won't last long. Here's another.'
He took it and mumbled, 'Fanks.'
'What yo' gonna tell yo' mam?' asked Terry.
Richard chewed his lip. 'I done it on some barb' wire *over tins.* Chrisser's mam stuck the plaster on.' He stood up and winced.

I took the surgical instruments over to the stream for a rinse. I also rinsed Richard's blood from my hands. Richard put the hobby knife into his jacket pocket.

Richard was wearing various sticking plasters for the rest of the week. He was also wearing a bruise on his right cheek. Terry told me that Alan had hit him. Alan knew that there should be twelve competition darts in the box. There were eleven. Only Richard could have taken it. Richard had denied the theft. Alan hadn't believed him. Alan knew that Richard told lies.

A man-at-arms in my toy box had recently been promoted. He was now wearing a bright red plume on his helmet.

Allotment

'Letter for you, Ken. It looks official.'

What she meant was that it was typed on a brown envelope. We never had bills through the post. Gas and electricity were both coin in the slot, and the rent was collected fortnightly. My Parents received hand-written letters and post cards. The postcards came only in August from one or other of my Aunties. It was always the same message: Having a lovely time. Digs fine. Weather good. The hand written letters were also predictable. My Grandfather in Yorkshire kept my Father up to date about working in the coalfields.

'Don't like the look of this. I hope it's not another flaming call-up. I'm too old for that now.'

I was suddenly excited about the prospect of my Father 'returning to the colours'. He had spent six years shooting at Germans before I was born. He was recalled during a national emergency in the early 1950's. The enemy was now the Russians. I could just about remember the disappointment of not receiving a weapon on his return. I got a stick of rock.

'It's from the council. They are offering me an allotment. Why? I didn't put my name down.'

'I did. Don't you remember a while back I read a notice in the Evening Post? I sent a post card. I told you.'

My Father laughed, 'Yes, but I never thought I would click. The list's as long as your arm for allotments. What would I do with an allotment anyway?'

When my Parents were just starting married life in a Council house, my Father had plans for growing food in the garden. Unfortunately, a month later, Adolf Hitler invaded Poland. There was a short spell before my father was conscripted: this time was spent planting an Anderson shelter where the vegetables would have been. It would have been little use having my Mother look after the garden as she went to work full-time making soldiers' uniforms.

Six years later my Mother was pregnant. The baby would need a lawn to play on. The ground for the main lawn was cleared and seeded. It was made ready for me to crawl about on. Later, when older, I would stare wistfully at the rockery at the end of the lawn and try to imagine the air-raid shelter hidden beneath the rocks. Of course it wasn't there:

the Council had removed the corrugated panels and the hole had been filled in.

I assisted my Father in preparing a second patch for lawn. This involved making a hole to take the garden rubbish. Digging over and raking flat was the next step. I was intrigued by the milk bottle tops which were threaded onto cotton. The cotton was stretched between short sticks placed around the perimeter of the lawn space. My Father told me that it was to scare away the house-sparrows from eating the grass seed. I had the best job: scattering the seed. Sadly, the lawn wasn't there the next day ~ it would take weeks.

My Mother returned the acceptance slip for the allotment. Another letter arrived saying exactly where the allotment was situated. The Council houses on the estate all had generous gardens, so there wasn't much land devoted to allotments. There was a slender stretch of land between the rec' and the backs of the first set of houses. This land could be accessed through the church grounds at the top end, or through a gate hidden in the privet hedge alongside Woodside Road at the other end.

'Come on, Sunshine, get your bike out and we'll take a look.'

I was surprised that Father said that we would cycle there because it was only five minutes' walk away, but it was Sunday: the day for bike ride, whilst Mother prepared the dinner.

We parked our bikes just inside the gate on Woodside Road. The ground rose steeply for a short distance and then more or less levelled out. It seemed very strange looking at the rec' through the railings and bushes.

'It says plot number three. Can you see any numbers, Hawkeye?'

There was no demarcation between the plots. The only way of telling where one ended and another one started was by the change in vegetation.

'There's a man, Dad.'

'Hello, we are looking for plot number three…'

The man, about my Grandfather's age, straightened up, 'Ah, that'll be owd Frank William's place. It's that un there behin' you, the one wi' the shed. Are you the new bloke?

'Yes, I am. Thanks.'

'Bit on a mess. Frank didn't do much towards the end. He were right poorly. He died a while back.'

We moved back to the plot. It looked desolate. Plants had grown and died without being harvested. Either side the plot was in good order. It was plot number three if the counting started on the left inside the gate. A shed stood at the back of the plot, close up to the rec's railings. It was a very small shed. It was about the size of a sentry box. The door had a small window with a cracked glass pane. My Father tried the door, but there was a rusted pad lock.

'Gordon Bennett. I'll bet he had the only shroud with a pocket.'

The plan was to return with a hack saw, a new lock, some territory pegs and string and gardening tools. This would have to be the next Saturday. I was itching to know what was in the shed.

It was Saturday morning when we set off again. This time we had all the kit. When we pegged out the territory we realised that a battered old dust bin and a compost frame were included.

'The bin's got holes in to let the air in when it's used for burning stuff.'

I quite fancied getting a bonfire going.

'And it's had a good while to rot down in the frame. It'll make good food.'

He grinned at my look of horror, 'Not for us: for the plants.'

We tackled the shed. The padlock gave up very quickly. It had been impossible to look in through the dirty window pane, but now all was revealed. I was disappointed. A grubby raincoat hung from a nail. A clutch of worn out tools slept in a corner. The creepy-crawlies scuttled from the intruding light. I had been hoping for treasure.

'I reckon these tools were used on the pyramids.'

My Father's tools were not a lot better. His had been bought second-hand at Sneinton market, along with a dolly-tub and a ponch for their first home.

He brandished our spade which had been strapped to his cross-bar, 'We'll need to clear the jungle before we can turn the earth.'

I pulled up the stalks while my Father began scraping off the vegetation. After almost an hour the plot was all but clean. The scrapings were shovelled into the compost frame.

'Well, corporal, that's enough for today. Do you fancy a pint?'

This was my Father's way of saying that we were going home.

In the following week I boasted about the allotment to my associates Richard and Terry, Richard declared an interest in seeing the 'new frontier.' I gave them a guided tour one afternoon on the way home from school. We would use the gated end, and exit the allotments through the church grounds to approach home from the other end of the street.

I began to wonder why Richard was showing such interest. He had little time for anything that was not an advantage to him.

'There's nowt growin'.'

'We haven't planted anything yet.'

Richard sniffed and scanned around, 'Ain't binnin 'ere before. P'r'aps one of the uvver plots is growin' summink int'restin'.

I could hear the cogs turning in his brain. He was plotting something. I wished that I had said nothing about the allotment. I could only think that he might have an idea to lift some produce and sell it 'on the black market.' This he had already tried out with scrumped apples.

My Father came home with several packets of seeds. I liked the peas. They were dry and hard, and would be just right for a pea-shooter: if only I had one. Of course the ground wasn't ready for planting: it still had to be dug over and hoed and raked. For me, the initial excitement was fading. There seemed to be far more work than I had expected.

The ground was dug over on the next Saturday. Father did the digging: I used the hoe to break up the lumps.

'We should take out the twitch, but I've only got the one lifetime.'

We returned on the Sunday morning to finish the hoeing and start the raking. It was beginning to look good. This time we did have a pint, or rather my Father had the pint and I had a small bottle of pop at *The Priory* across the road.

The next visit to the allotment was to begin planting and stringing bird-scarers. Whilst my Father was prodding little holes and filling them with seeds, I turned my attention to the shed. The door sagged open with the new padlock on the hasp. I stood inside pretending to be a sentry at Buckingham Palace. I pulled the door shut to experience the enclosure. It swung open. I gave it a good pull and it bumped shut. Something hit me on the head. The door was rapidly pushed open. There was no nasty spider in my curly hair. At my feet on the tatty piece of lino was a key.

'Hey, Dad, look what I found.'

He looked up to see me waving a Yale type key on a tag.

'It must be the key we couldn't find.'

'Wonderful, and a fat lot of use now. We slung that old lock and fitted ours.'

He went back to sprinkling tiny seeds in a long shallow trench. I examined the key tag. It was a grubby card edged with metal. Something was written on one side: *Box*.

'It says 'box' on the tag. Shouldn't it say 'shed'?'

'How should I know? Chuck it away. We're nearly done for today.'

'Why was it on the inside?'

'Dunno, p'raps the old man was a magician.'

I didn't do as he had suggested. The key was put into my pocket. It was a sort of souvenir.

'The man on the wireless said there's rain coming in. We're in for some heavy weather, Ken. Strong winds across the Midlands.'

'Hope it doesn't blow all our planting away.'

The sky darkened. Anything loose outside began to fly around. The rain came sideways. I hated this sort of weather. The gusting wind kept me awake. It rattled my bedroom windows. I hid deep under the eiderdown. A dustbin lid clattered across the yard.

By the morning the rain had ceased and the wind had dropped to a slight breeze. My Father said that we ought to take a look at the allotment. It was like a battle field cycling through the estate. Anything loose had been scattered about. A couple of ornamental garden trees looked like they had been bought in Pisa. There was even a vest in the gutter.

'Jiminy Cricket, the shed's gone!'

It hadn't disappeared altogether. It was several yards further along and on its side. On closer inspection it proved to be out of shape, but our new padlock had held the door on.

'At least we can get it back on our plot.'

As we were about to lift it, I noticed that there was hole at the bottom. It was not wind damage: it was a neat rectangle. The floor had seemed solid enough when I had stood on it.

We lifted the shed back to our plot and placed it on its back. Now it looked like an Egyptian sarcophagus. My Father unlocked and opened the door. The ancient tools and tatty raincoat were still jumbled inside. So was the piece of lino, and what looked like a little door. It fitted the rectangular hole.

'P'raps Mr Williams was digging an escape route like in *The Wooden Horse*.'

I went over to examine the site where the shed had stood. House bricks were arranged like a little fortress for the shed to stand on. Inside the perimeter the earth was bare. In the centre was a piece of metal chain protruding from the ground.

'Funny place to have a toilet. Why don't you give it a pull? I'll stand over here, away from the blast.'

I knew it to be another joke, so I held the chain with two hands and pulled. It came up so easily that I almost fell over. There had been only a thin skim of earth covering a box.

'Could be treasure in there, or it might still be a booby trap.'

The chain was looped around the biscuit-tin sized box. The box was wrapped in cloth.

My Father examined the find.

'It's oil-cloth to keep the wet out. Must be something worth going to all this trouble for.'

The chain was slack and could be easily slipped off. When the oil-cloth was pulled away there was a firm metal box. My Father gave it a gentle shake.

'Nothing loose in there, but the lid is locked down. Did you throw that key away?'

'No, Dad, I've still got it here.' I pulled it out into the light. He grinned.

He held the box whilst I tried the key. There was a click and the lid moved. He grinned again.

'What do you reckon, Sunshine? Jewels?'

'A Luger?'

'You think there's a German pistol in the box? Open sesame.'

He pulled the lid up for me to see the contents. He must have seen my eyes light up.

'Gordon Bloody Bennett. Do you know what we are looking at?'

I nodded, 'It's money like what Granddad had in the tin under his bed.'

Previously, on a visit to my Grandfather's, the old man had showed us the ARP medical tin under his bed. It was mostly black with a red cross on a white disc When My Father saw what was inside he was quite sharp with my Grandfather.

'What on Earth have you got this lot under your bed for? Why isn't it in the bank?'

'Happen I like to have it handy. Anyway I don't trust banks.'

My Father insisted that it was taken to the post office straight away. I hadn't recognised the large old fashioned white five pound notes: my Father never had any. These were in bundles held together with rubber bands.

'There's bloody hundreds here, Dad. Anybody could walk in and take it. You don't lock the back door most of the time.'

My Grandfather grumbled but did go with my Father to deposit it in his savings account.

Now I recognised the fivers in the tin. My Father closed the lid.

'Mouth shut, Sunshine. No names, no pack-drill. We need to do a bit of thinking.'

He straightened up and casually looked around. There was only one other person in sight. It was the man we had spoken to before. My Father re-wrapped the tin in the oilcloth and gave it to me. He winked.

'Hello, bit windy last night.'

'Aye was anall. Look it's knocked all these down.'

'The man who had our plot, Mr Williams. What do you know about him?'

The old man pinched his nose and clicked his tongue.

'Not a lot. Kept himsen to himsen. His wife died years back. He had a son what was killed at Alamein. He lived on Audley Drive, over yonder.' He pointed to the houses which backed onto the allotment. 'Some other people live there now.'

'I was wondering if he had any relatives. There's a few bits in the shed…'

The man grimaced, 'I wouldn't bother, mate. He never mentioned anyone, as I recall'

'Thanks.'

We stopped by the shed long enough to scrape some earth into the empty hole.

'I s'pose by rights, we should hand this in at the police station. He might have some relatives who would have a claim. Why was it all hidden though?'

'He might have been a bank robber.'

My Father laughed, 'Doubt it. Still keep your mouth shut, Jim-lad. Don't go telling Richard or Terry or anyone. For now we'll take it back home and count it. Right?'

'What would happen if you gave it to the police?'

'They would give me a chitty. And if it was not claimed, they would give it back after a few months.'

'How would anybody know that it was at the police-station?'

'I guess they would make inquiries about his relatives. But it doesn't seem that there are any.'

'Good grief, Ken, that's four hundred pounds. What are we going to do?'

My Father leaned back staring at the little piles of five pound notes and lit a *Park Drive*.

'What do you reckon, Geronimo?'

I had roughly calculated that with that amount I could get twenty posh Hornby train sets or over a thousand toy soldiers. I shook my head. The money wasn't really ours, but we found it. It was on 'our' plot.

'Don't know.'

After I had gone to bed my Parents sat and talked. In the morning a decision had been made.

'Your Dad said we'll keep the money. Most of it will go into your post office savings account. We'll keep a bit to spend. You'll get ten pounds to spend.'

She lowered her voice, 'You mustn't tell anyone, do you understand?'

The bulk of the money was paid into my savings account in small amounts over a period of time. My account was already bulging with money that I was not allowed to spend. I did not know then that this was my start on the property owning ladder. Ten pounds was given to me in smaller amounts. I was allowed to spend it as I liked. I liked Hornby's new Standard 4MT tank locomotive. It became mine, as did a couple of Dinky army vehicles and some more soldiers. Nothing was squandered on sweets. My Mother had a new long 'swagger' coat from Marks and Spencers. My Father bought a new sports jacket from Dunns. I kept my mouth firmly shut.

'Hey up, Chrisser. How yo' getting' on wiv that 'lotment?'

'The soil's too sticky to anything with. My dad says we'll leave it a while to dry out.'

'Y'oughta plant some pennies, an' lerrem growinta money trees.'

Richard began laughing at his own joke. Terry joined in with the merriment.

I laughed with them, but not for the same reason.

Anthony

'What have you got to say for yourselves?'

We just stood there looking dejected. I could guess what it was about. Mr Reeves glared at each of us in turn,

'I've been talking to Mrs Payne this afternoon. An*th*ony's mother.'

He pronounced 'Anthony' with a 'th'. We knew very well who he was talking about. I had guessed correctly. There was only one incident that week worthy of arraignment before the head teacher.

Mr Reeves rose from his desk chair. He was very tall and very imposing in the grey three piece suit. I chanced a glance to the right. Mrs Greenfield was hunched over her typewriter. I glanced to the left to view the line-up. I couldn't work out why Gary was there. Like me, he didn't do anything. I supposed that he was there because it was his garden hedge.

'Mrs Payne tells me that her son was viciously attacked by a gang on the way home from school yesterday. What have you got to say?'

'Sorry,' mumbled Terry.

'Sorry for what, Terence?'

'Sorry,' repeated Terry. He wasn't the one for words especially when an explanation was involved.

'I didn't do nothing,' blurted Gary. Gary King was the only other one of this line-up who was in my class. Terry was in the 'B' stream and Richard was in the year above. Richard and Terry lived on my street. Gary lived on the way home. We liked to sneak a look in the register which had our names in alphabetical order by surname. 'King Gary' was amazing.

'I was there but I didn't do nothing to An*th*ony,' he pronounced the name with the 'th' as Mr Reeves had. Miss Hilton had instructed us to do this. I had a friend called Anthony, but he pronounced it without the 'th'. He was called Tony anyway.

Mrs Payne had insisted that her son be addressed as An*th*ony. We all thought this was 'posh' and far too posh for a Council estate. If anyone actually wanted to speak to Mrs Payne's darling, the word 'fatty' was used. Anthony Payne was in the same class as Gary and I. He shouldn't have been. Early on Miss Hilton said that he was joining our class because he was far too clever for the year below. Someone said that he needed stretching. We thought so too.

He lived on the same Council estate and went to the same Council school, but he seemed to be from another planet. He never played out. During school playtimes he hung around on his own or with some girls. The girls barely tolerated him.

He was indeed clever. He already knew all the times tables and could spell difficult words. He read thick books too. Anthony knew all the answers.

Anthony was tall for his age, but he was also rather chubby. My Father said that he had been fed on 'Royal Jelly'. I assumed this was what had made him fat and different. I was intrigued with his academic abilities, but I didn't like his personality. He was disdainful about the short comings of other children. He spoke like the announcers on the wireless.

'Terence, you said you were sorry. Sorry for what?'

I glanced at Terry. I could almost hear his brain attempting to get into gear. He had learnt that if one 'coughed' early on the adult's anger might be lessened. He opened his mouth.

But it was Richard who spoke.

'He was askin' forrit.'

'Who was?'

'Payney, I mean Anfony, sir.'

'How so?'

'Well, we seen 'im 'avin' a go at this lickle kid.'

Terry's mouth was still open.

'Which younger child?'

'Dunno, sir, just a lickle kid. He was stranglin' 'im. Rahn the neck. Tight.'

'Who was strangling who?'

'Anfony was stranglin' the lickle kid.'

On the way home, the previous day, we had come across an incident. There was a scuffle on the street outside Gary's house. Several children were watching. Anthony was shrieking.

'I've had enough. Leave me alone.'

He was shrieking at a smaller boy. It was patently obvious that the smaller boy was in the game of teasing Anthony. He had gone too far. Anthony had both hands around the boy's throat. Richard bounded forward to the rescue. He recognised a good excuse for thumping Anthony. Richard grabbed Anthony's collar from behind. Now *he* was being choked. He always wore a tie.

'Ow, get off me.'

The little boy was released. He staggered away with red marks to his neck.

The watchers cheered.

'You bully, Payney.'

Anthony twisted around to meet his assailant.

Richard was two years older, but Anthony was almost the same height and weight. Richard was nimble and a street fighter. Anthony didn't stand a chance. I had little sympathy for Anthony. Terry was gleeful. Gary was on his own front door step.

'He was calling me names. He's always calling me. I have had enough!'

'You was stranglin' 'im, Fatty.'

Anthony shrieked again and began flailing his arms. Richard was in no danger. He deftly thrust both hands against Anthony's chest. Anthony was not able to deal with this. He was caught off balance. He fell backwards onto Gary's front hedge. The privet bent obligingly for the boy's bulk. Anthony rolled head over heels onto Gary's front lawn.

There was much laughter from the audience.

'Get out of my garden.'

Anthony regained his feet. His cheeks were very red and tear stained. He was in a quandary. The privet hedge had sprung back. So he had to use the gate.

'C'mon, let's go,' said the victor.

'So you decided to intervene and be a hero?'

I detected the controlled sarcasm.

'I didn't 'it 'im. Just pushed 'im, a bit'

'Pushed him through the Kings' hedge?'

I thought I heard Mrs Greenfield cough.

'Four onto one. That's not really fair is it?'

I wanted to say that it was only Richard, but it didn't seem right.

'Chrisser and Tez di'n't do nowt,' offered Richard, 'Nor Gazzer.'

I thought that Richard had got me off the hook, but Mr Reeves still seemed grim. Suddenly it occurred to me that Mrs Greenfield was typing letters to take home: Death Warrants. Richard and Terry would throw theirs away. But I couldn't.

My cheeks were burning. I was a good boy. It wasn't my fault that I lived near Richard. Even if I had decided to intervene, there wasn't enough time. It was all over in a minute.

'Now, what to do with you, Master Church?' Mr Reeves stared steadily at Richard. 'I am not at all surprised by your involvement. We have crossed swords before. You are going up to the Seniors at the end of the school year. You don't really want the knowledge of this sort of behaviour going with you.'

'No, sir.'

'So, do I have your solemn promise that you will keep away from Anthony Payne from now on?'

Richard was no longer slouching, he was now standing to attention.

'Yes, Mester Reeves, sir.'

'Good, let this be an end to the matter. I can report to Mrs Payne that her son will be spared any more abuse.'

'Sir, yes, sir,' Richard was going for full exoneration.

'Go home, boys.'

Outside school Gary soon scampered off. I was obliged to drift home with Terry and Richard. I was still delighted at not being told off and not to be carrying an envelope.

'The lickle fat sneak, he snitched to 'is mam,' growled Richard.

'He did get shoved through that hedge,' I replied.

'Yeah, but he deserved what 'e got. "'E shoun't ov snitched.'

The moral reasoning was sometimes baffling. I knew that there was a code of honour between criminals. It never made sense to an honest-john such as me. My Father had explained vendettas, blood feuds and honour codes. He said that that there was no obligation to cover for the wrong doings of family or friends. The Law must run its course and meet out punishment if necessary. I understood. I agreed, but it was difficult sometimes when my playmates were the wrong doers.

'I'm goin' ter friggin' well do the fat lump.'

'What?'

'Anfony- panfony the grasser, the snitch is goin' to get done.'

'But you promised Mr Reeves... and he'll tell his mam again.'

'I'll fink of summat clever.'

Terry beamed. He liked 'clever'. To him it was a branch of magic.

Mrs Payne escorted Anthony to and from school. I would hate to be taken to school holding hands with my Mother. We kept away from Anthony during playtimes. He spent his lunch break in what was optimistically called the school library. It was a redundant cloak room with the pegs removed. Word had spread about the incident. The verbal pot-shots had ceased. 'Fatty' Payne was allowed to increase the size of his brain in peace. I imagined him turning into the *Mekon*.

Richard didn't repeat his threat nor did he reveal any cunning plan of revenge. I had other concerns. As an 'A' streamer I would eventually transfer into Mr Hall's class. This was daunting because I had difficulty deciphering his 'posh' voice, and there was a rumour that he kept a slipper in his desk.

I associated more with Geoff and *Sacko* than with Richard and Terry. Geoff and I built a trolley together. I went trainspotting with *Sacko*.

One Saturday morning I bumped into Richard outside Woffington's on the parade of shops. He was chewing at a Mars Bar (which was probably not paid for). He had that special glint in his eyes.

'I've gorra great ideh. You know Fatty Payne never comes out wivout 'is mam. Well, he does sometimes, now.'

He grinned and tapped a finger to his head.

'I fahnd out that he started tekkin' vi'lin lessons. An' can you guess where?'

I shook my head.

'Dorothy-Grant's-School-for-posh-kids.'

This was a private preparatory school close to the boundary of our Council estate. It was on a lane which was also used to cut through to Beeston High Road.

'Fatty goes on 'is own on Sat'day mornings between arf pas' ten an' arf pas' 'leven. I fink he could 'ave a nasty accident.' He laughed.

What was he planning? I remembered being scared by Richard jumping out of the dark in our Close. He had a torch aimed up his face and he made a terrifying noise. He thought it hilarious. I almost wet myself.

'We can jump out on 'im. We'll pounce on 'im when 'e's coming back frough the twitchel. I'll bet 'is vi'lin cost a lot of dosh. It just might get trod on.' He laughed gleefully.

'Are you going to hit him?' Things seemed to be getting out of hand.

'Nah, won't 'ave to, only if 'e's stupid. He's gonna be so scared he'll shit 'is pants.'

'Won't he recognise you and Terry?'

'Nah, 'cos, 'ere's the clever bit, we'll be in disguise. Do yo' want to come an all?'

It sounded like a jolly good wheeze, a piece of harmless fun. I wasn't too sure though about wrecking an expensive violin.

'What's the disguise?'

'We got some masks. Horror masks. Tez's sister got them from a horror party she went to. An' we can have o'd sheets rahnd our sho'lders. Are you on?'

'Depends which Saturday. Sometimes we go shopping in town.'

'Well, can you come rahnd safto and see what we got?'

The masks were amazing. They were moulded in a thin plastic. Each of the four masks was painted in lurid colours. Inside them it said, 'Made in Hong Kong'. Richard chose the best. We tried them on. Richard and Terry looked alarming.

'An' I got theses o'd curtains from me aunty,' said Richard.

These too were horrible, but in a different sort of way. Richard and Terry practised jumping about, waving their arms and making fearsome noises. It was difficult not to join in.

'Right,' said Richard, 'Next Sat'day. Meet here to collect the stuff at 'leven o'clock. That will gi' us plen'y of time to gerrin position.'

I worried about this all week. What if we were recognised? What if the violin really got broken? What would Mrs Payne do? What would Mr Reeves do? What would my Father say? I thought about pretending to be ill.

'Put your coat on, Chick, were going into town.'

My mother had solved the problem. Whilst the gang of two were assaulting Fatty Payne, I would be trailing around Marks and Spencers with my Mother: Wonderful.

It wasn't until the Monday at school that I got to talk to the young assassins. I was expecting wide grins of triumph, followed by a full account of the ambush. It was not so.

'Fatty din't turn up. We waited an' waited, but we never seen 'im. A couple of people come past. They give us funny looks. We kep' peepin' over the hedge, but he din' come.'

Terry said nothing.

'Any road what 'appened to you?'

I explained about having to go into town with my Mother. Richard just frowned.

Anthony was not in class. Julia Billington told me that he had left. Miss Hilton confirmed this. She said that Anthony was at another school. He had been for a hard test. He had got something called a scholarship and was now at the Boys' High School in town.

'We could frow a brick frough 'is winder,' suggested Terry.

But Terry's subtle suggestion was thwarted.

'I was talking to Eileen on the shops. She told me that the Payne's have moved. You know, that clever plump boy Andrew.'

'Anthony,' I corrected.

'Wasn't he in your class? He spoke ever so nicely. They moved to Wollaton'.

Well, that was some relief.

'Eileen wasn't sorry they'd gone though. She reckons Mrs Payne was stuck-up. He was alright, but he was out working most of the time.'

I continued sorting through the pieces of my Meccano set, wishing it was the next size up.

'The Payne's are buying their new house. We nearly bought a house in Beeston, but the war came along and put a stop to that. Do you think we should buy a house?'

It was one of those daft questions like 'Should we go on a skiing holiday' or 'There's jobs at Boot's new factory in Airdrie, would you like to live in Scotland?'

Richard and Terry messed about in the masks for a while. They never really played at anything. The elastics soon broke and the masks were binned. Mr Hall was not as fearsome as I had imagined. If there was a slipper in his desk, I never saw it. I never saw Anthony again, but I saw his photograph in the Evening Post. He was posing with his mother at a school prize giving. He'd just been presented an award for his skill with the violin at such a young age. How lucky he was that Richard had not broken his fingers.

Big Top

They both froze. Eyes and mouths were wide, but no sound. Richard's right hand began to wobble slightly.

'Chrisser, keep still. Don't friggin' move.'

Terry just squeaked.

'Listen to this.'

My Mother liked reading stuff out of the *Evening Post*. My Father was tutting over something in *The Daily Mirror* and I was studying *Dan Dare's* efforts against the terrible *Phants* in the *Eagle* comic.

'There's a circus coming. But it's not going to be on the Forest. It's coming to Wollaton Park.'

I had been taken to the circus when I was much younger. The clowns were wonderful. But it was a trek to the usual site on the Forest in town. So, as with Goose Fair, I readily accepted the bribe not to go.

'It's not the usual one. It's Billy Kettle's. It's got everything: acrobats, animals and clowns.'

'We don't need to go the circus, Bridget, we've got all those round here.'

'Would you like to go to the circus, Chick?'

I wasn't sure. My Father was negative, but my Mother seemed to be making an offer. It would be very much nearer on Wollaton Park. The decision was taken out of my hands.

'Amen. Hands down, eyes open. Now, I've had a letter sent to me from a Mr Kettle. Some of you might have heard of Billy Kettle… Quiet please. Pay attention. I see some of you are aware of Billy Kettle's circus.'

Mr Reeves, our head-teacher, paused until he had our full attention.

'Well, Mr Kettle has kindly invited you all to see a show.'

All the children took a letter home. It explained that there was a free short show for junior children. The show was to be one afternoon fairly soon. Our school and a couple of others near to Wollaton Park were invited. My Father said that it was a good bit of advertising because the children would want to be taken to the full show by their paying parents. I was delighted.

'It's comin' at the weeken'. A parkie to'd us. Me an' Tez are gunna ay a look. Are yo' comin', Chrisser?'

I had already anticipated this. Richard was always keen to be with the action: especially if there might be some advantage.

'Yeah, when are you planning?'

'Right after school on Friday.'

This would be fine by me because my Parents would not be home from work until five-thirty, and it took only a few minutes from the Park: especially if we went over the wall as usual. I decided not to tell my Mother: she wasn't over keen on me associating with Richard and Terry.

'Hey,'urry up, ah can see 'em. There's loads o' vans.'

Richard was first up, of course, and was now straddling the Park wall. Terry and I scrambled up. We could see brightly painted circus vehicles parked neatly. Between the ha-ha, alongside the lake, and the cinder track up to the Hall was a very large flat space covered in grass. Several games of football could be played there at the same time. The circus vans and caravans were arranged in line near to the ha-ha. The ha-ha was a deep trench to prevent the Park's deer from wandering into the public areas. There was much activity around a massive white thing lying on the ground.

'Geronimo!' We dropped down and rolled to take up the shock of the jump.

As we approached the circus area we saw the great white thing rise. Men were heaving on thick ropes to pull erect the two main tent poles. The white poles were like telephone poles but twice as tall. Our way was blocked by a rope barrier. Iron spikes had been hammered in every three yards to hold the rope. We stood and watched.

I could just about set up my ex-army tent on my own in our back garden, but *this* was a staggering exercise. The big white tent grew wider. The circus folk pulled on more ropes. Smaller poles appeared through holes in the canvas. The ropes were secured to more long iron pegs. When the tent was completed, the erection team gathered around one of the vans which served tea and buns. This made me think: I looked at my *Dan Dare* watch. It was time to go.

The chosen date was the next Wednesday. I scoffed my lunch and raced back to school for the long march. The whole of the junior school would crocodile down Boundary Road and along Derby Road, the A52, to access a gated entrance to Wollaton Park. It was about a mile. We had had full instructions in the morning about how to behave, what to take and how to stay safe. I walked with Geoff. Terry was in the 'B' stream class and Richard was in the year above. Some mothers had been recruited to help keep the children on the pavement and stop them walking into lamp-posts. This didn't prevent 'Twilmop' and a couple of others from stepping into dog mess.

We stayed in formation from the gates right into the big-top. There was a circular central area covered in saw dust. Also arranged in a circular fashion were dozens of simple benches. We were guided onto the benches. A couple of other large groups of juniors from nearby schools completed the audience. The show began as the last children sat down around two o'clock.

It was the usual stuff. A ringmaster in a red tail coat did the announcing. Horses galloped around with girls standing on their backs. Between the acts, clowns dashed in and made the audience shriek. The buckets of 'water' were, of course, filled with little twists of cellophane. A small elephant did balancing tricks. Acrobats and jugglers did amazing stunts. Three acrobats performed high up on trapezes to lots of oohs and ahs. We were asked to be very quiet towards the end of the show. Tall railings were set up and a couple of tigers came into the ring. A young woman got the tigers to do tricks on command. The show was slick and fast and ended at ten past three. This would give plenty of time to march back to school for the end of the afternoon session at four o'clock. Nobody was allowed to slip off home, even if the crocodile passed close to their house.

'My best bit was the acrobats on the trapeze.'

'Ahr liked them gre't big tigers.'

'Ahr fought the clahns was good. I wanna be clahn when ah grow up.'

Richard laughed, 'You won't grow up, Tez, an' your'e already a clahn.'

Terry seemed bewildered.

'Ahr know, lets g'back nex' week when the circus is finished. We can pick up spilt dosh like after the fair.'

'Can we look at the aminals anall?'

Many children, Terry included, were a bit miffed that there wasn't enough time to visit the animal cages on the free afternoon. Paying customers and their children were invited to look at the animals before a proper show. The elephant was a favourite because it accepted vegetation from small hands. The scary tigers were kept in cages on the back of trucks. When the trucks were parked up, the sides and back end were let down to give the animals some fresh air. All around the two tiger trucks there were notices warning of the danger of getting too close. The ponies were happily tethered on the grass just waiting to be patted and fed sugar lumps.

The circus was scheduled to depart the following Friday. They had a booking in Derby. Richard reckoned that we could clean up the small change after school. So, as previously, we scampered to the special climbing place on the Park wall.

'Ay, guess what?'

This was difficult as Richard was on the top of the wall whilst Terry and I were still climbing.

The circus was still there. The big-top was down but the vans were still parked.

'Urgh, shalluz g"ome?'

'Nah, we c'n still ay a look-see. There's nob'dy abaht.'

Actually there were four men busy with the canteen wagon. We reckoned they wouldn't notice us moving stealthily like commandoes. We approached the target, scanning the trampled grass and also watching out for adults. Richard was quietly jubilant when he found a sixpence.

'The aminals!'

Terry forgot the search for coins and moved over to the elephant which was standing quietly munching. We followed him. Terry was delighted with holding out the elephant's feed for it to be taken up by the trunk. Richard scowled. I glanced around wary of being seen. The tiger wagons caught my eye. The sides were down and a tiger was glaring through the bars. I just had to get a closer look. I stood a sensible distance from the cage. A tiger was standing. It looked restless. I wondered if it could smell the Park deer.

'Where's the uvver one?'

Terry had abandoned the elephant and joined me. There was only one tiger in the cage. The next wagon was also posted with warnings. There was no tiger. The cage was empty. I noticed that the cage door at the end of the vehicle looked like it wasn't in line. It wasn't shut. I turned back to my chums.

'This cage isn't shut properly.'

Richard and Terry looked frozen. Eyes and mouths were wide, but with no sound. Richard's right hand began to wobble slightly.

'Chrisser keep still. Don't friggin' move.'

Terry just squeaked.

I sensed something behind me. Terry and Richard were moving backwards carefully and slowly. They looked terrified. As the penny dropped I felt some pressure against my right side. I glanced down. The huge missing tiger rubbed past me. My knuckles felt the fur. There was a warm wet sensation in my pants. The big cat took its time. It stopped and turned its head to the right and towards the other tiger. They both snarled.

'Keep very still, boy.'

It was a woman's voice. I dared to look away from the tiger. A young woman and several men were moving steadily towards me. The woman was holding a large whip. It was the woman who had made the tigers perform tricks.

'Rajah, roll over, roll over, Rajah.'

The great striped beast snarled again, and rolled over on its back like a pussy cat.

My arm was taken and I was pulled away. My feet were not helping.

'You alright, boy?'

I couldn't speak. Another man was talking to Richard and Terry. Rajah was being coaxed back into his cage. Three men were having an animated conversation by the cage door.

'I s'pose you ain't been that close to a tiger afore.'

He was smiling. I just shook my head: my teeth were jammed together.

Richard, Terry and I were led away to cups of tea and biscuits. I thought we were in for a good telling off, but the circus people were very friendly. A deal was stuck. They wouldn't 'report' us if we kept quiet about the tiger on the loose. It had been an accident with the cage door. It wouldn't be good for the circus if the story got into the newspaper. To seal the deal Billy Kettle, himself, gave us half a crown each. Richard was delighted. I felt very damp.

Of course I was a little late home. I thought about making something up about sitting in a puddle, but my parents read my expression. I wasn't ever concerned about leaving things unsaid, but I had reservations about telling actual fibs. It felt much better blurting everything out. The crying helped too. My Mother was shocked at first and gradually changed to being relieved. My Father said that he had been in some sticky situations in the war but nothing like rubbing up against a tiger. He seemed amused.

The next day I was quietly advised against getting involved with Richard and his schemes. My promises would be of short duration. Mother and I went shopping in Beeston. I spent Billy Kettle's half-crown on some toy soldiers.

Bleddy Boggers

'Tez come up wiv a gre't name. We'll call ahrsens *The Bleddy Boggers*.'

I winced at just hearing the name. It was close to being rude. My Parents would be very upset to know that their darling son belonged to such an organisation.

Mid-August was far enough away from the end of the summer term and nowhere near the start of the new school year. It was hot and getting boring. There was no seaside holiday or even a spell at Grandfather's in Cudworth. Most of my friends had gone away. My toy soldiers were nearly worn out with endless battles over the back lawn.

Richard never went on holiday. The best he got was a day at his aunt's house in Radford. I met him on the corner of the parade of shops when I had been sent on an errand.

'Hey-up, Chrisser, I've got a gre't ideh.'

Richard's ideas were something to be cautious about. They usually concerned generating money, but usually generated trouble.

He had that gleeful look.

'There's nowt to do, so we could mek it more lively.'

He had assumed that, because I was listening to him, I was in full agreement.

'We can mek a gang.'

'A gang?'

My Parents frowned on *gangs*. It was only naughty rough boys who joined gangs.

'Yeah, a gang. We could be really bad.'

Gangs were composed of several members. 'Who's in the gang?'

'Me an' yo' an' Tez. We'll get some more. I'll be the boss.'

(He didn't need to say that.)

'We'll have special outfits. An'a den. An' secret pass words.'

'What would the gang do?'

'Like I said, bad things.'

'Like what?'

'Swearin' an' shoutin' an' stealin' an' brekkin' stuff.'

'I've got to get some Typhoo for my Mum.'

The following day I met him again on the street. He was with Terry. I was half hoping that the gang idea had been dropped, but the other half was interested in being naughty. I wasn't naughty. It had been difficult for me to purchase some bubble-gum when I had been advised to stick to spearmint chewing-gum. Two hefty pink lumps were crammed into my mouth. They were difficult to chew at first. The taste was sickly sweet, but only for a few minutes. When the gum became pliable the flavour had gone.

'Hey-up, Chrisser. Tez come up wiv a gre't name. We'll call ahrsens *Bleddy Boggers.*'

I winced: he grinned, 'Good innit? Tell 'im arh yo' fought on it, Tez.'

'Ahr Glenys, when Arh 'noy 'er, she calls me a *bleddy bogger.*'

Glenys was Terry's big sister. She was sixteen and keen on ballroom dancing competitions. Occasionally a car would deliver a new dance dress. The dress was constructed of layers of brightly coloured net. This was exotic on the Council estate street in the early 1950's. Neighbours came out to stare. It wasn't too difficult to imagine Terry annoying his sister. He could be annoying standing still doing nothing.

'Tez wants to join. D'yo', Chrisser?'

Before I could give an answer he continued.

'New members of the gang 'ave to swear to keep it secret an' do what the boss says.'

(Of course).

'An' they 'ave to pay freppence subs.'

(I guessed who would hold the sub money)

'But firs' there's the test.'

'Has Terry done the test?'

'No, not yet. I fought it would be a good way ov sortin' aht who was second in command.'

(This would be easy: Terry was in the 'B' stream at school.)

'What's the test?'

'Well, firs' y'ave to nick a fag an' smoke it in front of the boss. Nex' y'ave to shout summat rude on the shops. Then, last, y'ave to pull a gell's dress up to show 'er knickers.'

Terry was smirking. I began to wonder if they were having me on.

'What's the rude word?'

The boss lowered his voice: 'Tits'.

Terry's smirk had grown into a grin.

'Yo' two on then?'

Terry nodded gleefully. I just nodded.

It wasn't difficult taking a cigarette. My mother kept a packet of *Park Drive* on the kitchen table. The cigarette was secreted in an empty *Smarties* tube. Luckily the packet had been started. I didn't smoke. I had tried one once. My Father gave me one and watched while I made myself sick. I was hoping that I wouldn't be 'poorly' during the test. Richard pinched cigarettes from his parents.

The performance was *over tins* away from prying eyes. Richard had a box of matches. Terry had a cigarette in his shirt pocket. His cigarette was bent and grubby. He pushed it between his lips ready for Richard. The boss struck a match and held the flame to the end of the battered cigarette. Terry heaved and the cigarette began to glow. The initiate took the cigarette from his mouth and blew out a wisp of blue smoke.

'Right, nah yo' 'ave to tek dahn.'

I was puzzled. Terry returned the cigarette to his mouth and sucked hard. His eyes seemed to wobble. He pulled the cigarette away and coughed out a great cloud of smoke. He also bent double coughing and gasping.

'Great, Tez. Nah your turn, Chrisser.'

Terry had dropped his cigarette and was clutching his knees and making puking noises. I put my pristine Park Drive between my lips. Richard gleefully struck a second match. I sucked and tasted the acrid smoke. I wondered why my parents did this. I wondered why most adults did this. I sucked hard and immediately felt giddy and sick.

'Good o'd Chrisser. Yo' passed anall.'

We hovered around Mr Leek's shop window pretending to be interested in the dummy packets of sweets. There were a few adults on the parade of shop: mostly mothers pushing prams and two older men talking about The Great War. Half a dozen young children were either trying to climb on the pillar box or just hanging about.

I clenched my fists and shouted. We turned to look accusingly at the climbers. A couple of adults looked shocked. I had got in first so I must be ahead of Terry. After a few minutes Terry yelled, 'Tets.'

We carried out the pantomime of seeming shocked and glaring at other children.

The final part of the test was more problematic: we had to find girls who did not know us. To do this we visited Beeston rec just below the

High Road. Terry was itching to even up the score, and I was determined to be second in command. Mothers were with smaller children but there were a number of juniors around the swings and slide. I targeted a girl in a gingham dress. With my heart pounding I approached her from behind, and with two hands pulled up her dress. I didn't see her knickers: I was too busy escaping the shrieks. Richard was convulsed. Terry looked glum.

Two girls were looking and pointing my way. Terry raced up behind them. He tugged at a dress with one hand. I saw a flash of navy blue. She lashed out at her assailant. Her hand hit Terry's face. He staggered on, but gained his balance enough to run after us.

'Looks like Chrisser's second boss.'
    I felt good. Terry didn't seem particularly bothered.
    'What about the gang outfits?'
Richard looked like a grandfather at the Pasach meal when the youngest asks why the evening is so special. He drew something from his trouser pocket. The boss pulled a lady's stocking over his head. The transformation was amazing. He could still see, breathe and speak but his facial features were distorted. His face seemed to have melted.
    'I got the ideh off a picture Ah seen. These 'Merican gangsters robbed a bank in masks like these.'
    Terry and I gushed with admiration. We both wanted to be similarly anonymous.
    'Jus' borrer one of yer mam's stockin's.'

With only slight misgivings I took a stocking from the linen basket in my Parents' room. I tried it on in front of the dressing table mirror. The figure in the glass was not me: though it did occur to me, that I could be identified by my clothes.
    'Yeah, well, Ah bin finkin' about that, Chrisser. 'An' you know what Ah got annuver gre't ideh. On Mondays the bin men come. O'd man Pretty puts rubbish aht the back on his shop. There's usually some sacks what spuds come in. The best are onion sacks. They not so mucky.'
    It took only a few seconds to walk down the service alley at the rear of Mr Pretty's and snaffle the redundant onion sacks. We cut slits on the edges for our arms and heads with Mrs Church's kitchen scissors. After trying on the outfits it was decided to cut slits up the side edges to allow freer movement of our legs. Of course the sacks were now

upside-down, but that didn't matter as it was printed in a foreign language.

'Gre't we're ready for the swearing in. Raise yer right han".'

Terry and I stood to attention, hands raised and facing Richard. We repeated the oath.

'I swear to keep the *Bleddy Boggers* a secret.

And never snitch on the others.

And do what the boss says.'

I was glad that nothing drastic like cutting thumbs and mingling blood was asked for.

'Are there going to be other members?'

'Bit diff'cult at the mo' 'cos uvver kids 'ave gone away. An' some kids, like your pal Twilmop, ain't tough enough. But when wo'd gets arahn they'll be flockin".'

Terry said, 'What we gonna do nah?'

The initial enterprise was a terrorist attack on the Baby Clinic in the church hall at the top of Boundary Road across from our school gates. Babies were taken there to be weighed and checked. There were always prams parked outside and nearly-mothers waddling about. The plan was to run in, shout the battle cry and run back out.

We lurked behind a low wall and donned the outfits. On Richard's command we bundled through the open doors.

'Hey, look what you're do…'

'Bleddy Boggers!'

'What do you think you're…?'

But we were gone and back behind the wall pulling off our outfits.

Flushed and beaming, with hearts still pounding, we sauntered down Wensor Avenue. The boredom of the long school holiday was certainly dispensed with. I felt elated and wanting more.

'What shall we do next, boss?'

The next stunt was to splash our name in paint.

'Yo' see there's this 'ouse on Baslow Drive where an o'd lady used ter live. Well, she's gone ter live in a nome or summink. The 'ouse is empty an' waiting on the Council to come and do it up. We'll do it up fer 'em!'

'How will we get in?'

Richard flashed his special grin, 'Arh back door key fits.'

He must have been trying his key beforehand. It was a well-known fact that on the council estate of five hundred houses there were only half a dozen patterns for the back door keys.

'Can yo' get some paint, Chrisser? An' some brushes? Bright colours.'

Whilst my parents were at work I collected the necessities from our garden shed. There were a couple of tins of pale emulsion. I settled for two small tins of Valspar. One was black and the other was red. Both were gloss paints. It didn't occur to me to take the white-spirit cleaner. I picked up two narrow brushes: the others were too wide to dip into the tins. Everything was secreted in an empty shoe box.

The *Bleddy Boggers* walked down the side of the target house. The back door opened easily. Once inside we robed up. The empty house was eerie. It was exactly the same shape as my own house. I was always intrigued how the uniform Council houses were so differently furnished and decorated inside. There was no furniture now, only the ghostly outline of where it had been. The decoration was bland beige flowered wallpaper to the living room.

'Right, Chrisser, let's see what yo' got.'

I removed the box lid. Richard pounced on the red paint, but the lid proved difficult because it had been sitting in our shed for months. He resorted to his pocket-knife. After some grunting and swearing the lid was prised off. The next problem was the skin that had formed. Richard stabbed around until he was able to flick out the tough dry skin. He looked like a killer holding the knife dripping red.

'Here, Tez, you do the uvver one while me an' Chrisser get to wo'k.'

He began to write *Bleddy Boggers* in large red capitals on the chimney breast. He got as far as *Bleddy Bog...* and ran out of space. The size of the letters was adjusted drastically. Richard had red paint on both hands.

'Soff,' proclaimed Terry.

'Pop up stairs and do the bedroom.'

Terry and I glanced at each other. Neither of us was too keen to go upstairs.

'What's a marrer wiv yo' two?' snarled Richard. 'Foller the boss!'

He surged out of the living room and we followed him upstairs. The two bedrooms were empty.

'Get cracking, Tez.'

Terry hesitated, and then had to admit he couldn't spell the words. So I said the letters, one at a time, whilst he slowly wrote in shiny black paint. Richard thrust the other paint brush into my hand. The paint was well down the handle and it was sticky.

'Baff-room.'

Before I could begin the 'decoration' there was a rattle at the front door. We froze. There were voices below: men's voices. The front door banged shut.

'Bloody hell, Frank look at this.'

'God Almighty that'll take some covering… it's still wet: can't have been done long.'

'How'd they get in? Best take a look round.'

Soon, very soon, they would come upstairs into Madame Tussaud's and see the three strangely dressed dummies with hands lathered in paint. Caught red-handed. Caught black-handed. I glanced at the boss. He had rubbed his nose with a sticky hand. It was now bright red.

'The back door's not locked.'

Richard put his finger to his lips. I was hoping the boss had an exit plan.

'We must have surprised them in the act.'

'Yes, they must have shot out the back as we came in the front.'

'They left their stuff: shoe box and two tin lids.'

As I was about to die, my past life swelled in front of me. Or at least the last few days did.

What was I doing? I shouldn't be in a gang with a rude name. I shouldn't be a nuisance and a vandal. I should be safely at home playing with my toy soldiers in the back garden. If I ever got out of this I would say my prayers every night and clean my teeth more carefully.

The paint, what of my Father's paint and his brushes? My hands were covered in rapidly drying Valspar. How could I explain this away.

Richard pointed to the window. Terry and I shook our heads. There was an expanding puddle around Terry's feet. I knew that he had been threatened with dire consequences if the police ever came to the house again.

'Do you think they done anything upstairs?'

Heavy boots started up the uncarpeted stairs.

Richard frantically pointed at the little cupboard that fitted over the stairs. Luckily the workman started in the bathroom. This gave us enough time to take rapid careful steps to the hidey-hole. The door was left slightly ajar, as shutting it would make a noise. We stood squashed together, holding our breath and peering through a narrow slot.

'Urgh, no, they've been up here too.'

The other workman came up into the main bedroom.

'Ah, well, we best get started.'

Two sets of boots clattered down stairs and the front door opened.

There was a slender chance. Terry whimpered. I began a silent prayer. Richard moved decisively. He paused at the top of the stairs. Muffled voices could just be heard in the front garden. The front door was wide open. We crept down hearts pounding with terror. Terry and I were still holding a tin of paint and a paint brush each. Richard scooped up the shoe box and headed for the back door. We slid out into the yard. Across the weedy lawn were the high pointed railings guarding the university grounds and a possible escape route. Unlike Twilmop's back garden there were no places to climb. We huddled against the corner of the house. Obviously we couldn't escape through the front. Two Council workmen in white bib and brace were unloading a hand cart.

I paused to press the lids back onto the tins and put them with the brushes into the box.

Richard did a double hand signal towards the privet hedge between the back gardens. He flung himself over and we followed. This had to be repeated over two more hedges to get to the other end of the terrace. I don't know if anyone saw three performing clowns from their kitchen window, or how I managed to keep hold of the shoe box. We had escaped.

Stocking masks and sack shirts were quickly dragged off. Some of the red paint had got through Richard's nylon mask. He looked like Rudolf. Carefully and casually we sauntered down the entry and onto the street. A man in white bib and brace was taking something out of the hand cart. He looked at us and then turned away. We strolled to the corner of our street. Once out of sight, we ran.

The clock in Richard's kitchen said four ten. My Mother would be home from work in just over an hour.

'Yo' two wait 'ere an I'll get the turps from arh Alan's box. And don't touch nowt wiv yer sticky 'an's.'

We rubbed the white-spirit over our painty hands. It was reluctant to come off. Richard found an empty jam jar for the brushes. He sloshed the white-spirit in and frantically worked the brushes up and down. Gradually our hands became clean and so did the brushes. Soap was used for the final stage: especially to get rid of the smell. It was nearly five o'clock.

As the slightly pink soapy water drained away, I blurted out, 'I don't want to be a *Bleddy Bogger* anymore.'

'Me neiver.'

Richard looked taken-a-back, but only for a moment.

'Yeah, right-o.'

I raced back home and rapidly washed my hands and brushes again. Paint and brushes were returned to their respective places in the shed. The messy shoe box was folded flat and stuffed into the dustbin along with the onion sack and the nylon stocking.

I sat on the lawn with a small army trying to regulate my breathing. The gate clicked.

'Hello, Chick. Have you been playing soldiers all afternoon?'

'Mostly. What's for tea?'

Bobbing and Jobbing

'Urgh, what yo' two up to?'

'It's Bob-a-Job week. Geoff and me have been earning money for Cubs.'

Richard's expression of mirthful contempt changed to focussed interest, 'How much yo' got, then?'

'Well, this morning we got a shilling each for getting rid of some sacks of hedge clippings,' boasted Geoff. 'We had to dump 'em *over tins*.'

I chipped in with, 'So far this week I got eight shillings and Geoff's got six.'

Richard's eyes gleamed. Terry continued to say nothing.

'How much d'yo' get to keep?'

'Nothing. It's all for the Cubs.'

Richard gave a burst of laughter, and Terry managed a grin.

'Yo' wo'k all the school 'oliday for nowt?'

Geoff started, 'Well it's not exactly…'

Richard cut him off, 'What's to stop yo' just keepin' the money?'

I held out my Job card. 'Everything has to logged on this card.'

Richard scrutinised the Job card. He grinned, 'If yo' had two cards, yo' could put some of the jobs on the fake card. And keep it.'

Geoff was about to point out the irregularity, when Richard cut him off again.

'Listen, these are cheap cards, anyone can mek 'em. Our Alan's got some card and a John Bull printing set. It's a cinch. Do you 'ave to be in uniform?'

'Of course,' I replied. Neither Richard nor Terry were in the Cubs, they weren't willing to be bossed about. They had enough of that at school.

Richard's plans for making money were coming thick and fast.

'Our Alan used to be in the Cubs. He kept his uniform for me. We just need another uniform for Tez. Got 'ny ideas?'

I suddenly thought of Mike. He had joined the Cubs with me, but he didn't like it. 'Mike might still have his uniform. I'm sure he would lend it to me.'

'When does Bob-a-Job end?'

'At the weekend.'

'Right, I mek the cards. Yo' get Mike's uniform. We can do some Bobbing and Jobbing for our sens on Sat'day.'

And so it was fixed. Geoff and I couldn't remember actually agreeing with the scheme. It didn't seem too bad, though, as we would be handing over most of our earnings to Akela.

As luck would have it I saw Mike the next day. We used to play together when he lived over the shop, but now he lived with his father and new mother. He did turn up now and again to visit his gran. Some of his stuff was still at his gran's. The hardly used uniform was there, and he was quite willing to lend it to me. It would make Terry look smart for a change.

We met, as planned, under the street lamp at the end of my Close on Saturday after lunch. Geoff and I were quite amazed to see Richard and Terry looking like real Cubs. We saluted each other.

'Nah, what d'yo fink of these?' demanded Richard.

He held out four recently forged Job cards. They looked like the real thing. They could have fooled the Gestapo. We nodded sagely.

'Had to do a few before I got it right. Good ain't they?'

We nodded again. I noticed that his fingertips were stained black.

'It's no good doin' rahn 'ere. They ain't got no money, an' the Cubs have bin at it all week.'

'What about Wollaton Vale and Park Side?' suggested Geoff.

Richard nodded, 'Yeah, possible, but I was finking more of Beeston High Road. There's some posh 'ouses going to the University.'

We set off in high spirits making guesses of how much we could collect. It took only five minutes to stride along Manton Crescent, cut through Salthouse Lane and exit onto the High Road. Almost opposite was Albert Road where the houses were large and detached. Most had cars in the driveways.

'OK, me an' Tez will do the ones on the left. Chrisser and Geoff will do the ones on the right, right?'

Geoff and I left Richard and Terry talking to a man cleaning his car. After half an hour we regrouped where Albert Road joined Lower Road. Four houses declined or were closed to callers, but we had three shillings between us. Richard grumbled about getting only a shilling between the two of them for collecting buckets of water and throwing them over a car. Geoff and I had a shilling each for moving a large pile of compost into another site.

'What we need is a big job,' declared Richard, 'or we'll be here all friggin afternoon gerrin' enough for a tube of Smarties.'

The marble in Terry's brain rolled into a slot, 'What abaht the big 'ouse at the back of Dorothy Grant's?'

'Tez, yo're a genius.' Richard patted Terry's head beneath the green Cub cap. Terry beamed.

Dorothy Grant's private preparatory school took up one side of Salthouse Lane. It was surrounded by fir trees and laurel bushes enough to restrict the view to the back. The bushes and trees continued around onto the High Road. There was a gap in the greenery after a few paces beyond the turn into the main road. A crumbling brick gate post rested either side of the gap. I noticed the kerb drop opposite this entrance. Hanging sadly from one of the gate posts was the skeletal remains of a wooden gate bearing an unreadable name. I had passed by many times without wondering what lay beyond. Beyond was a winding driveway which made the house barely visible. It all looked unkempt.

'Obviously they need a lot of jobs doing,' said Richard cheerfully.

'If there's anybody there,' said Geoff glumly.

Richard led the way for the rest of us cavaliers.

There was a big old red brick house with several chimneys, but more surprisingly there were signs of life. Parked in front of the main door were two vehicles. One was a shiny Morris Traveller in black, the other was a not so shiny Bedford three tonner. The truck was still wearing its army green paint but the military signs had been painted out. Trucks like this were sold off cheaply at the Ordnance Supply Depot near Beeston. I had one, but mine was the Dinky toy version. Standing between the two vehicles were two men. One wore a light coloured mac over a smart suit. The other wore a cloth cap and a grubby jacket.

'I don't think they'll want Bob-a-Jobbers,' I said to Geoff out the corner of my mouth.

Undaunted, Richard strode on. The men stopped their conversation and looked at us. Richard stopped and slung up a very precise salute. He could put it on when necessary.

'Good afternoon, gentlemen. We are Cubs trying to earn some money in Bob-a-Job week. We'll do anything.' He saluted again.

The smarter man grinned widely, 'There you are Mr Simmonds. The cavalry has turned up in the nick of time.' He reached into his jacket pocket and pulled out a wallet. From the wallet he extracted a brown ten shilling note. The note was handed to Mr Simmonds, 'Two bob each and a bonus when they have finished.' Then turning to us he returned Richard's salute and said, 'Have fun boys.' He got into the Morris and drove off. As he did so another figure appeared at the front door. A man, similarly dressed to Mr Simmonds, staggered down the steps carrying a large cardboard box. Mr Simmonds turned to help lift the box into the back of the Bedford.

'What do you want us to do?'

Mr Simmonds smiled at Richard. 'Come inside an' I'll show you.'

I caught Geoff's glance. He was radiating caution.

We trooped in through the front door. It looked like a set for one of those films that we were too young to see. In the hall way were many cardboard boxes. There were more to the rooms either side.

'There's more on the landing. Your job is to get them all to the back of the lorry. Me an' Bert have been packin' all morning.'

'They look heavy. What's inside them?' asked Geoff.

'They are not heavy. They've got old lamps and the like that need loads of newspaper packing. There's a couple of heavy'ns with books in. You can drag them.'

We worked in pairs to shift the boxes to the truck. After twenty minutes the Bedford looked full.

'Right you can have a break now. Me and Bert will tek this load and come back for the rest in about half an hour.'

'Who does it belong to?' asked Richard.

Mr Simmonds lit a Woodbine, 'Me now. It's 'ouse clearance. It belonged to an o'd bloke who died. That was his nephew I was talkin' with. I'm doin him a sort of favour. We clear the place, no charge. We get the money by selling the bits and bobs. Any good stuff went to auction. Shan't be long.'

The doors slammed and the Bedford chugged off down the drive.

'Right, come on let's have a look rahnd.'

We poked about the ground floor. The furniture was gone, except for a massive dresser that filled one wall. The dresser was empty. There were many doors standing open. It was obvious where furniture had been from the lighter carpet or the dents in the lino. Beyond the kitchen was a room with a hand pump. It didn't work.

We raced upstairs and examined the bedrooms to find more dents and grubby carpet. Some of the windows still had curtains which were not worth taking. The bathroom had an enormous iron bath perched on clawed feet. The white enamel of the bath was stained dark brown where the taps had dripped for years. They were still dripping.

'Hey this door is locked,' called Geoff.

There was a narrow door in a corner behind an open door to a bedroom. Richard rattled the door knob. He tugged and pushed. It didn't want to budge.

'It's just a clothes cupboard any way,' said Richard.

'Yeah, wiv a skellybob inside,' suggested Terry. He waved his arms around to look menacing.

Geoff said, 'No, it looks like a door to the attic.'

I looked inside the bedroom. The wall was definitely an odd shape. There could be another flight of stairs.

We heard the distinctive chug of the returning truck.

As the men came into the hall way, we were lugging the last couple of boxes down stairs. Together we got the boxes outside and onto the back of the truck. I noticed Richard wander over to the French windows that looked into the back garden. He deftly pulled the key from the lock and pocketed it.

'Right, lads that's it. It's pay day.' He pulled the ten shilling note from his shirt pocket. Richard held his hand out. Geoff glared at me. 'Wait. I can give you change. That would be easier for you.' Richard's hand slowly drew back.

Mr Simmonds pulled out a handful of coins. He carefully counted them out to the value of ten shillings and gave them to Geoff. Richard looked furious for just a moment.

'It's all locked up,' said Bert. The two men got into the cab.

'Come on, let's go home,' said Richard. He began to pace down the drive. The truck passed us. We waved and smiled. The truck turned right onto the High Road. We stood and watched it chug away. I thought there was going to be an argument about the money, but there wasn't. Geoff gave out equal shares. We got a florin each and then a further sixpence.

Richard smirked and waved the stolen key.

'Right, they've gone. Nah we can g'back an' see what's behind that lickle door.'

'How did you get the key?' asked Geoff.

'He took it out the French windows,' I said.

Richard was off back to the house with Terry close behind. I looked at Geoff. We both shrugged and then followed them. We followed them around to the back of the house. It was probably a nice garden before the war. Now it was overgrown with nettles and brambles. Here and there garden flowers struggled for space. Richard fiddled the key in the lock. The French window swung open. He grinned and plunged in. We followed. It was very empty now and very quiet. Richard was half way up the stairs.

'What if they come back?' said Geoff.

'They won't. They took everything. They locked up,' I replied.

'What about the bloke in the suit?'

'He's not bothered about the place. He won't come back. Not today.'

We clambered up the hollow sounding stairs. Richard was rattling the little door.

'It not budge. I reckon they missed it. Or couldn't find a key.' To Terry he said, 'Pop dahn into the garden. See if yo' can find a o'd spade or summink.'

Terry clattered down the stairs.

'What are you going to do?' asked Geoff.

'I'm goin' to get this flaming door open and see what's worth lockin' up.'

Terry clattered back up the stairs brandishing an ancient spade with no cross handle. Richard pushed the blade between the door and the jamb next to the key hole. He put his weight into levering the shaft to and fro. Very soon there was a loud crack followed by lesser snapping sounds. The door was open. It opened outwards to reveal a narrow staircase. There was daylight from above. Richard went first holding the spade at the ready. We followed cautiously.

'Crikey!' Richard exclaimed.

We stood bunched together.

'There's nowt 'ere,' he said with resignation.

Geoff said, 'Nobody's been up here for years, look at the floor.'

Except where we had kicked it up there was a smooth carpet of dust. The carpet of dust stretched a long way because the room was large. It must have covered several rooms on the floor below. The walls were short and the ceiling was angled down on two sides. On one ceiling side was a sky light window. It was dappled with dead leaves. Our eyes became accustomed to the limited light.

'There is summat 'ere,' said Terry. He took five or six paces towards the window: he was making for a chest of drawers. It had five drawers. The bottom one was deeper and was missing a knob.

'No, Tez, start at the bottom one,' was Richard's advice.

Terry knelt down and tugged at the single knob. It came off. Richard laughed. Geoff and I scanned the room whilst Richard went to

Terry's aid. There were odd things camouflaged by dust. Children's toys, mostly broken, lay forlorn in the gloom. I picked up a metal figure. It was a Britain's walking trooper in a dark blue jacket and a white foreign-service helmet. It seemed to glow in my hand. Michael had the full set. There were six of these, four mules loaded with field gun parts and an officer on a horse. I desperately wanted to find the others. Geoff had toed his name in the dust then decided against it. Richard was having difficulty with the bottom drawer, so he started pulling the drawers from the top. He pulled them out completely and dropped them to the side. Two of them broke as they hit the floor. There was nothing in them. At last he could get his hands inside the bottom drawer to push it forward.

''Ello, 'ello, what's this then?'

Geoff said, 'It's nearly five o'clock.' This was the notional witching hour.

I bent double scanning the floor for toy soldiers.

'It's a gel's nightie. Suit yo' Tez!'

Terry made an animalistic noise and pushed at the insulter.

'It's five o'clock,' repeated Geoff, 'We should get going.'

I went down on my knees to facilitate the search.

Richard was now chasing about flicking at Terry with the nightdress. Terry was laughing, but not for long. He stopped dead when he heard the voice. It came up the stairs from the hall way.

'Who's there?'

We stood as statues.

'D'yo' fink it's the cops?'

'It's your fault making all that noise.'

'We are trapped.'

'It's not the law. They'd be up 'ere by now waving their truncheons abaht.'

The stairs creaked.

'It's that bloke in the Morris.'

Richard eyed the sky-light. Geoff shrugged. Terry squeaked. I started down the narrow staircase, 'It's the Bob-a-Jobbers.'

The others followed. Richard muttered unkind words. The Morris man was standing on the landing, 'What are you still doing here?'

'Mr Simmonds and Bert went off in the lorry. They told us to wait here. Mr Simmonds said he'd come back and pay us.'

Geoff said, 'When we tried the door it was locked.'

Terry said, 'So we waited, but nuffink happened.'

'How long have you been waiting?'

''Baht a nour. Then we was worried 'cos we told our mams we'd be back by five.'

'And you didn't get paid?'

'No, sir,' we chorused.

'Well, I had my doubts about the fellow. You can't be diddled out of your hard earned money.' He pulled out his fat wallet again and handed over a ten shilling note. I took it before Richard could move,

'Thanks, mester. Can you sign our Job cards, please?'

He signed them with a smart new biro. I decided I needed one just like it for trainspotting.

'We found this. Don't know if it fit's anywhere,' Richard held out the French window key. The man took it. We saluted, two fingers to the cap, and turned about like soldiers on parade.

As soon as we were well out of view we shrieked with laughter.

We raced back home. The ten shilling note was changed at Woffington's corner shop, and the forged Job cards were dropped into the bin for lolly wrappers.

The house stood empty and boarded up for years. We kept away. Eventually it was knocked down and the site levelled. Apartment blocks were built in the huge space. I am still keeping an eye out for the rest of the mountain battery crew.

Bombs Away!

The one-armed man crawled under the truck. He loosened the fuel line and caught the escaping liquid in his empty whisky bottle. When it was half filled, he stuffed his neck-tie into the open end and shook the bottle. He clicked his cigarette lighter and threw the bottle as soon as the flame appeared.

As we walked home from the cinema my father explained about Molotov cock-tails. *Bad Day at Black Rock*, starring Spencer Tracey as the one-armed man, had been a tense film. The ending was spectacular. Robert Ryan, the villain, was caught in the fiery blast of the make-shift bomb as it exploded on a rock.

'The Russians invented them during the war. They hadn't got enough ammo, so they used glass bottles and petrol. They don't make much of a bang, but they could set a Gerry tank on fire.'

'Can we make one?'

'No we can't! They are very dangerous. Molotov cock-tails are not toys. And if you don't do it right you could end up getting badly burned yourself.'

There had been a short spate of water bombs on the street that summer. Richard had a good supply of small brown paper bags. These were filled with tap water and hurled about. Unfortunately the paper frequently disintegrated before the bomb could be thrown.

Richard switched to flour bombs. These were easier to handle, but his supply of flour quickly ran out.

'Yeah I seen it anall. We could mek some and lob 'em about.'

The others looked aghast. They were imagining Richard tossing Molotov cock-tails.

'My Dad says they are dangerous.'

Richard grinned, 'Yeah they're 'sposed to be. We wou'n't do it rahn' 'ere. Do it over tins, aht the way.'

Geoff was shaking his head, 'Still dangerous.'

Richard winced, 'Ah, well if yo' are all gonna be girls…'

Richard didn't make any Molotov cock-tails. At least we didn't hear about it. If he had he would have bragged about it. The next discussion on bomb making was a couple of weeks later. Richard had been visiting with his cousin in Radford. He was full of it.

'Hey, I know 'ow to mek proper bombs. I'm not talkin' water bombs or Molotovs. I'm talking about real explosives.'

Geoff and I looked at him. He was well known to 'romance'. We also knew that explosives were not readily available.

'Me cousin's gorra mate. He showed us how to mek 'em.'

He was really excited, but he spoke in a stage whisper.

'Very simple. Yo' on'y need two fings. Guess what.'

We knew about gun-powder. It came in very small packages called fireworks. I had experimented with these in the season. A tube, strapped to a gate post, loaded with a banger and a pebble made a small bazooka. I also lit a banger and covered it with a small rubber seaside bucket. The bucket was thrown up into the air. A banger tied to a rocket was unsuccessful because the extra weight interfered with the take-off. The primitive missile struggled sideways into the hedge bottom.

'Dunno.'

'Well, I'll tell yo'. Yo' can get bofe ov 'em dahn the shops.'

I glanced at Geoff. He was shaking his head slightly.

'It's sugar and the uvver is weed killer!'

'Sugar?'

'What's weed killer?'

Richard smiled that condescending smile that young children are given.

'On their own they're harmless. But if yo' mix 'em together that's diff'rent.'

He waited gleefully.

'My cousin's mate took us to this place an' let one off. Hell of a bang. An' it was on'y a lickle bit in a match box. He lit the fuse an' we hid behin' this wall. All the bi'ds flew about.'

Terry was beaming. Geoff and I were not sure.

'Wi can get sugar dead easy... your dad's gorreny weed killer?'

My Father dug the weeds out with a hoe. There was some powder to sprinkle on the ants if they decided to come into the house. I was fairly sure that it wasn't weed killer.

Geoff said, 'No there's nothing like that in our shed.'

Richard's garden was mostly weeds so obviously there was none at his house. Terry's was the same.

'Buy some?' suggested Terry.

'Yo' gorreny dosh?'
Terry shook his head.
'Me neither.'
'Same here.'

I had money, and so did Geoff, but not to invest in destruction. Nevertheless I was intrigued.

'Well, we'll have to gerrit some uvver way.'

The other way involved breaking and entering. Mr Adams lived in the house on one corner of our close. Poor Trevor lived on the opposite corner, but he never played out, nor did he go to school. My Mother said he was a bit simple. His head lolled to one side and his tongue flopped out readily. Trevor's garden was big and empty. Mr Adam's garden was equally big but full of roses. The roses were tended well because Mr Adams was retired. He cared very much for his plants, and very little for balls that frequently bounced into his garden.

'If your soddin' ball comes into my garden, I'll cut a hole in it!'

There was always consternation when a ball bounced out of the game on the street and landed amongst the roses. It was pointless going to the door and asking politely. Whoever had touched the ball last had the job of sliding into the garden and retrieving the ball without being seen. Of course we had no love for Mr Adams.

'Yeah well I bet o'd Adams 'as got some weed killer in his shed. It's the sort ov fing gard'ners 'ave.'

'Won't the shed be locked?'

'If it is we can easily pull the lock off. The wood's all rotten.'

'Isn't it stealing?'

'Neah, not really. He deserves it for keepin' all the balls.'

He looked at us expectantly.

'Yo' on, then?'

I could not contemplate what Mr Adams would do if he caught us in the act. Nor could I contemplate what my Parents would say if they found out. I also had difficulty in thinking of anyone whose ball had actually been slashed.

The plan was simple. It was permissible to play out in the twilight for a short while. Under the cover of darkness the commandoes would slip down the Simpkins' back entry. The privet hedges were high both sides, but it was possible to squeeze through. Mr Adams' shed was actually in his back yard but butted up to the hedge. Richard would do the necessary whilst Terry, Geoff and me kept watch.

Richard had a torch and a screwdriver.

'Hey, Tez yo' 'old the torch I've on'y got two 'ands.'

These two pushed through the hedge into the back yard. There was no kitchen light. Geoff and I dithered on the path.

'Not locked,' whispered Richard loudly.

The shed door creaked open. We could see the torch beam flicking about. Someone walked down the close about ten metres away. Calling a warning to Richard and Terry seemed silly. We held our breath and cringed into the hedge shadow. The figure continued away onto the street. Richard and Terry reappeared.

'No weed killer. 'E ain't got none.'

Our local shops did not sell weed killer so it was necessary to visit Beeston High Road. Just off the main road was Acacia Walk where Mr Pilgrim ran a general store. This store sold timber, nails and screws and garden stuff. We had reluctantly contributed to the scheme. Richard was the front man with the money. He also had a story.

'Me aunty's got loads of weeds all over her paffs. She tried pullin' 'em aht, but that weren't no good.'

'Well young man we have a couple of products that will do the trick.'

The man in a light brown ware-house coat placed two boxes on the counter.

'How much?'

'Well this one is three shillings and six pence, and this smaller item is two shillings.'

'I'll tek the small un. There ain't too many weeds on her paff.'

On the side of the box was a picture of a skull and cross bones with the word 'hazard'.

'Now you be careful with that stuff, son. It's poisonous.'

Richard pulled his cherubic face, 'Don't worry, Mester, I'll give it to me aunty straight away.'

I wondered if the investment was going to be worthwhile.

Getting the sugar was far simpler, though it was necessary to be a little devious to avoid questions. Richard, assuming the role of chief magician and armourer, began the lecture.

'OK, right, when the stuff is mixed it becomes dangerous. Yo' have to be dead careful mixing it. Just *rubbing* the stuff togevver can set it off.'

'How do you mix it then?'

'Very, very carefully wiv a lickle spoon on some paper. Then we very carefully tip it into one of these cigar cases.'

Richard had a small collection of single cigar tubes made of thin aluminium. They had screw on caps.

'Firs' we knock a nole in the lid. That's for the fuse. We poke a piece of twisted paper frough making sure it ain't too tight.'

Although we had all the ingredients, Richard was miming the procedure.

'We screw the lid back on and it's ready.'

He beamed around at the bomb crew.

'Tomorro' mornin' at ten o'clock *over tins*.'

Geoff and I climbed over the corrugated iron fence. Richard and Terry were waiting. Adults did not usually come into this scrub land beyond the fence. It belonged to the university but it wasn't used for anything. We walked well away from the fence and crossed the stream. In a flat area behind some bushes Richard set out the 'picnic'.

Geoff and I had discussed this enterprise. We recognised the possible danger, but we both thought that it was unlikely to succeed. We were fairly sure that it couldn't be that easy to cause an explosion and if it was, Richard had not got sufficient knowledge to do it right. That was another problem. He had cautioned against improper mixing, what if he made a slip? We decided not to touch anything ourselves and to keep well back.

'I fought we could mek a smallen, as a sort ov test.'

That was a relief, 'Good idea.'

The magician produced a redundant lipstick holder from his jacket pocket. He began to spoon out first the sugar and then the weed killer onto a piece of drawing paper. We watched him carefully stirring the two piles of ingredients together. Terry, the magician's assistant, held the lipstick case while Richard, in slow-motion, lifted the paper and tipped most of the mixture into the shiny cylinder. He screwed a twist of paper loosely and pressed it into the hole after the mixture.

'Phew.'

'Ready.'

Richard looked around, 'I fink we'll put it over there by that branch.'

He walked over to the fallen branch and selected a suitable place.

He waved us away, 'Yo'd better tek the uvver stuff furver back.'

Terry gathered up the ingredients and we retreated to a hollow well back towards the stream.

'Ready?'

We chorused an affirmative.

Theatrically Richard pulled out a box of matches. He lit one and stooped forward. He turned and raced over to the shelter of the dip. As he slid down there was a bright flash and a startling bang. Birds took off. Smoke spiralled upwards. Richard laughed.

A dog barked some way off. We looked around. There was no one.

'Chizz, that was a noise.'

'Great wa'n't it? Nobody'll tek no notice. They'll fink it's wo'kmen, or a car back firin'.'

We went over to examine the test site. Geoff and I were still cautious. There was no sign of the lipstick case. The branch had a charred break and the grass was singed.

'Let's do a proper'n, nah.'

Richard spooned out two more, larger piles of the ingredients. He was faster this time but still took great care. There was enough to make this device three times larger than the tester. Again, Terry held the case but this time it was a cigar tube. Richard had the fuse cap ready. The twist of paper was long enough to press down into the mixture when the cap was fitted. The cap was screwed on.

'Where shall we put this one?'

It was decided to place the device in a suitable hole in the ground. The earth was carefully pressed to the tube with just the fused top showing.

I had more confidence now. The first explosion hadn't attracted the attention of adults. Richard seemed to be well in charge. It was great fun.

'OK get right back. This is gonna be good.'

We scuttled back to the safety of the depression.

'Is this far enough away?'

Geoff shrugged his shoulders and pulled a face. He didn't seem worried though.

Richard went through the lighting ceremony and quickly joined us.

We waited. Nothing happened.

'Argh, bleddy 'ell it must have gone aht. Tez nip over an' tek a dekko.'

Terry dutifully got up and walked over to the device.

'Ain't gone aht. It's still smould'ring.'

'Terry, get away!'

'Terry, come back quick!'

'Tez, run!'

Terry must have picked up the alarm in our voices. He started to move fast.

There was a sudden flash and a very loud bang.

Terry was down. Face down. It rained pieces of earth through the cloud of dark smoke.

I clawed at the grass. My heart was pounding.

'Gordon bleddy Bennett!'

Geoff was the first up and moving towards the prone figure of Terry.

I was wishing that I hadn't been there. I was wishing that we hadn't been so foolish.

'Bleddy 'ell, what're we gonna tell 'is mam?'

I staggered after Geoff. As he got close to Terry, our playmate, lifted his head. His face was covered in dirt. He rolled onto one side. We helped him up. There was no blood, but he looked dazed.

'Yo' oright, Tez?'

Terry blinked and nodded. He spat out some earth, 'Ahr tripped.'

We batted the bits from his hair and pullover.

Richard's ready smile had returned. 'That was great.'

We stood around the blast area. There was a bowl shaped piece of the ground missing. A sharp smell hung around. There was no sign of the bomb case.

I glanced around again. The explosion had been much louder this time. Someone must have heard it.

'Let's mek anuvver. There's plen'y left.'

I caught Geoff's eye. He was thinking the same.

'I don't think you should.'

'Terry nearly got killed.'

Terry had a puzzled look.

'Well we know what we're doin' now. It'll be OK. C'mon...'

Geoff shook his head.

'Me and Geoff are going home. Are you coming Terry?'

Terry shrugged. We walked away leaving the mad magician and his assistant standing.

'He's going to make another one?'

'Yeah, probably blow himself and Terry up.'

We did not hear any explosion.

'Listen to this, Ken,' Mother was reading from the *Evening Post*, 'Some silly boy has been making home–made bombs and lost two fingers.'

I froze.

'They never learn. Where was it, Bridget?

'The boy was from Radford.'

She turned to me, 'I hope you don't get involved in silly dangerous things, our Lad.'

'Oh, no, Mum, not me.'

The next time I met Richard, I would count his fingers just to be sure.

Bournville Boy

It seemed very exotic to be arriving on the X99, much more exotic than the green 19 bus which we used. The X99 was a Midland Red coach which ran the express connection between Birmingham and Nottingham. This bus stopped at the edge of our Council estate about six o'clock, and then came to rest around 6:30 pm at the bus station in Nottingham.

Brian and his mother were to arrive a little after six, according to Paul. He was waiting for them on the street. Paul, who lived next door, was hanging around with us even though he was a couple of years older and in secondary school. We were out enjoying the newly dark evening after the clocks had been altered. The darkness added a thrill to hide and seek. Very soon it would be too cold to play out. I had to be in by 6:30 anyway. That evening the game had shifted up the street to the other close, near Terry's house. Not only was it dark, but a fog was forming and giving weird halos to the lamps.

A figure loomed in the shadow between the gas lamps at the head of both closes.

'It's our Brian,' announced Paul with delight.

They were cousins. Their mothers were sisters. The visits were rare. I knew very little about Brian. I knew that he was a year older than me and that he had an older sister. I knew that he lived in Birmingham.

Brian looked like a gangster from the cinema. He was wearing a tightly-belted grey school rain coat and a flat cap. His hands were deep in his coat pockets. Below the edge of the raincoat were long socks and plimsoles. He eyed the players.

'Hey oop, our Paul.'

'You got here, then?'

'Yus.'

He was saying very little and without much emotion. His West Midland accent was strange to our East Midland ears. Roger declared the difference.

'Yo' talk funny.'

A fist shot out of a raincoat pocket and connected with Roger's mouth.

'Now yow talk funny wiv a fat lip.'

There was some laughter, but most were shocked, especially Roger.

Richard seemed delighted with the swift response to a perceived insult.

I thought to go home and was delighted by my name being called by my Father.

In the warmth and security of our kitchen I asked about Cousin Brian and Birmingham. My Father told me that Birmingham was a large city much bigger than our own. He said that it was our country's second city after London and that it was famous for making things. My Mother told me that Brian's mother and Brenda next door were sisters, and that their parents lived a couple of miles away in a Council bungalow in Wollaton. I had seen Granny Jones when she had visited. I must have seen Brian on a previous visit, but I was not able to recall that. Apparently a visit would be made to Brian's grandparents. The Brummies were only here for the weekend.

Although it was Hallowe'en time it did not figure much in our lives back then. Nobody got dressed up or knocked on doors demanding treats. The main event to look forward to was Bonfire Night, but no bonfire building had been started yet.

Saturday morning was chilly but dry and bright. My Mother asked me to pop down to the shops at the end of the street and get a pint of milk. Our milk was delivered early morning, but Mother said we would need an extra pint. On the way back I met Richard and Terry.

'Hey up, Chrisser. We're goin' up Wollaton wiv Brian. Are you comin'?'

'No, I'm fetching this milk for my Mum.'

Richard grinned, 'Brian ast us last night after yo'd gone in. 'E 'ad loads of choc'late in his pockets. 'E gets it free from the Cadbury fact'ry where 'is mam an' 'is sister wo'k.'

I fondled the cold bottle and he continued.

'Brian's gonna see 'is gran. 'Im and Paul are goin' on the bus. 'Is mam is going later.'

I'd never been on a bus to Wollaton. Sometimes I had walked to Wollaton Village with my Father and Uncle Jim for a pint before Sunday lunch. It took about half an hour to walk. Catching a bus would be much quicker. Richard clinched the proposal.

'It's on'y fre'pence. Bet yo've got the dosh.'

I certainly had enough for the return trip, but I was bothered about asking permission… and Brian's quick fist.

Luckily Paul was leaning against his gate which was opposite mine. He agreed to speak to my Mother. After all he was older and sensible.

'You, Brian, Paul, Richard and Terry. Does Grandma Jones want all this tribe in her house? Don't do anything silly with that Richard. Make sure you are home for dinner at one o'clock.'

Paul nodded furiously, 'Gran's got a clock.'

It took less than five minute to walk to the end of Woodside Road (where the X99 stopped). We waited over the road at the first stop on Wollaton Vale. I was glad Paul was in the lead. He knew where he was going: I hadn't a clue. Brian was friendly now. He told us that his mother and sister worked at the chocolate factory.

'Me sister, Maureen, when shoi firs' startid shoi could ate as much choc'lit as shoi wantid. Shoi was nearly sick at the end of the doi. Shoi couldin't touch chocies for weeks. But the workers all get free choc'lit.'

To prove this he pulled an enormous slab from an inside pocket. Before he could begin to break it up a Corporation bus pulled up. Paul asked for a thre'penny one, so we followed suit. I was now anxious about where to get off, but Paul knew and even dinged the bell. It could have been another planet: I didn't recognise my surroundings. We followed Paul onto a street of Council bungalows. Terry's brain switched on.

'What does yer dad do?'

I sensed that this was not a good question.

'Oi aint gorra dad.'

Brian glanced at each of us.

'When me mam was 'avin' me, she told 'er 'usband that the boiby weren't 'is. So he boggered off. He sometimes come to see our Maureen 'cos he was 'er dad. He 'ad nowt to do wiv me. I don't know who moi real dad is.'

Richard asked, 'Did your mam get married again?'

'Nah, she has boifrien's, but they aren't dads.'

Paul stopped at a low gate and clicked the latch.

To my surprise Granny Jones seemed quite delighted with a gang of boys. We were ushered into the kitchen and offered biscuits. I declined, but Terry gobbled as many as he dared. We stayed standing as there was only a very small folding table and two chairs.

'I'll make us all a nice cup of tea while our Brian and our Paul go in to see Gramps. He's not been well.'

As Paul and Brian went through to the living room I glimpsed an old man slumped in an armchair. I realised why he hadn't been seen visiting his daughter Brenda. The kettle whistled.

'Any of you boys prefer coffee? I've got Camp coffee.'

'No fanks, Mrs Jones we all drink tea. These biscuits are very nice.'

She smiled at Richard. He knew how to turn on the charm.

'Oh, do have another one.'

Terry's hand shot out. Mrs Jones made mugs of tea. She took three into to the living room.

Richard scanned around the kitchen. I hoped he wasn't thinking of pinching anything. There wasn't much worth having. The contents were even less than my own house. On a shelf was a row of hand painted tins. Some had labels: milk, gas, electric, bread, rent, John. I guessed they contained money. Mrs Jones returned and asked us about our families. Richard was delighted to chat on about his brother Alan who was doing exams at secondary school. Usually Richard had nothing good to say about his brother who was apparently always thumping him.

Mrs Jones explained that Mr Jones had been poorly for a while and didn't go out much. She lowered her voice.

'He wouldn't go to our Brenda's anyway. He never got on with that Sid, her husband. He reckoned Sid was a rogue, and Brenda should never have married him.'

(My Parents were of the same opinion.)

This was all fascinating, but I was beginning to feel overloaded with family problems.

The door to the living room opened and the grandsons came out. Mrs Jones offered the use of the lavatory, for which I was grateful. We thanked the old lady and waved goodbye.

'Oi've bin wiv me mates down the choc'lit factroi. We climb over the fence an' gerrinto the deliv'roi vans an' get chocies. 'S'easoi.'

Paul looked a bit uneasy. Terry looked his usual blank. Richard radiated delight. I was shocked.

'Why do you steal chocolate if they give it free?'

Brian laughed, 'Cos it's excoitin'. Sometoimes woi get chased off.'

Terry said, 'What if yo' get caught?'

'Get smacked aroun' the head!'

Richard said, 'He's fibbin'. He's mekkin' it up to show off.'

Five boys stood as statues a few metres from the bus stop. Paul now looked very uneasy.

'No, oi'm bloody not. Oi tek worroi want.'

Brian's hand came out of his raincoat pocket. He was holding a small tin. It looked remarkably like the ones at Granny Jones' place. The lid was flicked off and the contents were decanted. The now empty tin and its lid were tossed over the nearest hedge. Brian waved a pound note, 'Anoi chippers aroun' 'ere?'

Paul, the nominal leader of the expedition, just gaped in disbelief.

Richard said, 'That tin was from your gran's kitchen.'

Terry moved quickly to retrieve it from someone's front lawn.

'Sow?'

'You nicked it from our gran?'

'Shoi don't need it. Shoi's got loads.'

Terry was back on the pavement, 'It's the rent money.'

'You've got to give it back.'

'Get lost, Pauly, or yow'll gerra thumpin'.'

I could see that Paul was confused and also scared of the smaller boy. I looked around for adult help but we were alone on the street. I wished that the situation could be diffused like the bomb-disposal soldiers did with dangerous ordnance. Richard stepped up.

'Yeah, Brian, you've got to give it back. It's not nice nicking money from an o'd lady.'

'Are yow gonna mek us?'

Terry stood clutching the rent tin. Paul looked embarrassed. My chest was pounding.

'If yo' want me to.'

I knew Richard was a street fighter, but Brian may well have been a killer.

Suddenly the two were tangling. Usually with fights there was a lengthy period of insults followed by a few flailing punches. Richard had grabbed Brian's coat collar and was pounding in the punches. Brian jerked his head forward and Richard's nose spurted blood. Richard, screaming blood, hooked a leg behind one of Brian's and threw all his weight against his opponent. Brian tipped backwards with Richard heavily on top. Richard's right fist connected hard and fast with Brian's left cheek. Blood dripped from Richard's nose onto Brian's face.

'Stop it!' yelled Paul.

He tried to pull Richard up but was batted away. Richard did get up, but in his own time. He was breathing hard. He drew his hand carefully over his nose before aiming a kick at Brian's leg. Brian lay whimpering.

'Get the dosh, Tez.'

Cautiously Terry pulled the rent money out of a raincoat pocket. Brian was in no condition to object. The money was replaced in the tin.

'Chrisser, yo' tek it back t'Mrs Jones. Mek summat up. Say yo' fahn' it, or summink.'

Terry gave me the tin. I was thoroughly frightened, 'Why me?'

'I'll come wiv yo',' piped up Terry.

'What'ya gonna say to Granny Jones?'

'Dunno, yet.'

I had about three minutes to think of something that sounded plausible.

Terry did the knocking. Mrs Jones opened the front door. She surveyed us quizzically.

'Hello, again, Mrs Jones. I dropped my bus fare. So Terry and me came back to look for it. Then Terry noticed this tin on your window ledge.'

I held it out.

'Yes, that's mine. How on Earth did it get out here?'

Terry and I tried to look like extras in the Nativity scene. I hoped nobody important was listening to the lies.

'I suppose it's got money inside. You'd better check it.'

'Yeah, there are fieves about.'

She examined the contents and smiled, 'Yes, it's all here. You are good boys. Thank you.'

My halo seemed a bit tight.

'Did you find your bus fare?'

'Oh, er, yes. It was on your path.'

She smiled and said, 'Just a minute.' She returned quickly brandishing the half empty packet of biscuits, 'A reward for being so honest.'

We moved quickly back to the bus stop. I gave Terry the biscuits. He was delighted.

'Wha'd'ya fink's happenin' wiv Brian?'

'Dunno.'

Brian was sitting on the pavement hugging his knees. Richard was standing wiping his nose with Paul's hanky. Paul was holding onto the bus stop pole looking like he would rather be somewhere else, 'Did you manage to give it to me Gran?'

'Oh, yeah.'

'She b'lieved him. Chrisser to'd her 'e fahn' it on her windersill.'

A green bus responded to our signals. The conductor said, 'Has there been an accident?' His eyes flicked from Richard's bloody nose to Brian's bruised cheek.

'Yeah, we was playing on a trolley an' it tipped over. It got smashed up. A fre'penny one, please.'

Richard sprawled on the anniversary seat just inside the lower deck. He looked pleased with himself. Brian sat opposite staring at the floor. We sat with them.

'Listen,' Richard said to the sullen Brian, 'We was playing on the swings on the rec. I got hit in the mush with a swing, an' yo' got it in your face. We don't say owt abaht the money tin. OK?'

While Brian was thinking about this, Richard looked for our support. We nodded consent.

'Roight,' mumbled the very subdued Brian.

'Hello, Chick, dinner is nearly ready. Your Dad'll be home soon. Did you have a nice time at Granny Jones.'

'Yes, Brian gets free chocolate because his mum and sister work at the factory.'

'Mmm, it's alright for some. Did you get any?'

Brian's mother and Mrs Daykin went Saturday afternoon to visit with their parents. Paul said that Brian wasn't feeling very well, so he was having a lie down with some ointment on his bruise. Later I met up with Richard. He was still wearing a blood spattered pullover, but his nose looked normal.

'Fancy nickin' from an o'd woman, his Gran even. He deserved what he got.' Richard certainly was no saint, but at this moment he seemed quite admirable.

Brian and his mother caught the X99 on Sunday morning. If they ever came to visit again, I must have missed them. I felt quite sorry for him. Having no father at home and not knowing who he was must have been dreadful. I was glad to know my Father.

Breaking the Ice

'Don't move. You're in a minefield!'

'Ken, it's not going down.'
   'What's not going down?'
   My Father was in their bedroom and my Mother was in the bathroom. I was tucked up in bed with an *Eagle* comic. My bedroom door was slightly open, as always. I preferred it to be closed, but Mother liked to be able to peep in to make sure I was alright.
   I heard her stand up in the bath and start singing as she towelled herself.
   'The bath water, I pulled the plug and it hasn't shifted.'
   I heard him cross the landing, and then some splashing.
   'Has anything gone down?'
   'No the soap's in its dish.'
   Normally I would have got out of bed to see what was happening, but the cold bedroom had me trapped in my cosy bed. I had my vest under flannel pyjamas and I was weighted down with a thick army blanket, over fleecy sheets, and a hefty eiderdown. It was winter, and it was a very cold winter. The bedroom window panes had lacy frost patterns on the inside. There was no central heating in our Council house.
   'I reckon the pipe's frozen. I'll boil a kettle.'
   This was too good to miss, so I scrambled out of bed and quickly into dressing gown and slippers.
   'Hello, Chick. Did we wake you?'
   'No I was still awake. What's going on?'
   Mother was wrapped in her dressing gown and had her hair bound up with a towel. She looked like an Indian princess.
   'Mind your backs, the cavalry's here.'
   My Father appeared holding the boiled kettle. He opened the window over the wash basin. I winced at the blast of cold air. Mother retreated to their bedroom.
   'The waste pipe is froz. I'm hoping this does the trick. Can you get your torch?'

I scampered back into my room to get the torch which rested on my bedside cabinet. *Cabinet* was a bit of an exaggeration: the piece of furniture was made from an orange crate covered in wallpaper.

'Right, let's have a look.'

My father leaned over the basin and shone my torch down into the box gulley which received the bath water. He made noises like the dentist did when examining teeth. The kettle was emptied into the gulley.

'Ask your Mum to boil another kettle, Corporal.'

Whilst the second kettle was put to boil, my Father stuffed Mother's first bath towel under the pipe which led from the bath drain hole to the where it disappeared into the wall just above the skirting board. The towel was to catch the second dose of hot water.

The bath water suddenly belched and began to gurgle away. He closed the window and grinned triumphantly.

'Didn't waste all the time in the army shooting at Jerries. Learnt a few tricks.'

On the way to school, there were a few frozen puddles to slide on. The school caretaker had ruined the playground slides with salt, sand and ash. The remaining leaves on bushes were rigid. We played at smoking by puffing out condensing breath. Unless it was really necessary, few people ventured out of doors.

'Hey Chrisser, did yo' know Woolley Park lake is froze?'

Richard was wearing a navy blue balaclava. It looked rather like the one his older brother had.

'No, I didn't…'

Wollaton Park was a place that was visited rarely by us in winter. Once, when the snow came, my Father had taken Mike and me sledging. During the winter months, when the Park closed early, we usually stayed home.

'Yeah, it's frozen 'ard right across. Me and Tez are goin' to 'ave a butchers on Sat'day. Yo' comin' wiv us?'

I was tempted, but I could guess what my Mother would say. She was never keen on me associating with the embryonic gangster Richard, and she would become hysterical if she thought I was going anywhere near a frozen lake.

'Well, I'd like to but…'

'Don't tell 'er where yo're going.'

He was a mind reader.

'Mek summat up: keep 'er 'appy. We're only gonna look.'
Terry stood quietly nodding, sniffing and smiling.
'When are you going?'
'Get there fo' ten o'clock. They don' nopen antil ten. We can get back for dinner time. Are yo' comin'?'
I nodded. He punched me lightly on the shoulder.
'Good man. We'll meet yo' at the lamp post at twen'y to ten.'
'Will the ice last until Saturday?'
'Yeah, o' course. It's gonna be co'd for the rest ov the monf. And the ice is dead fick.'

That evening I began the ruse.
'Is it alright if I go into Beeston on Saturday?'
'What for?'
'Alan Saxton says there's a new Hornby train in Appleby's window. I want to have a look at it.'
'Is Alan going with you?'
'No.'
She gave me a hard sidelong look.
'You're not going to Beeston with that Richard, are you?'
I replied truthfully to the question, 'Oh, no.'
'Are you going on your own, then?'
'Yes. I won't be long. It's the *Duchess of Montrose*. I'll be back for dinner.'
'You might see your Dad on the way back. He gets out at one. Don't go banging onto him about the train. It sounds expensive.'
'I only want to look.'
'Mmm, I've heard that before.'
I met Richard and Terry as planned. We jogged up the street to get warm and to remove myself from Mother's radar. Our usual way into Wollaton Park was over the wall, but today it was decided too cold and slippery. So we spent an extra five minutes going to the real entrance on Derby Road opposite Beeston Lane. The gates were only just being opened. The park keeper looked surprised.
The cinder track through the park normally moved under foot but today it was frozen tight. There was nobody about as we approached the lake. A new sign read, 'Danger deep water. Do not go on the ice.'
'Wow.'
What we were used to had gone. The dark shimmering surface had been replaced by flat white. It looked like concrete. Here and there

were scattered objects which had evidently been tossed onto the surface to test the strength. It seemed amazing for a house brick to be sitting there. There was a car tyre and a wooden box. Across the other side was a small island, almost separate, where the swans lived. The swans were standing around looking forlorn. Two swans were testing a gap in the ice next to the island.

'The keepers bashed an 'ole so the swans can get summat to eat.'

I wondered where Richard got his information.

A man appeared further round the lake side. He threw a tennis ball onto the ice. It bounced and bounced. His dog chased out after it. The dog slithered and wobbled on the smooth surface. When he caught up with the ball he was unable to stop. The man laughed and called him back. The dog regained his footing and dashed back.

The ice at the edge, where we stood, was thin. It broke with some foot pressure. We walked along to where the fishermen had a raised firm-standing area. Here the ice was white and solid up against the corrugated metal panels.

'Reckon we can stand on that. Looks fick enough. And that dog was OK.'

Richard got hold of a low branch and poked his foot down onto the ice. He stamped hard. Nothing happened. He grinned and let go the branch. He stood there like Jesus.

'See it's OK.' He did a clumsy pirouette.

Terry and I were not entirely convinced. Richard was laughing.

I looked around. The man and his dog had gone. There was nobody else in view.

'Come back, Richard. It's not safe.'

Richard continued his ice ballet accompanied by his own snorts of mirth.

To our great relief he did stop and return to the bank. Terry and I gave him a pull up. He was beaming with pride.

'We should go home now, it's nearly dinner time.'

We were about to move off when Terry spotted something.

'Look. Near that box. I fink it's a big ball.'

There was something round and orange peeping from behind the box.

'Yo' right Tez, it's like the balls we 'ave at school.'

I didn't enjoy football but I had coveted those PE balls. They bounced delightfully.

'D'yo' fink we could frow some stones at it and mek it roll?'

'Nah. Tek ages. I'll go an gerrit. Then, Tez, if yo're a good boy, I'll let yo' play wiv *my* ball.'

Richard heaved himself back down onto the ice.

'Richard, come back.'

Richard headed towards the ball sliding his feet as though he was skiing.

I could see the headline in the Evening Post: *School boy drowns under the ice.*

He looked very small and dark out on the middle of the lake. He grasped the ball and held it aloft, 'Mine.'

He drop kicked it back towards us. It travelled very nicely. Terry gathered it up. Richard started back. We all heard the sharp noise like a stick snapping. Richard stopped. He didn't need to say, but he did.

'It's cracking.'

His voice sounded wobbly. I thought of a war film I'd seen recently at the Essoldo with my parents. One of the GI's froze in the middle of a field.

'Don't move you're in a mine field!'

But he did move. He gingerly took a step and quickly pulled his foot back.

'Bleddy 'ell. It's breaking up.'

I looked around again. Where were the park keepers when you wanted one? There was a life- saving post close by, but the red and white life-ring was missing.

I'd seen other movies too.

'Richard, get down. Lay flat. Spread your weight out.

Terry, run and get some help. Anybody. Any grown up.'

Terry shot off, but Richard hadn't moved. He was staring down.

'Richard, lay down flat. Spread your weight.'

He looked up and then slowly began to descend.

'Richard, now try sliding along. Take it easy.'

He said something which I didn't catch. I desperately glanced around again. He began to move a little, like a seal. He made a high pitched noise. 'I can't move.'

I had no idea how deep the lake was in the middle.

'Richard, slide.'

'I can't.'

There was some commotion to my right. Terry had found someone. It was the man with the dog. I realised that I was tearful.

'Silly sod, what's he doing out there?'

He didn't wait for an answer.

'Take your belts off, boys.'

I pulled off my *Dan Dare* belt. Terry had an ordinary snake clip belt. The man tugged his brown leather belt from its loops. He fastened the belts together along with the dog's lead. The dog sat obediently watching. We watched the man test the ice against the bank. He began to move slowly towards Richard. Richard had started to make some effort now using his elbows and toes. Half way towards Richard the man stopped and got down on hands and knees. After moving a little more he threw out the improvised life line. It fell short. He edged further and said something to Richard. Richard lifted one hand. It took two more goes before Richard caught hold. Some more was said and Richard used both hands. The man swivelled sideways and pulled Richard towards him.

'Hold tight.'

The man rolled back towards us. It seemed to take hours but Richard was pulled to where it was possible to stand. He looked ashen. He was shaking. Terry and I hauled him up for a second time. As soon as he was off the ice, the man hugged Richard and rubbed him.

'You're alright now, boy. You're safe and sound.'

'Fanks, mester.'

The grin had gone, but there was colour back in his cheeks. He was trembling.

'You'd best get him home quickly. He needs to get warm and drink some hot tea.'

Terry and I nodded wisely and refitted our belts.

'What time is it, please?'

The man grinned, 'You should get a watch. It's just gone half eleven.'

We jogged back. Richard was subdued: Terry and I had nothing useful to say until we turned down Wingfield Drive into our estate.

'What you going to tell your mam?'

'Nuffink. Don't yo' go telling either.'

'I won't ~ because I wasn't there. I was in Beeston.'

Terry gave me an inquisitive look.

'I said I was going to look at a train in Applebee's window.'

Terry grunted, and then to Richard, 'Was it really breaking up?'

Richard scowled, 'Of course it was.'

'Were yo' really scared?'

'Yes. Now giz me ball. I gorrit.'

'Hello, Chick. You are well in time for dinner. You didn't wait for your Dad, then?
The kitchen smelled interesting.
'No. I wanted to come home.'
She laughed. 'Was the *Princess* worth it?'
She didn't notice me wince.

After the mid-day meal my Father said, 'Wollaton Park lake is frozen solid. We can do a bike ride tomorrow morning and have a look while your Mum gets the dinner ready.'
'Can we walk on it?'
'No, that would be silly. It might break. And then what would happen?'

Cock-Dancing in the Park

If I had been with my Father, we would have gone the regular way. I was with my friends, so the preferred way was over the wall.

'Mum, can I go to Woolly Park with Tony and some others? They're taking sandwiches.'
　'You want to have a picnic on Wollaton Park? Who else is going?'
　'Tony and Geoff, and Ray and his brother and a couple of other kids.'
　I was reluctant to mention that Richard was in the group. My Mother didn't trust him.
　'You'll be back for tea time?'
　'Yeah, Robert's got a watch.'
　'You'll be sensible near the lake?'
　I pulled my most sensible face, 'Yes, honest.'

A quarter of an hour later I was racing to meet the others. I wore a red and white striped tee-shirt and khaki shorts because it was warm. I had my cheese and tomato sandwiches and a bottle of pop in an ex – military canvas gas mask bag. Everyone had them ~ except Richard and Terry. Richard had some sandwiches wrapped in the waxed wrapper from a loaf. Terry didn't have anything. We all wore khaki shorts except for Richard. He wore what he always wore – short grey flannel trousers.
　We gathered outside Geoff's house which was only two minutes from the wall that surrounded Wollaton Park. We galloped along the bank between the wall and Derby Road. Richard, the self-appointed leader, called a halt at a stunted tree. He pointed to a pocket of grubby water between the divided tree trunk. Richard was the disseminator of wisdom. I never figured out where he got it all from, or how he knew all the swear words, even.
　'There, that's the secret wishin' well. If you put your best fag card in and mek a wish it'll come true.'
　He had told us to bring our favourite cigarette card. I was dubious about the outcome, and I had no wish to sacrifice my favourite card, so I carried a substitute, a swap. We each solemnly placed a card in the puddle.

'Nah, mek a wish, but don't say nowt or it won't come true.'

I screwed my eyes up and wished silently. I wondered what the others had wished for.

'You should always carry a sixpence wiv you.' Richard told us, 'In case a rozzer sees you smokin' a fag. You gi' 'im the sixpence an' then you won't get 'rrested.'

We nodded in appreciation of his wisdom. Richard did smoke. He took cigarettes from his mother's handbag and other places.

We wanted to climb the wall where the deer reserve fence joined it on the other side. This was no longer advisable as the workmen had smeared grease along the wall top. They had put up hefty supports to the failing wall nearby and realised this was too tempting. The greasing continued a couple of metres to cover our favoured spot. We found another sapling to climb further along. As there was no fence to give footholds, it was necessary to drop two metres and roll in the grass like paratroopers.

'Let's see if we can find some antlers.'

There was a sizeable herd of deer on the park and we knew that antlers were shed. They would never be lying around in the park open to the public, so we turned to the fenced off deer reserve. There was a sign attached to a five bar gate that advised the public to keep out. This was ignored after scanning around for park keepers.

Several fallen branches were mistaken for the objects of desire. No antlers were found this time, or any other.

'What's that?' Robert was pointing to what looked like a little green shed. We froze. All was quiet so we sneaked up to a green tent. It had flaps where windows might be. One side had a larger flap tied with a cord. Richard loosened the cord and opened the flap. It was empty. It didn't look the right shape for a tent. Then Geoff explained.

'It's a hide. People hide in it to watch animals and birds through the flaps.'

We crowded in and opened the flaps.

'Can't see no dickie birds,' moaned Richard.

'Well, you won't 'cos we frightened 'em all off,' explained Robert.

'If I'd got our Alan's airgun we could shoot some squirrels,' said Richard, 'we could cut their tails off and tek 'em to the cop shop. They give you sixpence for each tail.'

'Why?'

'Becos they are a nuisance.'

I wondered why they were considered a nuisance. They swung about in trees and looked nice. I was glad that Richard didn't have an airgun.

We fired a few rounds through the window slots at Japanese soldiers, before retreating to the regular path.

A gravelled track looped the lake. Across the lake we could see some riders. Four girls were on bikes. They were coming our way.

'Remember the free effs,' Richard said.

As we looked blank, he explained, 'Gells. Find 'em, fuck 'em an' forget 'em.'

The girls approached. I recognised them. They were from our school. The one in the lead was Barbara. She had the prettiest pale grey eyes. The bicycle bells tinkled.

Richard called out, 'Giz a go on yer bike, duck'

'No,' was Barbara's firm reply. She avoided running into him. They pedalled past.

I would have had to do something if Richard had stopped them. I was sure there would be a Spurius Lartius and a Herminius with me.

'Gerrof an' milk it,' he yelled after them. They just giggled and pedalled on.

To us, Richard said, 'Not wo'th it. All bleddy ugly.'

The retreat continued away from the frequented area towards a dead end that was seldom visited. This was a slope dotted with bushes that was almost surrounded by the golf course. Just over the golf course railings were a couple of sand pits. It was possible to find lost golf balls in the sand or round about. We poked about and found nothing.

'Let's play falling dead.'

'Yeah!'

One of us had the machine gun. The others attacked in turn. Each one died on the edge of the bunker and fell into the soft sand. The most spectacular death was the next machine gunner. This was tiring work in the sun.

'Shall we have our sarnies now?' suggested Ray.

Sitting on the edge of the pit seemed a good place.

Richard pulled his waxed pack from inside his shirt.

'Tez ain't got nuffink to eat. Let's all gi' him a bit,' said Richard.

'Like feeding the five thousand,' said Tony.

Richard stared at him as though he was speaking in Chinese.

We broke off sections of sandwich for Terry. He seemed very pleased.

'Why didn't you bring your own sandwiches?' asked Ray.

Terry's expression changed, 'Me mam wou'n't give me none.'

'Ahh!' interrupted Richard. He had red jam round his mouth. 'Giz a swig o' pop.'

This was aimed at Tony who had a bottle of Dandelion and Burdock. He handed it over. Richard tipped the bottle back and guzzled. When he took the bottle from his lips he belched loudly. He tossed the bottle back to Tony. He missed the catch. Some of the dark fizzy drink sloshed out onto the grass. Richard then tossed the stopper. I wondered if he was going to extort a drink from each of the group.

'Wanna drink? Robert was offering his lemonade to Terry.

'Yeah, fanks.'

I was glad Robert was there. He had a watch, and he was the same age as Richard.

With the picnic over we sauntered down the slope. The slope stopped a couple of metres before dipping sharply to the foot of the wall. Over the wall traffic could be seen on the Derby Road.

'Yeah, right, watch me,' exclaimed Richard, 'I'm gonna do a cock-dance!'

We gaped. Tony gasped. Geoff glanced my way and shook his head.

'Tez watch out for a bus, that's best.'

Terry dutifully stood on a tree stump so he could see down the road. Richard unfastened his fly buttons and pulled it out. This was outrageous.

'Bus comin'.'

As one, we dived for cover in the lee of the wall. Richard began the performance. He wiggled his hips to make it bounce around. He waved his arms as though he was demented. He wore a silly grin. We heard the Corporation double decker the other side of the wall. Richard gave a good performance for the passengers on the top deck. Suddenly he froze. His arms fell and his grin disappeared. We stared at him as the noise of the bus faded.

'Me auntie. Me auntie was on the bus. She seen me. She'll tell me mam. Me dad'll kill me.'

Nothing was said. I could guess what the others were thinking.

Richard looked deflated. 'Urh, bleddy 'ell.' He adjusted his nether region.

Nothing was said, but the silent consensus seemed to be that we should make for home. It was only a short distance to the Lodge House Gate. Scrambling over the wall seemed inappropriate and there were no foot holds on the park side. Over the other side of Derby Road was another lodge house on the corner with Beeston Lane. Richard brightened.

'I know, let's go an' ask for a glass of water. We can say we're 'ot and firsty an' we bin walkin' for miles. They might give us ginger beer or summat. Might be summat wo'th nickin, eh Tez?'

Geoff gave me another one of his glances.

Tony said, 'I'm going home.' He ran off.

Robert made a show of looking at his watch, 'Look at the time. We had better be going, Ray.'

Geoff and I quickly left Richard and Terry contemplating the path to the back door of lodge.

'What do you reckon his dad will do to him?'

'Give him a belting. That's what he usually gets,' I replied.

We stopped and re-crossed the road when we were level with the 'wishing well'. The cigarette cards were sogged together. The water had loosened the gum on the backs.

'I didn't put my best one in,' I confessed.

'Me neither,' replied Geoff.

We both laughed.

'Do you think the wishes will come true?'

'Nah, or there would be queues here.'

'What did you wish for?'

'If I tell you it won't come true.'

We laughed again.

'Well, I wished that summat would happen to Richard.'

We laughed all the way back on to the Council estate.

Darfield Road

It was always thrilling to visit with Grandfather. The journey involved riding on a train from the busy Midland Station to the almost rural Cudworth station. Then it was only a five minute walk to Grandfather's prefab which was one of many that formed a community on the edge of the village. Grandfather lived in the last prefab on Summerdale Road. He lived with Ethel who for all intents and purposes was my Granny. Beyond the prefab was a large oval of grass for Summerdale Road to loop around, and beyond that were a farmer's pastures. One side of the loop was different. These homes were brick built houses: four sets of semi-detached.

Sometimes we visited at Christmas for a few days. This time my Mother decided that 'it was good to get away at Whit'. This was good for me too as it was possible to play out and explore. I could renew my friendship with Alex who lived in one of the brick semis. His name was really Alexander. He told me that his father gave him that name to balance his surname which was Shorthouse. Alex lived up, or down, to his family name because he was a head shorter than me. We had met last Christmas in the street. We both wore identical Davy Crockett hats. He also told me that when he was older he would join the army. He was quite sure of this. Joining the army seemed to be the only way out of becoming a coal-miner.

After the initial welcoming ceremonies, I managed to slip out. I intended to return to the railway. I was an avid train-spotter. I had the 1955 edition of Ian Allan's combined volume. It contained all the locomotives of the British Rail regions. The place to spot trains at Cudworth was a grassy bank just inside the gate to the slope down to the station.

'Hey-up, Chrisser, thi granfaither told us tha was coming t'day.'

Alex was ready and grinning at Grandfather's front gate. When I told him where I was going, he laughed and said he would come with me. Alex was not a train-spotter, but he could indulge me in my interest. He was impressed with the images of the larger Midland Region engines. I was not expecting to see any of them rattling through Cudworth station. Perhaps the best that could be hoped for was powerful ex-military 'Aussie' with a long train of coal wagons.

To keep any spotters alert the shuttle between Cudworth and Barnsley came and went frequently. It was known as the Pull and Push because the diminutive engine pulled three rickety coaches to the city, but had to change ends to return backwards because it didn't have access to a turntable.

There were several children at the spotting place. They didn't appear to be train-spotters. Two girls were picking daisies. Three boys were clowning about. The largest of the three seemed to be having fun pushing the other two over.

Alex's grin disappeared, 'Uh-ho, it's Lenny. He's a wazzock.'

Lenny paused when he saw us. 'Hey-up, Short–arse. Who's that wi thi?'

'He's my friend, he's stayin' at his grandad's.'

Lenny stared at me. 'What do they call thi?'

For a moment I didn't understand, 'My friends call me Chrisser.'

Lenny responded to my accent, 'Thas not from Cuddeth, then?'

'No, I came on the train.'

'What's that in thi 'and?'

My combined volume was protected by a red plastic cover.

'It's a book, a book for train-spotters.'

'Giz a goz.'

I hesitated with the book pulled against my body. It was a treasure, and he was a wazzock.

Lenny smiled. 'C'mon, giz a look. You'll gerrit back.' He held his hand out.

I didn't trust him. He took a step towards me. He was big. He must have been twelve.

A train whistle sounded.

'Don't give it to him.'

Heads turned to see two boys who had come up the slope from the station. One was pushing a bike.

Lenny's face twisted into a sneer, 'What's it t'thee?'

'Hey-up, Colin.' Alex sounded gleeful.

'Piss off, Lenny, while thi can.'

The two girls and the other two boys had already disappeared. Lenny looked like he might explode.

He glanced around, 'Four onto one?'

'No, just me.'

Lenny spat into the grass, and like a cat which was wary of tangling with another, He began to move slowly towards the gate. He spat again and thrust the gate open. It banged back as he slouched off.

Alex quickly did the introductions, 'This is Colin and Robert. This is Chrisser, he's staying wi' his granfaither: Mester Marley.'

The two boys nodded and smiled. Being related to old Mr Morley seemed to have value. The two boys also lived in the brick houses on the green.

Robert, in a grey knitted zipper, was the one pushing the bike. Colin was the one who had seen off Lenny the wazzock. Colin was handsome. He wore his tawny hair loose and longer than the usual *short-back-and-sides*. His blue eyes gleamed. Colin was wearing a navy-blue shawl collar zipper top: it was shop bought.

'Does tha play cricket, Chrisser?'

'Well sort of, I know how, but I'm not very good.'

'No matter, we'll have a game s'afto on the green. You can be first bat.'

Robert swung his leg over the bike. Colin slipped onto the saddle. The bike lurched forward with Robert standing on the pedals, and Colin with his legs stretched out. Alex and I caught up with them at the green.

'D'you want a go?'

I was offered the bike. It was not new. When I held the handlebars they moved independently of the bike frame. I cautiously pushed off to do a circuit of the green. Steering was tricky and the brakes were slack. They grinned when I returned the bike.

'Teks a bit of getting used to,' said Robert. 'It was me big brother's, but he's off wit' lasses now.'

After lunch Robert and Colin were already setting up stumps.

I asked Alex about Colin and Lenny.

'Colin is a really nice lad. He's never naughty. And he won't have any nonsense. He's not frightened of even the bigguns. Everybody likes him.'

'And Robert?'

'Yeah, he's best butty with Colin. They do everything together.'

He chuckled, 'He's not as good looking as Colin, though.'

'C'mon Chrisser, you're batting first.'

A few more children came onto the green. There were three girls. Colin happily invited them all to play. There were no arguments. Everyone had a turn at batting and bowling. It was fun.

At tea-time, when the cricket ended, Robert suggested that he should go to the local rec the next day. I had been briefly to the rec with my Father when Grandfather wanted us to see the 'reet big bonfire' which was being built for the coronation celebrations. According to Grandfather there would be fireworks, lights in the trees and a real Scottish piper in full kit. I was desperate to witness all this, but my father said that we had to return home. I did see the enormous pile of the bonfire. It looked like a wooden pyramid. I understood that Cudworth park had the usual children's slides, swings, roundabout and rocking-horse. Also there was plenty of green space to have adventures in. Robert's suggestion was taken up.

The next morning we met up outside Grandfather's front gate. Robert had his bike. Colin said that they would give Alex and me five minutes start on a race across the village to the park gates. The park gates were a short way down a lane between two shops on the Barnsley Road in the village. Alex and I agreed. Colin had a watch. We dashed off convinced that we might just beat them. We turned up Newton Road, and again onto Darfield Road. It was downhill now until we had to turn again a short distance up the main Barnsley Road towards Grimethorpe. There was a shriek from behind.

'It's them, they are catching us up.'

We ran harder.

They raced past yelling triumph, with Robert standing on the pedals and Colin with his legs splayed.

'Ah, s'no good,' gasped Alex.

We slowed to a walking pace and watched them go. We had nearly got to the Barnsley Road. They would have to stop to cross, but they didn't. Alex and I watched them hurtle out onto the main road. We saw the single decker Yorkshire Traction bus to Barnsley hit them.

'Christ!'

Colin was thrown up into the air. Robert and the bike disappeared under the front wheels of the bus. We heard the locking squeal of the bus brakes. Everything was suddenly still and quiet. The bus conductor plunged from the rear platform, He met the driver who had scrambled from the cab.

Alex and I walked slowly towards the scene. We said nothing. Passengers began to get off the bus. A woman began screaming. People emerged from the shops. I was expecting to see Robert wriggle out from under the bus, and Colin get up and brush himself down. Colin was sprawled against the kerb. He was quite still. His head was at a strange angle. His blue eyes were wide open. Two men, one in a white shop coat, pulled Robert by his feet, from under the bus. There was a trail of blood. His chest was flat. The grey pull-over had turned maroon.

Alex and I stood and stared.

The man in the white coat knelt down next to Colin. He stood back up and shook his head. A woman put her head scarf over Colin's face. The screaming woman was now sobbing. She was being consoled by another passenger. The conductor was consoling the driver who had sat down on the kerb with his head in his hands. The man in the white coat removed it and placed it over Robert. Red spots began to show through.

'Christ. They are dead. Them bleddy brakes. They're dead.'

My throat was dry, my heart was pounding and my head felt light. I didn't want to believe Alex, but I knew he was right. I felt myself rocking slightly. I felt sick. Tears rolled.

A policeman arrived on a bicycle. He soon took charge. He herded the passengers towards the next bus stop down the road. The sightseers were shooed away. Statements were scribbled into his note book. Alex calmly approached the policeman. What he was saying was written down. Alex pointed at me. I was beckoned.

As I approached I saw that the headscarf had slipped down to reveal a dark abrasion on the side of his head. Colin's blue eyes were still open. Blood was spreading out from under the white coat that covered Robert. I told the policeman my details and what I had seen. It was difficult for me to form the words.

Two men in miners' work clothes were pulling the bike from under the bus. A third man in a butcher's apron had a bucket and was sprinkling sawdust around Robert. The bike was completely flattened.

Two sets of emergency bells sounded. An ambulance and a police car drew up. Two police officers conferred with the constable. The ambulance men stooped over the boys. The white coat was quickly dropped back.

'No chance.'

A little more time was spent with Colin but the response was much the same.

'Dead. Looks like a neck break and a heavy blow to the side of the head.'

'Better get 'em in't wagon.'

'You two best get off home, and tell thi parents.'

I turned away and began walking back with Alex. We didn't speak. The sun shone, birds twittered and people walked past us as nothing had happened. When we turned off Darfield Road Alex spoke.

'Jesus Christ. Do we have to tell their mams. What's gonna happen t'bike?'

'I don't know. I don't know.'

We didn't need to tell Colin and Robert's parents. The police car was already there. Nobody was out playing on the green. For a moment I watched Alex walk over the green towards his house, before I pushed open Grandfather's front gate. Inside the prefab I began to recount the events, but my words were lost in the sobbing. My mother hugged me.

My Father said, 'C'mon we'll go for a walk with Grandad.'

We walked up the alley at the side of the prefab and out through the old houses to a lane where my Father and Grandfather talked about being soldiers in two different wars, and I discovered harebells.

Grandfather wrote to tell us that there had been a double funeral. Two big black hearses with two small coffins covered in flowers. Everyone came out to watch.

My Father showed me how to adjust the brakes on my bike. When I went out on it my bike, Mother told me to be careful. I refrained from asking the barber for a *short-back-and-sides*, and asked for just a trim. I asked my Mother for a new top from Marks and Spencer's. I wanted a navy blue zipper with a shawl collar.

David

'Don't say that, it's rude.'

***

Now it was my turn to shine. I had managed to remember a little piece of silliness which my Father had taught me. I was word perfect and I had an audience in the school yard.

> 'God said unto Moses
> All the Jews will have long noses
> Except Aaron
> He'll have a square un
> Except Peter
> He'll have a gas-meter
> Except John
> He'll have none.'

My audience squealed with laughter, but David didn't.
   'Say it again,' said one of the girls.
   I got as far as, 'God said…', when David butted in.
   'Don't say that it's rude.'
   I started again.
   'Stop!' and he pushed me with both hands.
   I wobbled backwards, taken by surprise. There were more squeals of laughter from the audience. David looked really agitated. There were tears in his eyes. I couldn't work out what was going on. Was there going to be a fight? I avoided fights, and David didn't look the type. What had upset him? It was only a silly rhyme.
   'It's rude,' he repeated.
   The audience drifted away.
   'What was rude?'
   'You were rude about God and Moses.'
   I had heard about God and Moses from what was said in our Council school assemblies. They were in the Bible. They were in stories of long ago in a land far away.
   'Sorry,' I said.
   He wiped a tear from his cheek.

'Sorry,' I repeated to make sure.

The whistle blew and everyone froze to listen for which class would lead in first.

On the way home I ran the silly poem through my mind to try and understand how it was rude. There were no naughty words. People made jokes about everything. My father had even introduced the poem to me. He wouldn't say rude things. I caught David up at the bottom end of Meriden Avenue. He would take the left turn along Hathern Green, and I would take the right.

'David, wait.'

He turned.

'Why was it rude?'

'Mummy says that we shouldn't make jokes about God and Moses.'

He seemed very sure about this. I nodded. God and Moses were never mentioned at my house. My Parents would say 'God Almighty!' if something went wrong. We were not religious, though. My Father was strictly agnostic, whilst my Mother kept her options open.

After the evening meal and when my Father had lit a Park Drive cigarette, I recounted the incident over the poem.

'Rude? It's not meant to be rude. It's just a silly verse.'

My Mother added, 'P'raps it's because David's mother is a Jew.'

I was vaguely aware of David's parents. They looked quite ordinary. Except that Mr Wilson looked very smart in his policeman's uniform. My Mother continued.

'I met Rose Wilson at the Welfare when you were a little baby. She had her baby about the same time. She had more of an accent back then. She met her husband at the end of the war. He was a military policeman.'

'A red-cap,' said my Father.

'Poor soul, she told me that all her family were dead,' she paused for a moment, 'They were all taken away to them camps, and were never seen again.'

My Father continued the story, 'The Gerries tried to get rid of all the Jews.'

'Why?'

'Because the Germans had silly ideas about the Jews.'

My Mother cut back in, 'But they weren't bad. They were just ordinary people like us. Rose Wilson was lucky to have escaped them rotten Nazis.'

'Six million were murdered in the concentration camps,' said my Father solemnly.

'Yes, very lucky to have met a nice British red-cap who wanted to marry her.'

I thought that I might become friendlier with David. This would be to make up for upsetting him, and perhaps find out more about his parents in the war. An opportunity came when my Mother suggested that I show David my drawings. Lately my drawings had been focused on making a suit of medieval armour in kit form: like Airfix, but much bigger. I had planned to draw out the pieces on cardboard, and fasten it altogether with split pins. I thought to collect the silver paper from discarded chocolate bar wrappers and glue them on to look like metal plates. A glut of films featuring knights-in-armour had recently filled the screen at our local Essoldo cinema. The latest was *The Black Shield of Falworth*. There were some exciting fight scenes, but the strange American accents bothered me.

I targeted David in the school yard and suggested he saw my plans for the suit of armour project. He was delighted to be involved. He came to my house the next day after school. Our homes were only a few minutes apart. He lived on Baslow Drive, on the corner with Olton Avenue. I showed him my collections of toy soldiers and toy weapons. He was impressed.

I spread out the roll of old wallpaper with the diagrams of the armour on the back. I explained that most pieces were rectangular and curved: an easy thing with cardboard. The cardboard would come from Mr Pretty's yard. Pretty's shop always had a ready pile of squashed card boxes. I had a small box of split brass pins which Aunty Nellie had donated. David was excited.

'Can I borrow your plans to show my dad? I'll be careful with them.'

I readily agreed. My Father hadn't been too enthusiastic. He said that if it all fitted together, I wouldn't be able to move without it coming apart. I needed some positive endorsement.

David returned the diagram roll the next day at school.

'My dad says it won't work. Cardboard is too flimsy, and the split pins would pull loose very quickly.'

I was crest-fallen. The plans were shelved. First my Father, and now a policeman had reduced my enthusiasm.

On the brighter side David did ask me to his house. I cycled there on Saturday morning. His house was an end terrace like mine, but was at the other end of the block and so it was the reverse. I was more intrigued by the differences inside the Council houses. I measured the interiors against my own. Some appeared to be grander than ours, others less so. The Wilson's home was nice, clean and tidy. I met Mrs Wilson. She wore a pinafore like my Mother. She offered a glass of squash and a biscuit, with a nice smile. She looked like all the other mothers on the estate, but there was a hint of foreign accent. I was itching to ask questions but refrained. David was keen to show me his possessions.

He had a cardboard box containing a dozen Dinky toys. None of them were military. He handed me a book. It was well worn. I started to open it and he laughed.

'No. It has to be read from the back to the front.'

He took the book and began to turn the pages from what I considered the back. It looked like a child's book. The pages had a large illustration, with text in large print opposite. I couldn't read any of it. It certainly wasn't English.

'It's the story of Moses,' he explained.

As the pages were turned I began to recognise parts of the story.

I recognised the angel, pharoah, signs over the Israelite's doors, the plagues of locusts and the parting of the sea.

'It was mummy's book. She had it since she was a little girl. She gave it to me.'

He handed it back to me. I held it reverently.

'The words are in Hebrew. I can read some of them. Mummy taught me.'

'She's Jewish?'

'Yes.'

'Is your dad Jewish as well?'

'No, he's Christian. But mummy says that I am Jewish because it's passed on by the mothers.'

'What do Jews do?'

'Nothing much. Mummy doesn't go to church. The Jewish church is called *syn-a-gogue*. There's a synagogue in Nottingham. It's near the fire-station. Mummy says she will take me there when I'm older. Oh, we do have a Star of David on the Christmas tree. It's Jewish. It's got six points.'

I was overloaded with information. I could hardly wait to see their tree at next Christmas. I wondered what it was like inside a synagogue. All the usual churches that I had visited had the same sort of things.

'Why will she take you to the… synagogue when you are older?'
'So that I can become a proper Jew.'
'Do you want to be a proper Jew?'
'Yes.'

As I cycled home I wondered how David would be made into a proper Jew. At the corner, where I turned right onto Anslow Avenue, I was greeted by Richard and Terry.

'Hey-up, Chrisser. We seen you coming out the rozzer's house. Yo' bin a naughty boy?'

Terry sniggered.

'No, I went to see David.'

'What, that lickle weed?'

'He's not a weed. He's nice.' I felt my cheeks burning. I almost said something about his book and the tree decoration, but I held my tongue. I hadn't been sworn to secrecy, but I thought it best not to let Richard have any information. He knew about lots of things, but he didn't seem to know about Mrs Wilson, or he would have made some comment.

Back at home I told my parents about the Wilson's household.

Mother said, 'I think she's Belgian or French. She was sent to live with a Christian family during the war. She had to pretend not to be Jewish.'

Father said that when boys got to be thirteen they had to readout a prayer in the synagogue. After that they were considered to be adults.

I imagined David standing at a pulpit reading out the prayer. As he got to the *Amen* bit he got bigger and sprouted a beard. It all sounded scary.

I spent the afternoon cutting up cardboard and fixing pieces together with split pins. It was not successful. It didn't take much handling before the pins worked loose. Perhaps I should abandon the cardboard suit of armour, and stick to Meccano.

We visited each other's house. David enjoyed my train set, collection of toy soldiers and toy weapons. I enjoyed the biscuits and talking to Mrs Wilson at his house. She avoided talking about the war or her family. David and I became good friends. David was more sensible than Richard or Terry.

One Monday, in the school yard, David was beaming. His explanation for his delight took the wind from my sails.

'Chrisser, we are leaving. We are going to live in Africa.'

'Africa?'

'Yes, daddy has got a new job. He's going to be a policeman in Africa.'

He was brimming with excitement. He told me that his father had seen an advert. He would get more money and they would have a grand house, perhaps with servants too. It seemed like a fairy-tale. I had a sudden thought.

'Will you turn black?'

He laughed. 'No, only the tribes are black. There are lots of white people. They are in charge.'

'Will you come back?'

'No, daddy says it's going to be better living there.'

'What about the synagogue?' I was grasping at straws.

He shrugged, 'I suppose there will be one in Johannesburg.'

I guessed that was where he was going to live in South Africa.

'When are you leaving?'

'Soon, when school finishes for the summer.'

That meant he would be gone before Christmas, and I wouldn't get to see the special star.

I trailed home miserably, kicking at anything on the pavement. I told my parents.

My mother said, 'I wish we could go to South Africa, or anywhere away from this place.'

There had been some talk, previously, of going to live in Australia, or Canada, or even Airdrie in Scotland, but nothing came of it.

'Dad, you could be a policeman in South Africa,' I suggested.

'What, me be a policeman?' He was grinning. 'I wouldn't know how to start.'

This surprised me because I thought he knew everything. And what my Mother had said about getting away from our home surprised me too. I knew she wanted more and better things, but I thought they were just for our house.

My Father leaned forward with his arms on the table.

'Africa is a very big country a long way away. It's quite different. There will be trouble in South Africa, mark my words, Son. You see, the natives are fed up with being bossed about: they want to run the country themselves.'

This seemed quite different to the paradise which David had described.

Mrs Taylor, our Year 4 teacher, said a special goodbye to David in class. On the way home he promised to write a post card. He never did. I never knew what happened to the Wilson's. I wondered if David ever got to a synagogue, or became a proper man. Their house on Baslow Drive stood empty for only a week. A young couple moved in with two little girls.

***

My parents took me to our local cinema. The Essoldo was showing an exciting film about Romans. One Roman soldier's armour caught my interest. His breast-plate was made up of many overlapping silver discs. They looked rather like milk-bottle tops. It wasn't a whole suit of plate armour. Surely, a breast-plate could be easily made. I began to collect milk-bottle tops.

Dead Dog Pond

'Richard's set 'imsen on fire!'

It was Terry shouting at the end of our Close.

'Hey, Chrisser, come and see. Richard's on fire.'

This was quite possible. Richard was always involved in something out of the ordinary. There was the time that he acquired a hypodermic needle and threatened to inject anyone near him. He brandished the needle and squirted liquid into the air as we had seen in medical dramas at the cinema. Of course everyone shrieked and scattered.

'S'only water,' he proclaimed.

Another time he and Terry had been stealing apples. Scrumping a few from a garden orchard was *almost* acceptable, but Richard had an ex-army kit bag full. He was attempting to sell them. His chosen pitch was directly in front of Mr Pretty's greengrocery. Mr Pretty took a dim view of this and suggested Richard should disappear before the police were called.

Richard had seen a war film in which petrol was syphoned from a vehicle's tank. Armed with a length of rubber tubing and some empty lemonade bottles he set about syphoning from car tanks. Unfortunately he sucked too hard and made himself vomit.

Undeterred, he had now set himself on fire.

As I sped toward the commotion on the street I wondered if his latest escapade had somehow gone dreadfully wrong.

In the centre of a knot of admirers was the grinning magician. Richard was on fire. He held up a blazing hand. Strangely he was not shrieking with pain. He was positively gleeful.

'Doesn't it hurt?'

'Nah. I'm tough.'

The flames subsided. The magician held out his hand for all the Doubting Thomases.

'See norra mark.'

He grinned at me, 'Hey up Chrisser. D'yo' want a go?'

I just gaped and shook my head. There had to be a trick.

'S'easy, Jus' watch this.'

By his feet was a cotton bag intended for marbles. Inside was a box of matches and a small glass bottle containing a very purple liquid. Richard tossed me the matches and the bottle was given to Terry.

'Nah, when ar Tez sloshes some o' this on me 'and, yo' put a match to it.'

I carefully pulled a match free from the box as Terry unscrewed the bottle-top. He seemed to know what to do. There must have been a rehearsal. He dribbled the liquid out onto Richard's open palm.

'Nah!'

I struck the match and as I gingerly guided it to the purple stain. I caught a strange smell. The flames danced orangey blue. I felt a pain on my finger tip. I had forgotten to drop the match.

The audience cheered as Richard waved the flaming hand about.

'Sounds like meths: methylated spirit,' said my Father.

I was wishing that I hadn't said anything. It was turning into a lecture.

'Meths is very flammable. But it burns away quickly without making any heat. It's still dangerous to mess about with chemicals though. You didn't try it, did you?'

There were more questions about how Richard had got hold of the meths and the matches. For a moment I thought my father might go around for a word with Mr Church, but he didn't.

'Keep well away from Richard when he has barmy ideas. You might get into trouble ~ or worse,' said my Mother.

I understood the advice, and generally accepted it as common sense. However Richard was an attractive character. There was hardly ever a dull moment. Sometimes the moments were scary, but never dull. So when I was asked to go on a small expedition to investigate *Dead Dog Pond* there was not much deliberation. I had been often to Wollaton Park. It was only ten minutes away, and there was no mention of thieving. What could there possibly be to upset my Parents?

'Hey, Chrisser, yo' wanna come wiv us. We goin' over Woolly Park.' Richard was bright- eyed.

'Yeah we goin' to tek a look at *Dead Dog Pond*.'

I knew about Wollaton Park lake and the Ha-Ha which collected water.

'What's *Dead Dog Pond?*'

'Yo' kno' that bit the ovver side of the lake track, well there's a pond dahn there.'

There was a cinder track around the lake. On the other side of the track there were sections of the park which were not open to the public. On the slope up to the park wall, where we climbed over, there was a wood reserved for the deer. Further along, the ground fell away fairly steeply to the backs of the houses on Parkside. The lake had an overspill facility which allowed for a small stream to descend and form the Tottle Brook. (The very same stream that emerged from a concrete pipe *over tins*.) Apparently, according to Richard, the stream pooled at the bottom of the slope to form a small pond before entering the concrete pipe.

'It's called *Dead Dog Pond* cos this bloke tied bricks rahnd a dog's neck an' chucked it in.'

'Why?'

Richard shrugged, 'Spect he di'n' want it no more.'

'Is it still there?'

'Dunno, that's to find aht.'

'Who's going?'

'Well, me an' Tez an' Keef Baker an' yo'.'

I was surprised at the mention of Keith Baker. He wasn't a regular member of the group. He was in the 'B' stream with Terry. Mostly he was referred to as 'Lanky' because he was head and shoulders above the other children. He was in the 'B' stream because he wasn't too smart. I wondered why he was suddenly included.

'Why Keith?'

'Cos he's a mate of Tez.'

I looked at Terry. He was undersized. They would look ridiculous standing together. Terry didn't hold many friendships. Perhaps it was the same with Keith.

'When?'

'Sat'day mornin'?'

There was nothing on my agenda. 'OK, nine o'clock.'

I couldn't see the point of asking for sandwiches. I'd be back at home for lunch around one. We followed the usual route into the park: this was over the wall near to Abbey Gates bus stop. It was easy scaling the wall from the road side because of the handy young trees. It was a matter of honour to drop down the other side and land like paratroopers. We scrunched along the cinder track ignoring a couple of fishermen and the swans.

'Dahn there,' Richard pointed down the slope beyond the simple wire strand fence.

The view was obscured by dense rhododendron bushes and many trees. This was why I had not noticed the pond before. I still couldn't see it.

'How did you find out about the pond?'

'These kids I kno' to'd me abaht it.'

Richard always kept his sources of information vague, as if he belonged to some secret club for chancers.

He glanced about to make sure there was no park keeper cycling along or anyone else likely to question our movements.

'OK, coast clear. Let's go.'

We slipped through the fence with ease and scrambled down the slope until the safety of the bushes was achieved. I looked back: there was no one watching.

Richard led the way. The ground soon became boggy. It sucked at our shoes. I wished that I had brought wellingtons. It felt cooler and was quite gloomy near the bottom of the slope. The overspill from the lake was channelled in a pipe under the cinder track but was soon allowed to freely wander about in streamlets until it regrouped at the pond.

The pond was still and dark. A few metres beyond was the grilled pipe for the start of the Tottle Brook. Beyond that was the park wall with glimpses of roof lines.

'There's nowt much 'ere,' said Keith.

Terry sighed, 'I fought we might see the dog.'

Terry had a morbid interest in the gruesome. I was glad I couldn't see the poor creature.

Richard picked up a stone and tossed it to the centre of the pond. It made a delightful 'plop'. The flat surface was transformed with a radiating ripple. Terry stooped to pick up another stone.

'What's that?' Keith was pointing at the water.

'What we lookin' at?'

'There.'

I followed Keith's out stretched arm. Across the pond near to a clump of weeds there was something just breaking the surface. It could be almost anything: a boulder, perhaps.

'It's the dog, the dead dog,' enthused Terry.

I glanced at Richard. He was craning forward squinting. Did he need glasses?

'Could be owt, Tez.'

I was beginning to think that this might be a good time to go home for lunch.

Keith was making his way around to the far side of the pond. It was hard going because of the boggy ground. His shoes were caked in dark soggy lumps. He wobbled about near to the target.

'Worrizzit? Izzit the dog?'

'Can't mek it aht. The water's too mucky. I need a stick.'

Richard casted about and found a suitable fallen branch. It was a little too far to toss successfully, so he gave it to Terry to take.

Keith began to prod. The thing responded by moving slightly.

'Is it the dog?'

'Dunno. Looks pretty manky.'

'If it had house bricks round its neck wouldn't it be on the bottom?'

'Don' kno' 'ow deep it is. The bricks could of come off.'

'It's not fur. Looks like a sack or a pully.'

'Perhaps there wasn't a dog. Perhaps it was just an old sack. Perhaps…'

'P'rhaps the bleddy dog's in the sack!'

I turned to look back up to the cinder track thinking to depart rapidly. That was when Terry shrieked. He sounded like a girl.

I turned back. Terry had his mouth open. Keith looked frozen. His poking with the stick had caused the thing to roll over. I could see what looked like a glove on the end of what looked like an arm.

It was Richard who broke the tableau.

'Friggin' hell. That's not a friggin' dog.'

Keith came back to life, 'It's a body. A 'uman body.'

Terry had turned away and was retching.

'What shall we do?'

Richard didn't speak. He just shook his head slowly.

Keith called. 'Shall we pull it out?'

'Neah. Leave it. It's dead. It ain't goin' nowhere.'

'We can't leave it there. We'll have to tell somebody.'

'Me and Tez don't want the cops rahnd ar 'ouses again. Ar dads will go barmy'

Terry and Keith made their way back. They looked ashen. Terry was trembling.

'We'll be in trouble, anyway, being down here.'

Keith said, 'Cou'n' we say we was kickin' a ball about an' it rolled down here?'

Terry said, 'We ain't gorra ball.'

I said, 'I'll go and find a park keeper. You three can go home. I'll say I was exploring on my own.'

Richard said, 'Neah, we're in this togevver. All fer one…'

'One for all!' we chorused.

Shattered we climbed up the slope to the cinder track,

'Was it a bloke or a woman?'

'Could be a kid.'

'How long's it bin there'

'D'yo' reckon it was murder?'

Terry's colour drained away again. I thought he might faint.

'We'll be in the paper.'

'Yeah, might get a reward.'

'Right, me and Tez will stay here to keep guard. You, Chrisser, an' Keef go find a parkie.'

Keith and I ran off towards the Hall where the uniformed people were.

'Sorry, you two are not twelve. You can't visit the Hall without a sensible adult.'

'We don't want to come in. We want to report a body.'

'Yeah, a dead drownded body in the pond.'

The man in the entrance cubby-hole glared at us.

'We are not kidding.'

He listened to our story. After a minute of our gabbling he called a colleague. Keith and I were lead over to the stable block where the police horses were kept. A police Land Rover was in the yard.

I thought that Richard and Terry might have scarpered, but they were still there. They both looked alarmed at the police vehicle. The two officers went down through the rhododendrons with Richard as the guide. One officer carried a hold-all, the other carried a pole with a hook on the end like they have for boats. One of them and Richard came back after a few minutes. He took names and addresses. Richard actually gave true details. We were told to go home and that the area would be closed as it was now a possible crime scene.

A policeman did call at our house. My parents were not surprised. I had recounted the tale several times. It was confirmed that the body was that of an old man who had been reported missing for a few weeks. The police did not suspect foul play, it was considered misadventure. The old man was known for being vague and wandering.

Local newspapers carried the story. They reported that the body had been found by children playing in the park. There was no reward.

'When the copper came to ar 'ouse, me dad di'n't go bananas. I'd tol' me mam that we was jus' walkin' arahnd the lake an' we seen somefink funny. Dad was rather pleased cos I wa'n't in no trouble. The cop said I was a *good citizen*. Me dad give us sixpence,' Richard grinned.

'Yeah I fought me dad was gonna kill me 'til the copper tol' 'im. Di'n't get no sixpence.'

We didn't hear of what Mr Baker said to Keith.

My Parents went on and on. They weren't cross. They were anxious about me being easily influenced by others.

Of course they meant Richard.

Dolls' Hospital

The Dolls' Hospital was at the top of Alfreton Road near to Canning Circus. I had been aware of it ever since we had taken to visiting friends at Bobber's Mill. It was necessary to catch a trolley bus, and the stop was almost outside the Dolls' Hospital. Waiting for the trolley bus gave me enough time to gaze at the window display. The Hospital was really a shop front of one large window, a recessed entrance and a much smaller window. Boards obscured the interior of the premises but afforded shallow display areas. On display were mostly dolls and teddy bears. Some were bandaged or had an arm in a sling. One teddy with a leg in plaster was propped up on a crutch. Some dolls wore old fashioned nurses' outfits and tended patients in shoe-box beds. The main fascination for me was the small group of lead soldiers that represented the Army Medical Service. A wounded redcoat was being carried by blue tunic stretcher bearers towards a Florence Nightingale figure waiting at the entrance to a white medical tent. I wondered if there were more soldiers to be seen inside, but the Hospital was never open when I was there. There was a notice on the drawn down door blind that said that the hours were 9:30am to 5pm, with a lunch break between 12:30 and 1:30. Also the Hospital was open only Tuesday, Wednesday and Thursday. We visited our family friends on Saturdays. Anyway I didn't have an excuse to go inside because I had no dolls that needed treatment, and I would never dare just go in for a look.

Miss Hilton said that it would be nice to hear some diary entries read out. I shrank down hoping I wasn't chosen, not because I couldn't write or because I was nervous of reading aloud. I never seemed to have anything suitable to write about. Playing at soldiers and going to the cinema with my parents seemed so common place. Julia Billington was eager to read her diary. It was a sad account of her pet Chow-Chow who chewed off an arm belonging to her favourite doll. I sat up. I resolved to speak with her on the way home.

    I caught up with Julia and Lorraine. Lorraine glared at me when I broke the rules and spoke to Julia. Julia beamed and listened.

    'You can get your doll's arm mended at the Doll's Hospital.'

When I told her where it was her ready smile faded. She had no idea where Alfreton Road was, and her parents wouldn't let her go far without a suitable escort.

'I could take you next week, it's the holiday.'

Lorraine's eyes bored into me. Julia resumed her smile and agreed to meet me at the bus terminus opposite her house on Tuesday to catch the 9:40 into town.

I fretted about this adventure all weekend, but was reassured when I saw Julia waiting beside the Number 19 with a parcel under arm. We sat downstairs on the left so as to be ready to get off. She peeled back the brown paper enough to show where the missing arm should be.

'I told my Mother I was going to play with Mickey Hazeldine. What did you say?'

'Oh, I said I was going to look at new dolls in Beeston with Lorraine. I'm allowed to go to Beeston if I'm with a friend. Lorraine's really gone to her cousin's.'

'Tickets, please.'

The conductor was looming with his ticket machine. It was the one that my Mother said was lairy. He certainly was full of himself.

'Two halves to Canning Circus, please.'

He grinned as he wound out the tickets, 'Family outing is it?'

'Yes,' replied Julia, 'We are taking baby to the hospital. She's got polio.'

The conductor backed off. Julia was quick. Being a redhead she had had plenty of practice batting off silly remarks.

We got off just after the Drill Hall where the Territorial Soldiers met. It was only a couple of minutes' walk around Canning Circus to get onto Alfreton Road. As soon as we turned the corner we could see the sign for the Dolls' Hospital standing out from the wall. It was just about ten o'clock. There was a light on in the Hospital, much to my relief. The door pinged when I pushed it open.

The inside of the place was amazing. Behind the counter was a wall of wooden shelves crammed with shoe boxes. Each box had a glued label with the patient's details. At the back was a brown velvet curtain draped over a door. Most of the counter was covered with trays of small body parts and sets of tools. The proprietor behind the counter was an older man, about my Grandfather's age. He had very sparse grey hair and round lens glasses. He wore a dark blue suit waistcoat over a grey flannel shirt. He was talking to a woman and a girl of about my age. The mother handed over some cash and then the two turned to leave. The girl was tightly clutching a doll which looked complete. She seemed delighted. The door pinged again and it was our turn. Julia pressed up against the counter holding out her doll. As she explained the problem I noticed a tray of lead soldiers on the counter. Most of them had been wounded in battle. Pivoted arms were missing, but most had a loose head posted on a match stick into the body. They looked like human giraffes.

'Ah, yes, we can fit a new arm and it will be a good match. This is a popular size doll. We carry a lot of spares. It will be two shillings.' He paused for a moment. 'Can you afford that?'

I slid my hand into pocket and squeezed my silver coins.

'Yes, of course, when will she be ready?'

I released the grip on my coins.

'This time next week. What's her name?'

'Angela.'

Only when the door had pinged behind us did it occur to us that we would be back at school the following week. Julia's smile was fading.

'I can get her back for you.'

'How?'

'Well next Tuesday after school I can run and catch the ten past four bus. I'll be back by five. I'll tell Mum that I'm going to Michael Hazeldine's house to see his train set. I know it's a sort of fib, but it won't hurt. It'll be dead easy.'

Julia beamed. She unzipped her purse and gave me a shiny florin.

The next day I happened to meet Richard and Terry on the street.

'Hey up, Chrisser, what you doing with that ginger lump? I seen you ahtside the Dollies' Hospital.' Richard grinned, 'I was on a bus goin' dahn Radford wiv arh mam to see me auntie. You was all over... what's 'er name?'

He very well knew her name. Terry started to laugh.

'Julia, Julia Billington...'

'You goin' aht wiv 'er, then. Are you goin' to get married?'

Terry was doubled up with laughter.

I contemplated telling the truth. I also contemplated punching Richard's mouth. I decided not to follow the second course of action because Richard was a year older than me, he was rough and he had his side-kick with him. I went for the truth.

'I was taking Julia's doll to the Dolls' Hospital. It's lost an arm. Her dog chewed it off.'

They looked at me in total disbelief.

'Friggin' 'ell, Tez, he's playing wiv dollies now.'

'Chrisser's turnin' into a gell.'

They were both convulsed with laughter. I turned and walked away. I wondered how Julia would have handled that exchange, but they would never have even spoken to a girl.

The following Tuesday I was tense all day. I had taken cash from my money box for bus fare and spun the tale about seeing a train set after school. As soon as we were released I hared off to the bus stop. I sat gasping on the green leatherette seat with two minutes to spare. It was less than two minutes to run the last few yards to the Hospital. I pushed the door and it jingled. There was nobody behind the counter.

'Hello,' I said.

Listening hard I stood and waited. Still nothing happened. I glanced about. There was an eye on the counter. It was a large brown eye, the sort a teddy might wear.

I sensed a movement to my right to the back of the room. The brown velvet curtain moved and a giant doll appeared.

The doll was the size of a man. It was wearing a man's clothes. Its face was smooth and shiny like a celluloid doll. There was no hair or eyebrows and one ear seemed to be crushed. It was missing one eye. I gripped the edge of the counter. I was riveted to the spot. It spoke.

'I'm sorry dad's had to go out, and I was in the back. Can I help you?'

The featureless face twisted up into what might have been a smile.

'Don't be afraid. It's not catching.' He was now behind the counter and I could see that he was a man. He was a man with a terribly disfigured head.

I found my voice, but not my usual voice, 'I'm here to pick up my friend's doll. It's called Julia Billington. It belongs to Angela.'

The man turned to the shelves and selected a shoe-box. He placed it on the counter. Angela lay inside. She now had two arms. She looked perfect.

'It's a mess, isn't it? My face I mean.'

I didn't know what to say, so he carried on, 'You should have seen it before they patched it up - well perhaps not... It was in the war, right at the end. A round from a Jerry Panzerschreck exploded on the Sherman I was standing by. I was knocked over and sprayed with blazing oil. Do you know what a Panzerschreck is?'

I nodded. I knew very well. I had two miniature Airfix German soldiers both using the weapon. 'It's a sort of bazooka, to punch holes in tanks.'

He nodded and picked up the teddy eye. 'I could use one of these.' He laughed.

'That will be just two bob, sir.'

I placed the florin on the counter. When he scooped it up I noticed two missing finger tips. I wondered what more damage was hidden under his clothes.

I had to run hard to catch the bus. I had spent more time in the Dolls' Hospital than I had predicted. It was difficult crossing the busy Derby Road to get to the bus stop. I managed to scramble in just before my Father arrived home from work on his bike. I would have liked to present the doll to Julia that afternoon, instead I secreted it under my zipper jacket. I quickly transferred it to the bottom of my wardrobe whilst my parents greeted each other. During the meal I told them briefly about Michael's train set. He may well have had one but I based the description on Alan's train set which I had admired. I really wanted to talk to my Father about the scarred man. He had told me about the wonders of plastic surgery that had been developed for such people. Later I dreamed that all my class-mates had turned into celluloid dolls with only one eye each and they were all glaring at me.

Julia was delighted with her doll. Her smile faded when I told her about the encounter. She said that she was glad that she hadn't gone with me. She brightened and said that I was brave. I just grinned lamely. Then I turned and walked away from her and Lorraine. I moved to the football end of the playground because I had noticed Richard and Terry pulling faces my way.

Frog in the Sky

'Bleddy 'ell, Tez!'
 'I di'n't mean to do that.'
 I watched my treasure disappear.

My father had shown me how to make paper aeroplanes. For pennies I bought a simple balsa kit in a packet. There were only three pieces to slot together. A paper clip could alter the flight pattern. I built plastic Airfix kits, but they were static display models. The Spitfire could be adapted to appear to be ready for take-off by snipping off the propeller blades and fitting a transparent disc just behind the nose cone. It was still only a display model.

Things got off the ground when I saw a model aircraft kit in Applebee's window. Apart from electrical goods, this shop sold toys and models. The shop window was greasy with the prints of small noses. This kit was different. The plane had to be built almost from scratch, but it was described as a 'stunt' plane. That sounded good to me. There were two versions: the more expensive model had an elastic wind-up engine and propeller, the cheaper one was a glider. My piggy-bank could supply only the cheaper version.

'It won't be made in an afternoon, you know.'
 On examining the contents of the box I realised that it was going to take a while to construct and there were necessary extras to obtain. The balsa strips would need balsa cement. The paper tissue skin would need banana oil. Whilst drying, the balsa strips would need to be held in place with map pins. The construction took place on a board supplied by my Father. He also supplied a sharp craft knife.

The strips of balsa had to be measured against the paper pattern and then cut to size. When the skeleton of one side of the fuselage was ready all the pieces were cemented together and pinned directly to the pattern on the board. It took forever. I persevered.

When the skeleton frame was rigid it was covered in tissue paper. The tissue was tightened by coating it with banana oil. It smelt like my Mother's nail-polish.

Eventually all the separate constructs were glued together. The wings were built in the same fashion but not permanently attached to the fuselage. The nose had to be carved from a cube of balsa.

'You be careful with that sharp knife.'

There were no landing wheels. Neither was there a cockpit with a smiling pilot figure.

The finished model was quite large. All it needed was a test flight.

At school I had talked about the model with Alan Saxton. 'Sacko' was more than delighted to witness the maiden flight. Our garden was not suitable, so we ventured *over tins*. The wing unit was to be held in place with elastic bands. I launched the aircraft carefully into the gentle breeze. It glided about fifty metres, veered to the left and slithered to a graceful halt.

I launched it again. I told Sacko that he could have the next go. He never got it. The aircraft was launched with more gusto and at a steeper angle. It *was* a 'stunt' model. I thought it was going to loop-the-loop, but it suddenly dived sideways and straight down. The wing unit was wrenched off. The nose cone was knocked off. The tissue paper skin was torn in several places.

'You can mend it.'

'Yeah.'

I could, but in my mind I saw all subsequent flights coming to similar grief. It was parked on the top of my utility wardrobe.

Another shopping trip into Beeston gave another chance to gaze into Applebee's window. There it was: the answer to a young aviator's dream. The answer was in a cardboard box with the company logo emblazoned in the top corner like a large postage stamp. It said, 'FROG.' Below the logo was the image of an aeroplane with landing wheels and a motor driven propeller. I could just about read the essential words: clip together, sturdy construction and complete kit.

Inside the box was a silvery finished monoplane ready to be clipped together. It was indeed sturdy: being made of something like the stuff they use for ping-pong balls. The wings were separate and clipped into reinforced slots in the fuselage. The wheels, with spindly, but durable, wire legs also clipped on snugly. There was a transparent cock-pit, but alas no pilot figure. The best feature was the propeller which was driven by a hefty elastic band. Now we were flying.

I learned from the instructions that FROG meant 'flies right off the ground'. In a controlled test, with only a slight turn of the elastic band, the plane raced along the ground. It could take off like a real aeroplane. But what about landing?

'Pop down to Pretty's and get a packet of Typhoo.'
   On the way back I met Richard sauntering down the street.
   'Hey-up, Chrisser. How's that airy-plane yo're mekkin'?'
   I guessed he was talking about the ill-fated balsa and tissue one. So I told him of its maiden flight and subsequent demise. He had a feint smirk on his face. Other people's disasters were always a source of mirth for Richard. I told him of the latest acquisition.
   'Y'ain't tried it yet?'
   'Well, no, not a test flight. I don't want to go *over tins*. The grass is too bumpy.'
   'An' the rec?'
   'Too many kids chasing about.'
   'How abaht ar school field?'
   He must have seen the surprise on my face.
   'It's perfect. Flat and cut short. And there's nobody there.'
   We were all on school holiday. Children didn't usually go near in the holidays.
   'What about the teachers?'
   He grinned. 'They are on 'oliday an all. They don't live there.'
   I hadn't thought of the school being empty.
   'Yeah, let's try it out. You go an' get the plane, an' I'll call for Tez.'
   I wouldn't dare go into the school grounds on my own.
   'OK'

It was strange entering the school gates on Boundary Road without hordes of other children. I started to fret about the caretaker lurking, but Richard was full of confidence. Terry was happy to be included. We walked along the little road that serviced our junior school, the infant school and the boys' secondary school. We took the first right to enter the junior area. Our educational careers had started in the infant school. Aged seven we had been marched through the double doors on the corridor which separated infants from juniors. Being a year older, Richard was there to greet us. There were double doors at the other end of the infant corridor which gave access to the secondary school. I had only a hazy idea of what was beyond. It was not the place for City children. Only County *boys* went there. They were louts.

The long yard down the side of the school was empty and quiet. On the right were green metal railings to separate the school from the back gardens of Boundary Road. Half way down the yard there was a heap of coke leaning against the wall. It was for the school boilers. This was where the caretaker usually lurked. He had a den in the boiler house down the steps. All was quiet.

The yard sloped down to the field. The field stretched along the back of the school complex. Access to the field was usually down some brick steps because the field was lower than the schools. Now the field was quiet, empty and vast. Juniors keep to their end. The Secondary school end was a no-go area. Once, when the snow came, secondary boys invaded. Juniors screamed away from the snow ballers until gruff teachers restored the situation. All was quiet now.

I opened the box and clipped the aeroplane together. Tension mounted as I wound the propeller. It was ready. Keeping hold of the propeller I placed the aeroplane on the recently mowed grass.

It bounced away and then lifted free. It soared away for a few seconds until the elastic band unravelled. The plane glided down to a bumpy but happy landing. It was a winner.

All thoughts of 'trespassing' disappeared. The flight was repeated successfully. I was ecstatic. Richard and Terry seemed pleasantly amused.

Each launch took us further up the field: past the infant steps and as far as the big boys' steps. I let Richard have a go. He tried launching from shoulder height. It was a spectacular performance. The plane did a graceful curve before making a bouncy landing. The construction was indeed sturdy.

We realised that we had progressed almost the length of the school field. The end of the field was marked by more green metal railings and scrubby bushes. It was unknown territory.

'Fly it back, Terry, your turn.'

Terry carefully wound the propeller. The familiar end of the field seemed far away.

Terry made an aerial launch. He released it almost vertically. It soared into the blue for a second before rolling side-ways. We watched it level out shooting off the wrong way.

'Bleddy 'ell, Tez.'

'I di'n't mean to do that.'

I watched my treasure disappear.

It buzzed over the bushes and railings and out of sight. All the triumph of the afternoon drained away.

'Soz, Chrisser.'

'Do'n jus'stan' there. Let's gerrit back!'

Richard pushed through the bushes. The railings were high, taller than a grown-up. We looked for footholds.

'Here, dahn here.'

Terry was on his back and sliding under the railings. There was a depression, probably made by kids or a badger. He scrambled to his feet grinning. Richard and I followed. It was a squeeze for Richard. We stood on a grassy verge.

'What's this road?'

'Dunno, don' marrer.'

I scanned the road for signs of a squashed aeroplane.

Terry had his arm out. 'Must of gone straight over there.'

I looked in the direction he was pointing. If the plane had continued in the straight flight path, it would have crossed the road and gone into the garden of the house facing us, if the lorry hadn't been in the way.

As we crossed the road behind the lorry, I looked underneath. The vehicle suddenly sprang into life and we dodged the exhaust fumes. We watched it move away from the kerb.

Terry was suddenly shrieking and pointing. 'It's on the back!'

On the back, just behind the cab, were some boxes standing higher that the lorry sides. Perched on a box was a silver aeroplane with its nose down like it was sniffing.

It was Richard's turn to be shrieking and waving. 'Stop. Stop!'

The yellow Bedford continued. I read, 'Pilgrim,' lettered on the back end boards.

I was so close. I wanted to cry.

'Friggin''ell.'

We became aware of an audience. There was a man standing in front of an open garage. He had stopped organising his delivery to watch the pantomime. The lorry had turned the corner so we looked at him. He was about my Grandfather's age. He was very strange. He had a beard. Only baddies and dangerous foreigners had beards, according to the cinema.

Richard stage whispered like a gangster, 'Mad professor or child murderer.'

Terry squeaked.

'What's the matter, boys?'
'That lorry, what's jus' gone 'as gorrow aeroplane, Mester.'
'We were flying it on the field and it went over the railings.'
'Ah seen it on the back of the lorry. It's Chrisser's.'
'Chrisser?'
'That's me. My name is really Christopher.'
The man smiled. 'That's my name too. I used to have curly hair like yours.'
This was hard to believe. He was bald, and the hair on his face was grey.
'You could get your plane back'
'"Ow?'
'That was Mr Pilgrim's delivery truck. I've just had some bits delivered. The truck is going back to Pilgrim's yard on Acacia Walk. If you're quick...'
We were quick. We knew where Acacia Walk was. It was known to us as Ack-Ack. It was just off the High Road, near Applebee's toy shop.
We galloped after the lorry and quickly recognised Wallett Avenue. Wallett Avenue led onto Marlborough Road, which was a straight run to the High Road. We ran down the middle of the road to avoid tripping on the uneven flag stones of the pavement. Once on the High Road it was only two minutes dodging shoppers to get to the narrow lane called Acacia Walk. About half way down on the right was a protruding board indicating 'Pilgrim's Timber Yard and Iron Mongery'. Beneath the sign was a parked yellow Bedford lorry.
We walked towards the lorry breathing hard.
'S'not there.'
'Must have blown off.'
'Course it bleddy is. It's fallen dahn in the back of the soddin' lorry.'
My hopes were riding a roller-coaster.
'If it ain't, Chrisser, I'll nick yo' anuvver from owd Applebee's.'
Richard was wearing his roguish grin. I was quite sure he meant it though. He turned and scrambled easily up one of the big wheels.
'Yes!'
'Oi!' A man in overalls was coming out of the yard gates. He didn't look friendly.
Richard stooped and then reappeared. His arm jerked and the silver plane floated down. Terry caught it and swiftly handed it to me.
'Just what do you think you're...?'

But fly-boy Richard was already leaping to the tarmac.

'Hooligans!'

We legged it back to the safety of the shoppers on the High Street.

The aircraft didn't seem to have sustained any damage. Sturdy, it was. I was ecstatic again.

'Thanks, Richard.'

He beamed.

'Sorry,' said Terry.

Richard laughed and ruffled Terry's hay-stack.

'Soright, Tez. It woz a good laugh. Yo' can g'back an' tell the mad scientist we got the plane back.'

Terry looked aghast.

Richard laughed again. He was high on the escapade. He thrived on excitement.

'Nah, Tez, only kiddin'.'

Much later, and back at school, I stood on the field at lunch break with hundreds of shrieking and cavorting kids and tried to recall the empty space of that afternoon. It was difficult.

The FROG did buzz about the sky again. It eventually retired to a place of honour on my bedside cabinet.

Frogmore Street

'Keep it wrapped up, and don't go showing it to anybody, 'specially that Richard.'

I was rather delighted with the gift from Mr Bellamy. The Bellamy's lived next door. They were quite old, so they were moving to somewhere more suitable. They were disposing of much of the little they had gathered over the years. As a parting shot Mr Bellamy gave my Father a shirt. It was very long without a collar and was made of striped flannel. My Father was not impressed, but I was. It was perfect for dressing up as a Berber tribesman. A tea-towel around my head completed the ensemble. I was absolutely delighted with Mr Bellamy's gift to me. It was a German bayonet, in its scabbard, which had been brought back from the First War. My Mother was not delighted.

'You are not playing with that!'

I was allowed to examine it, under supervision. I tried fastening it to my wooden toy Lee-Enfield rifle. It was far too heavy. So it was secured in my Parents' wardrobe.

After the Bellamy's left, it was suggested that 'my' bayonet should be exchanged for cash at an antique shop. We knew of one, in town, on Mansfield Road. When I was younger we had passed this junk shop on the way to Goose Fair. The window display was probably more exciting than the candy-floss and the other magic in the annual autumn fair on the Forest grounds. The display contained all the things which little boys craved. I had my eye on an open biscuit tin full of old toy soldiers. A sign said, 'Antiques bought and sold'. My father said that we would go together on a Saturday. It wasn't quite confirmed that I could spend the resulting cash as I wished. Usually any spare cash went into my savings account for a rainy day.

The chosen Saturday looked like being abandoned as My Father was offered overtime. Time and a half on Saturdays was not to be missed. My Mother had an appointment with a hairdresser in Beeston that day. After some deliberation it seemed that I was a big boy and quite capable of taking the bayonet to the junk shop. It was a rite of passage. I was to be trusted. There was a note to show my Parents' approval of the potential deal.

'Keep it wrapped up and don't go showing it to anybody, 'specially that Richard.'

Unfortunately I couldn't keep my mouth shut. I had to boast about owning a German bayonet, swapping it for cash and travelling into town on my own. Of course Richard and Terry were intrigued.

'Hey, Chrisser we'll come wiv yo'.

That was the delightful bit. I was a little nervous of travelling alone on such a mission. The daunting bit was, 'Let's 'ave a goz at it before yo' sell it.'

One afternoon in the week Richard and Terry came with me from school. My Parents were working until five o'clock. I decided to take them both upstairs away from neighbours' eyes. They waited while I took the bayonet from its place in the wardrobe. I pulled the gleaming blade carefully out of the scabbard.

'Wow, imagine having that shoved in yer guts.'

Richard took it from my hand. He waved it about, and then made to stab Terry. He grinned when Terry flinched.

'Did O'd Bellamy kill a Jerry to get it?'

I shrugged. My Father had said that Mr Bellamy most likely would have picked it up at the end of the war. The bayonet was returned to its scabbard and then secured in the wardrobe.

On Saturday they were waiting at the end of my Close. Together we caught an early bus at the terminus at the end of our street. I had my return fare and a little extra. Richard and Terry paid for themselves. I had the bayonet wrapped in brown paper and carried in a shopping bag.

From the terminus on Mount Street we walked down St. James Street. We crossed Slab Square diagonally to get to King's Street. We crossed Parliament Street and started on Mansfield Road. It would be only a penny fare on the trolley, but we decided to walk. It wasn't far.

''Ow much d'yo reckon to get forrit?'

'I've no idea. My dad said not to expect much.'

We reached the shop and spent a few moments goggling at the displayed items. The door pinged as we entered. It was an Aladdin's cave inside. There was heaps of interesting old stuff. A deep sea diving suit stood in one corner, another corner had a red-Indian tepee, and the floor space was covered with trestle tables full of all sorts. The proprietor stood up from behind a cash register. He was balding like my Father, and wore an open grey cardigan. I noticed hideous carved masks hanging next to a couple of Samurai swords on the back wall. The proprietor eyed us warily: he had probably lost some stock to naughty little boys. I held the bag up. There was no room on the shop counter.

'I've got a German bayonet. I want to sell it. I've got a note.'

I pulled the note from the bag and handed it over. I pulled the bayonet from the bag and held it out. He took it and examined the scabbard, complete with frog. The gleaming blade was pulled and examined. He nodded.

'Mmm, nice and clean. I can give you, er… five bob?'

My father had told me I'd be lucky to sell it, and to accept any offer. Five shillings would buy ten toy soldiers from Woolworths, or four of the new smart plastic ones from Applebee's.

'Yes, please, sir.'

He smiled, opened the till and handed me two half-crowns.

'Do you want to look around. There might me something you like…'

As much as I wanted to, I shook my head and said that I had to take the money home.

Outside the shop I held the two half-crowns tightly with my hand stuffed deep into my pocket.

'Chiz, Chrisser, that was easy. Whatcha gonna do with the lolly?'

'Take it home.'

'Ah, c'mon. It's yourn innit?'

'Yes, but I said I would take it home.'

Richard shrugged. Terry spoke, 'Loads of stuff in there. Wish Ah'd got loadsa money.'

'Well yo' aint, Tez. Best yo' can do is nick it.'

Terry grinned, 'Ah did.'

He opened his fingers to reveal a medal complete with ribbon.

'Christ! Tez yo'll gerrus shot.'

Richard closed Terry's fingers, and glanced back at the shop.

'Best get goin', boys.'

He lurched out across Mansfield Road. We followed quickly. Back in those days the traffic was light, but still someone hooted. Safely on the other side, Richard laughed.

'Ah know where we are. That's Frogmore Street. It's a dead lickle cut fru to Huntingdon Street. It's only a couple of shakes dahn Hunto to get to Central Market. Ay?'

I knew the covered Central Market well. I spent happy times in there with my nose against the window of one stall while my Mother rummaged for bargains on the knitting wool stalls. My stall had electrical goods one side. The other side displayed the latest Dinky and Britain's toys. I coveted the Long Tom 155mm artillery piece. It had separate shells, but it cost 17/6. It was way beyond my dreams.

'OK, but we mustn't be long.'

'Berra run, then.'

It was not easy running with one hand stuffed into a pocket and the other clutching a shopping bag. I pulled my hand free, and promptly dropped the two coins. Richard heard the cry and turned. Terry, who was behind me, saw what happened. I staggered after the coins which rolled swiftly along the sloping pavement. Richard's foot stamped down. He missed, but the second attempt stopped a coin. The other coin continued its escape. It veered to the left and was stopped by the grill which covered the access to a coal cellar. It lay still straddling an iron rung. Richard handed me the first, and went for the second. He wasn't quite careful enough. The half-crown piece disappeared into the Black Hole of Calcutta.

I just stood there staring. My chest was heaving and my eyes began to blur. The loss of the coin was tragic, but explaining to my Parents would be awful.

'We'll gerrit back, Chrisser. Honest, we'll gerrit back. Not we, Tez?'

'Arh. We can try knocking on the door.'

The house which the coal-shute belonged to was number 3. The even numbers were across the road. The road was empty. The houses looked asleep. Number 3 was different in that the curtains were still closed. There was no answer to Terry's knocking. He put his ear to the door panel. He shook his head.

Suddenly Richard brightened, 'Ah know. We guz rahn the back.'

There were no entries in the short length of terraced houses.

'Dahn the end, rahn the corner. There must be a back entry or summat.'

We chased off down the short street and ran around the end house. There was an entry for all the backs. On the left was a brick wall with wooden gates for each house, on the right was a very high brick wall. The entry was scruffy. Litter and junk were decorated with wild plants.

We went to the far end and counted back. Terry tried the latch. Nothing happened.

'It's bolted. I'll give yo' a leg up, Tez.'

Richard laced his fingers for Terry's foot, and Terry was quickly leaning over the top of the gate.

'There's a bolt, but it aint on.'

When Terry had dropped back down, Richard gave the gate a hefty shove. It creaked open. The yard was closed in by an outside toilet on the right and a dividing wall on the left. There were several plant pots near the back door. The plants were overgrown and looked desperate to get out. The downstairs curtains were closed. Terry tried the back door. 'S'locked.'

Richard pointed at the plant pots, 'Eeny-meeny, miney-mo.' He chose the only pot which was upside down, 'Hey presto.' He picked up a back door key.

I said weakly, 'We can't...'

The key was already in the lock and the door swung open. The kitchen was gloomy and quiet. Richard touched the gas-stove, 'Co'd.' Cautiously we peeped into the back room. That too was gloomy, and smelly. It looked like a film set for a film about Victorian murderers.

'Nob'dy here. There's the cellar door, Chrisser, go get your half-crown.'

I took a step towards the door and froze. I heard a voice.

'Help.'

It was faint and far away. The others had heard it too. We didn't make a sound.

'Help.'

I turned to look at Richard. Terry looked scared, 'Ghost!'

'Nah, Tez, It's an o'd dame's voice.'

'Help.'

'Forward the Valiants.'

We crept carefully beyond the back room and into the hallway. There was a front room, but the voice was coming from upstairs. Richard led the way. On the first landing a bedroom door was slightly open.

'Help.'

It was obvious that the voice was coming from the front bedroom. Richard pushed the door open. I had time to notice the wallpaper in the stair-well billowing away from the walls. It was gloomy in the bedroom. We saw a form on the floor beside the brass bed. It moved slightly.

'Oh, thank God.'

Terry switched the light on. An old woman was underneath a counterpane. We could see a frail face with wispy grey hair. A bony hand clutched at the edge of the counterpane. One bony white foot protruded. There was a smell of unflushed toilets.

'What happened?'

'I fell. I think my leg is broken. I can't move. It hurts so.'

'When did you fall?'

'Last night, when I was going to bed, after I'd switched the light off.'

'Yo've bin there on the floor for over twenny four hours!'

'I managed to pull this cover over me. Thank God you came.'

There was a blank few seconds before Richard assumed command.

'Right, this o'd lady needs 'elp. Tez, yo' leg back onto the main road. Fin' a phone-box an' call a nambulance. Y'know 999. Yo' don' need no money. Tell'm the address: free Frogmore Street. Tell'm there's an o'd lady down Then wait at the front. Oh, an' click the Yale up, so's yo' can get back in. Chrisser, see if yo' can fin' owt to eat, an' mek a cuppa. I'll stay here wiv 'er an' try an mek her more comfy. An' while yo' are dahn there, see if yo' can get your half dollar back.'

It must have been because Richard was a year older than Terry and me.

We clattered down stairs. Terry went for the front door as I dived into the kitchen. I found a coronation mug with an image of George V. I put the filled kettle onto a gas ring and light the gas. In a bread-tin I found some bread which needed the green mould trimming away. On the kitchen table was a box that looked like a rabbit-hutch. The door was closely perforated metal. Inside the 'cooler' was a piece of cheese. That, too, needed trimming. Also there was a squidge of yellow stuff in greaseproof paper which was likely to be butter. I brewed the tea. The only milk didn't smell right. So I loaded the hot tea with sugar and turned my attention to making a cheese sandwich. I carried the snack on a tin tray very carefully out of the kitchen to the stairs. The front door bumped, and a panting Terry followed me to the bedroom.

Richard had put the pillows down for her head, and found a blanket as extra cover. He was kneeling beside her holding one hand. Her other hand grasped the little cross on a chain around her neck. She managed a smile.

'He's an angel. An angel sent in the hour of need.'

I didn't disabuse her of this notion. I put the tray down. Richard held the tea for her to sip.

'There's a nambulance comin'. I'll go an' wait forrit.'

Richard looked at me, 'The half-dollar?'

I followed Terry down stairs. Terry went to the front door, and I tackled the cellar.

Looking down the stone steps into black-nothing was scary. I turned around and opened the curtains. It didn't make much difference. My eyes began to get used to the dark. There was some light wriggling through the pavement grill, but not enough. I wondered how the old woman had managed to get coal in the dark. My hand was on the door jamb. My fingers were touching a round metal lump. The light switch! I clicked it down and the cellar was just about illuminated by a very low wattage bare bulb dangling on twisted cotton covered wires. I ventured down the steps. I could not see what might be waiting for me around the corner at the bottom. I clenched my teeth and fist and continued down. There were many spider webs, but no monsters. I started the search and very quickly found the coin. Gleefully I returned it to my pocket and scrambled out of the cellar.

I was just in time to meet Terry guiding a couple of ambulance men towards the stairs. They wore dark blue uniforms with peaked caps and white medical satchels. One of them carried a rolled up stretcher.

'We'll take over from now.' He ushered us out of the bedroom. 'You've done very well, she might have died. You best get off home, but wait a bit, lads, 'cos someone wants to talk to you.'

That someone appeared in the next minute. Standing on the doorstep was another dark blue uniform. I thought Richard and Terry might bolt for the backdoor. Richard might be arrested for breaking and entering. Terry might be arrested for stealing a medal.

'Well done, boys. Tell me all about it.'

Richard took command again, 'We was walkin' past this house on us way to Central Market. Chrisser had just so'd summink at the junk shop. We heard this cry for 'elp. We cou'nt gerrin the front, so we went rahn the back. The back door weren't locked, wassit, Tez?'

'Nah, so we gorrin to 'elp the o'd lady. Chrisser made the tea, an' Ah ringed for a nambulance.'

'An' Ah looked after 'er while we was waitin'. Can we go home now?'

The policeman nodded. He pulled out a notebook, 'I need to take your names and addresses, lads'

Richard took command again, 'Richard Smith.' He rattled off an address in Radford.

Terry followed suit, 'Terrence Brown.' He gave an address in Beeston.

When it was my turn I told the truth about my name and address.

Out on the pavement Richard scowled at me, 'Dumbo, yo' should never tell where yo' live an' what you real name is!'

I felt stupid and confused. I wished that I had used that outside toilet. We turned towards Mansfield Road. The cream coloured Trojan ambulance was parked on the street. A stout black bicycle was leaning against the wall. I clutched my two half-crowns tightly.

'You are a bit late, my lad. What kept you? Your Dad's had his dinner.'

I burbled on about selling the bayonet and going to look in GeeDee's toy shop and the toy stall in Central Market.

'And didn't keep an eye on the time. Did you spend any of it?'

I shook my head.

'Good. You've got enough toy soldiers. We can put the money in your savings account.'

For the next few evenings I scanned the Evening Post. I was looking for any report about boys saving the life of an old lady. I wondered if I should tell my Parents the truth, but decided not to.

A week later there was a knock at the front door. Only the insurance men came to the front door.

'See who that is, Chick.'

I opened the door to a policeman. I felt faint. I knew what he was there for, 'Mum'.

Even with his helmet off, the policeman seemed to fill up the room. My Father put the Daily Mirror down. My mother twisted a tea towel. The officer smiled.

'Well you have an excellent young man here. A regular hero. Someone the City should be proud of.'

This was not what I had anticipated. I felt dizzy. My Parents looked at me quizzically. I just wanted to be somewhere else, Australia perhaps.

The policeman outlined the rescue of the elderly person.

'But he didn't say anything to us. Have you got the right person?... Chris?'

I could not speak. I was wondering how many years I'd get.'

'Well, the other two boys, we didn't seem to be able to contact. Mrs Bailey, a widow, is making a good recovery in hospital. She had a fractured hip. She might have died if it wasn't for your son's intervention. She felt that she wanted to say a big thank you. Since your son is the only one we could contact, I'm to give you this.'

He handed me an envelope. I opened it and found a ten shilling note inside. (Perhaps the Moon rather than Australia.)

The rest of the evening was spent telling the truth and answering searching questions. I said nothing about the medal. At the end I burst into tears. My Mother hugged me.

I thought to tell Richard and Terry, and perhaps give them a share of the reward. My Father advised me to say nothing. They had lied their way out of the reward, and so got their just desserts. This didn't seem quite right, but I said nothing to them.

Five shillings for the bayonet, and ten for the reward made fifteen shillings which was three quarters of a pound, but still two and six short of the artillery piece. I knew that once the money was in my savings account it was no longer available. I was saving for something sensible in the distant future, apparently.

In the end they said that I had been brave, but not very sensible to go along with Richard and Terry. Of course I promised to keep away from them, as far as possible. Whilst I was promising I kept my fingers crossed.

Richard and Terry hardly mentioned the adventure. But a little while later Terry came up to me in the play-ground. He had something in his hand.

'Ere, Chrisser, yo' can have this. Ah don't really wannit, an' yo' like that sort of thing.'

He handed me the medal. On closer inspection I saw that it was a medal issued to soldiers who had fought in the Great War. A treasure.

Fun Fairies

'Tell you what, I'll give you ten bob not to go?'

This was my first lesson in *realpolitik*. It was a no-brainer, so my response took only a few seconds.

'Yes.'

'Are you sure?'

I nodded furiously. I was agreeing not to go the Fun Fair, and be rewarded with ten shillings. Ten shillings could be spent on increasing my army of toy soldiers. Truth be known, going to the Fair wasn't that much fun.

For the last three or four years my Parents had taken me to the Nottingham Goose Fair. It was claimed to be the largest Fair in the land. It started in the distant past with farm produce and the attendant attractions being for sale in the City's Market Square. Geese were walked from Norfolk with their feet protected with tar. The Fair outgrew the City centre and was moved in 1929 to a new site. It was an open space on the periphery named *The Forest*!

Each year, on the first Thursday, Friday and Saturday in October, small Fun Fairs gathered to create a sea of amusements. It was best to see these at night when thousands of coloured lights adorned the rides and stalls. There was the bus trip into the City, and then a walk up Mansfield Road. It was possible to travel by trolley bus, but it was more exciting to approach slowly. The glow in the sky was evident and the smells grew stronger as did the throb of the power generators. Coming away from the Fair were very young children armed with sticks of candy-floss, fluffy toy winnings and bought hats.

Once over the brow of the hill the great glow could be seen. My hand was held tightly because of the dense mass of people. I rode around on the *Golden Galloping Horses* whilst my parents waved and smiled. The bigger rides were too scary. Eventually I was prised away from the throbbing generators to go home wearing a small police helmet and covering my cheeks with candy-floss. I was warned off toffee apples as they were hard unripe fruit coated in seductive rich brown toffee.

My Parents had little interest in the Fair and I was too young to go alone. So my Father came up with the solution. He must have calculated that giving me half a pound was a good deal. Everyone was happy. I avoided the Fair for the next few years. The ten shillings were put into my money box for some future event…

Interest in the Fair was revitalised when Mother read out an item in the local paper.

'They're going to have a Fair on the field on Woodside Road.'

This was *over tins* territory. A new link road to join Woodside Road and University Boulevard was started. The boundary wall of corrugated 'tins' had been removed and bull dozers had created a pilot scar across our playing fields. After the initial burst of energy the enterprise seemed to slow down. The new road wasn't going to be instant. As the Summer began to fade into Autumn, drains had been laid, kerb stones set in place and lamp post erected. The lamps were not yet working and the road surface was still only compressed ballast. An arrangement had been made with Local Authority and Archie Cobb to have a four day Fun Fair on the open flat field which now had access from Broadgate as it joined University Boulevard. Archie Cobb owned a small Fun Fair which would make up part of the Goose Fair.

'There's one on Woffo's window!'

The new game was spotting *Archie Cobb's Fun Fair* fliers which the advanced party had been pasting around. Woffington's was the corner shop at the bottom end of my street.

'It's gonna be here nex' weekend.'

My playmates and classmates were fired with enthusiasm. It must have been infectious. I began to seriously reconsider my attitude to Fairgrounds.

Archie Cobb's outfit began arriving on the Monday morning. Everyone at school knew by the afternoon. So just after 4pm hordes of kids were standing on the un-metalled new road, to watch the action. Huge maroon and red vehicles, most of which were ex-army, had been strategically parked and the Fair Folks were busy setting out the amusements and rides. At the edge of the field were caravans and generators. I was smitten.

Richard, of course, had the details.

'They're 'ere til Sat'day. Starts on Thursday. Friday afternoon is for the lickle kids. Me an' Tez are goin' Friday night. What yo' doin', Chrisser?'

I really wanted to go to the Fair, but I was a little uneasy about telling my Parents. Their permission was necessary for anything out of the ordinary.

'I changed my mind.'

'Who are you thinking of going with?'

'Geoff, and maybe Alan.'

'What about Tony?'

Mother was always keen to include *Twilmop*, but I knew already that he was going with his mother on Friday afternoon straight from school.

'Oh, Tony's going on Friday afternoon.'

'When were you thinking of going?'

After tea it would be still light, but the evenings were closing in. I was not allowed out on my own when it was dark ~ except to go to Cubs.

'Friday, Friday after tea.'

'It'll be dark.'

My Father folded his daily paper.

'He's going with friends. It's only a quarter of a mile away. And he's a sensible boy.'

Mother didn't look convinced.

'That road's not lit…'

According to my Mother there were legions of 'funny' men, murderers on the run and mad people lurking in every dark corner ready to pounce on the innocent.

'Bridget, he's got to grow up. He'll be alright, and anyway he'll be back home by 9 o'clock.'

'Mind you are, Sunshine… Is Richard going?'

I hadn't lied about Geoff. He was definitely going with me. I had not mentioned Richard and his 'pet' Terry. They would of course be going to the Fair on Friday evening, as was everyone else we knew. Saturday evening was the preserve of the big kids ~ the teenagers ~ the lary ones.

Choosing an outfit was not difficult. I had school clothes, play clothes and best clothes. The choice was play clothes. I thought to wear my black blazer too: it might be cool, and I thought that I looked more grown-up. My informants had told me that Barbara 'Grey-Eyes' would be there. Now, that might be worth the effort.

117

Geoff called for me at half past six.

'How much you got?'

I'd spent the previous hour checking over my five shillings.

Geoff's eyes gleamed, 'My dad gave me ten bob.'

That was twice my pocket money, but I knew he wouldn't spend it all. Like me, he was keen on toy soldiers.

We had checked out the Fairground through the week on the way home from school. Archie Cobb had a modest helter-skelter, a big-wheel, a horsey round-about, a couple of smaller ones for little kids, a dodgem track, a ghost train, swing-boats and a scary machine that waved long 'arms' up and down as it rotated and spun the cars. Intermingled were shies for shooting pellets, throwing darts, tossing rings and hurling wooden balls. Prizes could be won. There were trailers selling toffee apples, candy-floss and hot-dogs. Tucked away were the fortune teller's booth, and another booth with the *Snake Girl* that only grown-ups were allowed to see.

The noise and the smell were intoxicating. We hurried along the un-made road with many others. Little children were coming away with their parents. I spotted Julia Billington's red mane. She was with Lorraine and Angela. I didn't see Barbara.

The lights were on even though it was still light. The sun was way down. Bill Haley was belting out *Rock around the Clock*. My parents would not have enjoyed themselves. The field was full of people, mostly kids who we knew from school. I was pleased to see Mickey Hazeldine a fellow artist and class-mate. We wandered about taking it all in.

'Let's go on the dodgems. We can bump Lorraine and Angela.'

Giddy-up-a Ding Dong blared out and the car lurched into life. A greasy looking 'roadie' took our sixpences, and the over-head pick-up crackled and sparked. Geoff chased Lorraine and Angela. We hit them several times. The girls squealed. When we climbed out the cars, Julia was waiting for her friends.

'Why don't you go on with Julia?'

I nobly paid for her. She was wearing perfume. As I piloted the car about I caught sight of Barbara 'Grey Eyes.' She was with her two friends watching the dodgems. Julia waved. I tried to concentrate on the driving.

Now Bill Haley was booming out *See you Later Alligator*. These 'degenerate' pop songs were squeezed into *Workers' Playtime* and odd slots on the Light Programme. There was no dedicated time for Rock and Roll on the wireless back then.

I scanned around for 'Grey-Eyes'. I thought to impress her with a gift. Perhaps a teddy-bear won by my shooting skill would do.

Geoff and I blazed away at the metal pegs. Geoff was certain that he had hit one, but it had not fallen. We heard the ping of the pellets on the metal back wall. It was necessary to knock down two pegs for a prize. I had no success with my one shilling out-lay.

We moved on to the coconut-shy.

'I reckon the nuts are glued on.'

Half my money was now gone.

'Hey-up, Chrisser.'

It was Richard. He was trying to wreck his teeth on a toffee apple. At his side was Terry barely visible behind a huge pink candy floss. They were all grins.

'We bin on ev'ry fink. Even 'ad a goz at the *Snake-Girl*.'

'How did you get in?'

'Di'n't. Sneaked rahn the back wiv Tez an' 'ad a peep.'

Terry cut in, 'She ain't got no clothes on.'

'Yeah, but she 'ad this snake wrapped arahn 'er. You can't see nowt.'

'Ah fink it's a rubber snake anyroad.'

I could see that Geoff was interested, so we readily agreed to let Richard show us where to peep in.

At that point a bunch of girls approached. It was Lorraine, Angela and Julia again. They were also with three others. One of them was 'Grey-Eyes'.

I hoped none of my pals would start blathering on about peeping at a girl wearing only a snake.

'Can we talk to you? Those boys keep following us. We don't like them.'

Hovering near were four boys. They were not from our school, but I did recognise one of them. He had been Richard's accomplice on the infamous firework stealing trip. I noticed that another boy had a sheath knife tethered to his belt. He definitely was not a boy scout.

'Hey up, Dickie, 'ow yo' doin'?'

Richard winced. He was not happy with anything other than his given name. He quickly retrieved his smile.

'What time is it? I whispered to Geoff. The lights were glowing bright in the evening gloom.

'Half eight.'

Richard was a big boy, but these other four were even bigger.

'We was aying a good time til yo' turned up.'

I glanced at Geoff. He was frowning at me. We figured what was going to happen next. There were plenty of people around, but most of them were kids ~ oblivious to what was about to unfold.

The girls started to edge away.

'Nah, don't go. These goons are going to shove off… right nah.'

They didn't look like they were going anywhere. What was Richard thinking of?

He dropped the remains of the toffee apple and slid his hand inside his jacket. I saw the flash of a blade. Angela squeaked. The boy with the sheath knife flicked the release stud.

Richard said, 'I'm dangerous, yo' know.'

One boy laughed. Another said, 'Yo' an' whose army?'

My brain was screaming for me to run, but I was fixed in position.

'Don't yo' laugh at me.' Richard suddenly became very wild. The blade was waved about. He turned towards Terry, who was grinning. 'I tol' yo' not to laugh at me. I'm bleddy dangerous.'

He stepped towards Terry and plunged the blade into his chest. Terry's face contorted. He made a ghastly noise, folded up and lay face down and quite still.

'Who want's it next?' The blade glinted again.

Six girls shrieked in unison, and then again.

Four big boys turned and fled.

Adults surrounded the scene.

A Fair worker said, 'What's going on?'

Richard lowered the blade.

'Nuffink, mester. We was just playin' abaht… You can gerrup nah, Tez.'

The 'corpse' sprang up grinning.

Richard was grinning, 'The gells fought he was really stabbed. It's not real.'

To make his point, he pushed the point of the blade into the palm of his free hand. The blade disappeared. When he pulled the weapon back the blade reappeared. It was bloodless. So was Terry's shirt front.

There was a loud gasp from the girls. Richard took a bow. The man shook his head. Other adults muttered, 'Silly, bleddy kids,' and began to drift away.

'Yo' done good, Tez.'

Terry beamed.

To me he said, 'They're sellin' 'em at the Fair. Me an' Tez was gonna scare yo'. Bit of a lark, see. We 'ad a practice. Just as well…'

He handed me the knife. On closer inspection it was a cheap toy made of plastic. The chromed blade pressed into the handle.

The girls were still staring in disbelief. Geoff nudged me, 'It's nearly quart to nine.'

Our group began to drift towards the unfinished road. The girls were chattering. Richard floated along on the wings of victory and the loud speaker wailed, *'Why do fools fall in love?'*

Geoff grinned, 'Shall we put all this in our school diaries on Monday?'

My heart was still bouncing.

Away from the Fair Ground it was dark. I had never been *Over Tins* in the dark. Archie Cobb's glowed and throbbed behind us. Beyond the darkness ahead was the lesser glow of the street lamps of the Council estate. It was chilly but magical. Richard was still full of himself. Terry re-enacted his 'demise'. He probably had a career future in being a 'stiff'. The girls giggled and chattered. There were several teenagers going the opposite way. The Fair would continue for another hour or so.

All too soon my feet were onto a metalled surface. I glanced at 'Grey-Eyes'. She was clutching a pink, fluffy toy. It could have been a rabbit, or a cat or a teddy-bear. She grinned.

Lorraine said, 'Mickey Hazeldine gave it to her. He won it on the rifle-range.'

Mickey had a young sister 'Lulu'. Why didn't he take it home for her? Why did he give it to Barbara Allen?

Julia peeled away to the right, and 'Grey-Eyes' went left with her friends. Richard and Terry cavorted about with the plastic knife. I walked up my street with Geoff. Lorraine and Angela followed at a discreet distance.

Archie Cobb packed up and moved off early in the next week. Richard and Terry combed the flattened field for spilt change. The new road received a dressing of tar-mac. I couldn't bring myself to ask Mickey about the pink, fluffy toy.

Galley Slaves

'Wham'

'Whatever's that?'

Mother had dropped a stitch when the quiet had been broken by a single loud bang on the front door. Father was reading the Daily Mirror and I was memorising every detail of *Dan Dare's* latest escapade. The wireless was playing light music, but very softly.

'Sounds like the front door, Bridget.' He got up and went to see. I felt the cold night air breeze in. 'Nobody.'

'Well it must have been somebody, or something to make such a noise.'

I fancied it was a member of the *living dead*, or a very small space craft that we would find stranded on the path in the morning.

There was a knocking on the front door. Regular three raps of the letter box knocker.

Father was up again quickly. 'Are we expecting anyone?'

Nobody ever came to the front door at 7:30pm. The insurance man called around 6:00pm, once a month. The *God Squad* would never come in the dark.

'Sid.'

It was the man from next door. The two end of terrace houses were at right angles in the corner of our Close.

'Ken, did you just have a bang at your door?'

'Yes, but there was nobody there.'

'Bleddy kids. I 'spect.'

The door was closed and Father came back into the living room.

'It was Sid. He reckons it was kids playing about. Spirit-tapping.'

My father had told me many tales. Usually of the time he'd spent in khaki. He also told me of his younger days. I was amused with the tales of spirit-tapping. Apparently it was too easy just to knock at someone's door and run away. There had to be some adventure. A wooden clothes line prop could be leaned against the door, or string tied across the street to door knockers. I was, of course, cautioned against such naughty activities. Though I did get a buzz with sneaking out in the dark to tap on our kitchen window. Mother would open the curtain to be shocked at the sight of a 'ghoul'. I shone my torch up my face to produce the ghastly effect. I never dare try it out elsewhere.

The following night was more or less a re-run of the previous. After listening to *The Archers* episode the wireless was re-tuned to a light programme music station. Mother continued knitting a sweater. My Father sat in an armchair blowing smoke rings. I rummaged through a shoe-box containing toy soldiers.

'Wham.'
'Again?'
Father moved like lightening.
'The bleddy little varmints. Look what they've done to our door.'
Sid's voice was loud and angry.
When Father moved out for a closer inspection of number 23's door, he stepped on something smooth round and hard.

Mother and I crowded behind Father. Sid's hallway light clearly showed the broken door glass. Sid was waving a fair sized stone. Father stooped to pick up a similar stone from our path.

'Look, Ken, a panel's cracked on our door.'
'They must have come down the back alley off Olton Avenue.'
'And thrown stones. Then run off.'
The two parallel streets had blocks of terraced houses in fours. To get to the backs of the middle two houses in each block it was necessary to walk the back alley. Alleys were not connected. The alleys of the two streets were separated by wooden fencing. This fencing had seen better days. Here and there a piece was missing, making a gap big enough for a child to squeeze through. Sid stepped swiftly to the fencing and pulled off another fence board. He ducked through. My Father followed.

As they disappeared I heard, 'Throwing wouldn't do that sort of damage. It was catapults.'

Mother and I returned to the warmth of the coal fire. Father returned after a few minutes.

'Nobody to be seen. Not a soul. Sid was furious. Good job they weren't there or he'd have killed them.'

I could believe that. Sid was easily roused. His background was dubious. He had a regular job at a factory making synthetic cloth, but he also had money making side-lines. Mother said that he was a crook. He'd seen heavy duty military action in Italy.

'We'll have to report the damage to the Council.'

At tea–time the next day my Father was drumming his fingers on the table top.

'What time did it happen last night, Bridget?'

'Same as the night before, about half seven.'

'Right. I shall be ready for them at quarter past.'

'Do you think they'll come again?.'

'Yes, they've got a good enough escape route.'

'What are you going to do?'

'I'm going to wait the other side the fence behind the hedge.'

At seven fifteen Father put on his demob raincoat and ratting hat, and got into position.

He was back at a quarter to eight with no success and in need of a mug of tea.

'P'r'aps they won't come again, Ken?'

My Father wasn't so sure. So on the fourth evening he was in position with a thermos flask. He said he'd had lots of practise doing guard duty watching for enemy paratroopers.

Mother turned the wireless off and we listened There was a sort of noise dead on half past seven. We waited for the bang on the door.

Three minutes later my Father returned. He was excited.

'Bloody hell. Nearly had my hands on them. Heard them whispering down the alley and getting closer. Then blow me if Mrs Edwards doesn't open her bathroom window wide.'

He tossed his cap into the arm chair and lit a cigarette.

'Must have got the wind up. They turned and ran. I followed. Just managed a glimpse of two lads. About fourteen. By the time I'd got onto Olton there was nobody in sight.'

'Yeah', said Richard the fount of knowledge, 'Wooden galleys are old 'at. Yo' can get meckluns now. Much berrer.'

I had had a go at making a galley. It was necessary to find a 'Y' shaped piece of fallen wood. After trimming and smoothing, the elastic had to be fitted. Knicker elastic from the sewing box had no power.

'Yes, we sell 'proper' elastic. How much do you want? We sell it by the yard'.

The man in Applebee's shop put a large spool of rubber strip on the counter. The elastic was about three eighths of an inch wide.

'A yard, please.' That would be plenty.

He cut off a length and popped it into a small paper bag, 'That'll be sixpence.'

The elastic was difficult to tie to the wood. It proved to be impossible for me. Drilling holes was also an impossibility. So the project was abandoned.

'Yo' can gerrem from the fishing shop in Beeston High Road. But yo' have to be twelve. They are dead good. *Really powerful.* This kid let me 'ave a go wiv his.'

'Who was that?'

'Urgh, just a kid I know, can't remember his name.'

Either he was lying or covering his tracks.

The break-through came from Paul. Paul was Sid's eldest boy. He was five years older than me and was in secondary school. Apparently he had heard two older boys boasting about their catapults on the bus home from school. The boys were impressing others with a tale of daring over a couple of nights in the week. Paul knew them by sight, but didn't know their names or where they lived. But someone else did.

Andrew Wilson told Paul that the boy with the curly hair was called Stephen and that he lived on Olton Avenue.

Sid's blue eyes gleamed, 'That's enough to find the little boggers. I'm going round there now to sort 'em out. You coming, Ken?'

My mother interrupted quickly, 'Not just now. I'm serving up the tea.'

Sid grinned, 'Right I'll see yo' later.'

'I didn't want you going round with Sid. You know what he's like. Anything could happen. You could smell he'd had a drink.'

Sid didn't return, as promised, full of triumph. He came to give an account in the evening of the following day.

'I gin him a piece of my mind. I to'd him what I'd do with his friggin' kid if he ever so much as looks over the bleddy fence. He was an ignorant bogger, that Nicholson. He wouldn't have it his Stephen would do such a thing. An' he reckoned the brat didn't own a catapult. He was quite belligerent. I nearly stuck one on him. Ignorant, bleddy ignorant.'

But we had already heard an account from a different source.

My school friend Raymond lived on Olton Avenue. He and his brother Robert were just about to go indoors, as it was quickly getting dark, when they were approached by a man. Raymond recognised him as our neighbour. He wanted to know where Stephen, a boy about fourteen lived. Robert pointed out the house. They watched Sid thrust open the front gate and pound on the front door. They sensed that something was up so hung about. There was much swearing and gesticulating. The voices got louder. Mr Nicholson was heard to say that he would summon the police. Sid flounced off, kicking the gate as a he went. It was better than TV.

'Stan, the Council workman, said he would drop round next week to mend the front door.'

'What about Sid's broken glass?'

'He didn't say anything about that. Though Brenda taped some cardboard over it.'

'That won't last long when it rains. Hasn't she talked to Stan?'

My Father sighed and folded up his paper.

'I suppose I'd better go and see him.'

'Who, Stan? Why?'

'No, not Stan. I mean Mr Nicholson.'

'Whatever for? Sid's been there and got nowhere.'

'Precisely. I don't want Sid Daykin speaking for me. I think I should have a word about teenage boys and catapults.'

Mother looked anxious. She looked even more anxious when Father said. 'Our lad can come with me. Give me some company.'

I was thrilled and also quite alarmed at the prospect.

'Ken!'

'Get your coat, Soldier.'

I stuffed a small automatic pistol into the raincoat pocket. It felt right.

'You see, Son, this will be a bit of an experience for you. You can learn something. I've no idea what's going to happen.'

I clutched the automatic tightly. Perhaps just waving it about might halt the juggernaut enough for us to make a getaway.

My Father rapped the knocker on the front door. I heard him take a deep breath. The door opened. A curly haired youth, who I guessed was Stephen, appeared.

'Good evening. Is your father in?'

The boy just stood there for a moment. He turned his head and called, 'Dad, there's a man at the door.'

Mr Nicholson looked stern.

'You anything to do with that bloke who came the other night?'

'Only that Sid happens to be my neighbour and both our doors were damaged.'

'He was very rude. I nearly called the police.'

'Sid doesn't speak for me. I have evidence that your son was involved in deliberate damage using a catapult. I wanted you to know about his behaviour.'

Mr Nicholson's face softened a little.

'My lad has told me all about it. It won't happen again. He doesn't own a catapult anymore. I'm sorry for the trouble that he's caused. Was there any other damage? I'll pay for it.'

I released the grip on the automatic.

'Only the split panel on the front door. The Council is coming in the week to mend it.'

Mr Nicholson turned his head and called, 'Stephen.'

Stephen appeared quickly. Obviously he had been listening. He looked crestfallen.

'I think you've got something to say to this gentleman.'

'Sorry, mester.'

My Father and Mr Nicholson shook hands.

'You are very different to your neighbour.'

My Father nodded.

'Phew. That went better than I thought. It was a real compliment to say that I was different to Sid. You see, Son, things can be solved without starting a war. I hope you don't get tempted to do such naughty things. Fancy a pint?'

I knew he was only kidding about the pint.

Stan turned up the following Thursday. He replaced the split door panel and gave it a coat of grey undercoat. It looked strange against the rest of the green paintwork for a while until a painter came and finished the job. Sid's front door glass was not fixed. It hadn't been reported. The card board fell off several times and had to be put back with fresh tape. It was like that for months.

'Hey-up, Chrisser. Yo' know them galleys I was telling yo' abaht? Well I've got one. I got one for Tez, anall. I can get you one, if you want…'

Gypsy Woman

'Go on, she won't bite you.'

She must have read the terror in my face. I was really apprehensive about most new situations, especially when talking to strangers was involved.

'All you have to do is knock on the back door and tell her that your Mam sent these.'

My Mother held out the brown paper bag which held several copies of the *John Bull* magazine. As I gingerly took the packet my Father spoke.

'I don't know why you bother, Bridget. The woman probably can't read anyway.'

My Parents never said her name: they referred to her as the *Gypsy Woman*. Some called her Mrs Smith on account of her living with a Mr Smith. My Father reckoned they were not married, and his name probably wasn't *Smith*. She wore a ring but it was thought to be a curtain ring.

The Gypsy Woman lived in our Close at number 17. It was only four houses from mine but it might as well have been on the moon. I had never been there. The nearest I had been was to Mrs Spears' who lived the other side of the path at number 15.

'I don't like to speak ill of folks, Bridget, but that woman doesn't know how to live in a house.'

I had seen Gypsies on the cinema screen, and read about Rollo the Gypsy boy in the Rupert Bear annual. Rollo looked like any other child except that he had a spotted handkerchief tied around his head rather like how pirates wore them. Rollo lived in a hooped caravan which was pulled in and out of the storyline by a piebald pony. Occasionally, when shopping in town with my Mother, we would be asked to buy 'lucky white heather' from a pair of women selling in the street. Usually my Mother would cross the road to avoid them.

'Gypsies. I don't want any lucky white heather, but if you refuse they'll put a curse on you.'

I didn't understand why she didn't want luck. We could do with some luck. My Father explained.

'They probably weren't proper Gypsies: more likely to be Irish tinkers. White heather isn't lucky: they've got baskets full and are still working out on the street in scruffy clothes. They can't put curses on people. People just believe they can.'

He pulled a face at my Mother. She pursed her lips.

'You see, Son, real Gypsies came from India. They like to travel about. Gypsies came to our country hundreds of years ago. They said they had come from Egypt, so that's how they got their name. We should really call them *Romanis*.'

I wondered if that was anything to do with the Romans: we were doing Romans at school, and they were exciting.

'Do the Gypsies live in the rounded-over caravans like Rollo in Rupert.'

'Most of the ones I've ever seen do. But I've seen a couple of Gypsy families in old army Bedfords too.'

Both styles of living in caravans or army lorries seemed very exotic.

'They like to travel about and not live in a house like us.'

'But what about… the Gypsy Woman?'

It took less than a minute from my back door to hers. The garden resembled a farm field complete with dandelions, daisies and butter cups. There were odd items dotted around in the long grass. The back door was open to the kitchen. Being a Council house it was similar to ours, but it was nothing like ours inside. Parked against a grubby grey wall was a rickety wooden table covered with newspaper. Under the table was a pile of empty tin cans. Two people sat at the table. I recognised them both, though I had never spoken to either. The woman was the Gypsy Woman. She was barefoot and not wearing stockings. The man, Mr Smith, I had seen only a few times. He was in a white unbuttoned shirt. They looked across at me. I took a deep breath.

'Mummy says I have to give you this.'

The Gypsy Woman stood up. 'Come in, duckie.' An empty can rattled along the floor.

I took two steps into the porch and halted on the threshold to the kitchen. She took the proffered packet.

'Oh that's nice. Look, Stevie, it's the ones with lots of pictures.'

Stevie's stern face broke into a brief smile. He had a gold tooth.

'Tell, your Mammie, thanks.'

I grinned and turned.

Mrs Spears had been correct with her observation of her neighbour's house.

I had little else to do with Mr and Mrs was Smith. They had no children to play with. He went out every day early and came back late. She was seldom seen out. A few times the house was in darkness for a couple of weeks. My Father said that they had gone off again, but he had no idea where to.

'Hey up, Chrisser, ay yo' seen that Gyppo carryvan?'

Richard was delighted that I hadn't. He took pride in being the dispenser of news.

'Me an Tez was up Woolly Park. An' when we come aht the gate-house it was there. A real un parked on that bit of grass on the corner o' Beeston Lane.'

It must have been quite an experience because it prompted Terry to string some words together.

'Yeah an' they 'ad a noss anall.'

'Black an' white, an' on a lead.'

'Did you see any Gypsies?'

'Yeah, we did, an' we talked to 'im.'

''E 'ad a lickle fire wiv a keckle on it. 'E said 'e was c'lectin' meckle. And if we crossed 'is palm wiv silver 'e would tell us ah fortunes.'

'We di'n't 'ave no money on us though.'

'But we're goin' back when we got some dosh.'

Richard was really excited about the prospect of looking into his future. My Father had said fortune telling was a trick. He scoffed at my Mother when she read out the *stars*.

''E asked us if we knew anybody called Kezia. But we di'n't. Do yo'?'

I shook my head. The name was new to me. It sounded foreign.

'Mum, can I go to Wollaton Park, please.'

It was a necessary formality for going beyond the end of our street.

'Who are you going with?'

'Terry and Richard.'

She scowled. 'You be careful with that Richard. Don't get led into something silly. Keep away from the lake and don't talk to strangers. Lunch is at half past one.'

***

We galloped along the well-worn path that snaked along the top of a small retaining bank against the Park wall. From Abbey Gates, which marked the edge of the Council Estate, to the Lodge Gate entrance to the Park it took only a few minutes. As we rounded the bend in Derby Road we saw that the caravan was gone.

'Ugh, it's gone. Bleddy 'ell.'

We examined the caravan site. The grass was trampled, and there was a scorched place. Richard carefully fingered the ashes like a good frontiersman.

'Friends of yours?'

The voice came from behind. A policeman was standing by the Park gates holding a push bike.

'Cripes.'

Richard was very wary of the Law. He had had some previous contact.

'No, not really. We seen the 'oss, an' we wanted to pat it.'

'Well, they *moved on*. Down there.'

The policeman pointed to Beeston Lane. He mounted his bicycle and pedalled off.

'Good, the rozzer's gone. Them ashes was still warm. They can't have been gone long. Bet 'e moved 'em on.'

'Why?'

''Cos Gyppos steal stuff an' they carry knives.'

'Shall we follow them?'

'Yeah, we can always cut back *over tins* or dahn Salt'ouse Lane.'

Beeston Lane was not used by proper through traffic. It was too narrow and was covered in sand in some places. It was the best place for collecting conkers. We whizzed down the winding lane with our arms held out and pointing back. We were USAF Sabre jets.

The caravan was standing at the end of the lane just over the bridge where the Tottle Brook vanished into a tunnel. It was parked on the wide verge. The man was tethering the painted pony. A boy was fitting a black, old fashioned kettle to a frame over a pile of sticks and twigs. He looked up. We stopped and stared. He said something that I didn't catch. The man glanced our way for a moment. We edged forward. The boy stood up. I guessed him to about Richard's age. He had tousled fair hair. He wore a grey pullover and short trousers. The pullover had loose threads. He wore black plimsoles without socks. As we got nearer he moved his hand to the hem of his pullover and lifted it enough to reveal a sheath knife.

Richard spoke jovially, flashing his best smile, 'Hey up, we seen your carryvan, Can we 'ave a closer look. I'd like me fortune to'd. I've got some silver.'

The boy said nothing, but the man spoke.

'I was talking with you yesterday. I'll see your silver.'

Richard had come into a sudden fortune: most likely from his mother's purse. The man took a half-crown and left the rest.

'Come.'

He walked to the caravan and lifted out two small stools. Richard sat on one and had his fortune told. The boy studied Terry and me.

'Are you Gypsies?'

'We are Roma. Are you Gorgers?'

'What are Gorgers?'

'People what are not… Gypsies.'

He spoke with a slight accent. It reminded me of next doors' cousin from Birmingham.

'Do you go to school?'

He shook his head. 'Did one time. Not now.'

'Yo've gorra knife.'

The boy glared at Terry.

'My name's Chris. What's yours?'

He turned his attention to me, 'Dan.'

'Is that your dad talking to Richard?'

Dan shook his head.

Richard and the man stood up. Richard was beaming.

'I'm goin' to gerrinto loads of trouble, but I'll wriggle out on it.'

'You can pat the nag and have a closer look at the van. But you are not allowed inside.'

He smiled and opened the doors wide for us to peep in. It was as shown at the cinema: everything was fitted in neat and tidy. It was so colourful too: every surface was patterned. We admired the paintwork to the exterior and the useful items, such as painted metal buckets, dangling on hooks. Terry took great delight in pulling tufts of grass from the other side of the fence and feeding it to the horse. He turned smiling and threw a brick into the conversation.

'We got Gyspies on ahr street.'

The boy and the man froze for a moment. They exchanged looks.

'Gypsies living in a house?'

'Well, they reckon she's a Gypsy. They call her *The Gypsy Woman.*'

The man concentrated on Richard. 'Does she have a name?'

'Yeah, calls hersen Mrs Smiff. But we don't fink she's married to Mr Smiff what lives wiv 'er.'

I sensed that this was no casual inquiry. The man said something to Dan which again I couldn't catch. To us he said, 'Can you find out what her name is. I'll make it worth your while.'

Richard recognised a chance to retrieve the half-crown, 'Yeah, sure we can. Ah long yo' gonna be 'ere?'

The man shrugged, 'Depends. Depends on whether we get asked *to move on*. But we'll be around. You will find us.'

I felt that it was my turn to speak, 'Do you think she might be a friend of yours?'

The man smiled, 'Might be.'

On the way home, using the *over tins* route, Richard declared that he would find out the woman's name by asking her.

'But she's a grown up. You can't just ask her.'

'No law against askin'. It's a free country.'

'How long has she lived at that house do you think?'

I could only remember her being there, but Richard was a year older, and he always seemed to know everything.

'Me mam reckons she's been there 'baht four year. The people what was there before 'er got chucked aht 'cos they was always fightin'.

That I didn't know. I had not started school at that time. My parents might have more of the story: they had had our house from 1939.

Richard had resolved to take the most direct line. At the end of the Close we turned left down to the end of the terrace. As we turned the corner of the house we nearly fell over the Gypsy Woman. She was sitting on the back door step with a tin can and some pliers in her hands.

'Hello, boy.'

She seemed to remember me. She smiled at Richard and Terry.

We three chorused a greeting. Richard got to the point.

'We don't know what your name is…'

'Says Mrs Smith on the rent book, I be told.'

'Yeah, we know that yo're called Mrs Smiff. But what's your first name?'

The Gypsy Woman tipped her head to one side, 'No secret, but why do you want to know it?'

'We bin talkin' to this Gypsy man, an 'e finks 'e might know yo''

Terry had done it again.

She put the things down next to a couple of twisted cans. 'What Gypsy man, what is his name?'

'Huh, don't know his name… he di'n't tell us.' Richard sounded wrong footed. I felt embarrassed and a little stupid. Terry had probably used up his vocabulary for the day.

'What does he look like, then?'

'Well, sort of tall and dark and thin. 'Bout as old as you…'

Terry's brain clicked on, ''E 'ad a boy wiv him called Dan.'

The Gypsy Woman's eyes closed and I heard her gasp. 'That be Daniok, for sure. And the man be Del.'

'Yo' know 'em, then?'

'Oh, yes, I know them.' She stood up. On the path, beside her, lay a pair of pliers and four tin cans twisted into the shape of roses. They would look nice if they were painted. 'You can tell them my name. It's Kezia.'

'Not a - bleddy -'gain.'

The wagon was indeed gone. We scanned around. They could have gone back up Beeston Lane, or up the High Road into Beeston itself, or along University Boulevard. Terry noticed the sign.

'Hey, look 'ere.'

On the well chewed grass was a pile of little stones laid out in an arrow formation. It was pointing towards the Boulevard. Beeston High Road turned onto the start of the Boulevard, but there was also the start of Beeston bypass swinging off to the right. We walked to the junction. There was no sign of a caravan, but now we were looking for clues. I spotted another arrow of stones pointing to the bypass. We hurried along. Just around the corner on Tattershall Drive we caught up with Daniok and Del.

Richard did the talking: the Gypsies did the listening. Del smiled and nodded.

'You done good, boy.'

He handed over the promised reward. It was the half-crown. Richard was ecstatic.

We tried to explain exactly where we lived, or more to the point: where Kezia lived. The Gypsies seemed at a loss when we rattled off street names. I suggested that we guide them. It would have to be the afternoon, though. We would meet them back where we first made contact.

The midday meal seemed to take ages, but we three were quickly running through the estate. The caravan was in position with the horse still in harness. They waved and smiled as we approached. Dan led the horse. Richard and I walked with him. Terry was allowed to sit on the wagon with Dan. We proceeded down Derby Road and turned on to Woodside Road. The gaily painted wagon drew much attention: it was a very rare sight.

We stopped on the wide grassy verge close to the parade of shops. Del said that he would go to the house on his own, but Richard would have to point it out. Terry and I stayed with Dan around the wagon.

'How do you know Kezia.'

Dan shrugged. 'She ran away. She went off with a Gorger she met with at a fun-fair. We Gypsies should stick together. She is dead to us now.'

'Is Del going to kill her?' Suddenly an alarm was sounding in my brain.

'He should, I suppose, but he *wants* her.'

He put his hands to his face. 'They were to be married. They were promised to each other, but she ran off with the Gorger.'

I looked a Terry. He seemed to be having difficulty with the explanation. I was struggling with it too.

By now the painted wagon and dappled horse had collected an audience. Adults gazed from the shops, but children came closer. I was beginning to feel uncomfortable. My discomfort grew when I saw Mr Atherley striding towards us. Mr Atherley was the pharmacist who also ran the post office.

'Is this, this wagon yours?

Dan stared at him for a moment before replying, 'No, it isn't.'

'Well, who's in charge?'

'My uncle Del. He's not here.'

'You can't stay here. You'll have to move on.'

Dan shrugged and took hold of the horse's bridle.

'Why's 'e 'ave to move?'

Mr Atherley turned his attention to Terry, 'Because they are Gypsies and they are not welcome here.'

Terry persisted, 'Why are Gyspies not welcome?'

Mr Athereley looked like he was about to explode. 'Gypsies are dirty. They steal things. They leave a mess. If he doesn't go right now I'll call the police.'

Prior to this I had always seen Mr Atherley as a nice old man who ran one of our shops. My Mother did one morning a week cleaning for the Atherley's. Now I felt compelled to speak.

'Dan hasn't stolen anything. He's not dirty. And he hasn't left a mess.'

Mr Atherley glared at me. 'Right that's it, I'm calling the police.'

As he stalked off back to the post office, I saw Richard running towards us.

'Hey, ah showed Del where the 'ouse was. He tol' me to go, but ah hid behin' the 'edge.'

Dan stood still holding the horse and listening intently.

''E knocked on the front door. I di'n't fink nobody was in. Took ages for the door to open. The Gypsy Woman opened the door and I heard her squeal.'

'Did 'e stab 'er?'

'No, Tez. She come aht and they just stood there talkin'.

I quickly told Richard about Mr Atherley and the police. His excitement turned to desperation. He glanced about.

'Crikey, where did this lot come from?'

There was quite an audience now: obviously waiting for the police, in force, coming to arrest a boy and his painted pony. We decided it would be best to *move on*. The only place nearby that seemed safe was behind the Essoldo cinema at the start of Woodside Road. Dan left a sign and said that Del would find us. I started to worry about the time slipping away towards tea-time.

We didn't have to wait long. Del turned up looking very excited. He nodded to us and spoke to Dan. At first he spoke in words that I didn't understand, but he soon switched to English.

'That *was* Kezia. She was surprised, but she knew I was around. I asked her to marry me. She said she would have to think about it. Kezia will give me an answer tomorrow at noon.'

'But what abaht the bloke, Mr Smiff. Ain't she married to 'im?'

'*He* won't be a problem for Del. Kezia is the problem.'

'She isn't married to him. His name isn't Smith. He works for a scrap merchant in Beeston, but sometimes goes off to work with funfairs.'

Richard suggested that they took the caravan across to Wollaton Vale. They could find a wide verge to park on.

'Oh, there you are. Your tea's ready and your Dad's waiting.'

As we sat down at the kitchen table for mother's minced beef pie she said, 'What was going on in front of the shops this afternoon? Mrs Daykin said there was a Gypsy caravan.'

I tried very hard to not lie, but I had learned not to 'worry' my Mother.

'Mmm, yes, there was a Gypsy caravan. All the kids went to have a look. I went to look as well. We talked to the Gypsies and Terry patted the horse.'

'Did they sell you anymore pegs?'

My Mother pulled a face at my Father. We had a set of twelve handmade clothes pegs that my Mother had bought from a Gypsy at the back door. She didn't really need them, but she was cautious about being cursed. They were handsome pegs made from two wooden blades held together with a 'wedding band' of copper. They lasted a long time: even longer than my Mother.

After tea I mooched about in the garden until I was attracted by some raised voices across the Close. It was unusual to hear raised adult voices. I went to our gate in time to see Mr Smith storming away from his house. The Smith's, I guessed, had just had a row and he was going off to the pub: or he might be of looking for Del. I went in to listen to *The Archers*. Mr Smith would be no problem for Del, according to Dan.

The plan was to hang about at the street end of our Close to see what transpired.

'What d'yo' reckon, Chrisser? D'yo' fink she'll go off wiv Del?'

'I hope so. He's nice. And they are both Gypsies.'

Mrs Spears approached on her way to the shops. We chorused a polite greeting. She looked like she was gasping to say something to anyone who would listen.

'Well, what a right ta-ta. Did you hear the row yesterday evening? And he came back drunk banging the doors. But she had gone. I saw her go off when I was closing the curtains. She had a bag with her. Good riddance, I say. Hope he goes too. Hmmmm.'

'What if Del comes here at twelve o'clock, and she's gone?

'D'yo' fink she's gone lookin' fr'im.'
'Crikey, stannin' 'ere gabbin' ain't gonna help.'
'Shall we go looking for her, or find Dell and tell him what's happened?'
'She c'ld be miles away by nah. An' we don' know which way.'
'Finding Del and the caravan will be best.'

Finding the caravan was very easy. It was parked at the near end of Wollaton Vale on the wide grassy verge near the entrance to the rec. Del was just about to start out to meet with the Gypsy Woman. We gave him a breathless account. He seemed very concerned.
'And you have no idea which way she went?'
'No, but Mrs Spears says she had a bag. She left home last night.'
'An' she ain't bin seen since'.
It was Terry's turn. He had been hugging the horse, 'There she is!'
We all turned to the direction of his outstretched arm. Kezia was standing on the sloped entrance to the rec. She looked a bit nervous and dishevelled.
'She's bin on the bleddy rec all night sleepin' rough.'
Dan said, 'Travellers can sleep under the stars. I like to sleep outside.'
Del was up close talking. Kezia was smiling and nodding. Del did a little dance around her.
'Yo' said Del was your uncle. Why aren't yo' wiv your mam and dad?'
'They are both dead. I never knew my father. My mother died when I was very young. Del took me in and learned me how to be.'
'We'd better be off now. There's a wedding to organise. So, thanks boys for your help. I'd like to reward you but I am a poor Gypsy.'
'I can give them something.'
Kezia scrabbled in her large bag. She pulled out a card-board shoe box. From the box she produced three roses made from tin cans.

Mr Smith stayed on in the house for a couple of weeks. He told Mrs Spears that he was going travelling with a fun-fair. The Council people came to tidy the place up. Mrs Spears was delighted when a 'proper' young couple moved in.
Richard and Terry soon lost their tin roses. I painted mine with bright colours and gave it to my Mother.
'Oh, Chick, that's nice. Where did you get it from?'

'A passing Gypsy gave it to me.'

My Father rattled his newspaper. '*Gave* it to you? Pull the other one.'

I stayed away from Mr Atherley's shop as much as I could.

The Gypsies, I never saw again.

Hemlock Stone

Geoff's map was good, but not good enough.

'It must be just off the edge of the map. Damn!'

The map had served us well on the cycle ride to Ruddington Military Supply Depot.

Another idea went down the drain. It was August, we were not at school and neither of us was going to the seaside, so Geoff and I had thought of an adventure. We had been inspired when Mrs Preston had given the class some ideas about what to do in the big six weeks holiday. Wollaton Park and Nottingham Castle were both old hat, but the Hemlock Stone was new to us. Mrs Preston had told us how the Devil had been so annoyed by the chanting of the monks in Lenton Priory that he had hurled this enormous stone from Castleton in Derbyshire. It was so heavy that it failed to hit the target and came down in Bramcote. This was good news as our Council estate was built on the priory land, and Bramcote was not much further than our 'playground' of Snakey Woods.

My Father didn't have a car, neither did Geoff's. The buses out of the city limits were too difficult. It would be possible to walk, if we knew the exact location.

'Sacko might have a better map!'

Alan Saxton was in our class. He was a pal who lived only two minutes from Geoff's house. Mrs Saxton called Alan. We explained the need for a good map of the shire. His father had several Ordnance Survey maps. He opened out the suitable one.

'There! There it is. It's marked as *Stone.*' There was a dot just over the road from Bramcote Hills and almost opposite the secondary school. It really was not much further than the picnic field off Sandy Lane. It suddenly became a possibility. We could go on bikes but that would mean the busy A52. Anyway we were quite familiar with three quarters of the journey on foot.

Geoff pencilled in the position of the Stone on the margin of his city map. Alan said that he would like to come on the expedition too.

'Why don't you ask Tony as well?' said my Mother.

Tony had been a close friend when I was younger, but now we had less in common.

'Well, his mum doesn't like him going off and getting mucky.'

'You could ask.'

To my surprise Tony was interested and Mrs Wilmott didn't object. Tony wasn't in the 'A' stream class so he hadn't heard about the Hemlock Stone.

Geoff grinned when I told him about Tony joining us. 'Twilmop is wet. I bet he won't go at the last minute.'

Four musketeers seemed about right for the adventure. I had been cautioned about involving Richard and Terry. They could well become a liability. Especially Richard, who was a year older and was impulsively inclined. After the summer holidays we would be in the top classes of the juniors, but Richard had the unenviable prospect of starting the dreaded Cottesmore secondary school.

Unfortunately Twilmop had boasted to Terry about the proposed expedition. Terry, of course, had reported to Richard.

'Hey-up, Chrisser a lickle bi'd to'd me yo' are goin' on a nexpedition.'

He wanted to muscle in. As a bribe he promised to behave. He had been useful in previous situations and he did promise. So Richard and Terry became the fifth and sixth musketeers. As a precaution, I didn't tell my Mother.

It was calculated that it would take an hour to walk there, and an hour back. We might spend an hour admiring the Stone, so it was possible to do the expedition in a morning, if we started early.

The route seemed straight forward. It was easy to get to Snakey Woods from Sandy Lane. Sandy Lane used to be bordered on both sides with gorse covered hillocks inhabited by rabbits and buzzed by sky-larks. Recently new houses had appeared, and Sandy Lane had been made into a proper road. We would approach the picnic field by the track along the ridge behind the Garden Nursery on Derby Road. The next step would be to use the track between the tree plantations. We could skirt around Moor Farm buildings at the top of the rise and drop down onto Coventry Lane where the Stone would be obvious: it was twenty eight feet high!

There was a choice of the return journey. We could simply retrace our steps, or follow Coventry Lane down to turn left at the T-junction and walk until we found the A52 Derby Road. There would be lots of buses going our way. It would be nice to ride on a red Barton's bus to the Essoldo stop. The estimated walk would be about three quarters of a mile.

We decided to take cash for bus-fares, and a packed lunch just in case. As it was so hot it was decided to wear 'jungle' kit. For me this consisted of my short sleeved tartan-check summer shirt and khaki shorts. I selected my Clarke's strapped sandals and, on my Mother's prompting, a hat. It had to be the cotton peaked cap which my Father had brought home from work. It was originally white but had been soaked in cold tea to become a military colour. My sandwiches were to be carried in the khaki cotton cash bag from my bus-conductor's outfit.

Wednesday was the day, and 9 o'clock was the starting time.

'Now you be careful crossing the roads. Look right, look left, then right again. Don't talk to strangers: you never know. Watch out for cow-pats. And don't do anything silly.'

She said this, except for the cow-pats, even when I went to the corner shop.

We met on the dot at Geoff's house at the top end of Baslow Drive. From there it was a straight walk down Audley Drive to the Essoldo cinema on Derby Road. I was early, but Geoff was already sitting on his front gate. Tony loped up, much to the surprise of Geoff. Next to arrive was Alan. I was amazed. He was wearing a foreign legion kepi complete with flap. He grinned.

'My dad got it from a shop in Beeston. It's not real.'

'Could of fooled me.'

'Looks great.'

The other three were in T-shirts and khaki shorts. They carried slung snap-bags with bottle necks protruding.

'Crikey.'

We turned to see the last two approaching. Terry was wearing his too-big jeans and a cowboy hat. Richard was in grey shirt sleeves, grey worsted short trousers and a handkerchief with the corners knotted. Neither of them appeared to have a bag.

And so the adventure began at 9:02 on an already very warm day. We trotted quickly down Audley Drive, crossed the end of Woodside Road and scampered across the Derby Road. It took only a few more minutes to pass Dr Brigg's surgery and get to the turn off which ran along-side the Garden Nursery. This was like Sandy Lane but was tighter and had brambles over hanging.

We emerged onto the moorland. The house builders hadn't got to this bit yet. A track ran along the ridge between gorse bushes. We saw no rabbits or snakes. We could see way over to the horizon where steam engines chugged. The sky was completely blue.

'I need a shit.'

We stopped and turned to Terry. He was wearing a pained look.

'Urgh, Tez, why din'ya go before we started?'

'Arh did, but now arh need to go again.'

Geoff rolled his eyes to the heavens. Alan smirked. Tony looked alarmed.

'Any yo' gorrenny lav paper?'

Geoff, Alan and I reached into our bags. Terry looked relieved. Tony still looked alarmed.

'G'behin' a bush Tez, an watch out for snakes. An 'tek yer spade.'

'Spade?'

'Yeah, a spade. Y'afto to bury it out in the wild.'

'What time is it, Geoff?'

'Nine forty one. Extra time waiting for Terry.'

We all laughed, except Terry.

Sandy Lane was now a proper road but only up to the ridge. The lane continued as a track down across the picnic field and to the houses of Wollaton in the distance. We kicked through the pale yellow sand and crossed the field to the gated farm track through the trees. The dense woodland afforded plenty of shade. It looked quite gloomy. Richard began to climb the five bar gate.

'I don't want to go.'

Now it was Tony's turn. He was looking down at his feet. His white cotton sun hat was in his hand.

'What?'

'I don't want to go to the Hemlock Stone.'

'Yo' scared?'

'Yes.'

He was obviously not going any further.

Geoff said, 'Told you so.'

I said, 'What are you going to do, then, Tony?'

'I'm going home.'

'On your own?'

Alan said, 'Come on Tony. We are nearly there. It'll be great.'

'No.'

He was shaking his head. I saw the tears.

As he turned to go, Richard called, 'Leave us yo' sammies, then!'

But Tony was crossing back over the field fast. I watched him until he disappeared into the gorse bushes. He didn't look back. I felt really sorry for him. We couldn't make him continue with us. I wondered why he came anyway. Was he suddenly scared by the gloomy woods? Would he get back home safely on his own?

'Ah, c'mon. We don't need the lickle twerp anyroad.'

We quickly mounted the gate. In the cooler shade of the trees we realised how warm it was getting. This was unknown territory. There might be Japanese patrols about, so we moved stealthily, watching for any signs. We were not sure if we were trespassing. After a few minutes of not meeting any of the enemy we saw signs of habitation. The track was leading into a farm yard. There was the back end of big old shed to the right where the trees finished. Over to the left there was the chain mesh fence of tennis courts.

'That must be Bramcote School,' said Alan, 'We are getting close to Coventry Lane.'

'Shall we walk frough the farmyard? There might be some *aminals*.'

'Yeah, Tez, there might be some animals oright: big dogs.'

'What shall we do?'

'We could run through the yard.'

'And look like crooks.'

'We could do a big swing round to the right and miss the farm yard.'

'That's going miles the wrong way.'

Richard had a brain wave. 'Nah, we walk back'ards frough the yard. An' knock at the door. We tells 'em that we bin walkin' fer hours, an' we are 'ot an' firsty. An'…'

'And can you spare us a glass of water, please?'

Richard looked stunned.

'You tried that before when we went to Woolly Park, remember?'

'Oh, yeah. Me an' Tez.' He grinned. 'But we gorra drink, di'n't we, Tez?'

'Argh.'

'Why walk backwards?'

'So'zit looks like we come off the Lane an' not trespassed frough the woods.'

I decided. 'No, we just walk straight through the farmyard. If anyone says anything we say sorry and we'll go. If a dog starts barking, keep going.'

After a half minute of no more suggestions we marched on into the full sunlight. We passed more sheds and the farmhouse. There was some washing hanging limply, but there was no challenge or barking guard dog. The track took a sharp right. We continued straight on through an orchard. Richard grabbed a couple of fallen apples, and so did Terry. I glanced back towards the farm house. The windows were blind. A hawthorn hedge marked the edge of the field. It also marked Coventry Lane. We scanned the horizon.

'Bleddy 'ell, s'not there.'

But there were plenty of tall trees. We wriggled through the hedge. There were paths either side of the road. A few commercial vehicles passed.

'It's got to be on the other side and down a bit.'

Coventry Lane was long and straight in both directions. Terry chewed on an apple. We crossed the 'Chindwin'. Looking back we could hardly see anything to do with the farm. We walked in single file peering into the trees. It was getting hotter.

'What time is Mr Wolf?'

'Gone quarter past ten, and nowhere near dinner time.' The laughter was half-hearted.

A bloke came pedalling towards us.

'Hey, mester, is the Hemlock Stone round here?'

'Yeah, down there, not far. Can't miss it.' He pointed in the direction we were headed.

'Fanks mester.'

I shifted my bag onto the other shoulder as we quickened the pace. On the other side of the road a there was now a sturdy wall and more trees.

'Yes!'

Ahead was the start of a clearing in the trees. It became possible to see beyond. Further back was an open clearing. The ground sloped up. And there it was, the 'Holy Grail'.

'Gosh'.

'Is tharrit?

'What were you expecting?'

It was higher than my bedroom window. It was a massive lump of grizzled sand-stone twenty-eight feet tall. The bottom half was a reddish colour, but the top half was dark grey.

Even if Richard was not impressed, the rest of us were. We stood and gaped.

'What time is it, Geoff?'

'Twenty to eleven.'

We circled the stone. It was fenced in with iron railings. Attached to the railings was a well –weathered notice for visitors.

'It says witches were fought to come 'ere an' do 'uman sacrifices. Don't worry, Tez, they wou'n't 'ave yo'.' Richard guffawed at his own joke.

'Can we climb it?'

There was the fence, but that was no problem. The pitted surface of the monolith afforded many foot and hand holds.

'I don't think it's allowed. There's a fence.'

'Ain't no notice sayin' yo' can't. Let's ay a go.'

I looked around. We appeared to be the only ones there. It was a week-day.

Richard was inside the railings. Terry was still climbing them. We scrambled to catch them up. Close to, it seemed very large and very alien. Five boys patted it like it was some big pet. Richard was away, scrambling up. It was hard work in that heat and I was soon feeling scared. Alan was struggling too.

'Done it! C'mon Sherpa Tez.'

Richard was at the top but I couldn't see him. I looked again at Alan. He shook his head. I nodded and we began the descent. Geoff was already down on the ground. It was necessary to climb out of the fenced area to be able to see Richard and Terry. They were both performing a victory dance.

Geoff grinned. 'If he falls off...'

Richard lurched backwards and let out a howl. We tensed, anticipating the screams as he bounced off the Stone's side and came to grief on the metal railings. Terry burst out laughing as the comedian sprang up. 'Fooled yo'!'

We sprawled around looking up at the Stone. Richard was still grinning with his triumph. Geoff told us that it was just gone half past eleven.

'Shame Twilmop isn't here.'

'Wonder where he is now.'

'In the back kitchen having his lunch.'

'Let's have our lunch now, shall we?'

Geoff, Alan and I had packed lunches. Richard and Terry had scrumped apples.

'Let's share it out.'

Grease-proof packets were opened and the contents pooled. Alan and I had small bottles of water. Geoff had a can of orange pop.

Richard and Terry presented their remaining apples. Richard also produced a pen-knife for the slicing up.

'So which way shall we go back?'

Alan waved his OS map. 'It looks quite a way down to the A52 Derby Road. Nearly a mile.'

'The road looked long and straight. Couldn't see the first turn even.'

'We don't know the times of the buses.'

'There would be lots going from Derby way to Nottingham. One every ten minutes or so.'

I quite fancied riding home on a red Barton's bus, even though it was a long stretch to the first bus stop, but I was out voted. The decision was to return the way we had come. At least we knew what to expect.

It was nearly mid-day when we crossed over the road to find the place where we had left Moor Farm orchard. Our packed lunches were not large and sharing them further didn't help. It was also extremely hot now. I was a little worried about going back through the farm yard. Perhaps they would be home for lunch. Richard's suggestion to present ourselves as weary and thirsty travellers now seemed about right. Richard and Terry picked up more fallen fruit. The track into the farm yard was dry and hard. I guessed it would be quite different in winter. I crossed my fingers as we neared the farmhouse. All was quiet. The washing was still dangling. I was much relieved on passing the last big shed. It was a little cooler being between the trees again. We were as good as home.

The home run proper started over the gate to the picnic field. It was still hot, but I felt elated.

'We done it, Chrisser.'

'Yeah we found the Hemlock, and got back alive.'

'Shame about Twilmop. What do you think he'll tell his mam?'

I shrugged and grinned. I didn't care.

Alan said to me, 'I'm going with my cousin to Crewe when we go back to school. It's better than Tamworth cos there's GWR sheds to bunk. Do you want to come?'

My elation swelled. Crewe station was many miles away and two train rides. To train spot the LMS west coast main line and do the GWR engine sheds would be fantastic.

'Yeah Al, that's terrific. I'll have to work on my Mum.'

There was a good chance that she would agree because Richard was not at all interested in train spotting, and I had returned safely from a previous spotting trip to Tamworth station.

We were now on the track along the ridge behind the Garden Nursery when Geoff spotted it.

'It's a summer hat. Looks like Tony's.'

I picked it up. It did have AW written in indelible ink on the inside band. It also had reddish brown marks on the outside.

'That's blood.'

My heart skipped. It was definitely Tony's. Why had he left it? Why was it smeared with blood? Had he met one of those 'funny men' that I had been warned about?

'Praps his bin murdered. Got 'is 'ead bashed in.'

'Where's the body, then?'

'Better look around.'

We cautiously began to search around in the gorse bushes. Nothing was found.

'Praps he just got coshed and then taken away.'

'We should have stopped him going off on his own.'

I felt the happiness of the day drain away. Surely I would get most of the blame.

'We should report it to the police.'

'I'm not goin' nowhere near no rozzers!' Richard, and Terry, had good reasons for steering clear of the Law.

Quietly we continued the trek home. I glanced around hoping to somehow see Tony, but only the larks twittered above.

We marched down Baslow Drive. Together we would go to Tony's house, but it was me who would tell his mother.

'Mrs Wilmott we have some bad news. We think Anthony has been murdered. Here's his hat. It's got blood on it. We are ever so sorry.' I rehearsed it in my head. She would probably collapse on the door step.

Over the high privet hedges I could see that Tony's front door was open. When we got to his front gate there he was, large as life, sitting on the door step guzzling fizzy orange pop. He saw us and gave a weedy smile. It was then that I spotted the large plaster on his knee.

'Fought yo' was dead.'

He shook his head and carried on grinning, 'Fell over and bumped my knee.' He pointed to the plaster. 'It was efto bloody, so I wiped it on my hat.'

'Why did you leave the hat?'

He just shrugged.

'Friggin' 'ell, Twilmop. We fought yo' was a gonna. Got yo' 'ead bashed in or summat.'

Tony looked bemused.

'You missed the Hemlock Stone. We got there. It was great.'

Tony shrugged.

'C'mon, let's go.'

'Phew.'

We separated, and walked away. The happiness returned. It was still very warm and well into the afternoon. I started to plan the expedition to Crewe station with Alan.

Kodiak

On wet afternoons, when not at school, I sometimes rummaged through the old brown hand-bag which lived in the sideboard. This hand-bag contained photographs. We didn't have anything fancy like an album. The images were mostly of people face on. Some were of good definition but the people looked like statues. The others were poorly focussed. These too were mostly face on, and appeared to be grimacing. I learned that the 'statues' had been photographed in a studio by a professional. The other images had been made with a bought camera wielded by a family member. It was necessary to ask my Mother about names and locations because only a very few photos had any notation.

We had a camera. It was a Box Brownie which my Father had bought before the war. The Kodak company, started by the American George Eastman, had cornered the photography market. The simplest and cheapest camera was the Box Brownie. The Brownie was brought into action only on special occasions. We had images of new babies and family members: all smiling and screwing up their eyes. The photographer needed the sun behind him. The procedure took so long that the posers developed grim false smiles. My Father would stand holding the camera close to his stomach. His head was bent down, as if in prayer, so that he could look into the little hole on the top of the box. Each 'snap' could take up to ten minutes of preparation: it's no wonder that the targets developed a glazed look. The last time our Brownie was used seriously was on our summer holiday to Mablethorpe in 1951. My mother had noticed that other families had superior modern cameras. The Brownie was relegated to slumber in the sideboard.

Fortunately Kodak brought out, in 1952, a flashy new product for the cheaper end of the market. My Mother declared that our family should invest in this new-fangled piece of photographic equipment. Unfortunately my Mother referred to it as a *Kodiak*. My Mother had the same problem with words as did Mrs Malaprop. After a holiday visit to Caldy Island, off the Welsh coast, she told everyone that she had been to Coney Island.

The camera was not a birthday present: it was to be shared by all the family. I would be allowed to use it, in due course, when I could show that I knew how to use it and knew how to treat it sensibly. (This also applied to my pocket money which languished in the PO.)

The Brownie 127 was a modern looking streamlined camera. It was small, compact, rounded at the corners and made in smart black Bakelite. It came in a brown canvas satchel which could be slung over one shoulder or dangled around the neck. There was no more squinting down. This camera was held up to the eye to make the shots, though my Mother still referred to 'snaps'. Being a cheap camera it had a fixed focus. An additional lens was eventually made available. This could easily be screwed onto existing aperture to take 'close-ups'.

My Father came to grips with new camera. We had sermons on how to operate it, with much reference to the instruction booklet. I was disappointed with the first set of photographs. The prints were quite small. Some were dark, so it was still necessary to have sunlight. One could request larger prints when the film was processed.

I wanted desperately to breeze out with the new camera slung casually over my shoulder. I dreamed of taking photographs of really interesting things such as military vehicles, railway locomotives or bank-robbers making a getaway. Although I despaired with the notion of recording family members, I was stuck with the idea that photographs should be noble and worthy. Photographing the common place such as our street, the Redgates delivery lorry or the postie emptying the box on the parade would be a waste of film.

I was taught how to load the 127 twelve frame film. This had to be done out of sunlight. The winding on, after each take, had to be precise. I practised lining up the camera and peeping through the eye piece. I was given the opportunity to take some actual photographs. This was in our back-garden under supervision. My Mother posed sitting on the swing.

'Hold the Kodiak straight. Don't let it wobble, Make me look nice. Tell me when.'

'Say cheese.'

'Click.'

'Now let your Dad take a snap of you holding the cat.'

I took another 'snap' of Mother and Father together. The cat had sensibly disappeared.

When the film was developed and printed, I was quite pleased with my efforts. I was surprised that the images looked like the people. Of course they were monochrome, black and white. Colour film would be way too expensive.

When I turned ten in the summer I was deemed capable and sensible enough to take the camera into the wide world. I would have liked to have gone with Mike, but he was not available.

'Now you look after that Kodiak. Don't go dropping it, or leaving it somewhere. Take some nice snaps. Don't let anybody else handle it, especially that Richard. Be back for dinner at one. And don't talk to any strange men.'

I wondered why folks took photographs. Ours were just stuffed into the old handbag. There was not one framed in the house. I was wrong, there was an image of a younger me taken in a studio in town. It didn't look like a photo because it had been hand-tinted. My friends didn't appear to have framed photos. Mike's granny had a framed image of Captain Pretty in his army uniform. My step-Granny in Yorkshire had two photos framed. One had my Grandfather and his brothers Jack and George. All three were in uniform. The other photo was a portrait of a sour-faced little girl who died. Aunty Lizzie, in Nottingham, had several dark photos of groups of 'statues'. I didn't recognise anyone. I didn't realise that they were my family from many years ago. The older man would be my Great-great-grandfather William Henry. The younger people around him would be my Great-grandfather Charles Henry, his brother William who ran away to join the Coldstream Guards, and his sister Sarah, known as Lizzie. These precious images were all binned when Aunty Lizzie died.

There was nothing of any consequence to be photographed on our Council estate, so I decided to venture into Wollaton Park. It was only ten minutes' walk. As I turned the corner at the top of our street I heard, 'Hey up, Chrisser.' Of course it was Richard. He clocked the camera bag straight away.

'Yo' goin' on a pic-nic?' He was pointing at the bag. 'Got yo' sammies then?'

'No, it's a camera. A Kodak 127. It's brand new.'

Just for a heart–beat Richard was speechless.

'It's a camera. A new sort of Kodak camera. It's called a 127.'

I was tempted to get it out of the bag, but thought better of it.

'Let's see it.'

I shook my head, 'I'm on my way to Woolly Park. I'm going to take photos of…the swans.'

The swans were noble creatures worthy of using up 127 film.

'We'll come wiv yo', not we Tez?'

Terry, standing in Richard's shadow, nodded agreement.

I was out-gunned. Everything would be fine if I kept my hands on the camera and got back by one o'clock.

'Where'd yo' gerrit?'

'My Dad bought it. It's a sort of birthday present.'

Richard growled. He had never mentioned any of his birthday presents. I suspected that he didn't get any.

When we got to the usual spot for climbing over the Park wall, I hesitated. I didn't want the camera to come to grief accidentally. Carefully I followed Richard and Terry up the little twisted tree and over the wall. I held the camera close to my chest as I dropped down. Three minutes later we were standing on the lake-side path. The water seemed polished in the sunlight. Across the lake the swans were grouped on their island reserve. I pulled the camera from its bag and aimed it at the swans. Richard and Terry watched eagerly. I could see hardly anything in the view finder. The swans were too far away. The camera could not cope. I lowered the camera.

'Did yo' tek the snap?'

'No, they are too far away.'

Richard pulled a face, 'Yo' need to be closer, then.'

Terry made a suggestion, 'We could go rahn the lake.'

'But we're not allowed on the reserve, and you can't see them from the path because of the trees.'

Richard grinned. He was quite capable of trespass, but he suggested something different.

'The deers. They'ed make good snaps.'

'Yeah, Arh like reindeers.' Terry spanned his hands with his thumbs touching either side of his forehead.

If we followed the ha-ha towards Wollaton Hall we would get to the railings which separated the deer from the public. We ran and arrived gasping. The Park had a large herd of deer. They were a lovely mix of russet dappled with creamy spots. We always kept an eye out for discarded antlers but never found any. This time there were no deer. Not one. We stood on the bottom horizontal of the iron rails and scanned about.

'There they are!' yelled Terry.

I followed the direction of his pointing finger. Away across the enormous empty field the deer could be just seen. The herd was resting in the grass. I didn't bother to point the camera, I knew that they would be just tiny specks on a photograph. Richard didn't suggest anything irregular he knew about the keen Park wardens and the protective stags.

Terry tried again, 'Yo' could tek a picture of me.' He screwed his face around and waved his arms about. Richard fell about convulsed. I had to grin. Richard joined Terry's lunatic dancing. I pulled the camera out and aimed. I had no intention of taking their photos. They changed contorted poses as I pretended to shoot. Eventually they had let off enough steam and flopped onto a nearby bench. I joined them.

'Can we see the snaps when yo've gorrem?'

'Yes of course,' I lied knowing that that would be quickly forgotten.

'Hello, boys, looked like you were having fun.'

Unnoticed a middle-aged man had approached. He was smiling, but an alarm-bell rang. I thought he might be one of those funny men I had been warned about.

Richard replied, 'Yeah, we was gonna tek some photos, Arh mean Chrisser was gonna tek some photos of the deers. He's got the camera. But they've gone.'

The man looked at me. 'Nice camera. Is it one of those new ones?'

Anxiety welled up. I was sure that he would ask to look at it.

Terry unwittingly broke the spell, 'What time is it mester?'

As the man glanced at his watch, I kicked Richard's foot. He understood.

'It's twenty-five to one.'

'Oh, I have to be home by one. We'd better go.'

'Yeah, or arh mams'll be upset. C'mon Tez.'

We were up and moving away: not running, but not dawdling.

'Bye, boys.'

'Traa,' we returned in unison.

After only a minute or so, I suddenly felt a wave of unease. My camera bag felt light. It was empty.

'My camera!'

It wasn't in my hand. Richard and Terry were empty handed.

'Where is it?'

Ricard and Terry looked at me blankly.

The wave of unease turned to terror. My smart new camera was gone. I tried to push away the horror of having to explain to them back home.

'Yo' dropped it?'

We looked back towards the deer park. The grass was short, smooth, flat and empty.

'D'yo' leave it on the bench?'

I focussed on the bench. The man was sat there. He seemed to be examining something.

'He's got yo' camera. We'll gerrit back.'

The self-appointed hero became fired up. I followed Richard as he trotted back to the bench. As we got nearer the camera was pointed at us.

'I thought you'd be back. I did call but…'

He held out the camera. I gingerly took it. He smiled.

'Thanks, mister.'

'Too nice to lose. I think I'll get one myself.'

I secured the 127 in its carrier. I was trembling. We turned and ran back along the side of the ha-ha. We almost fell over the swans. Four swans had crossed the lake to investigate the weed on the water trapped in the ha-ha.

'Gret, Chrisser, snap 'em quick.'

I fumbled with the camera bag stud, and then the camera. I was still trembling as I raised the camera. The image looked just right.

'Click, click and click again'. Did I do it right? The swans watched us race off to the Park wall.

I bounded through the back door at 5 minutes to one.

'You look hot, chick.'

'Yeah, I ran home, what's for dinner?'

Over the spam fritters, mashed potatoes and peas I recounted the tale of taking the photographs of the swans. I omitted the bits about Richard and Terry, and the diversion to the deer park.

'How many snaps did you take?'

'Three.'

'Oh, you'll have to wait while we take the others on the film.'

Then she added, 'Your Aunty Dot and Uncle Jim and little Clive's coming over on Sunday. You can take some snaps of them. That'll be nice, mmm.'

It wouldn't be nice, but I didn't argue.

It wasn't really worth the wait because the swans had no heads.

- Kodiak Island, off the coast of Alaska, was originally a Russian settlement.

- Kodiak brown bears are the largest of the species.

Lemonade Lads

Lunchtime was at noon, prompt. I would run home for my Mother's cooking rather than sample the stuff turned out by the school canteen. There was ample time. I could be home by ten past twelve, and the afternoon session started at one twenty-five.

My street connected with the parade of shops. On the corner was Woffington's where cigarettes, cakes and sweets from glass jars were sold. Mr Woffington also sold several varieties of chilled goodies from a cream and blue fridge big enough for a body.

The ones that had my attention were the *Archie Andrews* iced lollies, though we called them 'suckers'.

Archie Andrews was a dummy operated by Peter Brough. He wasn't a very good ventriloquist, so it was just as well that Archie rose to fame on the wireless. He had a weekly show called *Educating Archie*. During the show attempts to put some sense into Archie's wooden head were made by the likes of: Tony Hancock, Benny Hill, Harry Secombe, Dick Emery, Bernard Bresslaw, Bruce Forsyth, Beryl Reid, Max Bygrave and a fourteen year old Julie Andrews.

Archie was so popular that he toured the country. My Parents took me to the theatre in town to see my hero. Going to the theatre was a very rare treat. During the show very small harmonicas were thrown from the stage into the audience. I wasn't quick enough to catch one, so Mother bought one at the box office.

The real interest was the iced lollies, or rather the wrappers they came in. Archie's portrait featured on the wrapper. These could be collected, and eventually exchanged for 'prizes'. The more collected achieved a greater prize. It was a long haul collecting the 250, but I was delighted with a pictorial encyclopaedia.

Obviously it was impossible for me alone to lick and suck my way to such a 'prize'. It was necessary to lurk around Woffington's for some ingenoue to carelessly caste away a wrapper. The 'litter' was immediately snatched up, rushed home, wiped clean and stored in an envelope.

On the way home I inspected the area around the corner shop for wrappers. As I drifted up the street I was caught up by Richard and Terry. They were interested only in scoffing the lollies.

An open lorry pulled up at the kerb. It was a delivery of fizzy drinks from *Redgates* for Mr Pretty's shop.

As ever, Richard was looking for the main chance.

'Hey-up, mester, d'yo' wan' any 'elp?'

'Yeah, nip down the alley and gerrus the trolley.'

Mr Pretty owned a trolley. It was a wooden platform about the size of a door. It rode on a single central axel. At both ends were small wheels which didn't quite touch the ground. When the trolley was at rest one wheel did touch the ground. Both ends had tubular metal frames to prevent the cargo from slipping off. They also acted as handles. The trolley had a mind of its own: it was best to pull rather than push to get it to move in a straight line.

When I played with Mike Pretty the trolley served as a tank, a spaceship, a boat or a see-saw. The real function was to transport goods from the curb-side to the sheds at the back of the grocery shop, and also to remove empty crates and bottles.

We hurtled to the end of the service alley. Richard and I pushed whilst Terry rode. Of course the trolley zig-zagged, and it was bumped up and down to give Terry a better ride.

The delivery man was pulling on a Park Drive cigarette when we returned. The appropriate side had been dropped. He pointed at Richard, the largest, 'You, gerrup on the back and get what I tell you.' He had a clip-board under his arm, 'You two, catch, an' don't drop nowt.'

Richard scrambled up the side of the lorry using the huge wheel for footholds.

'Nah then. Four lemonades.'

Terry and I stood ready whilst Richard heaved the wooden crates around. They were orange coloured and held six glass bottles. The first crate was positioned. As Richard heaved it over the edge Terry and I reached up and then swung it down onto the trolley. We banged down a dozen crates of dandelion and burdock, orangeade and cream-soda.

Lugging the trolley back was harder work. We were told to leave the crates on the trolley for Mr Pretty to sort. A copy of the delivery note was placed in one crate.

The delivery man was looking at his drop list. He grinned.

'Ta, lads, ay this.'

He held out a bottle of pop. The contents were bright red: it was cherry-ade.

'It fell off an' got broke.' He grinned again.

Richard grabbed the bottle.

As the lorry backed away to turn, we stared at the shiny red bubbly liquid.

'Ah kno', we'll hide it in the hedge-bottom. Then we can guzz it on the way back to school.'

This seemed fair and sensible, so Terry and I nodded sagely. Richard secreted the bottle amongst the tangled privet root, old leaves and litter.

'Where have you been? It's half past twelve gone.'

I explained about the assistance that we had given, but I didn't mention the reward. My lunch of spam fritters, mashed potato and tinned peas followed by a glass of milk disappeared quickly. When the wireless news came on at one o'clock it was time to depart. A kiss, and I was off.

I was the first there. Something was amiss. I raked around in the debris but there was no bottle.

'What's up, Chrisser?' Terry appeared. There was a gravy splash on his shirt front.

'It's not here. It's gone.'

'Y'lookin' in the right place?'

'Yeah, I watched Rich put it here. You did too.'

'Anuvver kid could of seen us.'

'Don't think so. We looked around. We were careful.'

'Oh, 'ere comes Richard.'

Richard trotted up.

He looked from me to Terry, 'What's a marrer?'

'It's gone. The boccle's gone.'

Richard looked shocked, 'Bleddy 'ell. Somebody's nicked it. Well, no use crying over spilt pop, eh?'

Feeling disgruntled we ran off for the afternoon session.

School finished at 4 o'clock. I didn't play army around the Welfare Rooms, nor did I linger outside the house where the monkey lived and nor did I search for 'dead rainbows' in the road gutters. I went quickly to Woffington's to search for lolly wrappers that infants might have dropped (infants finished the day at 3:30). There was just one to be had. I also rummaged along the length of hedge where the bottle was supposed to be.

'What are you looking for, Christopher?'

It was Angela. She was in the first year of the juniors and she was a girl, which usually meant that I did not acknowledge her presence.

'Oh, something that got lost around here.'

'A bottle of pop?'

'What?'

'I was watching you helping the man. I was upstairs looking out of mummy's window. I saw you hide the red bottle. I saw Richard come back for it. Richard took it.'

I stared at her in disbelief. Was she fibbing? Did Richard really take the bottle? How could he? How could he lie to his friends? What happened to the cherry-ade? What could be done?

'Thanks. Thanks for telling me.'

Angela smiled and said, 'I don't like Richard. Mummy says he's naughty.'

These were exactly my thoughts too.

'What's a matter with you? You've hardly touched you tea.'

'Oh, er, nothing,' I polished off the rest of the beans on toast. I also continued to think about the injustice done to Terry and me by a supposed friend.

'I'm going out for a bit. I'll be back soon.'

I walked up the street to Terry's house. He was sitting on his front gate eating an apple.

'I know who took it.'

Terry stopped chewing.

'It was Richard. He went back and got it. Somebody saw him.'

Terry slid off the gate. He looked surprised.

'Nah, not Richard. He wou'n't do owt like that.'

'Yes he did. He must have drunk it at home. She saw him.'

'Who seen 'im?'

'Angela. The little girl who lives at number six. She was watching through the bedroom window.'

Terry shook his head slowly. He had a far-away look.

'We'll ask 'im, yeah, we'll ask 'im.'

'He'll only lie. You know Richard.'

I could not see where this was leading. Terry was Richard's disciple. Richard was tough. Terry suddenly became animated. Richard was out on the street near the lamp post. He saw us and waved. We walked towards him. As usual, he was grinning. Terry got straight to the point.

'Yo' 'ad that pop, di'n'yo?'

'What, what yo' talkin' abaht?'

'Yo' kno' very well.'

Richard pulled his bemused, innocent face. He turned to me. '"What's 'e on abaht, Chrisser?'

'You took the bottle of pop. You went back for it. You were seen.'

Richard's smile faltered for a moment. 'They're telling fibs. Who is it?'

'Yo' are telling fibs.'

Richard was smiling again, 'I di'n't tek it, 'onest to God.'

'Yo're a cunt.'

I nearly jumped out of my skin. I'd heard swearing, but there were some words that children didn't use. Richard had told us previously that under-twelves were not allowed to say 'pregnant'. We should say 'having a baby'. I believed him. I was surprised that Terry came out with that word. I was aghast at how Richard would react. Richard looked shocked. For a moment he was lost for words.

'Wha'd'yo' call me?'

Terry repeated his words and added, 'An' yo' nicked the pop we was s'posed to share.'

'Yo' can't prove that.'

'Yes we can. There's a witness. And she doesn't tell fibs.'

I could see that Richard was sizing up who he would punch first. Of course it was going to be mouthy Terry. I would be the next to get hammered. My Father had advised me to run from situations like this, but if it was inevitable: strike first, keep at it until they went down and then make sure they stayed down. It all made good sense, in theory.

It was Terry who moved first.

Terry wagged his finger just short of Richard's nose, 'Yo' can gerrus ah share.'

Richard's face was blank. He took a step back. His head began to nod, 'OK.'

Terry pulled his finger back. Richard thrust his hands into his pockets and gave a little smile.

'OK. Ah took the pop. Ah thought it was safer indoors. But ah Alan was at hom' an' he took it off of us.' He looked shifty.

In one move Terry had made his point firmly; defused the situation; and given Richard a golden bridge to escape over. This was amazing for a 'B' streamer who couldn't recite the alphabet.

The following day I saw Richard coming up our path. At the backdoor he handed me a full bottle of cherry-ade.

'Am I to share this with Terry?'

'Nah, Tez has got one an all.' He pulled his impish grin, 'Ah foun' some dosh.'

Later I saw Terry. He seemed to be starting a pink beard.

'Hey-up, Chrisser, yo' got one an all?'

'Yeah…You know he said his brother had taken the pop from him.'

Terry tipped his head to one side to demonstrate that he was listening.

'Well, I don't think Alan would be at home at that time. He goes to a bi-lateral school. It's miles away. A bus ride away. And do you think Richard really *found* some money?'

Terry nodded wisely. Then he brightened and said, 'Good though wa'n't it?'

I agreed, but I had been disappointed with the taste. It didn't live up to the promise of the bright red colour. I had decided to stick with lemonade.

'Hey-up.'

Terry and I greeted a smiling Richard.

'When yo've finished, giz the boccles back.'

There was three pence returnable deposit on each bottle!

The incident was never mentioned. I was not aware of being cheated again, but I tried to be on my guard when involved in any of Richard's schemes.

We did see the *Redgates* delivery truck from time to time, but the driver was different and he declined our offers of help.

No Smoke Without

'Go on ay one.'

This was new. I had seen him with a single one on previous occasions. It was usually slightly bent from being in his pocket. He would keep the activity secret: away from adult eyes. There was never enough to be generous. Now Richard was openly smiling and offering a brand new whole open packet of *Park Drive* cigarettes.

I was shocked and not shocked. Shocked because of his flamboyant style, and not shocked because I knew that Richard pinched the odd cigarette from his parents.

While I hesitated, Terry reached out and took one of the pristine white tubes.

'Good man,' and then to me Richard said, 'Yo' gunna ay one, Chrisser?'

Back then everyone smoked. It was a legacy from the War, just like most everything else. My Parents smoked. All the adults I knew smoked, except for Uncle Jim. When Dr Briggs visited, he would accept a cigarette from my Mother after examining me. During the interval at the cinema a big girl would appear with a selection of sweets and cigarettes on a tray. The audience smoked during the film-show. The ascending trails of smoke were caught by the projection light. The cinema made smoking look glamorous and 'grown-up.' All the tough guys smoked.

It was acceptable to smoke indoors. Public bars were a haze of blue smoke. My Father would light up a cigarette as soon as he had finished his evening meal after work. Everyone smoked: except children.

Children were forbidden to smoke. If they were caught doing so, punishments were given out. These ranged from a clip around the ear, or freedom curtailed, or worse. Apparently some children were made to sit at the kitchen table and were obliged to smoke cigarette after cigarette until they were sick.

'Why can't I smoke?'

'Because you're not old enough.'

'How old do I have to be?'

'When you are grown up.'

I had realised that growing up was not an instantaneous thing. There was the process of getting taller, featuring teenage spots and eventually having a beard. On the way to being grown up there were rites of passage. One moved from the Infants to the Juniors. At the age of twelve, according to the Rec' notice board, we were not allowed on the swings or slide. By fourteen we would be charged full-fare on the buses. At sixteen one could get married with parents' consent. The Sunday newspapers always had a story about sixteen year olds running away to Gretna Green where the Scottish Law on marriage was different. It seemed such a long haul to being able to go into pubs and drink beer at eighteen. Being twenty-one was the last hurdle to being truly grown-up. People had a special party and 'got the key of the door', and could do as they pleased.

Nobody, though, said when it was permissible to smoke. If children fancied smoking, it had to be done secretly. When I had expressed an interest, my Father had given me a cigarette to try. Of course I coughed and spluttered and felt sick. He grinned, and I was cured of interest. Obviously smoking was truly an activity for grown-up tastes. I couldn't understand why folks would want to subject themselves to such a grizzly experience.

Sid, our neighbour, gave advice, 'Drink as much bleddy ale as you like, but never start bleddy smoking!'

This was rich coming from him. He was frequently incapable, and smoked like a chimney.

When I related this homespun philosophy to my Parents, it was explained that smoking was addictive. Once one started, the drug got into the system and one could never easily stop. Every New Year many people vowed to stop smoking. Few did. My Father lasted three days without a cigarette. He became so bad-tempered that my Mother lit one and gave it to him.

'Aw, come on, tek one.'

Richard was still holding out the packet of *Park Drive*. Terry was blowing out blue fumes.

'Where did you get them from?' I was playing for time, and I knew that Richard would not have sufficient funds to splash out on a whole new pack of twenty.

'What, you fink ah nicked 'em?' Richard put on his hurt expression.

I began to feel uncomfortable. We were sitting in my garden shed which doubled as my den. My Parents were both at work. I didn't want them to come home to find evidence of 'evil' doings. Richard wasn't easy to control. I had been warned many times about being in his company and being led astray, but he was the nearest play-mate. Terry was Richard's none too bright protégé. Richard pulled himself a cigarette and lit it nonchalantly with a match.

'Yo' got summink we can use as a nashtray?'

I pushed an odd cracked saucer along the work bench. He dropped the dead match into it, and Terry quickly flicked his ash.

'Well… I mean… it's a new pack…you don't…'

He grinned, 'Yeah right. Well, nah Ah've gorra source o' supply. Cheap an'all.'

He flicked the open packet along the work bench. Richard was lording it on the old kitchen stool, I was perched on the up-turned dolly tub and Terry was sprawled on the narrow Utility bed.

'Ah can let yo' ay a packet cheap. If yo' wannit.'

The penny dropped. Richard would buy the cigarettes cheaply and sell them to his customers to make a profit. Of course he knew that the young customers would become hooked. He still hadn't said where they came from. I suspected that they had been stolen in the first place.

Richard blew out smoke in my direction. Terry started to cough.

'He needs more practise. Don't yo', Tez?'

'Arh.'

Richard suddenly stood up, 'C'mon, Tez, we best be goin'. To me he said, 'Yo' 'ave 'em on the 'ouse. Ah'l talk wi' yo' later, Chrisser.'

When they had gone I buried the contents of the ash tray in the garden and opened the shed door and window wide. I took the abandoned cigarette pack and secreted it in my Meccano box which lived in the narrow gap at the base of my Utility wardrobe. Mother would be home soon from the afternoon shift at Boots factory in Beeston.

'Well I never.' Mother was reading out pieces of interest from the Evening Post.

'What now, Bridget, are we getting a rebate on the rent?'

'No, listen, somebody pinched one of Players' wagons right out of their yard. They just waltzed in, as bold as brass, and drove off with a load of cigs. It was full with thousands of packets of cigs going for export.'

Later, when the coast was clear and I was supposed to be reading the *Eagle* in bed, I pulled the Meccano box out and looked at the packet of cigarettes. Down one side in bold black lettering it read, 'Export Only.' In smaller print it said that it was prohibited to sell the cigarettes in the UK. I had a mental picture of Richard, and possibly Terry, sneaking into Players' lorry park and driving off. It couldn't be. My dream was full of policemen bursting into my bedroom looking for stolen goods. I wondered what the penalty was for 'receiving'.

In the morning I thought to dispose of the contraband goods. I couldn't slip the pack into my Father's coat pocket or one of my Mother's several handbags because of the message down the side. Anyway I would have to account for the cigarettes with Richard. I could give them back or pay for them.

It was easy enough to disguise the packet in a brown paper bag and stuff it into my coat pocket. The hard bit would be handing it back and setting myself up for ridicule as a wimp.

I hung about under the lamp at the end of our Close. I cruised along the parade of shops but didn't see Richard.

Later, after the evening meal, my mother continued with the story, 'The police have found the stolen lorry, you know, the one from Players. It was found not far away in Radford. It was parked between two old warehouses. Back doors were open and everything gone. Hmm.'

My Father threw the last tiny end of his cigarette into the fire, 'Sounds like a well-planned job. Probably somebody on the inside. Of course the fags would have been switched to other vans. Must have been several to move that load quickly.'

'I'll bet Sid's got some already.'

'Well I shan't be buying any cheap smokes off Sid.'

'Not with *Export Only* stamped all over them.'

I busied myself with tying my shoe-laces, and prayed that my mother wouldn't decide to tidy up my coat.

Richard was no saint. He had an uncle who lived in Radford. He had some dubious friends who lived in Radford. Perhaps he was part of a gang that stole to sell on. Maybe there were other kids, like Richard, selling cheap cigarettes around Radford. It was the sort of district where questions were not asked. I had instructions to keep well away from Radford. My personal knowledge of the place was limited to the view from the top deck of a trolley bus.

There might be a reward for information leading to the arrest of the gang of thieves. I imagined shaking hands with the Chief Constable and accepting a thick envelope. Then I imagined Richard coming round to beat me up for snitching. Who could I tell without getting myself involved?

Richard was out on the street, 'Hey-up, Chrisser.' He held his hand out. It was palm up. I placed the package on his hand.

'What's this?'

'The cigarettes. The stolen cigarettes.'

He had a quick look inside the paper bag, 'Who said they was stolen?'

'The Evening Post did the other night. There was a lorry load nicked from Players.'

'Nah, these aren't the same uns…'

'They've got *Export Only* along the edge. The lorry load was for Export Only.'

I was sure a faint flush came briefly to his cheeks. He shook his head.

'Chrisser if they is stolen, Ah din't know. Ah gorrem off of a mate. Ah had to pay forrem.'

He was wriggling. I was not sure whether he was lying or had been caught out on a money making racket.

'Yo' 'ad any out the pack?'

I shook my head, 'No they are all there, except the ones you and Terry had.'

'Yo' to'd anybody?' His eyes had narrowed, he was thinking fast.

'No, but I was thinking of taking them to the police.'

This was a dangerous thing to say, or it just might squash him.

'Yer wou'n't! Not the rozzers.'

I shrugged. He pushed the package under his pull-over.

'Ah tell yo' what, Chrisser me o'd mate, if yo' don't say nuffink to nob'dy…'

I raised my palm as if to stop him, 'Don't bother, I'll keep quiet.'

I wasn't sure if he was about to threaten me or offer me a bribe. In any case he grinned.

'Listen to this, Ken.'

'I'm all ears.'

'You know that lorry of cigs that was robbed, well they've got them back, or most of them.'

'Mmm.'

'It seems that they were hidden in an unused shed down Radford not far from where the lorry was found. Some bloke was flogging cheap cigs in the *Denman*…'

'…And he picked a plain-clothed policeman.'

'How did you know?'

'I could see it coming. He must be a simpleton.'

'Well, he must have talked, because they got the gang and most of the stuff back. It was all in sealed boxes.'

'Except for one.'

I knew where some of that box had ended up. It wasn't too difficult to work out how. I wondered how many packets Richard had actually got, and what he was going to do with them now.

Richard had a cunning plan. He had speculated with buying six packets of twenty, which he was going to sell on and make a profit.

'Hey up, Chrisser.' He was all smiles. 'Your mam an' dad smoke *Park Drive*. When they've finished a packet, can yo' gerrit for us?'

'What do you want empty fag packets for?'

He didn't hesitate. 'Ah'm gonna mek a garage for my lickle cousin's toy cars.'

'How many do you need?'

'Oh, 'bout 'arf a doz. Not squashed uns.'

I agreed to help. I chose not to press him on how he would make a reasonable sized garage with only six packets. Richard was not known for his handiwork, charitable or otherwise. I pictured him struggling with the exchange of the outer sleeves, all six.

'Mum, why doesn't Uncle Jim smoke?'

'He never has. He was in the Navy. The sailors all got free cigarettes. Your Uncle Jim gave his away. He said he didn't like the taste. He likes the taste of rum though, at Christmas.'

Later, when I asked Uncle Jim, he said that it was a mug's game, a waste of money and he was sure that it didn't do the lungs any good.

Uncle Jim lived well into his nineties, but Dr Briggs died at fifty-five with lung cancer.

Not So Smarties

Miss Hilton gave us the usual reminder about putting coats on. We were out of winter, but the weather was still miserable. Today was a good day: we could actually have playtime outside. The boys who played football in the yard didn't bother with coats. I didn't play football, so standing around for fifteen minutes necessitated wearing an extra layer. I headed for the cloak-room across the corridor. There were a pair of cloak-rooms, one either side of the steps down to the hall. My cloak-room was intended for the two Year 5 classes. The other was for the two Year 6 classes. Years 3 and 4 had cloak-rooms at the far ends of the corridor. Each cloak-room had benches down the sides. Two more benches back to back made an island. This island had a beam which held the coat hooks. The girls tended to use the island while the boys used the hooks on the two long sides. At the end of the cloak-room were four wash basins with windows above to see into the quadrangle. Coats and PE bags hung close together: seventy children would use each cloak-room. The painted hooks were worn down to the metal.

I reached for my navy blue gabardine raincoat. It was like all the rest. It wasn't school uniform. There was little choice back then.

'It's gone. I'm sure I had it in my pocket.' Julia, with the marmalade hair, was rummaging in her coat pocket.

'What's gone?'

Julia and I had our birthday month in common. No other child in our class was born in July.

'A Kit-Kat. I got it from Woffo's this morning. Now it's gone.'

I left her turning her pockets out and looking under the bench. We weren't supposed to bring sweets to school. Having chewing-gum or bubble-gum was a serious crime. Even so I felt sorry for her.

Outside in the play yard I mooched about with Geoff, and Mickey Hazeldine. We chatted about toy soldiers and train sets. It was good to get back in the warm class-room. We were set the task of writing a story with the emphasis on starting each sentence with a different word.

At the end of the school day the Lenton Abbey Estate children spewed out of the gates onto Boundary Road. Julia was just in front of me with Lorraine.

'Did you find it?'

'No, and it's not the first.'

'What?'

Lorraine chipped in, 'Last week I had a lipstick in my pocket, and that disappeared.'

The following week Keith, in the second Y5 class was moaning about his missing collection of cigarette cards. Luckily they were a small bunch of 'swaps'. Even so, Keith was not happy.

I thought that it was quite silly to keep valuables in coats left in the cloak-room, and that it served the victims right. I changed my mind when I couldn't find my gloves. I was sure that I had stuffed them into my rain-coat pockets. Joyce was beside herself with indignation when her knitted hood vanished from the cloakroom. She told Mrs Taylor straight away. Joyce was from a very religious family and had a firm sense of right and wrong.

After the morning assembly Mr Reeves had something to say about the spate of pilfering from the cloak rooms. He promised to deal with the culprit most severely, without specifying what the punishment would be. Geoff, Mickey and I speculated on what it might involve.

'He gets his fingers crushed in a vice.'

'No, that's too much. It will be caning, hard across the hands.'

'He might be expelled, and have to run-the-gauntlet past all the kids who had stuff nicked.'

'Might be a girl.'

So far the culprit was a boy, but it was possible that it could be a girl.

We made a provisional list of boys and girls who might the villain. We left out anyone who had been a victim. Most of the possibilities were in the other class: the 'B' stream. Most of the names belonged to children which we didn't like.

'What if it's not a Year 5 kid. What if it's somebody from Year 6?'

That widened the field. There were lots of villains in the top classes. I thought of Richard straight away, but dismissed the idea because Richard was not into petty pilfering. He was more ambitious with his schemes for becoming rich.

After Mr Reeves' presidential speech the spate of pilfering stopped. Or perhaps the children were less careless with their treasures. For a couple of weeks only school stuff happened.

There was a commotion in the play yard. Joyce was standing on the bottom bar of the iron railings which separated the Infants from the

Juniors. She was pressed against the bars with one arm stretched out into the Infants' space.

'There's my hat. That girl's wearing my hat. She's got my hat!'

It was easy to spot the hat. It was hand-made: knitted wool by Joyce's mother. It was the only one of its kind. The infants seemed perplexed when dozens of Juniors squeezed against the bars.

'Cavalry to the rescue,' declared Mickey. He pressed on the latch of the railing gates. We regarded these gates as special gates which were there for the ceremony of Top Infants graduating to the Juniors early in September. Mickey swung the gate open and stepped through. By this time Mrs Moody who was on Infant yard duty was striding over. The little girl wearing Joyce's hat began to realise that she was the centre of attention. Geoff and I galloped after Mickey. Mrs Taylor called us back and told the rest of the Juniors to come away from the railings. The two teachers, the girl in the hat, the indignant Joyce and the three cavalry troopers met at the frontier gate. When asked about the hat the little girl, Susan, said that her brother had found the hat and given it to her as it was a girl's hat. The hat was handed over to its rightful owner. Susan's big brother was in the Juniors. Names were mentioned.

'Now we've got him,' said Geoff.

'Yeah, I know him, he's in class 4,' said Mickey. Class 4 was the other Year 5 group.

'Let's get him. We'll make a citizen's arrest,' I said. My Father had explained about a citizen's arrest.

Mrs Taylor said, 'Not so fast. Colin is in my class. I will deal with it.'

I was disappointed at not making an arrest, but delighted to be a close witness when Colin was summoned away from the football game. He looked sheepish. He admitted straight away that he had found the hat, and that he had given it to his sister. He said that he had spotted it on the edge of one of the old air-raid shelters. He totally denied any thieving. He apologised for not handing in lost property and said he was sorry for Joyce.

'Well, if Colin isn't the culprit, some other kid is.'

'It must be a boy, 'cos he chucked the girl's hat'

'Why did he take it in the first place, then?'

'And why did he nick Lorraine's lippy?'

We were stumped. There didn't seem to be any sense in the pilfering spree.

Geoff came up with an idea, 'We could set a trap.'

'What do you mean?'

'We could keep watch in the cloak-room. Stuff got nicked in the mornings.'

'It has to be when everybody's in class.'

'So somebody goes to the toilet?'

'Yeah, they pretend to go to the toilet, and go through pockets.'

It was not easy going to the toilet in lesson time. It was frowned upon by the teachers. If toilet paper was needed it had to be asked for. Only three sheets were given, and they were the nasty stiff Izal brand. The toilets, boys and girls, were outside of the main building. The boys' was open to the elements. There were roofed cubicles, but the only light came through the gaps at the top and the bottom of the doors. Of course I had no idea what the girls' toilets were like, but I suspected that they were just as primitive.

'So, how are we going to keep watch?' I asked.

Mickey and Geoff looked blank.

'If a kid asks to go to the toilet, one of us could ask, and follow them.'

'What if it's a kid from another class?'

Blank looks all round.'

'I know. One of us doesn't come into the class but stays in the cloakroom until playtime. Then after play he says that they over slept.'

'What about after play?'

'One of us doesn't go back into class.'

'Won't Miss Hilton notice there's one missing?'

'If she does, we say that so-and-so felt poorly and went to the toilet.'

It was an hour and a quarter between playtime and dinner break. Miss Hilton was a new teacher, but she wasn't stupid.

'One of us could volunteer to go find him. He's brought back moaning and groaning.'

'Yeah, well that's one day. It wouldn't work a second time.'

'Why can't the spy stay there all the time? Then when he comes back to school he's lost his sick note.'

'That's two days sorted. We should have got the thief by then.'

In my mind I had already received the reward and made a statement to *The Evening Post*.

'OK. When do we start?'

'Tomorrow. I'll bring some Smarties, and make sure they are seen.'

'Who's going to be the spy?' I asked.

Geoff and Mickey quickly agreed that it would be me. Of course I was honoured but also a little apprehensive.

The next morning Mickey was making a show of offering around a tube of Smarties. 'It's OK I've got another couple of tubes.' His generosity was an attraction. The performance ended abruptly when Mr Hall appeared with his whistle. When our class number was called we trooped into school. We three secret agents lingered in the cloakroom until all the other children had gone to the class-rooms. I scrambled onto the bench between two of the largest coats. Geoff and Mickey made sure that I was well hidden. I waited. After five minutes the classes emerged to go two by two for morning assembly in the hall. As the noise of feet faded a figure appeared in the cloakroom entrance. It was a girl. It was Barbara with the pretty grey eyes. My heart pounded. Surely it was not her? She dipped her hand into a coat pocket. It was her own camel-coloured duffle coat. Barbara scampered away clutching her handkerchief. I heard the hymn and then the marching feet. I had to shuffle my feet: I was getting cramp. It was tiring and boring. I began to think about abandoning the project. Suddenly I was made aware of another figure. In fact there were two hovering by the entrance to the cloakroom. I recognised two boys from Year 6. They belonged to Class 2, the 'B'stream. One of them stayed by the entrance, while the other, very quickly, began dipping into coat pockets. I had recognised them, but I didn't know their names because they were from the Beeston side. What was I to do? They were Year 6 and big boys. The dipper suddenly held the trophy tube of Smarties. I had to do something, and quickly. The dipper turned back towards his associate. 'Stop thief!'

The dipper stopped and spun round. He looked startled. I had sprung from my hiding- place.

'You are under arrest, for stealing.'

Then there were two of them coming at me.

'Shut yer gob, Curly. Yo' ain't seen nowt.'

'If yo' snitch you'll get a good duffing.'

I was shown two clenched fists, and two sets of bared teeth.

'Hey up, what's goin' on?' I recognised Richard's voice. He was in the same class as the two thieves. 'Mester Bateson sent me to see 'ow yo' two was gerrin on.' To me he said, 'They s'posed to be sorting the salvage.'

Back then *recycling* was called *salvage*. It was another left-over from the war. Children were asked to bring newspaper and aluminium milk bottle tops which would be collected from time to time. Year 6 was responsible for keeping the salvage store tidy.

I wasn't sure how this was going to go. As he lived near to me Richard was a sort of friend, but he could be naughty, and they were in the same class.

'They are the thieves. They are the ones who have been taking things out of kids' pockets. I saw him take Michael Hazeldine's Smarties.' I pointed my finger. 'And they threatened me.'

Eyes flicked about. The dipper looked livid. Richard looked amused. I felt like pissing my pants.

'Church, I sent you to do a job. What's going on?'

Richard snapped to attention, 'Mester Bateson, sir, these two was nickin' stuff from pockets, sir.'

The two thieves sagged. They knew that the game was up. It would be little use lying to the well experienced teacher in charge of the Year 6 'B' stream.

Mr Bateson turned his attention to me, 'What's *he* got to do with this?'

'Chrisser seen 'em nickin' Smarties jus' nah, sir'. 'So he made a cit'zens arrest.'

A faint smile appeared on Mr Bateson's face.

'Richard was helping me, sir'

Richard beamed. Mr Bateson's eyebrows lifted, 'Well, I think this is a case for Mr Reeves.'

As we emerged from the cloakroom on the way to the Head teacher's office I noticed that the clock was not yet at ten o'clock. After I had explained why I was in the cloakroom, I was told to go back to my class, escorted by Mrs Greenfield, the school secretary. She spoke to a surprised Miss Hilton. I was aware of a host of inquisitive eyes. I gave a discreet thumbs-up to Geoff and Mickey.

At playtime I recounted the apprehension of the villains to goggle-eyed Mickey and Geoff.

On the way home I was caught up by Richard and Terry.

'Cor, did they gerrit in the neck. Mester Reeves freatened 'em wiv the rozzers, an' the cane, an' tellin' their dads. They 'ad to promise to stop nickin' stuff, an' to bring stuff back. And they had to keep away from yo'.' Richard was gleeful.

I was relieved.

It seemed that they had readily admitted to the cloak-room thefts. They had taken the opportunity every time they had to tidy the salvage store. Some items were returned to their delighted owners. Keith got his cigarette cards back. Lorraine was obliged to explain why she had a lipstick at school. I got my gloves. The sweets and chocolate bars, alas, had been consumed. Children were reminded about what was not allowed to be brought to school, and how we should take care of our 'treasures.'

Richard generously provided Julia with a replacement Kit-Kat. He was still basking in the praise for his part in ending the crime wave. I suspected that the chocolate wafer had been pinched, though, from Woffington's shop.

O'd King Wenceslas

As soon as the last sparkler had spluttered out all eyes were on the supreme target. The tinsel appeared in Woffington's window. Pretty's had stacks of biscuit tins featuring images of Regency shoppers in the snow. Signs appeared urging folks to place Christmas orders. The off-licence had special offers on beers, wines and spirits. My thoughts turned easily to Dinky military vehicles, toy soldiers and Hornby trains. I didn't need to write to Santa: my Parents knew only too well.

There was little playing outside. The sky was darkening as we left school at 4 o'clock. It was also too cold to hang about.

'Hey, listen, Arh've gorra gret ideah.'

Richard was always having great ideas for making a fortune. Usually they ended in disaster for all concerned.

'We can go carol singin'.'

As Terry and I didn't seem initially impressed, he continued.

'We bin learning all the carols. So nah we can make some dosh.'

Ever since Harvest Festival had been cleared away, Mrs Taylor had been drilling the juniors with the carols. She was accompanied by Miss Hilton on the piano. This took place in the hall on Wednesday afternoons. Wednesday afternoons were usually for games lessons but now the weather curtailed them. Sometimes Mr Hall would show his face to terrify any miscreants, but Mrs Taylor was more than capable of controlling the eight classes. We were rehearsing a carol service for parents. One dark evening the school would be open. Children were expected to return in the company of parents for a six o'clock start. This was to accommodate teatime and those parents who were working. The school would be dark again by seven. The Nativity play was performed by infants during an afternoon in their own hall.

My favourite carol was *Soul Cake*, which was sung all on one note as a round:

A Soul cake, a Soul cake
Please good missus a Soul cake
Apple a pear, plum or cherry
Any good thing to make us all merry
One for Peter, two for Paul
Three for Him 'as saved us all.

After the first round other singers took up *God Rest Ye, Merry Gentlemen*. I was amazed that the two quite different carols could be combined. The *Soul Cake* round was usually sung through three or four times.

In the rehearsals a couple of classes would stand on the stage to sing to the rest of us. It was on one of these occasions that Louise Dale, standing in the centre of the front row, pissed herself. It was entertainment for some and a horror for others. Lulu was led away in tears. She had been too scared to ask to go to the toilet.

After school lunch on the day of the Carol Service, the caretaker, assisted by some trusties from the boys' secondary school next door, would fill the hall with chairs for the parents. My Mother would come along, but my Father was invariably working overtime at Boots factory.

On the last afternoon of the autumn term, bedlam would be acted out in the disguise of a Christmas party. I was not thrilled by the noise, silly games, watery jelly and meat paste finger rolls.

'Quiet down or you won't get the ice-cream or see the film.'

A movie projector was hired and the kids sat on the floor sucking ice-cream and watching cartoons until home time whilst the adults cleared the sticky mess off the classroom desks.

'There's only three of us.'

'Well, wi can get some uvvers. Not too many or wi get less dosh. 'Ow abaht your mates, Twilmop and Geoff?'

'Geoff would I suppose, but I think Tony might not. What about some girls?'

'Gells?'

'Yes, they are good at singing. There's Julia…'

'The ginger lump?'

'Julia has friends: Barbara and Lorraine.'

Richard screwed his face into a scowl which changed quickly into a merry grin.

'OK, Chrisser, but the gells get less dosh.'

'Why?'

''Cos they're only gells.'

Terry spoke the wisdom, 'That's not right.'

Richard scowled again, and again produced a grin. 'OK, Chrisser, you chat the gells.'

Julia was up for anything. She said she would ask Barbara. When I spoke to Lorraine, who lived across the road from our Close, she flatly refused to be involved in anything with Richard. She said that he was an uncouth thug. I could not readily disagree with her.

Geoff was happy to join the carollers, especially as Richard would be outnumbered by sensible people. He also said he could bring a prop in the form of a lantern on a pole. Twilmop's mother said that she didn't like Tony out in the dark.

'So are we going to do this it in the dark?'

'Yeah, carol singin' is allus done at night.'

'When?'

I hadn't given any serious thought to when and where the project would take place. I had pictured us working our way up our own street in the hour before tea time. Richard had a master plan, of course.

'It's dark at six, so we sing 'til seven.'

This would need some negotiation with parents, especially with the girls.

'An' it's useless doin' it on the 'state 'cos they're all poor, an' ev'ry uvver Tom, Dick and 'Arry will be doin' it.'

I remembered previous years when my Father became annoyed with one line of a carol followed by rapping of the door knocker, 'Not again! That's five times in the last ten minutes.'

'So, where?'

Richard beamed, 'Miggleton Crescent, of course.'

'But that's the other side of Derby Road.'

Middleton Crescent looped off the better side of Derby Road. It started just past the parade of shops where the Pretty's had their third shop, and finished opposite Central Avenue which led into Beeston. I had walked past the beginning and the end of the crescent many times on the way to Snakey Woods. I had actually been in the first house on the corner. Doctor Briggs had his surgery in part of the ground floor of his huge home. There had been no reason to wander into the crescent: it was unknown territory. Richard reckoned that there were about thirty large posh houses for us to visit.

'Yeah, but you don' tell yer mam where wi goin', lerrer fink it's on the 'state.'

Richard and Terry's parents were not too bothered about them being out after dark as long as they were not brought home by the Law. I now had serious doubts about Julia and Barbara.

'Since Lorraine won't come, shall I ask Jo?'

'Tom Boy? Yeah, why not? She can be arh body guard.'

Richard and Terry were really both still in awe of her martial arts skill.

A meeting was necessary. It took place in the rec shelter on a dreary Saturday morning. I was surprised to see Lorraine. She said that she had changed her mind since Jo, her friend, was keen. I was delighted to see Barbara with *the grey eyes*. Geoff had been busy with his lamp. It was a broom stick with a kerosene lamp attached. The lamp had been converted to hold a night light. The girls were so impressed that Julia suggested that we all wore woolly hats and scarves. It was also agreed that carol sheets were not needed because we all knew the words. The carols chosen were *Away in a Manger*, *We Three Kings* and if necessary *Oh Come All Ye Faithful*. I was disappointed that *Soul Cake* was not included.

'Nah, we sing only the firs' verse of *Away* an' then *Three Kin's*. Then we bang the door an' chant *Christmas is a comin'*. When they come aht, we sin' *We Wish You*. If they are dead keen they get *Oh Come*, but on'y the firs' verse. OK?'

'*Christmas is a coming?* That says *please put a penny in the old man's hat.*'

Richard acknowledged Julia's observation.

'Yeah, well, we can change it to... *please put some silver in the young gell's 'at.*'

'Which day?'

The day after school finished seemed a good choice. It would be a Thursday.

The girls worked together to persuade parents to agree. They said that four sensible boys would be with them, and they promised to be home before 7:15. They refrained from saying that the carolling would be in the next district beyond the main road.

It seemed like a slick operation. Richard said that we would need to clear four pounds to make it worthwhile. Terry had to ask how much we would each get. I doubted that we could even achieve a pound.

The school Carol Service on Tuesday evening ran smoothly. It was really important that we used the last chance to polish the chosen carols. I was surprised to see Richard and Terry: they were reluctant to do anything extra. Neither of them had a parent in the audience. Mother and I had to scamper home quickly to organise a meal for my Father's return at 7:30.

The school Christmas party was as I had anticipated. The film was good. It was in colour and a bit scary with witches. Only three children were sick, and only two went home tearful.

It was agreed that we would meet at the front of the Essoldo cinema at 5:45 (*The Searchers* starring John Wayne). On the way I caught up with Lorraine and Jo. I noticed that they both were wearing Lorraine's lipstick. I preferred Jo when she used to dress like a boy. The others arrived on time. We all had gaudy scarves and woollen hats with pompoms. Geoff practised lighting his lantern. He would also be the time keeper because he had a watch.

'Right, let's go. We'll start at o'd Briggs' an' wo'k arh way rahn the ahtside. An' we do the miggle on the way back.'

We crossed the A54 easily and were at Dr Brigg's house by ten minutes to six. Middleton Crescent was only about a quarter mile from our home territory. For me, the initial excitement had dissipated as soon as I had left the warmth of our kitchen.

'You be careful, My Lad. And be back here before 7:15. Your Dad won't want to come looking for you when he gets home.'

Now the excitement had kicked in again. The cold was ignored. It was exciting advancing into foreign territory with chums, and a task in mind.

Middleton Crescent was lit by feeble lamps like the ones on the Council estate. The light was increased by porch lights fitted to every front door. Some houses had tasteful Christmas lights at the ground-floor windows. A few gardens, with appropriate trees or bushes, displayed more lights. The houses were huge and detached. They were all set back with drives and immaculate lawns. I thought that whoever lived there must be very rich.

We stood ready and dithering at Dr Brigg's front door.

The self-appointed leader raised a hand and began, 'One, two, free'

Together we sang, '*Away in a manger...*'

We moved on to, '*We Three Kings...*'

Richard banged the knocker.

'*Christmas is a coming...*'

The door rattled and light flooded out. There was a woman.

'Oh, that was very nice, do you know any more?'

We took up with, '*Oh come all ye faithful...*'

Another figure joined the woman. It was Dr Briggs. It dawned on me that the woman was the receptionist in the surgery office and that she was Mrs Briggs.

Julia held out her up-turned woolly hat. Dr Briggs dropped in some coins.

We backed away to the gate singing, '*We wish you a merry...*'

'Arh much we got?'

Julia counted the coins, 'Three shillings.'

'Not bad. Let's get on.'

We moved on to the next house. It was one with a decorated fir tree in the garden. The house lights were on, but there was no response to our efforts. Richard banged the knocker again. He stooped and peeped through the letter box.

'They're out an' left the bleddy lights on.'

Geoff said wryly, 'Or they're deaf.'

The girls giggled.

'Snot funny. We are wastin' time.'

The third house was more successful. They didn't ask for an encore. We achieved a shilling. Now that we were veterans we moved faster. Five more houses produced much small silver which amounted to four shillings and six pence.

'What's the time now?'

Geoff looked at his watch, 'Ten past six.'

We missed out two houses without lights.

At one house a couple came to the door before we knocked, 'Oh, you sing beautifully, which charity are you collecting for?'

Richard managed, 'Er...'

Geoff piped up quickly, 'Children in Need, sir.'

'Splendid, such a worthy cause,' he said and dropped a lot of coins into Julia's hat.

We sang the rest of our repertoire.

'Arh much was that?'

'I don't know. It's all mixed in.'

Jo said, 'Shhh, listen.'

We stood still straining our ears. It was quite audible. Someone else was singing carols.

'*Silent night, Holy night...*' was coming from further along the crescent.

'Bleddy 'ell, they're on arh pitch.'

'They must have started at the other end.'

'We had better get a move on.'

We ran up the next driveway and burst into song.

Richard rattled the letter box knocker, 'Come on, come on.'

When the door opened Julia thrust her hat at the woman. We turned and skipped away chanting, '*We wish you a merry Christmas.*' It sounded like a record on the wrong speed.

After two more houses we were very close to the opposition. They, of course, had clocked us: especially with Geoff's lamp dancing about. We met on the pavement. There were six boys.

'Who are yo'?'

'We're carol singing, like you. We're from Beeston.'

They were not recognised, 'Which school?'

'Roundhill Junior. Which school are you?'

Roundhill Primary School was on Wollaton Road, opposite the County Library, in the town centre. It took children from central Beeston.

'Beeston Fields Junior. Yo're on arh pitch.'

'It's a free country.'

Lorraine nipped the bud, 'Have you done the other side of the crescent?'

'No, we only done this side.'

Richard abandoned any idea of fisti-cuffs, 'Oh come... on.'

We swooped over the road to the inner rim of the crescent. There would be fewer houses, so we had to work quickly. The first house looked very promising. It was mock Tudor like all the others but appeared larger. There were plenty of lights on. I noticed that the Roundhill group had gone next door.

Richard had barely made one knock when we were flooded with light. A woman had answered the door. Several other people were standing behind her. They all had glasses in hand. We sang, '*O come all ye faithful...*' Our audience of six adults clapped. The woman said, 'Oh, that was really good. Can you do another one?'

We glanced desperately at each other. We had no plan for an extended performance.

Barbara touched my arm and sang out, '*A soul cake, a soul cake.*'

I joined in with the second line. Jo and Terry helped finish the first round.

Richard, Geoff, Lorraine and Julia cut in with, '*God rest ye merry gentlemen...*'

We stopped singing *Soul Cake's* fourth round just after the final '*...comfort and joy.*'

Our audience were delighted, 'I'm sorry we don't have any soul cakes, but I have made some lovely mince pies. Do come in and try them.'

I heard Richard growl, 'Bleddy 'ell.'

Free mince pies would be high on his list, but silver coins would be higher.

We advanced into a spacious hall way. My hall at home was about a yard square: this one was big enough to hold a car. The adults were obviously having a small party somewhere. It was very warm inside and smelt of fresh baking, cigars and perfume. We were offered a mince pie on a paper plate. This was followed by a fizzy drink in a paper cup. There was a frenzy of unbuttoning outdoor coats and juggling mince pies and drinks. The adults were merry, and happy to dip into pockets and purses at the suggestion of the hostess. Silver clattered into Julia's hat. Richard, now cheered, had a second mince pie. Terry was onto his third. Barbara turned to Geoff, 'What time is it?'

'Ten past six.'

'You said that last time.'

'Crikey, it's stopped.'

I had a brief vision of Santa Claus stuffing my presents back into his sack. I looked around. There was an old fashioned grandfather clock standing by a door. It was showing seven o'clock. It began to strike. We sang, '*We wish you…*' as we moved towards the front door.

I was level with Julia who said, 'Oo, look: mistletoe.'

I paused to look up at the large bunch hanging over the door. She kissed my cheek.

We were back out into the cold and dark. Geoff kept tapping his watch. Terry was now carrying the lamp. We galloped back around the crescent and turned left at Dr Briggs'. We jogged along the side of the A52 as far as the Essoldo. There was much gasping as the effort made us hot inside our winter gear. A breathing space was had while waiting for gap in the traffic. The last leg along Woodside Road was straight forward. Geoff, complete with lamp, peeled off left into Audley Drive. The rest of us continued to the No. 19 bus terminus. Barbara turned right for Bosley Square. Julia crossed the road to her house, and the remainder of us bounded up Anslow Avenue.

'Hey,' as the ginger lump still got the dosh?'

Lorraine pushed her front gate open, 'Yes, of course she has.'

Jo raced another few yards home. I turned into our Close, leaving Richard and Terry under the street lamp muttering about rightful shares. I had no doubt that we would get them.

'Ah, there you are. You're cutting it fine.'

I looked at the new-fangled plastic kitchen wall clock which had recently been acquired. It displayed, 'Seven fourteen.'

'Lay the table, Chick, your dad will be home in a jiffi.'

Richard and Terry were already hanging around the lamp post when I ventured out. I guessed that they wouldn't go to Julia's house.

'Arh seen 'er las' night. She gev yo' a kiss at the door.'

'There was some mistletoe hanging. It's… traditional.'

'Oh, yeah. Let's go an' get the dosh.'

Terry sniggered.

I was now embarrassed. The day before, I had been surprised and delighted. Though I wished it had been Barbara *Grey Eyes*. Julia was a fun friend: Barbara was something else.

Julia was on the corner of the parade of shops. She was grinning.

'That was good last night, real fun. And we got back in time.'

''Ow much?'

Her smile widened, 'Four pounds, two shillings and sixpence.'

I tried to divide that by eight, but I was struggling. She was way ahead.

'We get ten bob each and the half-crown goes to Children in Need.'

Richard looked gloomy, but he shrugged and said, 'OK'.

Julia handed over ten shilling notes, 'I've just changed the silver in Woffo's'. She gave me an extra note, 'Can you give that to Geoff? I'll see the girls.'

'Fought yo' might spen' some ovit on mistletoe, eh?'

Julia blushed.

Richard played with his ten shilling note for a minute or two before saying, 'Yeah, well that was a good sing song las' night. We mek a good team. Come on, Tez.'

They turned towards Woffington's confectionary shop. Richard started to sing,

'O'd Kin' Wenceslas
Knocked a bobby senseless
Wiv a fist of ste-el…'

Old Valvone

'Guess what.'

Before I could even begin to think of what might be of interest to me on a short shopping trip she carried on.

'There's a poster in Woffington's, on the board where they advertise what's on at the pictures.'

She placed the green shopping bag on the kitchen table. My Mother looked at me expectantly. There was nothing in my head. The initial excitement of the long summer holiday had faded away. Geoff had gone away, so had Tony. I was wallowing in the dubious luxury of being bored.

'There's a Punch and Judy show coming. It's on Wednesday. On the rec. At two o'clock.'

She began to fill the kettle, 'And it's free.'

'Free?'

'Yes, the Council pay for it.'

I remembered the free midsummer show the previous year. A man did some juggling and a few magic tricks. He got all the kids singing too. The finale of the show was him doing large drawings with charcoal on sheets of paper. He drew some kids' portraits. They were very good. All this was on the back of small lorry with the side down.

'You should go. I'll be at work. You like Punch and Judy.'

I wasn't so sure. I had seen a Punch and Judy show on the beach at Mablethorpe. It wasn't free. The show didn't start until there was a reasonable amount of cash in the *bottler*'s tin. I had a vague memory of being bewildered and alarmed with Punch when I was much younger. The Mablethorpe experience reminded me of what I had difficulty with. It was supposedly for children, but the sausage machine and the beatings seemed to be unsuitable. It was made worse by the audience shrieking with delight at the gruesome events. Punch had a strange voice made by a little gadget in the *professor*'s mouth. My Father later explained the use of the *swozzle* and how it was sometimes, inadvertently, swallowed in the excitement.

Before confirming that I would go to the rec on Wednesday afternoon, I decided to look at the poster for myself, and perhaps meet someone else who was going. I was uneasy about being on my own in new or strange situations.

A couple of girls stood at the entrance to Woffington's. They were reading the poster. One of the girls had carrot coloured hair. Julia was reading out the details to her friend.

'Professor Valve One presents Punchinello.'

'That's not right,' I said.

Julia turned her ready smile. Her friend, Lorraine, just glared.

'It says 'Professor *Valvone* presents Punchinello.''

'Valvone?'

'Yes, it's Italian. That's why it says *Punchinello.*'

I was not a linguist, fluent in Italian. My Father had seen the poster on his way home. He had noticed the name was the same as our local chimney sweep. *Old Valvone* was the man who did everyone's chimney. Everyone on the housing estate had coal fires. He was a man of few words, and these were accented. My Father told me that he was a left-over from some war, but I could not figure out which one. It was difficult to assess his age because I saw him only in his grimy work clothes, jungle hat and sooty face. I must have seen him at the weekend but didn't recognise him all cleaned up.

'Are you going?'

'Yes, I think so.' Lorraine was radiating hostility, so I quickly added, 'With some friends.'

Right on cue the friends appeared from around the corner.

'Hey up, Chrisser.' Richard ignored the two girls.

I greeted Richard and Terry. Julia and Lorraine moved swiftly into the sweet shop.

'Me an' Tez are goin' to the Punch-up wiv Judy. Are yo' goin'?

Because I hesitated for a moment, he went on, 'Urgh, come on Chrisser. It'll be a laugh. It's great when Punch starts smackin' everyone wiv 'is truncheon, an' he shoves 'em in the sausage machine.'

Just then, the girls re-appeared sucking lollipops.

'OK,' I said trying to sound enthusiastic. 'Have you seen the name of the professor?'

Terry looked his usual amiable vague. Richard peered at the poster.

'It's *Valvone.*'

Terry switched on, 'Is arh sweep doin' it?'

'Don't think so. It's just the same name.'

As the two girls sauntered off Lorraine stuck her tongue out. It was bright red.

'Don't yo' fink it's funneh that there are two Wops wiv the same name?'

I spent some of the weekend wondering about the Valvone's. Questioning my Parents wasn't very productive. All that they seemed to know was that the man lived with an English woman on our Council estate and he swept chimneys. My Father suggested that during the war he might have had to report to Beeston police station every week for a while.

On the Monday I bumped into Richard and Terry on the street.

'Yo' know it starts at 2 o'clock. Well, me an' Tez fought we'd get there early. Then we can see 'em set up. We wanna see what's inside the striped tent fing.'

'We could go to the rec at half past one and sit on a bench.'

Richard nodded approvingly. Terry became animated. He was pointing at the sky.

'Look, there's 'is brush.'

Sure enough, there was Mr Valvone's black sweeping brush sticking out of a pink chimney pot. It disappeared and then quickly re-appeared.

'Ah know, let's go an' ask 'im if he's gorra relative what does Punch and Judy.'

Old Valvone's bike was parked against the hedge. It was like a butcher-boy's delivery bike. Over the front wheel was a metal frame basket. The triangular space below the cross-bar was filled in with a metal plate advertising his name and address. We waited patiently until Old Valvone appeared at the gate carrying his brushes. He eyed us with eyes that seemed very bright in his dark face.

'Mr Valvone.'

'Yez, you want sweep?'

I wondered if he recognised us: he had been to our houses often.

'No, fanks. We was wond'rin' if yo' knew owt abaht Professor Valvone what's doin' the Punch an' Judy show on the rec.'

Mr Valvone looked perplexed even under the coating of soot. '*Come?*'

Richard was about to start again, but I cut in with, 'Punchinello. Professor Valvone.'

The man blinked, '*Pulchinella Professore Valvone?*'

It sounded very Italian.

'Yes - on Wednesday- at two o'clock- on the play park.'

He looked at us carefully, closed his eyes and shook his head. 'No, don't know *Professore Valvone.*'

Old Valvone slung his sack of rods onto his shoulder and took hold of his bike. '*Ciao.*'

We watched him pedal off to his next job. Richard shrugged, Terry sniffed and I wondered.

Happily Wednesday was a bright sunny day. I had a quick lunch with my Mother before she went off for the afternoon shift. Richard and Terry were waiting by the lamp-post. It took only five minutes to reach the Children's Recreational Park. On the corner of our Council estate was a field for games. At the far end were tennis courts and a bowling green. Against the other end of the field, standing on asphalt, were the usual array of swings, round-about, rocking-horse and slide. A path edged the field on both sides. Behind the path were bushes and spiked railings. The park-keeper, who wore a dark blue uniform including a peaked hat, had a den near to the bowling green. There was no sign of a Punch and Judy show.

'We're too early.'

'Is it the right day?'

'Course it is!'

A car appeared up the slope between the bowling green and the park-keepers place. It drove slowly across the field towards us and stopped on the grass opposite one of the several slatted benches. The car was actually a small van with a man and a woman in the cab. When they got out, it was clear that he was older than her. She was wearing a brightly striped dress with a plain apron. He was in his shirt sleeves with gaudy braces holding up his tan corduroy trousers. Both of them had very dark hair. His was quite bushy.

Richard made his move, 'Are yo' the Punch and Judy people?'

The woman smiled and spoke, 'Yes, we'll be ready soon.' She had the hint of a foreign accent.

'Can we help?'

'Yes, you can help Sep with the tent.'

Sep was at the back of the van pulling things out. We carried wooden poles, rolled up striped cloth and several leather bags to a spot opposite the park bench. We held the poles whilst Sep hammered them into the ground at the corners of a small ground sheet with a large wooden mallet. The striped cloth was unfurled and deftly slid onto the poles. Now there was a little tent. The front had a sort of window space. The woman clipped a window-sill in place. Sep fixed four guy ropes to the poles and pegged them to the ground. He said, 'OK Angel.'

Angel put the leather bags through the opening at the back of the tent. I desperately wanted to see the contents of the bags. My boredom had vanished.

The audience had begun to arrive. Most were juniors, with some infants with mothers and prams. I spotted Julia and Lorraine who were sucking more lollipops. There were other children who I recognised. Two old men came to sit on the bench. The park-keeper plodded around his domain just to check. Four teenagers stood at a discrete distance pretending not to be interested. Sep disappeared into the tent. Angel collected a squeeze-box from the van. She began to play. The audience packed onto the grass in front of the tent. The music quietened them down. Suddenly a weird voice said, 'That's the way to do it.'

The audience was silent, peering up at the window ledge. They erupted when Punch popped up. The audience squealed with delight as Punch bounced around shouting things which I could not catch because of the children's voices, his *swozzle* -distorted voice and the scampering musical accompaniment. The story began to unfold. Judy had to go out and leave Mr Punch to look after the baby. He wasn't very good at it. He was better at beating the policeman with a truncheon and pushing the doctor into the sausage machine.

I glanced around. Terry was transfixed: it must have been his first experience of Punch. Richard was shrieking and calling out. The teenagers seemed to have forgotten to be disinterested. The mothers were locked on too. So was the man.

I hadn't seen him at the start of the show, but he was there now standing on the path. I did a double take. He had very dark bushy hair just like Sep's. In fact he looked just like Sep. It couldn't be Sep because Punch was still cavorting. The dark haired man was not laughing like everyone else. Angel had her back to him and was busy with the accompaniment.

Eventually the show came to a frantic end. The crocodile was fed the sausages and Punch was very sorry and promised to be good, but not very convincingly. The audience applauded and Angel switched to soothing music. As the audience began to disperse, the dark-haired man spoke.

He spoke out very loudly, '*Sciocchezze, sciocchezze!*'

Some departing children gave him a glance, but didn't understand what he said. Angel turned and gaped. He spoke again.

'*Desidero le sue scuse.*'

Mr Punch slowly reappeared on the window sill. His strange voice said simply, '*Sal?*'

Angel said, 'My God.' And with her free hand she touched her forehead, '*Madre mia.*'

We three stood transfixed. It was like another show. I suddenly realised who the dark-haired man was. 'Richard, that's Old Valvone.'

'*Si, Salvatore, Salvatore Valvone.*'

Punch disappeared and Professor Valvone appeared from behind the little tent. The two men stood staring at each other. Apart from the clothes they looked exactly the same. The spell was broken by Angel who gave a shriek of joy. The two men flung their arms around each other. They jabbered away in Italian and danced about, with faces beaming.

As we helped Angel pack up she explained. The men carried on talking fast and loudly.

'Giuseppi is my father. Salvatore is his twin brother. Their father had married an English girl. They were separated a very long time ago when Salvatore came to England. My father didn't hear from him, so thought he was dead. After the war, it was difficult, so my father came to England with his Punch and Judy. I came with him. My mother had died. He was restless.'

She placed the glove puppets carefully back into their bags, 'My name is really Angelina. My father tells people that his name is Joe. Giuseppi is Italian for Joseph, Joseph in the Bible.'

I said, 'Where can I get a *swozzle*?'

Angel grinned, 'From me.' She dipped into her apron pocket and produced the strange gadget. 'We always have spares just in case.' She grinned again, 'Don't swallow it.'

My pals stood open–mouthed at my luck.

She glanced towards the brothers who were still gabbling, 'Sep, Sal.'

To us she said, 'There will be a party tonight.'

All three squeezed into the cab and the van moved away. We watched it go back down the slope and out of sight.

Richard said, 'Gordon bleddy Bennett.'

Terry said, 'Which'n' was the real Valvone?'

I said, 'I'm going home.'

'Hello, Chick. What was the Punch and Judy show like?'

But I waited until my Father came home from work, a little later, before telling the tale. They were spell-bound. It took a while to learn how to use the *swozzle*, mostly because I was afraid of swallowing it.

Old Valvone, the real one, continued sweeping chimneys, but now he waved and smiled. I could also recognise him when he was cleaned up.

Panther Boys

'Good grief, what happened to you?'

My mother looked alarmed. There was no way that I would tell her what really happened.

'Fell off me bike.'

She put the tea towel down on the draining board and came over to inspect the damage.

'You've got a bruise on your forehead and your cheek's all grazed. Are you hurt anywhere else?'

I held my right hand out. My knuckles were skinned and the little finger was red and tender.

'Right let's get you patched up. Was there something wrong with your bike?'

When I was five I had a new red bike for my birthday to replace a three-wheeler. I grew out of the birthday bike even though the saddle and handlebars were raised to the maximum. My Father came home with a second-hand adult bicycle. I wasn't delighted with the black paintwork but it had dropped handlebars. To my great disappointment my Father changed the handlebars for straights.

'We'll keep these 'drops' for when you're older.'

Over the following week he checked and adjusted the bike. I was allowed to wind white plastic tape the length of the handlebars and fit a bell. Later I acquired a saddle bag and a pump. This machine was then ready to take me train spotting or fielding errands.

That fatal Saturday morning I had pedalled the short distance to Aunty Nellie's. Sometimes she would want errands doing. I would earn some pocket money. The sixpence reward was in my pocket and I was cycling home down the gentle slope of Baslow Drive. I spotted the boys ahead on the pavement my side. I recognised them. They were three of the Panther Boys. Strangely they were not on their awful track bikes. They were laughing and brandishing bamboo sticks. The sticks lashed out at any flowers daring to peep above the privet hedges.

I decided to spurt past them quickly. It was best to avoid the Panther Boys. As I attempted to flash past I came to a sudden halt. My bike stopped abruptly, but I didn't. I continued over the handlebars, and face first onto the gritty road surface. The Panther Boys were convulsed with laughter. When the sky was back in the right place I looked at my bike. A bamboo pole was jammed through the back wheel. It was pulled free and the villains continued on their way. I started to feel the stinging pain and the acute embarrassment of being so easily un-horsed.

The Panther Boys were so called because of the American style casual jackets emblazoned with the head of a panther and the words *Team Panther*. I coveted the jacket, but was not allowed. How they came by them was a mystery. The boys were not a team. They were a gang of Council estate boys who had banded together because nobody wanted to play with them. They were considered rough and dangerous.

The Tate's lived next door to the Mitchell's. The Stokes lived across the road on Olton Avenue. Ralph Tate was the eldest. He was in the first year of secondary school. His next brother Dennis was the leader though. He was in the top juniors. Their youngest Ronald, was in the same year as me but he was in the 'B' class. They were all 'B' streamers. The Mitchell's had Melvin in the same class as Dennis Tate, and Eric in my year group. Leonard 'Lenny' and Daniel 'Danny' Stokes were twins, also in my year group. They were twins but not identical.

In school they could be more or less ignored. Out of school they wore the Panther Jackets and scruffy jeans. Boys usually had their hair well-trimmed and short at the sides and back. The Panther Boys always looked like they needed a haircut. They greased their hair into weird styles. All three sets of parents worked long hours and spent their money and free time in *The Red Lion* in Beeston. It was the sort of pub my parents wouldn't dream of entering.

The Panther Boys usually rode together on customised bikes. These bikes were probably stolen and stripped of anything deemed inessential. The bikes had tall cow-horn handlebars.

'Leave your bike here for your Dad to check and you pop down and get a *Wonderloaf* from Woffingtons.'

I limped off to the shop on the corner of our street. My grazed cheek stung but what really bothered me was the incident. I went over and over it thinking how it could have been avoided. I was feeling angry and frustrated.

'Hey up, Chrisser.' Richard and Terry were sucking sherbert fountains outside the shop. 'What happened to you? Did you try summat with that ginger lump, what's her name?

'Julia Billington,' suggested Terry.
'No. Came off me bike this morning.'
'What? Fought you could ride proper.'
I shrugged, 'I can. I was knocked off.'
'Knocked off?' He looked at me shrewdly.

I didn't tell my Mother the truth because my Father would wade in and get out of his depths. On the other hand Richard was bound to find out. He always did find out. So I told him. I expected him to snigger and say that he wished he'd seen it. He looked aghast. We didn't always see eye to eye. This was an outrage to have a street pal attacked by hooligans from another street. Revenge was necessary.

'Which ones was it?'
'It was three of them. The two Mitchell's and Ronnie Tate.'
'Who did the bamboo stick?'
'I think it was Ronnie. He pulled it out anyway.'
'Right, don't you worry, Chrisser. Monday, I'll do that Ronnie at school.'

Richard Church was a street fighter.

Monday morning break we *three caballeros* followed Ronald Tate into the outside toilets. Richard paused to let Ronald begin peeing in the channel, then, he shoved him against the wall. Other boys disappeared quickly.

'You knocked my mate off 'is bike on Sat'day, Nah it's your turn.'

Richard pushed the back of Ronald's head so that his face collided with the gloss painted brick work. Ronald squealed. He squealed again when Richard punched his lower back.

'Leave my mates alone you lickle shit.'

The retribution did not come from the teaching staff. It came from Dennis Tate aided by the Mitchell's and Ronald. They jumped Richard on the way home. I saw the aftermath. Richard was sitting on the curb nursing a split lip and a darkening eye. Terry looked terrified.

'Bastards. I'll frigging do 'em.'

'I cou'n't do nuffing', said Terry, 'They was dead quick, an' the twins shoved me away.'

'Sallright, Tez. Not your fault. Too many on 'em.' He licked the blood on his lip.

'This is war. You wiv us, Chrisser?'

Richard had no need to ask. I was in. I was in from the beginning. I realised, though, that we were out-gunned and that the Panther Boys were ruthless.

'There's seven of them. An' they're mobile. We got to get some more sojers.'

'Tony?'

'What, Twillmop? Nah. He cou'n't punch 'is way out of a wet paper bag.'

Richard was right. My friend Tony was a light-weight.

'How abaht your mate Geoff?'

Geoff was no light-weight, but he might not like getting involved. The same would go for Alan. Most of my friends kept out of situations of this nature. Nobody would want to deliberately get in a tangle with the Panthers.

Richard had an established 'shiner' now, but his lip was not so swollen and the blood had stopped.

'OK, if we can't match the numbers, we'll have to use ah brains.'

Terry looked like Stan Laurel in a quiet moment. Perhaps he could pick up the bits.

'Yeah, we'll have to use ah noodles and get 'em wiv cunnnin'.'

Richard's cheek bone was settling to yellow. My cheek was peppered with little scabs.

'We could do 'em one by one. Even Dennis on 'is own. An' Ralph's norra problem.'

Ralph was the eldest and in Cottesmore secondary school, but he was quite small for his age and not at all bright. Dennis was the pack leader.

'Trouble is if we do one of 'em, they all come back as a gang.'

Terry spoke, 'We could use weapons.'

'What yo' finkin' of, Tez?'

'Ball bearians.'

'Ball bearings?'

'Yeah, an' Chrisser's got bone arrers.'

I did have two home-made bows and a set of arrows. The doweling arrows were sharpened and would be deadly.

'Owt else, Tez?'

'Water pistols.'

'Water pistols?'

'Yeah wiv summat nasty in 'em.'

Terry must have used up all his brain power for the day. I was impressed.

'Like tomato ketchup?' I suggested.

'Nah,' chipped in Richard, 'Not 'ard enough. Need summat like vinegar. Vinegar in the eyes would be good.'

'We can't do any really serious damage...'

'Why not, Chrisser? They'd do it to us. An' if we start owt they *will*. We gotta knock 'em down so they stays down.'

It suddenly felt like things were getting really out of hand.

'Right, let's mek a start. Find some ball bearings. Stones will do instead. I know where to get thick bamboos from: from the carpet shop in Beeston.'

Terry was sprawled on the pavement. The howling had alerted me. Two girls stood nearby. Angela was picking up the contents of a shopping bag. Lorraine saw me coming.

'It was some boys on bikes. They just raced up to Terry. They knocked him down and started kicking him.'

Terry was curled up now and sobbing.

'Was it the Panther Boys?'

'Yes. They were in a big gang.'

We helped Terry stagger back home with the shopping. I felt sorry for him and afraid for me. What if they came back for me? I wouldn't stand a chance. I glanced up and down the street. I imagined being beaten up every time I came out in the street. I thought about telling my Father. He would go round to the Tate's house and probably get punched in the face. We had to sort this out ourselves.

Richard was quietly livid, 'The friggin' rat-bags. Seven onto ar Tez. We gotta do summink right now. Looks like it's jus' yo' an' me, Chrisser. Tez ain't very well at the mo'.'

'What, just us two against all seven of them?'

'Gonna die sometime... nah, jus' jokin. Ha-ha'.

How could Richard be joking when we were about to hold the bridge over the Tiber against the entire Etruscan army?

He grinned and tapped a finger to his head, 'Been usin' me noodle, see. I've gorra plan.'

Richard had picked up much from weekly trips to the Essoldo cinema. His plan was to lure the Panthers onto a battle field which favoured us.

We would be waiting with our weapons hidden in the long grass. When they came at us we would pelt them with ball-bearings and stones. When they were stopped we would charge with the thick bamboo sticks. Richard would go for Dennis and give him a good pasting. When the leader was screaming for mercy the others would back off. My task was to cover Richard when he made his run at Dennis. I had my doubts. Richard's royal namesake had tried such a move against Henry Tudor at Bosworth. I had recently seen the film at the Essoldo with my Parents. It hadn't worked out too well for the King.

'What if *they* are armed?'

'They don't have none 'cos they're *so tough*.'

'What if you don't get Dennis?'

'Oh I'll get lickle Dennis o'right. It was him what split my lip.'

He grinned again, his eyes gleamed at the prospect of revenge.

'An here's the clever bit. While they are busy facing us they won't see what's happening to their bikes.'

Like a magician he produced a good length of chain with a padlock.

'All the bleddy bikes will be chained togevver and we'll chuck the key. We need anovver sojer. Can yo' get Geoff?'

Geoff listened to the whole story and the cunning plan. He agreed to lay low and chain the bikes. He was concerned that there were only two facing the Panthers.

'Where's the battle field and when is the battle?'

Whilst the proposed battle was being fine-tuned, Terry recovered and was thirsting for revenge. He showed us some of the bruises. He had a small bag full of ball bearings that he had begged from an uncle. We all trooped to look at the battlefield. I guessed that Richard would choose the unused field *over tins*. The grass was untouched and too long to ride bikes on. We knew where they would dismount. They would have to leave the bikes on the street side of the corrugated steel wall. Geoff was delighted with this. He would wait until they had scaled the wall, before lashing the bikes together unseen. We hid the weapons under a bush to be positioned properly later. A weekday evening, just after tea, was the chosen time. Richard suggested padding for protection just in case. All that was needed was the invitation.

The lure was made in the afternoon of the chosen day.

'Hey you, rat face I'm talkin' to you.'

Ronald was on his own again feeling secure in the false knowledge that nobody would dare touch him again.

Terry slipped behind him and crouched down.

'Yeah, yo' stupid.'

Richard shoved the startled boy. He toppled over Terry. Terry scrambled to his feet and used them on Ronald. He began to cry.

Richard leered down. 'Yo just tell your friggin brother who done this. An' tell him that we'll be ready *over tins* tonight at seven o'clock. Got it?'

Ronald whimpered in the affirmative. We all gobbed on him, and walked away.

'My bruvvers are gonna get yo' boggers!'

I could barely eat my tea. All I could think of was the looming battle. Of course nothing was said to my parents except that I was playing *over tins,* jumping the stream with Geoff. I promised to be back before eight o'clock. We reached the battle ground at six thirty. Geoff was left sitting on a fence rail with the chain in a bag. The weapons were laid out in three piles. There was a small cushion stuffed inside my shirt and I had a pair of leather gloves that used to belong to my Mother. Richard was sweating in a thick woollen sweater. Underneath was a piece of cardboard folded double. Terry wore a cowboy hat.

'Wait till I give the wo'd. Then we lob the missiles. Two in each hand. Do it again quick. That should gi'em sumfink to fink abaht. While they finkin', I'll go for Dennis an' yo' two cover me.'

'What you going to do to him?'

'Don't worry, Chrisser, He won't get killed. I'm goin' to shove this bamboo in his mush. Then I'll smack 'im rahn the head wiv it. If 'he's still standin', I'll shove him over an' give him a good kickin'.

'What about the others?

'Well that's yourn and Tez's job to keep 'em off. Swing the bamboos abaht.'

'What if it all goes wrong?'

Geoff gave the pre-arranged wolf whistle which meant that the Panthers were approaching. I felt like going to the toilet, but there wasn't any time. Heads began to rise above the parapet. Seven fiends dropped to our side of the *tins*. They all wore the dreaded uniform. They fanned out and began walking towards us. I was frightened, I wondered if the other two were. It was slow progress because of the tussocks of long grass.

'You're dead!'

It was Dennis in the middle. His brothers either side. On the right were Melvin and Eric. On the left were Lenny and Danny. Dennis was playing with a piece of chain. I wondered if Geoff was hobbling the track bikes. I wanted to be far away. I felt sick.

'I'm gonna do you, Churchie, for what you did to my bruvver.'

'It was me!' yelled Terry.

'Yo' an'all. Yo' gonna wish yo' ain't bin born.'

I was already wishing just that.

They had stopped to hurl insults. They began to move again.

I saw another face appear over the parapet. It was Geoff. He gave the thumbs-up.

'Nah!'

We stooped down for the missiles. There were more stones than ball bearings. Twelve missiles covered the gap. It wasn't accurate aiming. More were scooped up.

The attack line faltered. Eric shrieked and clutched his head. Twelve more missiles were sent home. Danny's hands went down to his thigh.

'Wiv me. Charge!'

The bamboos were snatched up. Richard ran the point of the attack straight at Dennis. He got within two strides of the Panther leader when he lost his footing on the tussocks. He sprawled forward, 'Shit.'

The Panthers realised that the missile barrage had ceased. They looked gleeful: except for Eric and Danny.

Dennis raised the chain above the prostrate Richard. Terry was shrieking. I closed the gap between the end of my bamboo and Dennis' face. I continued forward. Any moment I expected to be dragged down and kicked. It was Dennis that went down. He tipped backwards trying to avoid the bamboo stick which was being pushed into a nostril. Terry took an overhead swing to connect his bamboo with Dennis' head. Someone was clutching at me. I swung round to face Lenny. I brought my bamboo round on a level arc. It hit Lenny's upper arm hard. Richard was up again and laying into the Mitchell's. He turned his attention back to Dennis who was clutching his bloody nose.

'Friggin' bastard. Friggin' bleddy bastard!' He swung the bamboo twice before switching to his boots. Terry and I glared around at the enemy. My heart was pounding. They were backing off. Dennis was whimpering covering his head. It had taken only a couple of minutes.

'Go on, frig off. Take this piece of dog dirt. Don't come back or you'll really get done.'

Ralph and Melvin helped Dennis away toward the *tins*. The others followed without a word.

I was shaking. Richard gave a satisfied grin. Terry was looking for his cowboy hat. We watched the defeated Panthers climb the wall.

Richard leaned his head in that direction and cupped his ear. 'Wait for it.'

There was a massed shriek of disbelief and much swearing.

'Nah, let's go fin' good ol' Geoff.'

Geoff was elated. 'They didn't take no notice of my wolf whistle. As soon as they were over, I shoved the bikes together and chained them. I've still got the key. I nicked off to hide in the telephone box as soon as I saw them coming back. They were dead mad when the bikes wouldn't come apart. It was great.'

I strolled casually through the open back door just before eight.

'Whatever have you got those gloves on for in this weather?'

'Do you reckon they'll try to get us?'

'Nah, don't fink so. We done 'em proper. They wou'n't' dare.'

The Panther Boys still wore their jackets and rode around together on the severe bikes. (It had taken a good hour to cut the padlock off). There was no retaliation. They avoided us or ignored our presence. They seemed subdued, almost civilised.

Parkside Incident

'Walter Pretty asked me if you would like a job.'

I looked up from the *Eagle* comic. Dan and Co. was battling it out with the dreaded Phants of the Rogue Planet. She was beaming.

'I spoke to Walter on the shops this morning. He asked me if you'd like a little job.'

'Doing what?'

Walter Pretty ran the grocery and the green grocery on our Council estate. He also ran another shop not far away on Derby Road opposite the Essoldo cinema. Mr Pretty was the father of my 'blood brother' Michael. Unfortunately Mr Pretty, a widower, married again and chose to live miles away. Michael went with him of course. Just occasionally Mike would turn up at the shop near us to see his grandmother. We seldom met.

'Well, he wants someone to deliver leaflets advertising his off-licence.'

'Where to?'

'Up Wollaton Vale. He'll pay you.'

Cash registers clattered in my mind. I'd never been paid for a job before. Pocket money, such as it was, came my way regularly. I seldom spent it. Sixpences earned for running errands for Aunty Nellie didn't count.

'Ten shillings he said.'

That wasn't even a pound, only half a pound.

'It's only for a morning's work. If you want to do it, you'll need to tell him.'

The rate was acceptable. I wished it was more than a morning's work though so I could earn more. There was really nothing that I wanted the cash for. It was something to do.

Mr Pretty offered me his hand. I took it and was on the pay roll.

'We're trying to get the people this end of Wollaton Vale interested in visiting our off-licence.'

He was very tall, taller than my Father. He had dark crinkly hair pushed back and sported a tidy moustache. He smelt of cigarettes, as did most adults then. He always wore a tie. He was the boss. He had been an officer in the Sherwood Foresters during the war.

'So if you can come next Saturday morning, I'll meet you at the other shop. How about 9:30?'

It was a month before Christmas and quite cold. It was my last year in primary school. There was the 11plus exam to look forward to in the Spring and nothing much in between. The weather prevented playing outside, and I was starting to lose interest with indoor toys. Going to school was preferable to staying at home because the school had central heating. At home there was just the coal fire in the living room.

I cycled over to the other shop. Thankfully it was not raining. I had pondered over what to wear. My navy belted raincoat would be sensible, but I didn't want to wear it in daylight on a Saturday. So I settled for a black blazer over a knitted tank top and jeans. There really wasn't any choice.

'Here, take a Mars Bar with you. I'll get you something hot when you get back. Lock your bike up and don't do anything silly.'

Nobody would want to steal my bike, and I never did anything silly. I was well trained.

The other shop, on Derby Road, I knew very well. Mike had lived above the shop for a while. His Uncle Les had driven me over there in the Morris Traveller. We played with his amazing toys upstairs. Outside there was a garden with a pond. At the end of the garden there was a row of garages: but that's another story.

The shop was modern and larger than either the other two. It combined grocery, green grocery and off-licence. I chained my bike to the line post in the back garden.

Mr Pretty gave me a small sack with a strap rather like the postman's. Inside the sack were four bundles of flyers. They smelt of fresh printing ink.

'I'd like you to deliver them to Wollaton Vale and Parkside. Do one side of the Vale, then the other until two packs are gone. Then do both sides of Parkside. Only go as far as Parkside Rise. That's the road that joins the other two. I'll see you back on the estate at 5 o'clock.'

He grinned, 'That's when you get paid.'

Wollaton Vale was a main route to Wollaton Village and the up-market Wollaton area of the city. Wollaton was where posh folks lived. The houses were large and separate. They had gardens front and back with trees, bushes and drive ways. My Mother could only ever dream of living there. We didn't know anyone who lived there. It was a strange land that I was venturing into.

About two hundred yards from the other shop, I turned left onto Wollaton Vale. On my right across the road, was The Priory pub. I wondered if it would be too cheeky to put a flyer through their door. I came to the first house. I tore open one packet of leaflets and began the mission.

The majority of the houses had closed gates. They all seemed to have different catches. The letter boxes were all in different places. Some were sensibly in the centre of the door. Others were low down or in a separate fancy box. A few houses didn't seem to have a place at all for posting.

A couple of dogs yapped from inside. Considering that it was a Saturday there was hardly anyone about. Perhaps it was too cold, or they were off Christmas shopping. I avoided any place that was labelled 'No hawkers, canvassers or circulars.'

There was some advantage in working briskly. It generated warmth and diminished the load. The houses were set well back so the return walk up the drive was tedious. I fondled the Mars Bar but decided to keep until I was half way. It was not yet mid-day and the sky was darkening. I hoped it wasn't going to rain.

When the first packet was exhausted, I crossed over and worked my way back down to where Parkside branched off. I started Parkside with a few sheets left from the second packet. That was when I saw her.

I pushed the gate open and started up the drive. There was a girl my age. She recognised me too. We stood and gaped.

'Hello, what are you doing here?'

She was Barbara Allen. We sang a song about a cruel girl with her name at school. She pretended to be embarrassed during the singing. She had the most beautiful pale grey eyes. I admired her, but only from a distance. Now I was in conversation with her, or would be if I opened my mouth. It was open.

'I'm doing a job for Mr Pretty. Delivering adverts. I'm getting paid.'

She was wearing a tan coloured duffle coat and knitted beret in maroon. She looked like a para-trooper except for the lace up school shoes and pink socks. The pink socks were exotic: I'd seen girls in only white cotton or grey woollen socks.

'I'm delivering something too.' She waved a letter. 'It's been delivered to the wrong house.' She glanced back at the house. 'My

Aunty Margaret lives here. I brought my little sister Lizzie. Aunty asked me to pop this letter up the road.'

Exotic socks and an aunty at an exotic address… and beautiful eyes.

'You are always staring at me.'

I was taken aback. This was true, but I didn't think she'd noticed. I stared down at the gravelled drive. My cheeks were burning.

'You have very nice eyes, very pretty eyes.'

She giggled. I dared to look up. She was smiling.'

'Do you want to kiss me then?'

This was obviously a dream and I would wake up soon. I glanced around. There was nobody around, but there were several windows overlooking the driveway.

'Where?'

She giggled again. 'On the lips, silly'.

'Now?'

'Yes.'

I took a step forward and an alarm bell rang. Well, actually a bicycle bell. A bicycle bell was dringing behind me. I turned.

'Hey-up, Chrisser. There yo' are. Your mam to'd us what yo' woz up to. But she di'n't say nowt about yo' going gelling!'

It was Richard and Terry on a bicycle. I recognised the bicycle as belonging to Roger Green who had the misfortune to live almost next door to Richard Church. They had 'borrowed' Roger's bicycle to come and find me. Richard had propelled the machine standing on the pedals while Terry sat on the saddle with his legs splayed. This was, of course, dangerous but these two were not adverse to tempting fate.

The dream had turned into a nightmare. They dismounted.

'What's O'd Man Pretty paying yo'?'

I was reluctant to give Richard any information, especially when it was to do with money, my money.

'Ten shillings to deliver all these.'

Richard's eyes gleamed, 'I tell yo' what, Chrisser, if yo' giz me an' Tez a bob each, we'll deliver the rest on 'em. Not we Tez?'

'Arh'.

'You'll still 'ave eight bob. And you can spend the afternoon gabbing to Grey-Eyes.'

This seemed a very fair deal and a quick way of getting rid of them.

'OK, but you have to deliver them and not just dump them.'

Richard was a master of disguise. He offered his 'sadly offended' look.

'O' course. Wou'n't dream on it.'

The front door opened behind me. 'Is everything alright, Barbara?'

'Yes Aunty. They are boys that Christopher knows.'

Aunty Margaret was at the open door with a smaller edition of Barbara. Lizzie, Elizabeth, had not inherited the eye colour. Hers were pale green.

'Oh, and Christopher is my friend from school. He's delivering Christmas letters.'

My button was pressed so I stepped up and handed over a leaflet. Lizzie glared at me.

Out on the pavement the remaining leaflets were split. Richard was to do one side of Parkside and Terry set off on the other. The bicycle was left leaning against aunty's low front garden wall with Richard's assurance that it would be perfectly safe in such a nice neighbourhood. All that remained for me to do was to escort Barbara of the Grey-Eyes a few houses up the road to deliver the letter.

'Are they really your friends?'

'Sort of. They live near. We do sometimes play together.'

'I think Richard is a thug and Terry is stupid.'

'So do I.'

Barbara giggled. I dared to look at her face. I guessed the chance had vanished.

We dawdled along in unspoken agreement. This slow pace let Richard and Terry get well ahead.

'It's on the other side. There, it's got a name similar to Auntie's house.'

She was pointing out a good looking house that backed onto Wollaton Park. There were over- sized fluffy grasses growing in clumps on the lawn.

'Must be great living there. Dead easy to get into the Park,'.

The gate clicked open. I touched one of the floaty grasses. It was so very soft.

'They are called Pampas Grass. They come from South America. Aunty has some in her back garden.'

'Are you going to post it in the letter box?'

'Do you think we should knock?'

'There's someone in. I saw a head on the settee. I think you should knock.'

There was a bell. Barbara pressed it. We heard it ring. She pressed it again. We waited.

'Are you sure you saw somebody?'

'Yes, they have a settee in the bay window. I saw the head sticking up.'

'Might have been a cat. Let's have a look.'

We peeped into the side of the bay. There was a woman sitting on the settee. Her head was tipped back.

'She's probably asleep. Just pop the letter in the box and leave her.'

Barbara tapped on the window pane. She tapped again. The woman didn't move.

'She doesn't look very well. We should do something.'

'We could go in a find out.'

'Go in? How? The door's shut.'

'The front door is, but people don't lock the back door if they are in.'

She flashed her grey eyes and nodded. We moved around the side of the house. There was a rustic gate, but it was not locked. Neither was the back door. We heard voices.

'The wireless is on in the kitchen.'

Barbara called out, 'Hello'. There was no answer.

'What if she's dead?'

He pale grey eyes widened. 'We should find out.'

We walked carefully through the kitchen and through the hall. The door into the living room was open. The woman was still in the same position. She was wearing a flowery house-coat. There was a mug on a low table nearby.

'Hello, HELLO.'

Barbara moved up close enough to gently shake the woman. She did not wake, but her head rolled sideways. Her skin was almost white. I suddenly felt very afraid. I glanced around.

'What if she's been murdered and they are still here hiding?'

Barbara reached again and touched the mug.

'It's still warm.'

'Let's check if she's still breathing. Have you got a mirror?'

'No. There's one just inside the front door.'

There was but it was securely fixed in place.

'We need to get some help. An ambulance.'

'There's a telephone in the hall. Ring for an ambulance.'

I was forced to admit that I had never used a telephone. I did not know what to do. I followed Barbara to the phone. She knew what to do. She lifted the heavy black hand-piece to the side of her face. Her middle finger moved the dial on the solid black base. 999.

'Hello, yes. I want an ambulance, please.'

Barbara gave all the details including reading the address from the envelope and describing the situation. She was good. She put the phone down on the cradle.

'They will be about ten minutes. They asked us to stay here. I can phone Aunty Margaret and tell her what's happening.'

She knew the number by heart.

'Aunty's coming. She's bringing Lizzie.'

I suddenly thought about Richard and Terry. They might be nearly finished.

I looked at Barbara. She was looking at me. Her eyes were so, so beautiful.

'Are you eleven yet?'

'No, are you?'

'Nearly.'

She looked away and back at the woman on the settee.

'She still hasn't moved. She might have just died. She's old, she's got grey hair.'

She did look older than my Mother, but perhaps not as old as my Grandmother. I looked around the room. There was a television in a shuttered cabinet. One wall was decorated with several hammered brass dishes depicting country scenes. The doorbell rang.

Aunty Margaret took command. She instructed Barbara to keep Lizzie in the hall whilst she made an attempt to rouse the woman on the settee. I was told to watch for the ambulance. As I opened the front door a cream coloured Morris ambulance pulled up.

I waited with Barbara and Lizzie in the front porch. The woman was declared alive but needing to be hospitalised. Aunty Margaret said that she would secure the house and ask the neighbours about the woman's husband. (The letter was addressed to Mr and Mrs) Barbara was to escort Lizzie back to Aunty Margaret's. There was no role allocated for me.

I stood with Barbara and Lizzie to watch the ambulance pull away.

'Nah then, what's going off?'

Richard and Terry surprised me again from behind.

I told them briefly of the incident.

'When we seen the amb'lance, we fought Baa-Baa was 'aving a baby already, din' we Tez?'

They fell about laughing at the joke. I was aware of Barbara and Lizzie moving away. I followed.

'I'm sorry about that. They're...'

'Rude and stupid.'

'Who's having a baby?'

'Shut up, Lizzie. Nobody's having a baby.'

Barbara flashed her eyes at me. I saw only anger.

I trailed after them back to Aunty Margaret's. Roger's bicycle was still propped against the wall. It was retrieved swiftly, as Aunty Margaret was rapidly approaching.

'See yo', Chrisser. When d'yo' get paid?'

'Later, when I see Mr Pretty.'

Barbara didn't look back. Lizzie glared.

I retrieved my bicycle and pedalled home for a late lunch.

'Everything go alright, Chick?'

'Mmm, yes.'

Around five o'clock I found Walter Pretty clearing vegetable boxes from the shop front. I handed back the delivery bag and he handed me a brown ten shilling note.

'I understand that there was a bit of a problem this afternoon.'

How on Earth did he get to know? I was hoping he wasn't referring to Richard and Terry.

'A bit.'

He smiled, 'Seems more than a bit. A golfing friend phoned me. It was his wife you helped save. A neighbour phoned him at the club. His wife is in hospital. She'll be alright now. He's very pleased. He asked me to give you this.' He handed me a second ten shilling note.

'What about Barbara?'

'Oh, Barbara Allen, she is getting a similar reward.' He shook my hand. 'Nice young lady.'

It occurred to me that having a telephone was advantageous.

'A telephone? What for? Who would we telephone, we don't know anybody with one.'

The following day I went out on my bike armed with two one shilling pieces in case I met with Richard and Terry. Actually I was going to casually ride the short distance to Bosley Square, a close off Hathern Green, where Barbara lived somewhere.

There was nobody around because it was Sunday and it was cold. I didn't hang about.

Pelmet by Moonlight

'Starry is getting a pelmet.'

Mother said this with such enthusiasm that my Father looked up from the Daily Mirror.

'Starry's getting what?'

Starry was the name of the mother of my new friend Johnny who had come to live in a house at the corner of our Close. Mother took to her straight away. She was a jolly woman with an exotic name. It was the sort of name that American film stars had. After some time I discovered, from Johnny, that Mrs Withers' real name was Estelle. She had translated her name from the French for 'star', and become Starry.

I'd clocked the Withers family as having ambition. They had a television and were the first family on the street to use washing up liquid rather than thin soap flakes. *Sqezy* came in a squirt tub which could be used as water pistol. We switched to *Sqezy* soon afterwards, mostly because there was no need to rinse the dishes.

Pelmet was new to me. I imagined it to be the name of car. The *Austin Pelmet* or the *Morris Pelmet* or even one of those tiny cars from Europe, a *Fiat Pelmet*. The Withers family would just about fit into a tiny Fiat, and it would be quite suitable for people who lived on a Council estate. There was only one car on or street. The 'tin-lizzie' belonged to Mr Jones. It moved once a month. Mr Jones started it by letting the car roll freely down the hill.

'She's getting a pelmet. You know, those things that cover up the curtain tracking.'

'Yes, Bridget, I know what they are. What's it got to do with us?'

He should have fallen on his sword there and then: if he had one.

'I thought it would be nice if we could have one. They are very modern and fashionable. There's a piece about how to make them in this month's *Woman's Own.*'

'Make one?'

'Yes. They are ever so easy to make. George is going to make Starry's.'

'Why don't you make one, if they are so easy?'

It was really no use playing for time.

'You are good at making things. Look at all those things you've made for our Chris.'

My father had produced a couple of castles and a rifle with bolt action and a fixing bayonet. These were only toys, a sort of continuation of the wartime 'make-do-and-mend.' This had now morphed into DIY, where smart serviceable products were required. Tools and skill were necessary. My Father had very few tools and his skills were centred on stripping down Bren guns.

He turned to me, 'It's all your fault for getting friendly with Johnny.' Then he winked. He went on to explain how 'easy' it would be to make one.

I had never much thought about the curtain tops in the living room. Paper decorations were secured there at Christmas, and sometimes wasps tried to hide there through the winter. Our curtains were held on a wooden pole by brass rings. Modern curtains ran on plastic tracks. These tracks were efficient but were not necessarily attractive. So *pelmets* had been invented to hide the works. Enterprising timber suppliers were offering ready cut lengths of hardboard for the man of the house to cut to shape and decorate. The difficult bit was to get the thing to stay up in place.

'Go and ask George how he's going to fix their pelmet to the wall.'

My Father sighed heavily.

I was disappointed that the pelmet was not a vehicle, but I was delighted to be involved in a project with my Father. We visited the Wither's just in time for George to demonstrate screwing two angle brackets above the top line of the curtains.

'You'll need rawl-plugs, Ken. Have some of mine, I've got lots.'

He handed Father several short pieces of round wood.

'You can screw the pelmet to the brackets, but it's not really necessary. Get a piece of wood longer than the pelmet so you can make end pieces.'

As we came away my Father muttered, 'Should have stayed in the army.'

I knew he was only kidding.

During the week I met Richard at the end of our Close. He was a real clever-dick. He was never called 'Dick' though. He got really cross if anyone tried. I thought that I might put one over on him.

'Hey up, Chrisser, 'ow yer doin'?'

'Hello, Rich, we're going to have a pelmet.'

'You're going to have an 'elmet?'

'No not a *helmet*, a *pelmet*.'
'What's that?'
Wonderful, he didn't know. Now I could show off.
'It's a sort of long lid that goes across the top of the curtains.'
He visibly winced. He was supposed to be impressed.
I added quickly, 'They are very smart. Everyone's having them.'
'We ain't. What d'yo' need it for?'
'It's to cover up the new plastic tracking for the curtains.'
'What's wrong wiv curtain poles? It's a friggin' waste of money.'

The following Saturday I accompanied my Father to a hardware shop in Beeston. It was run by Mr Wood. His son, Alex, was in my class at school. The shop was an Aladdin's cave of interesting things. They sold paraffin, rolls of chicken wire, loose nails and screws, wooden bird tables and tools. There were several sizes of hardboard specially cut.

'And we carry several styles, sir. This is quite popular.'

Mr Wood held up a length of hardboard which had been pressed to give a ripple effect. He also showed us hardboard with a fancy edge which had been cut on a machine.

Father chose the basic style. He also made sure that the slender plank was of planed timber and long enough to make the vertical end pieces. He also bought three metal angle brackets. He declined the screws because we had a couple of *Oster Milk* tins full of reclaimed screws.

'Right that's enough for today. Fancy a pint?'
I knew he was only kidding.
'And don't go telling your Mam about the fancy ones.'

Sunday morning was the time to assemble the weapons. The chief weapon was a hand drill. The piece of hardboard was measured and cut to the exact length. A length of plank was sawn to match. It had to have an inch or so more cut off to allow for the end pieces to fit in. There were sufficient pieces of plank left over to make the end pieces. After it had been double checked, the assembly was put together with *seccotine glue* and panel pins. There were many of these, and they took a while to hammer home.

'Wash your hands, I'm serving dinner now.'
Sunday afternoon was not the time for DIY.

On Wednesday Mother and I met my Father from work. Together we went to the Co-op on Beeston High Road to buy the plastic tracking. It came in a long card box with an illustration on the side. I was allowed to carry home the *Easy–Glide* unit complete with fixings and full instructions.

'I hope the pelmet is going to fit over the tracking.'
My Father gave my Mother a withering look, 'So do I.'
Most of Saturday morning my Father checked and measured and made small pencil marks on the wall. After lunch he started in earnest. The curtains were slipped off the pole. The pole took some time to remove because the screws seemed to be 'hammered' in. I played with the tracking, checking the ease with which the pieces slid. My Mother changed the curtain rings for the little plastic hooks which would hold the curtain to the track.
The tracking was held in place whilst Father secured the position and its level. He marked the places were the screws would go. There were more places than had been anticipated. He set to work with the hand drill. It was really hard going.
Mother slipped off to the kitchen to make cups of tea.
'Have a look in the packet, Chris, and see if there's any rawl–plugs.'
'Can't find any, Dad.'
'Right. Pop down to Johnny's and ask Mr Withers for half a dozen.'
When I got back he was drinking tea… Mother was reading the instructions.
'It says to screw the track onto the wooden batten.'
'George didn't say anything about a batten…'
It would have made things easier, but we had no battens.
Father used his mallet to drive in six plugs. He used a bradawl to make a starter hole in each plug. I handed him the screws and the plastic brackets as he fixed each one.
'It's going to be dark soon. Are we going to have the curtains back up, Ken?'
'Yes, of course.' He pulled a face at me.
Once the brackets were up it was relatively easy to clip the track to them.
'Can we put the curtains back on now?'
'No, not yet. I need to fit the brackets for the pelmet. Switch the main light on.'

I switched the room light on, and a few minutes later the street light at the end of the close came on.

'I'll start to make the tea then. We are having pork sausages.'

'*Give me the tools and I'll finish the job*! Pass me the pelmet, corporal.'

He decided that two brackets would be sufficient. As the second was tightened into place our front garden disappeared into the darkness and the moon appeared over the Withers' roof top. Father took the pelmet and placed it on the brackets. It looked good: my Father looked triumphant.

'Bridget, we're ready to put the curtains up.'

Mother was well pleased with the results, and Father basked in the glory. The pelmet was taken down the next day in order to be painted. This was done in the shed over a couple of days. It was undercoated in white and then finished in cream gloss to match the rest of the paintwork. Unfortunately, at certain angles, the gloss paint enhanced the pin heads.

'Next time the nails need to be sunk with a punch and filled,' said the latter-day-expert. 'And we'll use battens.'

'Well since you've done such a good job, it would be nice to have a pelmet in our bedroom.'

'Of course, my darling Wife,' He pulled another face at me.

'That would leave just our Chris' bedroom. I'm not sure about the back kitchen… What do you think, Ken?'

'You don't really want to know what I think, especially with our lad listening.' He winked.

Philately

Very rarely did we receive parcels in the post. Usually it was something to do with knitting. My Mother knitted, and so did her three sisters. The parcel which arrived this time was for me. I couldn't remember ever getting a parcel before. My Mother looked at the handwritten address on the brown wrapping paper.

'It's from your aunty Joyce in Grimey.' She handed me the package. 'You open it. It's addressed to you.'

I tried to loosen the string, but the knots were too tight. My Mother gave me a pair of scissors. Once the string was cut, the brown paper unfolded to reveal a slender book. There was also a letter which my Mother read. I opened the book entitled *Postage Stamps of the World*.

'Joyce says it's from their Peter. He doesn't want it anymore, and their Davey is too small.'

I had seen the stamp album previously on a visit to Yorkshire. I was impressed, and also alarmed by Peter's method of attaching the stamps to the pages. He dipped his finger tip in *Carnation Cream* and transferred the sticky substance to the back of a stamp. My Father said, later, that it was more evidence that his sister's family were 'crackers.'

I leafed through the album. The jumble of stamps needed sorting and re-arranging. I was excited because most of my pals had stamp collections. I had some loose stamps in an envelope. Now I was justified in requesting a new album.

My Father readily agreed to buy the new album. He suggested removing the stamps from Peter's album by soaking the pages in water. The stamps would eventually lift off and could be dried and flattened. Happily we worked together: it seemed to take forever.

One evening, when he got home from work, he handed me a brand new album. He also had a packet of stamp-hinges. It was fascinating to identify the stamps with their appropriate page. At first the stamps were placed loosely in position. I wanted to have a complete set before sticking them down.

I had lots of British stamps, but they were mostly the same. I set about asking family, friends and neighbours to save their stamps for my collection. There was some swapping of surplus stamps at playtime. I goggled in the window at the foreign stamps for sale in a philatelist's shop window in Beeston. There were some beauties which were quite expensive. The more exotic stamps seemed to originate from small obscure countries. I was intrigued with the triangular stamps and the larger stamps. Our small stamps bore the young queen's head in one colour. The most boring stamps were from the Netherlands. They too featured the image of the monarch, but had very dull colours.

'Stan the plumber's coming today.'

He arrived just as I finished my breakfast. Mother cleared the kitchen swiftly. Stan worked for the Council. He had mended the burst pipe in the bathroom, and another time he had fitted a novelty in the bathroom: a wash-basin. He worked for the Council during the week, but he could be employed, for cash, privately at the weekend. My parents had decided to have the kitchen sink moved to the more sensible place of under the kitchen window. I took the opportunity to keep out of the way and attend to my stamp album in the living-room. For a break Stan was invited into the living-room for a mug of tea and a cigarette. He spotted my stamp album. He said that he was a stamp collector, and he had some spares which I could have. He would bring them when he was doing another job nearby. Stan finished our job by lunchtime, and was given cash. When he had gone my mother told me not to hold my breath for the stamps. She was wrong. One afternoon in the following week Stan knocked on our back door. Luckily I was home from school. He gave me an envelope full of stamps.

Gleefully I spread the stamps out on the dining table. There was about a hundred. I was delighted with higher value British ones, and a couple of the triangular types. There were the inevitable ones from the Netherlands, but there were many I had never seen before. I checked the envelope. A stamp was wedged in a corner. When it was pulled free I saw that it was unlike the others. It had straight edges: there were no perforations. The image was black. The woman's profile seemed familiar. Along the bottom I read 'one penny'. It had to be an example of the famous Penny Black: the very first gummed-back stamp ever. My heart skipped a beat.

I showed the stamp to my Father (I still believed that he knew just about everything).

'Might be... Looks like it, but I'm no expert. I've never seen one. You could get a stamp book from the library.'

The nearest library was in Beeston. I had joined when my class was taken on a visit. I had taken out a book on trains, but Foster Avenue was a bit of a trek. The best time to visit the library was after school. Beeston Fields Junior School was about half way. So as my chums poured down Wensor Avenue, I scampered off along Abbey Road which led into Wollaton Road. I turned right at The High Road. The next right, at the Post Office, was Foster Avenue. It took only ten minutes, but it felt very strange to be out of my own territory.

I remembered the children's section.

'Where are the stamp books, please?'

'Do you mean Stanley Gibbons?'

The librarian read my blank look.

'Stanley Gibbons is the expert on postage stamps. His books are in the reference section. I'll show you.'

I followed her to a set of shelves marked 'Reference.' She selected a hefty volume from the rows of very large books and placed it on a table.

'It's in the reference section. You can read it here in the library but you are not allowed to take reference books out.'

I thanked her and began. Story books were straightforward. They are read from the beginning and progress to 'The End.' How to tackle a reference book was not in my experience. I did have a child's encyclopaedia, but I only looked at the illustrations. I turned the pages of Mr Gibbon's book. Only a few pages in I recognised the stamp, or something like it. There were lots of Penny Blacks: several pages of them set in dense print which meant nothing to me. I couldn't quite remember what my stamp looked like. I would have to bring the stamp to the library.

The following day I was armed with the stamp secured in the envelope. In the playground I made the mistake of boasting about having a Penny Black in my collection, Alan and Gary were suitably impressed. Richard was less so. He questioned my veracity. So I gave him a peep of the treasured item. Richard was no stamp collector but he knew of things which might have value. He had heard of the first postage stamps.

'Could be worth a lorra dosh. Why yo' carryin' it abaht?'

I told him about the abortive first visit to the library, and the second visit that very afternoon.

'Well yo' need a couple of guards then. Me and Tez will come wiv yo'.

It was always best to be wary of Richard, but having two chums made the library visit much less daunting.

The librarian smiled. Perhaps she was thinking that I had brought two new recruits. I pulled the Gibbons book from the shelf and opened it at the appropriate pages. Richard and I gazed at the images and my Penny Black. Terry gazed about the room full of books: he could just about cope with *Janet and John*.

'Yeah, look it's gotta be one of the first uns cos it's got straight edges. An' it's gonna be wo'th loads o' lolly!' Richard was speaking in a heavy whisper. I was speechless.

I thought about returning it to Stan. He was a very nice bloke. It must have been a mistake to leave the stamp in the envelope. But avarice got the better of me.

My Father said that we should get some expert advice. There was a philatelist's shop in town. Perhaps it might be bought for a favourable sum. I thought of Hornby trains, and toy soldiers. That coming Saturday my Father was not doing overtime, so a trip into town was suggested. My Mother would go to M&S.

The philately shop was on Parliament Street. It was wedged in between two large shops. It was a just a glass door with a window not much wider. The window display was crammed with stamps. Inside the shop, the walls were covered with glass cases full of stamps. A man about my Father's age was examining some envelopes under a small lamp on the counter. He looked up as the door-bell pinged.

My Father explained the mission and presented the Penny Black. After a very brief examination the proprietor snorted and declared the stamp an obvious forgery. He leaned back in his chair leaving the 'dud' stamp on the glass counter top. I felt foolish and ashamed.

My Father thanked the man for his observation. I could tell that he was a little annoyed. Outside he said, 'He didn't have to be so blunt. How were we supposed to recognise a forgery from the real thing?'

'Never mind. I've got some nice things from Marks.'

I did mind. I would have to tell my chums.

'What, not real? We checked it wiv o'd Gibbo at the library. It look like the real fing.'

Suddenly Richard's face lit up, 'Ah gorra nidea.'

Richard was full of ideas. That most of them didn't end happily, didn't daunt him.

'We meks it *look* real'

This was beyond Terry, and I was struggling too.

'OK, so it's a fake, but if we put it ona o'd letter it would look real.'

'Where are we going to get an old envelope from?'

Richard grinned and tapped the side of his nose with a finger.

'Nah this is the good bit. Yer uncle Richard can lay 'is 'ands on one right nah!'

Richard had access to all sorts of interesting items, but I had serious doubts about a fifty year-old envelope.

'Yo' see, my mam and dad 'ave this shoe-box where they keep important papers. It's in the bottom of their wardrobe. An' Ah knows what's innit.'

Of course he would.

'There's some real o'd letters. All we 'as to do is swap stamps.'

He was glowing with anticipation. He led us into his house. There was nobody else at home. His parents had the smaller back room, while Richard shared the front bedroom with Alan his older brother. It felt creepy going into the Church's bedroom. On the lino there were a three quarter bed, a small wooden stand and a double utility wardrobe. Richard opened one of the wardrobe doors to reveal a few clothes on wire hangers. He stooped to retrieve a cardboard box. He pulled an envelope out,

'Ay, this'll do.'

The envelope had of course been slit open. It was yellowed and grubby. The writing on the front was difficult to read. It was in faded brown ink in an old-fashioned curly style. It was addressed to *Mr R. P. Church Esq.* at an address in the Radford district.

''E was my gret- grandad. Ah nev' met 'im.'

I focussed on the stamp. It looked like a proper stamp. There was the image of a man in faded red with the words *Edward VII.*

'Want 'e the king after Victoria, 'er son?'

I wasn't sure but I agreed with him.

He took out the contents of the envelope and stuffed them back into the shoe-box.

'Nah, let's get to wo'k.'

The work began with Terry putting the kettle on the gas stove in the kitchen. After a minute or so the kettle was whistling and steam rushed out of the spout. Richard held the envelope to the steam with the stamp closest. After another minute or so, the envelope was pulled away and Richard poked a grubby finger-nail under the perforated edge. The stamp lifted easily.

'Ta dah! Turn the keckle off, Tez.'

Terry jolted into action, 'What if the real stamp is wo'th moron the dud?'

This was enough to freeze Richard, but only for a second, 'Nah, if the reddun was wo'th owt ar Ralan would 'ave tecknit. Any road there's a fortune to be med wiv the Penny Black.'

Terry had a point. Whatever Richard was planning would be risky though.

'Ready wiv the Black?'

I pulled the envelope from my shirt pocket and tipped out the dud Penny Black. As Richard snatched it up, I did the same with the Red Edward and put it safely in my envelope.

'Nah we lerrit dry off a bit, an' then we can stick the Blackunon. Tez pop upstairs to Alan's cubby 'ole an' get the glue: that stuff wiv the rubber squeezy top. Oh, an' the *John Bull* set.'

When Terry had left the kitchen, Richard explained the next move.

'That stamp we took off was nicked on one corner by Post Office stampin'. That's what the Johnny Bull set is for.' He grinned.

Terry returned and put the bits on the kitchen table. Richard positioned the Penny Black. I could see that the franking needed to just touch the white margin of the stamp.

'What about the date on the franking?'

The Post Office franking was clumsy but one could still read the year.

Richard nodded, 'Well that can be smudged a bit more.'

He smeared a tiny drop of the glue to the back of the stamp and pressed it carefully into place. It was looking good. Richard checked that no glue had leaked. Next he prepared the *John Bull* printing set.

'If we use this as tis it'll look too new. So it needs scruffin' up a bit.'

He bumped the stamper onto the ink-pad. He opened out yesterday's *Daily Mirror* from the other end of the table. The stamper was pressed down on the paper until the print looked faded. Satisfied, Richard carefully touched the white edge of the stamp margin with just a corner of the stamper. He did the same to mask the date. It looked wonderful.

Beaming with joy at his handiwork Richard announced the next phase.

'There's a nantiques shop in Beeston what sells an' buys o'd stuff. The bloke what runs it is smart, but 'e aint no expert on stamps. Ah reckon he would pounce on owt what looked like a Penny Black. An'this one does, it's blinkin' good innit?'

Terry and I had to agree. For one dreadful moment I thought that he would give me the task of visiting the antique shop. I imagined being held until the police arrived to arrest me for forgery.

'OK, Ah'll do the talkin'. Yo' two jus' watch. If we do pull this off, Chrisser, Ah'll gerra cut cos Ah done most of the wo'k.'

I couldn't think that the scheme might work. I didn't care about any possible money. I was anxious about being discovered and having to face my Parents, 'OK.'

Richard grinned widely, 'Right, let's tidy up. We'll g' dahn Beeston tomorra after school.'

I told my Mother that I was going to look in *Appleby's* window after school. *RS Appleby's* window was a magnet for children: it was crammed with all sorts of toys.

'Be back for five o'clock.'

I couldn't concentrate on Mrs Hilton's end -of –the-day story. It was a relief to gallop off with Richard and Terry at four o'clock. The antique shop was on the High Road sandwiched between two much larger shops. I hadn't paid much attention to it previously: Appleby's was more or less opposite. The shop had one ordinary glass door. To the left of the door was a similar sized window. Among assorted bric-a-brac, stamps of the world were displayed on a piece of card. Also in the window was a neat sign which read, *Bought and Sold: Antiques, Curios and Collectables.*

The door jangled as we entered. A middle aged man wearing glasses was sitting behind a glass top counter. He was fiddling with a clock. He looked up. There was no welcoming smile.

'Good afternoon, sir. Me mam's been sorting stuff aht at 'ome. She come across this.'

With a flourish Richard pulled the letter from his jacket pocket and placed it on the glass top.

'She fought it might 'ave some value as it's really o'd.'

The man placed the clock to one side and picked up the envelope. He stared at it for a long few seconds. I thought about diving for the door. The man screwed his face into a sort of sneer, and put the envelope down. He shook his head.

'Well it *is* old, but there are lots of Penny Blacks around now. They don't have the value they used to have.' He stared at us. I clenched my teeth. Richard had one hand behind his back with his fingers crossed.

The man's expression changed. He made a little smile. 'It's not worth much, but I can give you… ten bob for it.'

Richard's crossed fingers twitched, 'Oh, as much as that. That's good. Ah'll tek it.'

I unclenched my teeth. I heard Terry sigh. The man's smile grew wider. He reached under the counter a pulled out a ten shilling note. The transaction was done. Richard quickly palmed the brown note. 'Fanks mester, me mam will be pleased.'

We exited the shop and turned right calmly until we had passed the window. Our pace increased until we could skid around the next corner. Richard was jubilant. I was exhausted. Terry was Terry.

'Wow we done it. That crook finks he conned free kids aht of a fortune.'

We laughed hysterically. With his breath back Richard said, 'OK nah it's pay time. We'll get this note split. I reckon I get five bob cos it was all my wo'k, and Chrisser gets five bob cos it was 'is stamp.'

I nodded agreement.

'Yo' 'elped a bit Tez, so Ah'll buy yo' some tuffees.'

The note was split at a sweet shop on the High Road. I didn't linger. I left them chewing, to visit *Appleby's* with two half-crowns. I bought six sitting toy soldiers to fit my military *Dinkies*, and I still had plenty of silver in my pocket. I remembered that I also had an Edward VII red stamp in a pocket. I would have to check out its value some time.

Picnic on Snakey Woods

'Nine'y eight, nine-nine,'undred ~ Comin'!'
I could see Joan. I was sure she wouldn't be able to see me. Anyway if she came my way, I could easily slither off into the gulley.

It was mid-August and very warm. After the first two weeks of school holiday we had run out of things to do. There was no trip to the sea-side or a visit to my Grandfather in Yorkshire. We had had a couple of days with Grandfather at Whitsuntide, and there was no money for the sea-side this year. My Parents worked: Father all day and Mother in the afternoons.

'Hey, Chrisser, tell y'mam ah mam's tekkin' us on a pic-er-nic. She's tekkin' uvver kids too. Yo' can come.'
It was Joan from next door inviting me. I was playing with toy soldiers in the garden. Joan was six years older than me. We didn't play together. She had taken me to school in the second week of the infants, and she was invited to my fifth birthday. According to my Mother, Joan was well-meaning but not very bright. Her sister, Christine, was a year younger and sharp as a pin.

'Who's organising it?'
'Mrs Daykin and Jeffrey's mam…mum, Mrs Perkins.'
I corrected myself. There had been a sea change with language. My Mother had been impressed by the way Jeffrey referred to his mother as 'mummy'. It was firmly suggested that I did the same. Mother thought it sounded so much more *refined*. It was difficult knowing which word to use when talking about other children's mothers.
'And Joan's helping too.'
'Where is the picnic going to be?'
'On Snakey Woods. In a field.'
'When is the picnic?'
'Joan said next Wednesday in the afternoon. The picnic will be at tea-time.'
'Who else is going?'
I didn't know. I guessed that Mrs Daykin's youngest David would go. Likewise Mrs Perkins would take Jeffrey.'

'I'll have a word with Brenda.'

The choice of picnic place was perfect. Many picnics were held on Wollaton Park, but Snakey Woods was untamed. Nobody had ever seen any snakes, and the parts we played in had no trees. The trees began over a fence that ran along the edge of a large fairly flat field. To get there one took a track from the Derby Road near to Bramcote. In fact this lane, Sandy Lane, began only half a mile from our Council Estate, but it seemed further away then. We played there often. We played in the scrubby hummocks rather than the green fields beyond.

After talking with Mrs Daykin, Mother said she would provide some potted meat rolls. Everyone was supposed to provide something. Mrs Daykin was making a cake, and Mrs Perkins would provide a jelly. So a spoon was necessary ~ just like the school Christmas party.

Over the next couple of days it became clear who else would be picnicking. Of course it was Jeffrey Perkins who was my age, and David Daykin who was only a little boy. Christine Daykin was going to the lido with some friends. Mrs Daykin had invited Richard and, of course, Terry. Also, because he was my friend, Tony Wilmot was invited. She had even invited some girls. Lorraine and her friend Angela lived on our street. Lorraine asked if her other friend Julia could come. I liked Julia: she wasn't pretty: she was happy and full of fun. Julia in turn requested that her friend came too. Her friend was Barbara, Barbara of the grey eyes. I liked her too: she *was pretty*. I would have liked Mike to be with us but he lived far away now.

'Good Heavens. You're not taking that. You're going on a picnic: not playing at cowboys and Indians.'

I took off the holster with the six-shooter. It seemed reasonable that we would play at something, and guns figured largely in my games. I wondered what we would do at the picnic. The picnics that I had experienced so far were family affairs. My father and Uncle Jim would organise a game of cricket while my Mother and Aunty Dorothy sat and gossiped. Perhaps Mrs Daykin and Mrs Perkins had some good ideas.

The sky on Wednesday morning was cloudless and there was no breeze. It would be perfect. I had a light lunch of spam and salad to leave room for the picnic feast. The gathering, in our Close was at twelve thirty. It was exciting to see so many known faces near my house.

Mrs Daykin and Mrs Perkins had big shopping bags. Children placed their contributions in these bags. The two women carried one between them. The second bag was carried by Joan and a rota of children in turn. It was like being on a school trip with the two adults leading a posse of paired children and a big girl at the rear. I partnered Tony. We talked about the rival merits of the Hornby Dublo and Tri-ang model railway systems.

Crossing the main road to Derby back then wasn't a big problem. We scurried across when a Barton's bus stopped for us. It took only about fifteen minutes along the footpath to the turn off up Sandy Lane just past the flower nursery.

Sandy Lane was well named. The deep yellow sand was kept in place by steep banks covered in gorse bushes. The lane climbed away from the main road and then dipped down towards Wollaton in the distance. Yellow sand gave way to green grass. The track more or less cut the field in half.

'Yeah!' The children surged onto the field of green grass, buttercups, clover and butterflies.

Mrs Perkins called us back. 'We need to check for cow-pats.'

There were no cows in the field, but there sometimes were.

After a few minutes of 'sweeping for land-mines', it was declared 'mine-free': though we hadn't been to the far end of the field where there was a five-bar gate and a stile. A suitable place was chosen half way between the track and the woods. Mrs Perkins spread out a blanket while the children gazed about. Behind was the sandy defile. On the west side was a deep wood. To the north the track continued over another field beyond a hawthorn hedge. To the east the land was in hummocks and covered in gorse bushes. The hummocks were referred to as hills. From a hilly vantage the track could be seen heading for the start of houses.

'Let's play hide and seek,' Joan was in her big girl mode. 'I'll close me eyes and count to 'undred. One, two...'

We scampered off in different directions. Tony and I raced to the woods. The fence was easy. It was gloomy compared to the sunlight field. There were some shafts of light dappling the interior. We pressed in deeper and hid behind a fallen tree. Behind us there was a long narrow dip in the ground. This would make an escape route. From our hiding place we could see Joan standing in the field.

'Six-free, six-four, six-five, six-six…'

'What shall we do if she doesn't find us?'

I shrugged. I hadn't given that any thought.

'I suppose we could run back to the picnic spot and shout one, two, three.'

'Nine-nine, 'undred. Coming.' Joan began to walk away from us and towards the scrubby hills.

'I put Penguins in the bag.'

I suddenly realised what Tony was talking about, and thought of my potted meat rolls.

'Come on let's go back to the fence and get ready to go over when she goes behind the bushes.'

Joan changed her mind and direction. She turned right towards Sandy Lane. She didn't walk into the sand: she climbed the slope where the big rock stood. It was a good vantage point.

We moved back carefully.

'Let's explore the wood.'

Tony didn't look keen, 'I'll wait here.'

I shrugged again and began to walk through the trees. After a few minutes I looked back. I could just see Tony's stripped tee-shirt. The bright green field was almost blotted out.

'One, two, free Lorraine. One two free Angela.' Two were caught.

When I turned back to my direction I saw something. It was a flash of bright colour. Yellow was the colour of Julia's dress. She was standing behind a tree. I saw another colour White was Barbara's dress. The trees weren't wide enough.

'Julia.'

Her beaming face appeared. And so did Barbara's.

I stood there like a lemon. The girls giggled.

'Is it tea-time?' asked Julia.

'Not yet. Only two have been caught, I think.'

Barbara spoke ~ to me. 'Are you on your own?'

'No, I'm with Tony. He stayed by the fence.'

I could not look directly into her pretty pale grey eyes. I might have been turned to stone.

'We didn't come over the fence. There's farm gate halfway down. It was open.'

'And there's a little track going up through the wood.'

'We'll take you back that way.'

'What about Tony?'

Both girls laughed. I wondered why.

I followed them through the trees and down to a track. We turned right and came to the open gate. We could see some children standing around the picnic spot. Only Richard and Terry were missing.

'Richard! Terry! Richard! Terry!'

They appeared at the bottom of the field climbing over the gate. As they got nearer, Jeffrey called out. 'We've done hide an' seek. Now we're gonna have something to eat.'

Terry put a spurt on.

Mrs Perkins and Mrs Daykin had put out some of the food onto grease proof paper. We were invited to sample. My potted meat rolls looked very nice and disappeared quickly. We sat or knelt on the grass and munched. The way Terry dived in made me think that he hadn't had any lunch. I didn't fancy the door-step jam sandwiches: even though they had been halved by Mrs Daykin. Richard pounced on these. He had to shake off a wasp which was also interested. The two women shared a flask of tea, and Mrs Daykin smoked a Woodbine. We children guzzled fizzy pop from waxed cardboard cups. It was idyllic.

'You can play some more. Then we'll have the jelly and the cake. We'll call you.'

Richard rubbed his belly and licked his jammy lips.

Joan pretended that she was an adult. The girls seemed happy enough to hang around the picnic spot making daisy chains. So did Tony.

Richard, Terry, Jeffrey and me wandered down the field towards the hawthorn hedge and the stile.

'There's a lickle stream the uvver side. Not as good as the one *Over Tins*.'

I looked back. Barbara had tucked her dress up into her knickers and was doing cart-wheels.

The stile had a longish plank to cross the stream. It was more of a trickle: a lethargic trickle. Five or six cows were chomping the grass. We jumped from the end of the stile to avoid the sticky ground by the stream.

Terry became animated, 'What's that?' He was pointing at the ground and took a quick step towards it. Suddenly he was all arms and legs. He sat down abruptly.

'Urgh.'

He had skidded on a cow pat, and had sat down on it.

Richard began shrieking with laughter.

Terry stood up. The seat of his jeans was covered in yellowy-green cow muck. He looked forlorn. I felt sorry for him.

'Urgh, Tez yo' got cow shit all over y'bum.'

Terry slowly moved sideways wiping his shoe on the grass. He twisted around to inspect his rear.

Jeffrey said, 'Let's find some dock leaves for him.'

I said, 'Best take your jeans off, Terry.'

As he began to unbuckle his belt the sunshine disappeared. We looked at the sky.

Clouds had sneaked up on us. They had come from the west over the trees in the wood. In just a minute the clouds had expanded. They were very dark.

Terry was kneeling in his underpants rubbing away with the dock leaves.

'Ah fink it's gonna rain.'

'Boys!' Mrs Perkins was shouting.

'Come on, let's go.'

There was a sudden intense flash of light which was followed immediately by a very loud bang. I wasn't usually frightened of thunderstorms, but usually I was watching safely through the window. Another streak of lightening seemed to stab down on the picnic field. The treble thunder roll followed without a pause. I was scared.

We started back to the stile. As Richard jumped onto it the first huge drops of rain hit my face.

'Wait fer me,' Terry was struggling back into his jeans.

I heard a scream and realised It was not the first time. We dashed across the picnic field. Mrs Daykin had her arms around Joan. Back home Joan would have cowered behind the sofa with her hands over her ears and eyes closed.

The whole sky seemed to be very dark. The lightening flashed again. The thunder exploded with it. The rain poured heavily. I was wet though in seconds. Mrs Perkins grabbed up the picnic. The girls huddled together. Their thin summer frocks were plastered against them.

Mrs Perkins was in command, 'Quickly back to the road. We'll try and catch a bus.'

There was a simple bus shelter near Sandy Lane, but the bus would take us only one stop. We would still have to walk into the estate.

Richard thought it was great fun running through the heavy downpour. Joan was still shrieking. Everyone looked like they had been in the bath with their clothes on. The fine yellow sand stuck to shoes and socks.

Everyone squashed in under the bus-stop canopy. Cars had their head lights on. The rain bounced high off the tarmac.

'Well that's got yer jeans washed, Tez.'

Terry was not amused.

'Where's Davey? Mrs Daykin twisted her head around. 'Where's our Davey?'

David Daykin was definitely not with us. He hadn't been seen recently. Mrs Daykin had been too busy calming Joan. Now it was her turn to be hysterical.

Angela piped up, 'He said he was going to look for rabbits.'

Mrs Perkins took command again, 'He must be still at the picnic spot. I'll go back, Brenda, while you get these kids home.'

'I'll help Mrs Perkins.'

Richard's heroic gesture galvanised Jeffrey, Terry and me into solidarity.

A Barton's bus pulled up splashing a wave from the gutter.

'Go on, Brenda, we'll find him.'

As the bedraggled group piled into the bus the rescue party turned back onto Sandy Lane. The rain still poured down. Thunder rolled around and lightening plunged.

'There's rabbits on the hills under the bushes.'

'Yeah, we seen 'em.'

Mrs Perkins listened to our local knowledge, 'Right we'll start there. But stick together.'

We were so wet it didn't matter anymore. The only thing that mattered was finding David. He hadn't started school yet.

'Why di'n't Tony come wiv us?'

I shrugged again. 'He wanted to go home I suppose.'

I pictured him squashed onto a maroon velvet bus seat with a couple of girls.

'David. David!'

The ground had turned sticky. The rain lashed down.

'Davey, Davey!'

Jeffrey saw him first. A little frightened face in the cover of a gorse bush.

Mrs Perkins pulled him out. He was sobbing. She cuddled him.

'Let's get you home, my lad. Get you dry, back to your mummy.'

Between huge gasps and sobs he managed, 'See wabbits.'

By the time we had descended to the bus shelter the storm had calmed. It was still raining, but not so hard. David told us that he had gone looking for rabbits as he had seen one in the bushes. When the thunder and lightning had started he was frightened and so hid under the bush.

'Just look at you. You look like a drowned rat. Take those wet things off.'

While I pulled off my sodden clothes in the kitchen, Mother went to fetch a clean towel from the airing cupboard.

We never got the picnic cake or jelly. I wasn't bothered. No more group picnics were suggested. The Perkins family moved away soon after. Mother said that she wasn't surprised as they were 'a cut above'. The other children on the picnic managed to get into more adventures with me sometimes.

Protect and Survive

The door behind us squeaked and strong light danced about. We were not alone.

'Hey, Chrisser ay a goz at this.'

Richard and Terry had moved rapidly from the school premises at the end of the day. I had caught them up outside the Welfare at the top of Wensor Avenue. They were studying the noticeboard. Usually there were curling notices about vaccinations and baby food. Now behind the glass was a rather different poster. It was entitled 'Protect and Survive' and beneath the words was a dramatic picture of a man holding a 'dustbin lid' to the sky. He was wearing a soldier's helmet and dark blue overalls. He looked determined. In smaller letters it said that volunteers were wanted to help in the event of an air attack.

'Why's 'e gorra a dustbin lid?'

Richard snorted. 'It ain't a dustbin lid, Tez. It's s'posed to be a shield.'

I had seen many war films at the Essoldo. I didn't think a knight's shield would be much use against bombs from the sky.

'Snot s'posed to be real. It's just a picture, innit?'

I liked the idea of the uniform even if it was really just a boiler suit dyed navy. I already had a similar helmet, but mine was not white: it was a dull grey green.

'Arh fought the war was over.'

'Tis, Tez, but there might be annuver'n.'

Terry looked puzzled.

'Wiv the bleddy Roosh'ans, see.'

'We might have to use the air raid shelters.'

It hadn't been explained to us that, in the event of a thermo-nuclear exchange between the West and the East, second-world war shelters would serve only as tombs. The shelters that I was enthusing about were in our school grounds. Our junior school was connected to the infant school which was connected to the secondary boys' school. It was line of brick buildings from Boundary Road to Central Avenue. There was a gated service road which could be accessed from both ends. Across from the service road there was a slender stretch of land given over to trees and bushes, and the air raid shelters.

Three shelters had been built in case the Luftwaffe paid a visit to Beeston. They were built in line. Flat concrete lids covered the long squat brick boxes. Most of each shelter was underground. Each shelter had a short flight of concrete steps at both ends. The steps were flanked by sloped walls. At the bottom of the steps a hefty door guarded the entrance. There were no windows.

Because the buildings were rather low and had convenient ramps, children liked to play on them. The flat roofs were used by the more daring as bicycle tracks. Mr Reeves, the junior school head teacher, warned us from time to time about the dangers. We were forbidden to go anywhere near them. Their interest soon faded when it was realised that they could not be entered. The doors were permanently locked, apparently.

'Whadja reckon's inside?'

There were many guesses.

'Guns an' ammo?'

'Skellingtons?'

Miss Hilton told us that they were empty, but she, herself, had not seen inside.

Richard was wearing his jubilant expression. It was necessary to be cautious when he was like this. It was an indication that he had had another brainwave. He was clutching something tightly in his left fist.

'Guess what, Chrisser.'

I shrugged. Terry looked his usual blank.

'Da-dah!'

His fingers uncurled to reveal a key. It was a mortise type key attached to a grubby and crumpled label. I suspected that it must be of importance.

Gleefully he told us that it was the key to one of the air raid shelters.

At the end of the lunch break Richard had been asked by Mrs Taylor to get the caretaker.

'Some stupid kid had puked up his dinner in the main door way. She to'd me to g'dahn to O'd Bradley's den an 'gerrim to come an' sort it.'

The caretaker, Mr Bradley, took his lunch break in the boiler room. This was his den down some steps beneath the school. In the winter months he shared his den with a huge pile of coke that started in the playground.

'Well, Arh guz dahn there. He's gorra lickle table an' a chair. An' a keckle on a gas ring. When Arh to'd him abaht the puke, he moaned summink abaht a mop an' a bucket. He went to get them an' Arh had a goz rahnd. There was a notice board wiv loads ov keys danglin'. Each on 'em 'ad a label. Arh seen free keys all covered in spiders' webs. There was AR1, AR2 an' AR3. Arh took this'n. AR stands for air raid. Arh was dead quick. He di'n't notice. Arh've only borrered it. Arh'll tek it back.'

He chuckled,

'Arh'll tek it back when we've 'ad a look-see.'

It all seemed so very simple. From past experience I knew that things never quite pan out like they are expected to.

'Which shelter is it?'

Richard shrugged. 'Dunno. It's AR1. We can try 'em all.'

'When are you going to try the key?'

'After school when all the kids an' teachers have gone 'ome.'

'What about the caretaker?'

'He 'as to go 'ome for 'is tea.'

I thought that Mr Bradley might live under the school, like I used to think that the teachers slept in the staff room.

Richard swung the key temptingly.

'Ah 'bout tomorrer after us teas?'

There was a gap after tea and before having to be home. The really dark nights had gone but it still got gloomy before bedtime.

'We'll meet under the lamp at six. Bring a torch: there might not be no lights.'

The school gates on Boundary Road were locked. This was a good sign: Mr Bradley may have gone home. The locked gates were not a problem. We could have easily climbed over, but it was far easier to squeeze through where a gate post was shy of the perimeter railings. It seemed very strange being without the clamour children. It was all still and quiet. Never-the- less we moved unobtrusively along the service road. I glanced down, over the wall, into the blind windows of the junior school. There was no sign of anyone. We approached the first air raid shelter. Richard paused and looked about before moving down the steps. Terry and I followed. I noticed dark marks on the door jambs where the hinges might be. The marks were not fresh but the hinges had been oiled at some point. Richard had the key in the key hole.

'Might not be this'n. No, wait, it wo'ks.'

The key turned all the way. There was no door handle, but the door moved slightly inwards. Richard pushed with both hands against the peeling green paint work. There was a squeak and the door opened fully against the inside of the end wall. Beyond the door was an empty small room. Almost opposite the peeling door there was a doorway, without a door. Now we needed our torches to see inside the shelter-proper.

It was very dark inside. Only a small amount of light could trickle down the steps and turn right.

"O'd the bleddy fings still.'

Naturally we had started by waving the beams about. It looked like a dungeon. The darkness seemed to swallow the torch beams. The ceiling was flat concrete festooned with spider webs. The floor was a reflection of the ceiling but without the webs. The walls were bare unfinished red brick. Along both walls were continuous benches made with slats of plain wood. On the left hand bench close to our vantage point were a few gardening tools and a yard brush.

'There's a light switch here.'

'Well spotted, our Tez'

'Shouldn't think it works…'

'Well there's only one way to fin' aht, Chrisser. Pop the light on.'

I was hesitant, but it looked like the ones we had at home. It was a small brass knob poking out of a Bakelite dome. I pulled the switch down: a light flicked on. We hadn't noticed the bulb held close to the ceiling by a sort of wire basket. The light was dim.

Terry traced the lighting structure with his torch beam. He picked out two more lights. Neither of these was on. The one in the middle had no bulb. A cable connected the three bulb fittings.

'Chiz, it don't 'arf pong in 'ere.'

It certainly did smell. It smelled of damp soil. We had ventured in a few steps. My eyes were getting used to the dark interior. At the far end of the shelter. I expected it to be the reverse of our end: the other entrance. There was a door.

'Imagine comin' dahn 'ere when there was a raid on.'

'Did your Alan 'ave to come dahn 'ere?'

Richard's brother was five years older.

'Nah, Tez, when he was startin' infants the war was nearly over.'

'There's a door.'

'Yeah, it's the uvver way aht.'

'Don't think so. It's in the wrong place.'

A couple more steps and we were at the door. The brick wall was only three quarters the way across. To the right there was an open door space. Terry ventured into it.

'Yeah the uvver way out is round 'ere.'

'What's behind this lickle door, then?'

It was the door to an inner structure which was built of brick.

Richard took hold of the door knob.

I suddenly felt quite frightened.

'Urgh, won't flamin' well open.'

'Pull it.'

Richard did as Terry suggested and the door creaked open. He burst out laughing.

Three torch beams targeted a lavatory pan. It was the cheap version with plain pieces of wood fastened directly to the ceramic bowl. Terry sniggered.

'A khazi, a bleddy khazi.'

'Do you think it still works?'

Richard tucked his torch under his arm and began to fiddle with his fly buttons. When he had finished baptising the dry pan he reached for the chain which dangled from a high cistern. Water gushed noisily. In his haste to re-button his flies he lost the grip on his torch. It dropped head first into the pan. The light was still working under the water.

'Urgh, Gordon-bleddy-Bennett.'

The light went out. I hadn't heard the tank refilling. I did hear something behind us. The door squeaked and a strong light danced about. We were not alone. As one, we slipped around behind the lavatory and doused our remaining two lights. We stood trembling in the smelly darkness.

'Hullo, anybody there?'

It was a man's voice. It wasn't the caretaker's voice. This one was authoritative. The beam flicked down to our end. It light up the other entrance: we were hidden behind the lavatory. Heavy footsteps sounded. He was coming our way. I desperately wanted to pee. Terry squeaked softly. The footsteps stopped. It wasn't Mr Bradley or big kids. I wondered about using the key on the door nearest to us. Would it fit the lock? Would the door open? Could this be done in less than thirty seconds?

'Hullo, hullo, what's this?'

Obviously the man was looking into the lavatory. We had left the door open. He would have spotted Richard's torch. The strong beam moved about.

'Ah, well, nobody here. Another case closed.'

The footsteps moved away. The single dim light switched off. After a moment the stout door banged shut. We waited silently for a few more minutes.

'Lights.'

Terry and I switched our torches back on.

'That was a rozzer.'

'I'm going to take a leak.'

'Not 'til Arh gets me torch back, Chrisser.'

Richard took my torch.

'Yeah still 'ere. The rozzer di'n't tekkit.'

'Does yo'r'n still wo'k?'

'Will do when it's dried aht.'

Making sure to keep hold of my torch, I peed in the pan. The flush didn't work this time.

'C'mon, let's go. We seen enough. Lead the way, Tez.'

Terry aimed his torch beam back the way we had come in.

'Yo' don't fink that rozzer locked us in?'

'Nah, still got the key. An' even if 'e 'ad, we c'n still unlock it from the inside, see.'

Whilst they were chatting, I followed and shone my torch about. I tried to imagine what it would be like squashed in there with dozens of other children. The little ones would be crying. The girls would scream every time a bomb exploded on the concrete roof. My beam caught something under the slatted bench. It was a small coin. I picked it up.

'Great, there's a nandle this side.'

Richard turned the handle and pulled the door open a fraction.

'All clear, men.'

We slipped out into the blinding light.

Richard remembered to deal with the door. He put the key in the lock and used it as a handle. I looked around rather expecting a policeman to be lurking behind a tree. There was nobody.

'Do yo' reck'n the shelters ever got used.'

'Nah, the Gerries came over durin' the night an' nob'dy was at school then. Me dad to'd me they was tryin' to get Chilwell Ord'nance Depot, and managed to flatten a few 'ouses dahn Beeston.'

We slipped through the gap and out onto Boundary Road.

'And now for something rather serious. You have been reminded often about not playing around the air raid shelters: especially after the schools are closed. I had a visitor yesterday. A policeman came to tell me that some children had been seen near the shelters. A lady who lives on Wallett Avenue had seen three junior boys up to no good.'

Mr Reeves was looking directly at me. I was about to be arrested, dragged away and forced to denounce my comrades. I would hold out as long as possible.

'The lady didn't recognise any of the boys. The policeman who investigated found that one of the shelters was unlocked, but the naughty children had fled. Now if you know anything about…'

I wondered if Richard had actually returned the key like he said he would. I dared to look over my shoulder to the class at the back. Richard was practising to be an angel.

'Yeah, course Arh did. Arh seen o'd Bradley fiddlin' wiv the water fountain. So Arh nipped dahn the boiler 'ouse and stuck it back on the 'ook faster than yo' can say *Jack Robinson.*'

The small coin was a silver three penny piece depicting King George V. These coins were no longer in circulation, but we had several at home. Every year they were polished up and added to the Christmas cake mix. My coin became part of the team. I guessed that a child had dropped it during an air raid drill. The drills must have been fun.

Richard the Conkerer

'Do I make myself clear on this matter?'

Mr Reeves glared down at the assembly.

'Well?'

A subdued response came, mainly from the boys, 'Yes, Mester Reeves.'

Later, at home time, class teachers reminded us to take our conkers home, and leave them there. Apparently things had been getting out of hand. There had been too many weeping children with bruised knuckles, and disputes that had become violent. It had been the same with marbles. There was disruption when bags of glass marbles had emptied onto the class-room floors, and disputes that had become violent.

Everything that seemed the current rage was eventually banned. Water pistols were banned. Whip and tops were banned. And now it was the turn of conkers.

'Gordon-bleddy-Bennet! Everyfink wot's fun is banned.'

Once outside the school gates the children reverted to being Council estate savages.

Richard was scowling and swinging his conker. It was a fourer.

'Play yo',' challenged Gary King.

Richard looked disdainfully at the Gary's shiny brown conker dangling on a shoe-lace.

'OK.'

Richard held his conker out for Gary's swing.

I was sure Richard's conker would resist the attack.

Gary swiped his hand down. Bits of smashed conker flew off the collision. It was Richard's conker that disintegrated. We stared in disbelief. Gary broke the spell.

'Now mine's a fiver.'

'Sod it. That's all I need.'

Terry and I caught up with Richard.

'Yo' know what? What we need is some super conkers and a competition.'

There were plenty of ideas of how to make conkers tougher. Some kids tried baking them in the oven. Others tried soaking them over night in vinegar. The ambitious tried both methods on their conkers. It was rumoured that some conkers had had their insides tweaked out and concrete or ball-bearings substituted. This last idea seemed a bit on the fanciful side. Richard was the sort of person to know about some special treatment.

'Yeah, wi can org'nise a competition, an' wiv ahr super conkers wi can win all the prizes.'

I glanced at Terry. He looked puzzled. He always looked puzzled.

'What prizes?'

Richard turned his radiant face to me.

'Ain't yo' heard of *sponsors*?'

'Sponsors?'

'Yeah, rich people who give money or stuff to people wots doing sommink.'

'We don't know any rich people.'

'Course we do. There's Mester Pretty fer a start…'

'And…?'

'Well we'll think of some more. Not we Tez?'

Terry nodded enthusiastically. His thinking for the day was used up now.

'You good at drawin', Chrisser, yo' can mek the posters.'

I didn't rush to make any posters, mostly because I didn't know what to write, and I had an idea that the whole scheme would dissolve. I was wrong.

Richard enjoyed hatching schemes especially if there was something to gain.

'Nah, this is the plan. The competition is to be held on Hathern Green.'

Hathern Green was an empty grassed space between the parade of shops and the terminus for the No. 19 bus. The Council in their wisdom had placed green iron railings around the neatly mowed space, but this was no problem for kids and dogs. The railings were easily climbed and some of the metals had been bent apart.

'On Sat'day mornin', between ten and twelve. We'll gerra grown-up to be the judge and give the prizes.'

'How about Mr Woffington?'

Mr Woffington, senior, ran the confectionery shop overlooking Hathern Green. He was a very nice old man.

'Yeah, o'd Woffo would do. P'r'aps he might gizzus one of the prizes?'

'How many prizes?' Terry had stuttered into action.

Richard looked at me.

'It's usually three prizes. First, second and third.'

Richard nodded his approval, 'We gorra mek sure we win 'em. We need some really good conks.'

There were very few horse-chestnuts in the vicinity. There were none on the estate. The nearest was *Over Tins*. There was another one on our school site behind the air-raid shelters. Both of these trees had been raided by conkering heroes. The most obvious place was Wollaton Park.

'Ok we'll go conkerin' on Sunday mornin'. That'll gi' us a week before the contest.'

Short heavy sticks were gathered for the dislodging of the choicest fruits. The ones lower down had already been removed. Sticks were thrown again and again with little luck. The spikey green balls refused to be separated from the parent.

'S'no good. We'll 'ave to climb. Tez yo're the lightest. Yo' climb, an' me and Chrisser'll tell where.'

Richard and I gave Terry a leg up to the nearest branch. Terry scrambled higher. His grinning face appeared through the leaves.

'Yeah that branch yo're on. There's some gooduns furver out.'

The leaves wobbled as Terry worked his way towards the outer layer. The branches became thinner away from the trunk. Terry tugged conkers free and dropped them.

'Great, Tez. A few more.'

Terry edged along the branch. It began to bend. He missed his footing. The leaves wobbled. Terry cried out. His feet appeared. He was dangling from the very flexible branch above. 'Help.'

We couldn't reach his feet. We couldn't scramble up after him to haul him back.

'Tez. Paratroop. You're only as high as the park wall.'

We had practised dropping from trees and walls, and landing like paratroopers.

'Geronimo!'

Terry dropped and rolled. He was unscathed and grinning.

'Yo' could gerra job in the circus, Tez.'

We gathered up the conkers and scampered home.

Richard took all the conkers so that he could perform 'magic' on them.

'No, it's your idea. You have to ask him yourself.'

I knew Mr Pretty very well, but I was still shy of asking a favour. I slouched off to the parade of shops and hung about until I saw Mr Pretty tidying the display outside the greengrocery.

He listened to my request. I tried not to gabble too quickly. He seemed amused.

'Yes, Christopher, I think we can find you something. Pop down on Friday and talk to Janet.'

It was as easy as that. I wondered how the other two were fairing.

I set about making some posters. Suitable oblongs were cut from an old wall-paper roll. On the plain side I wrote with a paint brush:

GRAND CONKER COMPETITION
THIS SATURDAY
ON HATHERN GREEN 10 TO 12
PRIZES
JUNIORS ONLY

It took ages. I made many mistakes and had to start afresh. Once the first good copy was complete it was relatively easy to produce seven more. There seemed to be more rejected duds though, and the *Quink* ink was almost empty when I had finished.

The idea was to attach them to the railings. They would be there several days. I hoped that it didn't rain or the big kids didn't pull them off.

My Father suggested folding the sides around the metal railings and gluing them.

During the week at school contestants were invited by word of mouth, 'Pass it on.'

There seemed to be considerable interest especially in the prizes. Rumours buzzed about as to what the prizes would actually be. By Thursday tea-time I was beginning to get a little anxious. I was the only one who had a definite prize: even though I didn't know what it actually was. There was also no evidence of super conkers.

After tea I went out to check on the posters. It had been a hard and tedious job gluing them into place. Only one had come unstuck on one side and was flapping like a flag.

I met with Terry who had a small package in his hand.

'Hey up, Chrisser. I gorra nuvver prize'. He held the package for me to see the contents.

Inside the cardboard package was a brass bell for an office desk.

'That's nice. Where did you get it?'

Terry beamed, 'Mester Atherley at the post-office was gonna chuck it out. He's got a new 'lectric buzzer.'

I quite liked the brass bell, but I could imagine Richard's disdain.

'Has Richard got a prize yet?'

We knocked on Richard's back door.

Richard bounced out. He had a small paper bag. He was beaming.

'These are super conkers. Prize winners.'

Terry and I looked into the open bag. I was slightly taken aback. There were three conkers: they looked quite ordinary. Richard pulled one out by its string.

'They are super conkers 'cos I varnished them. Loads of times. I borrowed arh Alan's modellin' varnish. I ginnum free coats of varnish every day fer the last free days. They're armour plated. And the beauty of it is it can't be seen.'

We marvelled at his ingenuity.

'We'll smash all the other conkers and win the prizes. What yo' got.?'

Terry showed the brass bell. Richard showed his disdain.

'Well I 'ope yo' win that Tez, 'cos it's no good to me.'

'I wouldn't mind winning it.'

Richard gave me a pitying look, 'What yo' got then, Chrisser?'

'Mr Pretty promised me something for Friday ~ I don't know what.'

Richard scowled, but his scowling was cut short by Terry.

'What prize 'ave yo' got, Rich?'

Richard beamed again. 'The best prize. I was talkin' to Mester Spears abaht the competition. He said he would give us ten bob.'

He paused to let that sink in.

'Ten shillings?'

'Yeah, great innit? We'll mek that first prize. And I'm goin' t'win it.'

Ten shillings was twenty weeks pocket money for me. I suddenly began to worry that the elderly and frail Mr Spears, who lived in our Close, would change his mind or forget.

'Where's the money now?'

'Mester Spears said he'll bring it dahn on Sat'day morning.'

Terry and I took our conkers from the bag as though they were cyanide pills.

My conker was truly very smooth. It still had a faint chemical smell. I put it into my right hand trouser pocket. Into the left I put my own ordinary conker. It was just before five o'clock on the Friday.

'What have you got there, Chick?'

I held the fruit box out for my Mother to see.

'Ooh, how nice, a box of fruit. Looks like you've got two of every sort. Just right for the Ark.'

I wasn't so delighted. Richard would be appalled when he saw Mr Pretty's contribution. I liked fruit, but a box full didn't seem suitable as a prize. We had run out of time.

Even before the allotted hour children had begun to gather. Richard was there with a little camp table just inside the arena. I had been right about his reaction to the box of fruit. He put it on the table along with Terry's bell. He was scanning faces, looking for Mr Spears.

'How's Mr Woffington going to get over the railings?'

Mr Woffington was an adult. He would never squeeze through the bent bars. He was an old man. He would never be able to climb over.

For an answer Terry appeared just ahead of Mr Woffington. Terry was carrying a dining chair. It was for the judge to sit on and watch the proceedings through the bars. It was five to ten and there were dozens of eager kids swinging conkers. They squeezed through onto the grass. Their places at the railings were taken by curious adults and a sprinkle of bemused secondary children. Dead on ten o'clock Richard slapped his hand down several times on the brass bell. The masses quietened.

'Welcome to this grand conker contest. There are prizes to be won.'

Mr Spears had still not shown up. I had sense of disaster. I checked the nearest exit.

'Mester Woffington will be the judge. He'll start it off.'

A few adults clapped as Mr Woffington stood up.

'Hello boys and girls.' Astonishingly there were some girls. I spotted Lorraine and Julia. There was no sign of the lovely Barbara *Grey Eyes*. I knew most of the boys. There were some from our school who lived in Beeston. There were a lot of children. I guessed about sixty.

Richard said quietly, 'Hey, we should've charged an entrance fee. Freppence each. That would mek us…'

I did the arithmetic, 'One pound three shillings and four pence.'

'In a moment I would like you to get into pairs for the first round. If you are a winner go and stand over there, and if you are a loser over here.'

As I followed his hand signals I spotted Mr and Mrs Spears. Mr Spears handed Mr Woffington an envelope. He in turn stretched through the railings and put the envelope on the table. We had decided that the ten shillings would be the first prize, the shiny bell the second, and the box of fruit the third.

'If someone doesn't have a partner, they can have a go at my conker.'

So, everything was sorted, the sun was shining and the prizes were in the bag.

I selected a contestant. I held my closed hands for Alan to choose. He chose correctly and got first swing. On the fourth collision Alan's conker shattered. He moved to the losers' side and I moved to the winners'. Whilst the first round was finishing I selected another contestant. Julia was delighted. Terry and Richard both were through to the second round. The super conkers were doing well. It bothered me a little that it might be cheating. It was too late to use my ordinary conker. No 'swaps' were allowed.

I squared up to Julia. She chose the correct fist and got first swing.

'My brother got me this conker.'

Her first strike nearly pulled my conker from my hand. She grinned. My hit was a glancing blow. Her second hit was fatal. My conker was broken in two. One half remained on the shoelace the other flew away. The conker was not the only thing shattered. I could hardly believe what had happened. Julia was laughing.

The contestants separated again. As I moved towards the losers' end I saw Terry. He looked dejected. There was an empty string still in his hand.

'It broke. Keith hit only once, an' it broke in lickle bits.'

I looked for Richard. He was not with the losers. If his conker was the same as ours he soon would be.

The contesting parties were reduced to four: Richard, Robert Pickard, Adam Young and Julia. The two finalists would get the first and second prizes. The two losers would fight it out with fresh conkers supplied by Mr Woffington. There seemed to be more adults watching now. The kids started chanting the name of their favourite. Mr Woffington stood up and tossed a coin a couple of times. This was to see who was opposite who in the semi-final. Richard was to play Adam, and Julia was paired with Robert. Robert looked gleeful. Adam was passive. Julia just smiled. Richard scowled. He had seen that Terry's and my conkers had shattered.

The semi-final began. It was only twenty to eleven. The crowd roared when Adam's conker disintegrated. There was second louder roar when Robert was left holding a length of knotted string.

Robert and Adam were supplied with fresh conkers. They stood like a couple of prize-fighters ~ which they were. It didn't take long for Robert to leap up gleefully. He had secured the third prize.

Now it was the final. I imagined the turmoil inside Richard. It would be an utter disaster if he lost out to a *girl* and missed the first prize.

The tension mounted. The crowd was still and quiet. As the two finalists faced each other ready to do battle, the chanting started. The calls were evenly balanced. Richard had quite a few enemies who chanted for Julia. If she won, Richard was most likely to thump her and snatch the ten shillings. He flashed a grin and made a 'V' sign. Julia scratched her nose.

Julia had the first strike. Richard's conker twirled around his fist. He uttered a triumphant gasp when his conker slammed into Julia's. It was wishful thinking and totally out of place. Julia's second strike destroyed the super conker. The crowd gasped, then shrieked. The adults applauded. I felt sorry for Richard: he had been trounced in front of many witnesses. Julia beamed.

Mr Woffington handed out the prizes. Robert, eating a banana, carried off Mr Pretty's box. Julia blushed with delight on opening the envelope and finding a brown ten shilling note. Richard stood awkwardly holding the brass bell down by his side.

Terry and I gingerly approached Richard as the on-lookers began to depart for their lunches.

'Friggin' 'ell. I lost out to that ginger lump. S'not fair. I should 'ave the ten bob. Not her.'

For a moment I thought he was going to cry. Instead he turned to me with a wistful smile.

'Yo' ave it, Chrisser. Yo' like it an' I don' need it.'

I took the brass bell happily.

Terry was eating an apple, 'Robert ginnit me.'

As we squeezed through the railings I saw Julia with her friends heading towards Woffington's sweet shop.

We walked back up our street with hardly a word until Terry said, 'Soon be bonfire night. We could mek a guy…'

Richard the Conkerer's reply was rather rude.

Saving the Eagles

'And that's an end to it.'

I couldn't believe that this was someone who professed to love me. I wanted to go on pleading, but as usual I had nothing to say. She turned away into her bedroom. She was in a hurry. I sat down on my bed and stared at the deep pile. After all this time I was supposed to just bin them?

The pile was a collection of *Eagle* comics, lovingly collected from November 1955 to March 1958. One hundred and seventy issues slumbered by my bed. The pile was about a foot deep. The comics contained three hundred and forty glossy full colour pages of Dan Dare, Pilot of the Future and leader of an intrepid band of Space Fleet personnel. Colonel Dare had struggled with many alien foes and saved Earth several times.

The *Eagle* was a different sort of comic. It had style. This comic was produced to counter- balance the ghastly stuff flooding in from America. Britain's own popular comics were simple funnies with limited colour. The *Eagle* won the market with its quality production and exciting storylines. Dan Dare, in full colour, occupied the first two pages.

I had come across the *Eagle* whilst waiting my turn at the barbers. Also my older cousin had sent a couple of the comics with other newspapers from Yorkshire. The glimpses of the strange future world were fascinating. The storyline was baffling, as it was a continuing drama. Why were all those Thorks massacred on Saturn?

The clincher, for me, was when I accompanied my Mother during a half term holiday. She was house cleaning for the Atherley's who ran the local pharmacy. She gained permission for me to look at Robert's Hornby 00 model railway. It was fantastic. I knew immediately what I wanted for Christmas. At the same time I saw a pile of *Eagles* in Robert's room. Robert had them all, right from the first issue in April 1950. My Father agreed to amend the delivery from Mr Leek, the newsagent, on condition that *Mickey Mouse Weekly* and *Radio Fun* were dispensed with.

My pile of *Eagle*s gradually grew. My Father constructed a suitable bedside cabinet to house the treasures. It was made from a couple of wooden orange crates covered with wallpaper.

'You can't take everything. We've got to get rid of the junk. We are going to a new house and we don't want to clutter it up with old stuff. You've read them all anyway. You are not taking them.'

My Mother was in a flap as the new house had been sprung on us. My parents had lived in this council house since they were first married just before the war. They didn't have any ambition, or money, to move elsewhere. It was the behaviour of the new neighbours that encouraged my Parents to request a transfer to another address. The request was actioned very quickly. We went to view a house which was much younger than the present one. It was miles away the other side of the river. I was delighted because it had three bedrooms. The spare bedroom would be just right for my expanding model railway.

The Council Housing Officer said that we should move before Easter. This was in barely three weeks' time. The new house was unoccupied, and our present house had nearly twenty years of accumulation. It wasn't much, but my Parents had little experience of house-moving. They both worked full-time, so sorting and packing was done in the evenings and at the weekends.

I was sad to see the garden shed being dismantled for sale. It had been a fort, a space ship, a tank and a submarine. I had slept in it too.

'How would we get it to the new house?'

I didn't see why it couldn't go on the Co-op van with everything else. My request to ride in the back of the van was turned down too.

The toy soldiers and plastic models fitted into a cardboard box. Later I would generously give the soldiers to my young cousin. These things did not weigh much. The *Eagles* did.

Mother was disposing of her magazines, old tea towels and things which were never used. In her mind the *Eagles* belonged with them.

'We'll have to get some new curtains, Ken. These won't be long enough.'

'Stop flapping, Bridget, it can wait till we get there.'

Whilst my Parents were out working I was at school. I was in the first year of Grammar School. I was initially proud to have passed the 11+ exam and to having progressed to making two bus journeys to the revered hall of enlightenment.

Being a Grammar School pupil I was cut off from my playmates of primary days. My new friends were spread across the city. At school the advice from Keith was, 'Chuck 'em, what do you want o'd comics for?'

Tony advocated smuggling them to their new home. Neither suggestion was helpful.

We didn't have a car, and I didn't know anyone who had one and was likely to help. I thought of taking a few at a time on the bus. That would mean several journeys on two buses, humping the comics and storing them near the new house. It had all the hall-marks of impossible. It would take days.

It was Saturday, I went for a walk. Our local parade of shops was close and it wasn't raining. I might bump into Mike. We had not been together since his family moved to Long Eaton. Mike's family were well off and had good connections. He was nowhere near his father's two shops. I would have phoned him if I had the courage, or knew his number, or even knew how to use a phone.

'Hey-up, if it ain't o'd Chrisser.'

In my gloomy mood I had failed to spot someone I'd rather avoid.

'I heard yo' was movin'. Where yo' goin'?'

I hadn't spoken to Richard since our last excursion together when he had stolen a Mars Bar and suggested that we did something obnoxious with a girl I knew. He had been around through my primary years. Richard was destined to be a first class villain. Terry was in tow as usual. Terry just grinned like the simpleton that he was. He was destined to be a third class villain.

'We are moving to Clifton Estate.' I wasn't prepared to tell him anymore as he just might turn up.

'Yo' don't look very 'appy abaht it. Gonna miss us, eh?'

Terry hoisted his jeans that were a size too big. I noticed that Richard was wearing narrow long trousers now.

'No, I mean yes… It's my *Eagles*.' I could have bitten off my tongue.

The budding villains looked perplexed.

'The comic. *Eagle*. Dan Dare.'

Richard grinned, 'Still reading lickle kids' stuff?'

Terry had still not started to read properly. He liked the pictures in the more dubious publications.

'Yeah, the *Eagle*'s good. I've got hundreds of them, but I'm not allowed to take them.'

'So what?'

'I want to keep them.'

'Why can't yo' tek 'em?'

'She, Mum, says they're junk.'

Richard's eyes twinkled, 'What's it worf?'

'What?'

'Ah much would yo' pay fer me and Tez to gerrem to the new 'ouse?'

I knew he wasn't joking. If there was money to be made he was right there.

I shook my head, 'It's too far. There are too many. I haven't got any money.'

Richard knew that was a lie, 'Me an Tez can do it, can't we?' He nudged the sidekick, 'Ah.'

I shook my head again. I really didn't want these two involved.

'Well, if yo' change yer mind…'

Time was running out. I called on Geoff. We had built a trolley together. I had given it to him when I lost interest. We hadn't made contact for months. Mrs Wheatley said he was out with a friend.

Back home there was nothing suitable to put the comics in. The suitcases were full of clothes. I thought to reduce the comics to just the front page with scissors, but that would be sacrilege. After another half hour of fretting, I went looking for Richard.

'How you goin' to do it?'

He grinned. There had been enough time for a plan to be hatched. He responded with his own question, 'How much can you pay?'

The money was in my pocket. I had emptied my money box. There was a savings account at the TSB, but that was for something special in the future, according to my Mother. What counted as special and how far into the future was never made clear. Any withdrawals would be noticed. My pocket money accumulated because very little was spent.

'Three quid?'

He grimaced and made a sucking noise, 'It's a big job. Tek a lotta effort. An there's Tez. Not worf doing fo' free quid.'

'Five.' My existing comics had a face value of little over five pounds.

'Nah yo' talking. Two pahn, ten bob nah, an' the ovver when it's done. Deal?'

He spat on his right palm and held it out. I didn't take it.

'How you goin' to do it?'

'Well, me an Tez are gonna borrer Weetabix's trolley and roll 'em over Clifton.'

'It's five miles. You can't push a trolley five miles!'

'Who said owt abaht pushin'? We're gonna pull it.'

I mustered my best expression of disbelief and shook my head.

'We're gonna pull it wiv our Alan's bike. He owes me a big one, so he'll lend it.'

It must have been very big. Alan treasured his bike and would normally not lend anything to his younger brother.

'Deal,' and I slapped his palm. He counted the money which was mostly in coins.

It wasn't going to work. My pocket money was thrown away on some hare-brained scheme. If, by some amazing stroke of luck, the *Eagles* arrived, I would have to produce another two pounds and ten shillings which I hadn't got.

'Right. Tell us when yo' movin' and we can get crackin'.'

What if it was raining? What if Geoff wouldn't lend them the trolley? What if Alan refused to lend the bike? What if they got lost? What if my Parents found out? What if...

The cash balance was not a problem. I knew where 'rainy day' money was secreted. It wouldn't be theft, the money would be returned... eventually. The nagging problem was how to get the comics into the house, and where to hide them until *they* were occupied with something more important.

The rehearsal was not a hundred percent convincing. The Raleigh bike was propped on its kick stand. A length of washing line was secured to the saddle bar. The other end was lashed to the front axle of the trolley. The idea was that Richard would peddle whilst Terry pushed at the back like he was working a dog sled in Alaska. When sufficient progress was made Terry had to jump aboard. I tried to imagine him performing this difficult feat with the trolley driver's space being taken up with the pile of comics. It was necessary to practise stopping several times so that the trolley didn't catch up with the back wheel of the bike. The trolley brakes were very primitive. Alan's legs were longer than Richard's so the saddle would have to be lowered.

'What if it rains?'

Richard grinned, 'We get wet. The comics are gonna be safe under a piece of tarp.'

I tried to imagine them proceeding over the much heralded and recently opened road bridge over the river. I began to realise that the comics would never be seen again and the River Police would be dipping for the bodies of two children.

Removal day was Saturday. Mother wouldn't dream of moving on a Friday.

'Friday flit, short sit.'

We spirited the comics out of the house when my parents were out. It didn't take three of us very long to take sheaves of comics down stairs and load them onto the trolley. The driver's cushion had been replaced with a piece of tarpaulin. The tarpaulin was lashed over with twine. The trolley was taken to be parked in Richard's back garden. His parents had little interest in his doings, as long as the police were not involved. I gave Richard the address and a simple hand drawn map.

The home was packed, but I still had to go to school on the Friday. We had fish and chips from the chippie for tea. I could hardly sleep.

At nine o'clock the Co-op van arrived. My Father supervised the loading whilst Mother cleaned the emptied rooms. There were no fond farewells, we were too busy. I wanted to slip off and see if the comics had started on their journey, but thought it wiser to stay. We locked up and went to catch the bus into the city. It felt strange making this journey for the last time. It felt strange catching a different bus to the new estate. The blue South Notts buses continued to use the old winding route, but the green City fleet had been rerouted to make use of the brand new bridge. It was a real experience sitting on the top deck as the bus turned onto the ramp. There would be a spectacular view of the river.

'What do those silly beggars think they're doing?'

We had chosen the front seats. The bus was steadily gaining on two boys riding a strange contraption. The bus slowed as there was no room to overtake.

'They ought to have more sense. They could get killed.'

My Mother gasped, 'It's Richard, Richard Church and another boy. What are they doing all this way over here?'

I could have told her.

The contraption began to speed up as it cleared the top of the span. It positively zoomed down the steep turn off the bridge. The road we wanted curled down and under the bridge. There were traffic lights where it joined the old main road. These were ignored. This caused a fanfare of indignant horns. When the lights turned to green our bus was able to catch them up. Over on the right was a cycle lane which they had moved into. As the bus drew level with the dynamic duo, the driver bipped the horn. Richard gave a two finger salute. Terry had one foot on the trolley, the other was pounding the tarmac. They both had flushed complexions. We left them struggling up the long incline to the estate. I guessed that they must have started quite early.

The van was waiting outside number 81. The crew dropped their cigarettes as soon as the doors were unlocked and began taking the goods in. We had seen the empty house a while back. Mother reckoned it needed a good clean. Father looked ruefully at the navy-blue kitchen ceiling and calculated how many coats of white it would need.

There were three bedrooms. My parents had the larger front bedroom with the built-in cupboard. I chose the other front bedroom because it was separated from them by the stair-well. The third room at the back would be my den where the model railway was to be built.

From time to time I slipped out onto the street looking for the *Eagles*. The gaggle of inquisitive local children had melted away. On the third venture I spotted a figure that I recognised. It was Richard wandering nonchalantly towards me. There was no sign of the *Eagles*. He stopped short of the house and beckoned.

'Fought it best not to arrive where you' mam can see.' He was grinning.

'Where's Terry?'

'Rahn the corner guardin' the load.'

'We saw you on the bridge. What was it like? When did you start out?'

He shrugged. 'Started abaht nine. It was OK when we got the 'ang of it. Tez moaned a lot. Be easier goin' back.'

They had been travelling for about three hours. Lunch had been missed. They might get back for tea.

'So, what we goin' to do wiv the comics, Chrisser?'

I had given this much thought, but not come up with a brilliant idea, or any idea. I didn't know anyone in the neighbourhood yet. There was nowhere outside safe enough from curious fingers and the weather.

'I'll get a box. There will be some empty ones by now. I'll smuggle them in a few at a time.'

'What, we gonna haf ter wait while yo' ferry 'em in dribs?'

'You can't help. I'll be as quick as I can. I can get you something to eat.'

He grinned. 'OK, an' don't ferget the dosh.'

There were some chocolate biscuits left by the removals men. I scooped them up. My parents were upstairs fitting beds together. Outside the back door were cardboard boxes that had been emptied. I chose two and spirited them away.

Richard wasn't there. I found them both a few yards away around the corner. Terry brightened when I produced the biscuits. I pulled off a handy wad of comics and placed them in a flat box.

'I'll be back in a tick.'

They were still upstairs. I tip-toed up and turned left into my room. My bed was made up. The box fitted. Stealthily I retraced my steps and collected another box from the yard. This box was exchanged for another which had comics. This second box was left under my bed with the first. I was beginning to feel triumphant.

'What have you got there?'

I was four steps up and she was stood at the top. It was an innocent question, but I felt like I was being grilled. I tried to hold the box as though there was nothing in it.

'It's an empty from the yard. I thought I'd get rid of some rubbish.'

'Don't put it in the bin, it'll get full, leave it at the side.'

When she had gone back to assisting my Father, I decanted the comics onto the first pile. There had to be two piles under my bed to suit the clearance. I made three more trips. Richard was getting a little tetchy. Terry had wolfed the last of the biscuits and now had a chocolate moustache. The last trip was made. I pushed the two *Eagle* piles as far back as they would go. They were not visible to a standing person. Quickly I shoved some wrapping paper in the empty box and took it down to the dustbin.

'Put the kettle on, love.'

'OK,' But I raced off to the delivery boys.

Terry was sat in the trolley. Richard was lolling against a gate post. I pulled the money out before he asked. This time it was notes. He examined it as though he wasn't sure it was real.

'C'mon, Tez we're off'. To me he said, 'Fanks. See yo'. Traa.'

I watched them ride off, Richard pedalling and Terry scooting.

'I thought I asked you to put the kettle on.'

'Sorry, I forgot to light the gas.'

I thought this would be a good time to ingratiate myself by volunteering to keep my room clean and tidy.

I don't know anything about the return journey or how much Terry was paid. There was no further contact except for a brief chance meeting in the city. I was with my parents so nothing was said about the *Eagles*. The treasured comics slept under my bed. They were handled only to put them back in order. They were not added to. Father said that if I wanted a comic I would have to buy it myself. It didn't seem to matter though anymore what Dan Dare was doing. He was a Pilot of the Future, but he felt like history. There were other interests looming.

'Ken. I think I'm going mad.'

He looked at me and winked, 'I can believe that.'

'I'm sure I had twenty pounds in the kitty. Now there's twenty three. Have you put some more in?'

'Not me. You've spent all my spare cash on curtains. P'raps it was our Sunshine.'

I turned away in case I was blushing.

'You should be happy, Bridget.'

'I am.' She was beaming. 'Are you happy, Chick?'

I shrugged and gave a noncommittal answer.

'What would make you really happy?'

This was a rare offer, she must have been intoxicated with the new house. A Hornby model 'Eight-Freight' locomotive rattled through my mind.

'Slim-fit black trousers?'

The new curtains arrived in the new-fangled polythene bags. These I acquired as they were just the right size. When my parents were both out, the *Eagles* were transferred to a distant corner of the loft space. This took some effort as there was only a decorator's step ladder available and the loft was not boarded. They are probably still there.

Snow Snow Quick Quick Snow

'It's too cold to snow.'

She was right, but then the weather changed.

It had been a great struggle. He didn't possess really suitable tools and his knowledge of carpentry was minimal. I watched my Father fit the second-hand storm-door to the open back porch. The Harrisons, two doors away, had up-graded their storm-door and we had acquired their inferior model. The door was in two halves with the top panels of both glazed. Of course, it was painted a dismal Corporation green. It was a good fit as all the Council houses were virtually the same. All that was necessary was to secure the frame with eight wood screws. Hand drilling into brick work was the hard bit.

'That looks good, Ken.'

My Father grinned, 'Yes, Bridget, but let's see if it works.'

It did. He opened and closed the two halves several times to prove it.

After a mug of tea, he set about finishing the job by checking the two vertical bolts and the one larger one across the centre. There was no lock. I was allowed to squidge putty into any gaps around the frame.

'Now we're ready for Old Man Winter.'

I recalled previous winters when the weather pressed into the open porch. The back door mat was soaked by rain. A couple of times snow had had to be shovelled out. It was no fun visiting the toilet which, whilst part of the house, was accessed through the kitchen door and across the square yard of open porch.

Not a moment too soon. The cold weather was upon us. In winter the house was easily chilled. There was only a coal-fed fire place in the living room. My Parents' bedroom had a smaller open fire place, but it was never used. The chill in the bedroom was relieved with a two-bar electric fire. This was switched on ten minutes before bedtime. My bedroom was heated with the same appliance.

Sometimes in the morning my breath had condensed onto the window panes and frozen into delightful crystal patterns. The floor lino was icy. So getting ready for bed was done rapidly standing on a small rug. If it was really cold I was told to keep my socks on. A hot water bottle made the bed possible. After a few minutes I would be warm under the layers of brushed cotton sheet, ex-army blanket, counterpane and candlewick bedspread.

It had been very cold for several weeks. I went to school under solid grey skies clothed in a balaclava helmet, gloves, scarf, gabardine raincoat, pullover, flannel shirt and woolly vest. Even so my knees were chilled. I wore grey short trousers. I did possess a pair of jeans but it was unthinkable to wear these to school. The best I could do was to pull up the turndown tops to my long socks.

School was good. The boiler house provided central heating in the huge pipe system.

It was too cold to snow. She was correct, but the weather changed. I should have paid more attention to the wireless.

'It's snowing at your Grand-dad's.'

It started in the afternoon at playtime. The grey sky had become much more menacing. Children began to shriek as huge white flakes struggled Earth-wards. Mr Hall looked desperately at his watch as children hurtled about trying to catch Heaven's gifts.

The last quarter of the school day was electric. We were advised to go straight home as the snow was settling fast. It was about two inches deep at home time. Some snow balls were flung, but most children scurried home.

My garden was blotted out.

'I suppose you're happy now, Chick.'

I nodded enthusiastically. After a cup of tea I watched the relentless descent through the new storm-door windows.

'Gordon Bennet! That was no fun.'

My Father was standing in the porch batting snow from his cap and demob raincoat. He had pedalled from work in the dark and the blizzard.

'Good job we got these doors.'

It continued snowing. The weather forecast warned of more snow: especially for the East Midlands.

'You'd better wear your wellies today.'

It was now four inches thick in the back yard. There were tracks where my Father had gone to work for eight o'clock.

Silence reigned. The snow baffled any sound and there were few people about. Lorraine Hooley was wearing a knitted hat with an enormous pom-pom.

'Chrisser!'

Richard and Terry caught me up. Terry also wore a balaclava. He had the benefit of his knees being covered by jeans. His raincoat was far too big: the sleeves had to be turned up. Richard was in his usual outfit of grey flannel short legged suit, but now with a hefty brown pullover beneath the jacket. He had gloves and scarf. Terry didn't, his nose dripped.

'Great, innit?'

We were ushered straight into school and instructed to leave the snow outside. Half my class was missing. At playtime the comics came out of the cupboard. At mid-day those children who went home for lunch were told not to come back in the afternoon. The school would be closed the following day too.

At twelve o'clock I went home as usual, with Richard and Terry. I had cottage pie with my Mother at the kitchen table.

'Your Dad's taken a packed lunch today. He reckoned it would be too difficult to come home at lunchtime.'

After lunch there was a debate about whether it would be sensible to play outside. I won with a promise not to bring any snow back in. I rolled snow into large lumps. The lumps were stacked to make a snowman. There was some ambition to make the figure more realistic this year. I got as far as fitting arms akimbo and cutting out a slot to suggest separate legs. I gave up because the falling snow was so intense. I returned to the warm kitchen.

'You're home early,' she said glancing at the wall clock.

My Father was in the porch batting off snow at twenty-five past four.

'Yes, the factories closed early, sent everyone home.'

There was no let up. Sometimes it thinned out, but never really stopped.

'Our lad's not going to school tomorrow. Are you going to work?'

'Yes, but they said it was OK if we clocked in late, and we're all home at lunchtime. The weather forecast said there's more to come.'

My Father came home early on Friday. After lunch he said we had a job to do.

Being a good citizen he reckoned to clear the paths around our house. I was the apprentice. We cleared the snow from the back door to the dust bin and coalhouse door. Next was the path leading to the Close. Mr Daykin, our neighbour, was equally responsible but he has not a good citizen.

'Here, take the spade and do Mrs Bays' front path.'

Previously we had done this together, but now it was all mine. I started at the front gate and worked towards the front door. The elderly widow waved and smiled through her living room window. I felt very proud.

Just as I was about to retreat, Richard and Terry appeared in the Close.

'Ah much she gi'in' yo'?'

I must have looked blank.

'Ah much for cleaning the paff?'

'Nothing. We always do it. She's an old lady.'

Richard pulled a face. 'Yeah, well, that's nice on yo'. But we could mek some dosh shifting snow.'

His eyes gleamed as he unfolded the scheme.

'Listen, yo' me an' Tez could be a team off'rin' to shift snow. Whatdya fink?'

Terry was nodding vigorously.

'People usually clean their own paths around here.'

'Yeah, rahn 'ere they do. I was finking of doing posh 'ouses.'

'Wollaton Vale?'

'That's jus' what I was finkin'. They got posh cars in driveways. Half a dollar to clean the drive?'

'That's a bit much…'

'OK, say two bob an' the paff to the back door.'

It sounded fine, but with Richard's schemes it was wise to be cautious.

'You' gorra spade, ah can get one, an' Tez 'as gorra shovel.'

I nodded.

'Right tomorra. Meet yo' at the lamppost at nine.'

The project was explained to my Parents. My Mother was dubious, but my Father said that it was the same as bobbing and jobbing.

'Lunch at one, mind. And don't do anything silly.'

Usually it took only a few minutes to skip through the estate and over Derby Road to get to the affluent area of Wollaton Vale. Now it was hard going trudging through the deep snow. Some good citizens had made an effort to clear the paths but later falls had covered their efforts. There was nobody about and it was very quiet.

We passed the first house because the driveway had been cleared recently.

'Good mornin', sir, we are offerin' to clear your paffs and drive for *only* two shillin.'

Terry and I stood like soldiers with our tools shouldered whilst Richard did the sales talk. I was a little surprised when the man agreed. We set to digging and shovelling with gusto. It was hard work. The job was about done after 40 minutes according to the watch my Mother had provided.

'Best get the dosh before no more bleddy snow comes again.'

Richard rang the door-bell.

I had done a quick calculation in my head. Twenty minutes here and twenty back home would leave three hours and twenty minutes for slaving. This first job had taken 40 minutes. If 5 minutes was allowed between jobs, we could do about another four jobs. We would earn ten shillings and be worn out. The take-home pay would be a princely three shillings and four pence each.

Richard was grinning and flicking the two shilling piece in the air.

'If we work to dinner time we'll get three shillings and four pence each.'

Richard caught the coin and frowned, 'Yo' sure, Chrisser?'

Terry's cheeks were flushed and his nose dripped. Flakes of snow began landing on his black balaclava.

Richard's tongue clicked. 'Best get cracking then.'

We trudged to the next snow covered driveway.

The man wanted us to scrape the snow off his car which had not been put in the garage. He gave us a soft broom and a dustpan and brush as he didn't want the paintwork scratched. We gave Terry the dustpan and brush because he was looking tired.

Doing Mrs Bays' path was fun. Doing the driveways was something else. It was hard and tedious. The snow started to fall in earnest.

Several people were not at home or couldn't be bothered answering the door. We collected a third florin. I was hoping the other two would suggest abandoning the project. Terry became quieter, but Richard continued to wear his ready grin.

We moved to the next customer. I glanced at my watch. There was still some time left, but I'd had enough. Terry was drooping.

'Yo' alright, Tez.'

He looked like an extra from film about *Stalingrad*.

'No, don't feel good, aching all over.'

'OK, Tez, we'll just do this one. Mek it the las' one.'

Terry grunted. I felt elated.

There was a snow covered car which was not mentioned when the price was agreed. Spades and shovel set to work. Snow was tossed onto where we imagined a lawn. Something was on my blade of snow. It was maroon with a brass clip.

'Whatcha got, Chrisser?'

'Looks like a purse.'

Richard moved quickly. He flicked it open. There was a partition for paper money. The green pound notes showed up well on the maroon leather. Richard pulled the purse to his chest and glanced around.

'Jesus, it's full of bleddy onecers.'

Terry seemed to brighten for a moment.

'The lady who lives here must have dropped it.'

Richard gave his crafty grin, 'Finders keepers.'

'You can't keep that. It belongs to someone else.'

He scowled back, 'We'll share it. Meks the mornin' wo'th it.'

'S'not yorn. Give it back.'

'Shurrup, Tez. Yo'll get your share.'

'No, it's stealing. Give it back.'

'Friggin' 'ell.' Richard flung the purse at me.

I rang the doorbell.

'Have you finished already?'

'No, mister, but we found this in the snow near the car.'

His eyes lit up. 'That's my wife's. She's been frantic looking for it. Thank you.'

He turned and called back into the house, 'Irene your purse is back. The snow-boys found it.'

She was delighted. 'Better give them a reward, Brian.'

Brian pulled some change from his pocket, and then changed his mind. The coins were pocketed and he fished out a ten shilling note from his wallet. He handed it to me. I could see Richard's mouth moving. I guessed he was about to ask for payment for snow clearance too.

'Thank you, sir. That's very generous.'

'That's five shillings and four pence each. I'll change the note at Woffington's.'

Richard sighed. He carried Terry's shovel because Terry was whimpering and dragging his feet. It was hard trudging back home with the snow up to our knees. There were hardly any new tracks and our earlier tracks had disappeared. After splitting the money at the sweet shop we saw Terry to his house.

I'd almost forgotten about the storm doors, so it was a bit of a surprise when I turned the corner of our house.

'Leave it out there. Bring the spade in. Your Dad'll be needing it later.'

The kitchen was beautifully warm from the cooking on the gas stove.

'Well, how did you get on?'

'We got five bob each. I found a purse. I think Terry's got the flu.'

'Ken, Captain Scott's back and I'm serving now.'

Rissoles, peas and chips lathered in ketchup never tasted so good.

Springing Mickey

Mickey was a prisoner. He was detained in a cell. It was solitary confinement. Nobody spoke his language. He brooded alone for endless hours. Sometimes he was the centre of attention. He would be offered strange food to augment his plain repetitive diet. Happiness must have long since departed.

Some Sundays we would walk to the *Maypole* in Beeston for a drink before lunch. Or we might stroll to the *Admiral Rodney* in Wollaton. On the way my Father and Uncle Jim talked of putting the world to rights. I tagged along trying to understand the conversation. It was of little use talking to my cousin Clive who was five years my junior and not interested in *Meccano* or the latest *Herald* toy soldiers. The soldiers were one shilling and three pence each. I had calculated that it would take a year to achieve the set. This might be shortened by donations of cash on my birthday, but it was a long time to my next birthday.

Today was different. Uncle Jim suggested that we try a pub on Derby Road by Abbey Bridge. He said it would be only five minutes on the bus.

'Make sure you're back by quart to two,' said my Mother.

She and Aunty Dot were busy in the kitchen. I think they quite liked a good gossip about medical matters and fashion, with the men and the children out of the way.

It was the simplest thing to catch the 19 from its terminus at the end of our street. It was bound for the city and had to cross Abbey Bridge. It took just five minutes.

I recognised the pub from previous trips into town for shopping. The pub faced the main road. We walked past the front and along to the side garden where there were some rustic tables and chairs and a couple of swings. The garden deteriorated towards a wooden fence which marked the railway line. We sat at one of the tables whilst Jim went inside to collect the drinks. Other families with children were in the garden. Many of them were gathered around a shed at the end of the pub building. Obviously there was something to see. I went over to see. The shed had a wire grill on one side. Through the grill I could see some creature sitting on a box. It was a monkey.

'C'mon Mickeh, ay a crisp.'

A father was attempting to impress his two girls by poking a crisp through the grill. The monkey took the crisp and ate it quickly. This delighted the audience. The floor of the cage was covered in sawdust. A couple of gnarled branches were fastened across the space. In one corner, on a raised platform, was an open box with a tatty blanket. Mickey picked up a bottle, the sort that babies have, and sucked the pink teat.

'Chris,' my Father called.

On the table were two pints of bitter in straight sided fluted jars and two small bottles of fizzy.

'What's in the shed?' asked my uncle.

'A monkey. He's called Mickey,' I replied.

'Can I see the monkey?' piped up my cousin.

As they went off to look at Mickey, my Father said, 'It's awful keeping a monkey in a hole like that. It shouldn't be allowed. He should be swinging about with his own kind, and not stuck in there.'

I hadn't thought about it before. Pets lived at home. They were treated as part of the family. I had been to a zoo once. The animals were in cages, but the cages were big and full of rocks and trees and ponds. The animals were fed regularly. I wondered if they were happy.

My Father went on, 'It's cruel to take wild animals from their natural places just so we can be amused.'

The next few times, when I was travelling past on the bus, I looked out for Mickey. I saw his little form sitting on the box.

'Urgh, yeah, I've seen Mickey the Monkey,' said Richard, 'I went to me Uncle Jack's in Lenton. He took me.' He laughed and added, 'Me Uncle gin him a drink o'bear through the bars.'

'Did he get drunk?' asked Terry, who then staggered about like a drunken monkey might.

'Nah, on'y had a sip.'

Trying to sound noble, I said, 'My Dad says it's cruel to keep animals like Mickey in a cage.'

'S'on'y a bleddy monkeh,' said Terry.

'Well. I think Chris' dad's right,' said Geoff, 'It *is* cruel. Cats and dogs can roam about...'

'Jut a monkeh!' interrupted Terry. He followed this with his impression of an ape. He pushed his tongue up over his top teeth and pranced about, bent back, swinging his arms from side to side.

'Shurrup, Tez,' said Richard firmly. "Ow'd yo' like to be locked in a cage?'

He was scowling at Terry instead of joining in the clowning. Terry returned to what he considered normal. Richard's face seemed to be radiating. I had seen this several times previously. It signalled inspiration. Usually this sort of brain wave was to do with enhancing Richard's fortunes.

'Mickeh needs saving,' he announced.

He had us hooked, so he carried on, 'Mickeh needs rescuing.' He looked at us expectantly.

'Rescued?' I asked lamely.

'Yeah,' said Richard sounding like he had been planning the D-Day landings for months, 'Break the lock off when nob'dy's lookin' an' lerrim aht.'

'Then what?' said Geoff, 'He'd starve to death or get run over.'

'Tek 'im to a zoo,' suggested Terry who had figured out which way the wind was now blowing.

'No zoos round here,' said Geoff.

'Who's going to get him out?' I asked, and immediately wished I hadn't.

'We are,' declared the self-appointed leader, 'we c'n do it like a commando raid. In an aht quick, snatch the monkeh an' go.'

'Then what?' said Geoff again.

'We'll think of that later, replied Richard, 'now put y'thinkin' caps on an' come up wi' some idehs.'

Terry mimed pulling on his thinking cap. We stood fast for a few moments until it was Terry's brain that spluttered into action.

'Our mam's still gorra pushchair. It's for our Glenys when she 'as a baby. We could get the monkey away in the pushchair.'

'Brilliant,' said Richard sincerely.

'My little sister's clothes might fit him. Dress him up like a baby going for a walk.' said Geoff.

Enthused, I joined in, 'My Dad's got some tools. We'll need them to break the lock.'

Richard was almost dancing when the bell summoned us back into class.

On the way home Geoff began to niggle about what exactly would we do with the freed monkey. I couldn't think of anything, but I had a feeling that Richard would come up with some solution. After all he was a year older than the rest of us.

The solution was to put Mickey into a tea chest (from Pretty's shop) with provisions, and send the chest to Africa. This was where, no doubt, monkeys like Mickey lived. As soon as the chest was opened, Mickey would spring out and swing away through the trees.

This solution was dismissed, even though it had been adapted to having air holes drilled. It was dismissed because we had no idea how many postage stamps would be needed. Also, Geoff had pointed out that Mickey would be uncomfortable in the chest for, probably, weeks.

I suggested that we take him to the PDSA. This was rejected because we would have to explain how we came by a monkey, and he wasn't sick.

We fished around cautiously for ideas. The best came from Julia Billington. Her big brother had a motorbike and sidecar. He took his girlfriend out at the weekends. He might be persuaded to take her to Whipsnade zoo. The monkey would go too. He would be handed over to a better life in a nicer place.

We promised Julia all kinds of things if she would work on her brother. As a sort of down payment we gave her two shillings and a packet of Rollo's (that Richard had pinched from Woffington's). Julia enjoyed the attention and the intrigue.

Now we got down to the fine detail of the operation, *Operation Mickey*. We would catch the bus to Abbey Bridge. The pushchair was to be folded up and placed under the stairs on the bus. If anybody asked, we were taking it to Richard's uncle for his new baby.

The operation was planned for a Saturday because there was school in the week. It would have to be about three o'clock because the pub closed at half past two, and the landlord would be busy tidying up or having a sleep before opening time at six.

I surreptitiously prised some cash from my money box.

'Mum can I go with my friends to Wollaton Park after dinner?'

This was fairly usual, and permissible.

'Yes, but keep away from the lake. Don't talk to strange men. Be back by tea time at five.'

We had agreed to meet at the Abbey Gates stop on Derby Road, where we were less likely to be spotted by neighbours. Richard and

Terry were waiting. Terry had the pushchair already folded. I pulled out a screwdriver and a pair of pliers from under my jumper.

'What, no 'ammer?' Richard said scornfully.

Geoff appeared with a duffle-bag stuffed with toddler's clothes and a baby's bottle.

'Four halves to Abbey Bridge,' said Richard who had now assumed the role of banker as well as leader.

We sat downstairs to keep an eye on the pushchair. I knew it wouldn't take long. The conductor helped lift the pushchair off the platform. The pushchair was unfolded with a little tugging and quiet swearing, and the tools and bag of clothes were hidden under the blanket.

We looked over the fence and down from the ramp of the bridge. It was five minutes to three according to Geoff's *Dan Dare* watch. There was no sign of life around the pub. Behind us some vehicles passed by. Nobody was walking about.

'Let's go!' said the commander firmly.

We advanced down the slope and onto the flat. Casually we paraded past the front of the pub. I felt better after we were away from the windows. We proceeded into the garden. So far, so good. Mickey was watching us. We turned towards him. I glanced around. It was broad daylight, we could easily be seen. Richard examined the lock. 'Giz the screwdriver.'

The lock was a simple arrangement. It would be easy to unscrew the thing from the wood. I glanced around again. Geoff had a little knitted coat ready. Terry was hanging onto the pushchair handle. One screw came away. Richard began on a second screw.

'Hello, boys, come to look at Mickey?'

I almost wet myself. He just appeared. Richard snatched the screw driver down and into his waist band beneath his jacket. He spun round with a huge smile.

'Yes, mester, we woz just on our way with this pushchair to my uncle's house. He lives on Dunlop Avenue. Me antie is havin' a baby. We thought we'd have a look at Mickey. Is that alright?'

The man was in shirt sleeves. He was about my Father's age. He was carrying a bowl of scraps. Geoff carefully had screwed the little coat into a ball behind his back.

'I've come out to feed him. Do you want to watch?'

'Oh, yes please mester. We love monkehs. Don't we?' said Richard with enthusiasm.

'Yes, yes, yes,' we sang, nodding furiously.

The man turned and spoke to Mickey who chattered back. He produced a key and unlocked the cage door. The missing screw seemed not to be noticed. I wondered if Richard would do something really silly now that the door was opening. The bowl was parked inside the cage and the door was locked. When he turned back to us he looked puzzled.

'You know you can't get through to Dunlop Avenue this way. It's a dead end. The railway's in the way. You'll have to go over the bridge.'

'Ah, right. Thanks. We'll do that. Thanks for letting us watch,' said Richard still beaming.

'Thanks, thanks, thanks', chorussed the rest of the commando brigade.

We pushed the pram back onto the slope of the bridge and started walking up. Richard, still smiling, waved back at the pub. 'Bleddy Hell!'

'What now?' asked Geoff.

Richard was not interested in defeat. 'We do it in the dark,' he proclaimed.

My heart sank. The nights were closing in. It was fully dark at six o'clock. I would never be allowed to wander about in the dark without a very good reason.

'Listen,' said the master conspirator, 'Chris and Geoff go to Cubs on Wednesdays. It's six til seven innit?' We nodded. 'Well, me an' Tez will meet you at Abbeh Gates at ten to six. We'll be there by six an' back in less'n hour.'

It sounded good. We had had a sort of practise. One screw was out. What could go wrong?

I was still scared. If it worked out my Father would be proud of me. If it didn't…

Julia was the key. She said that her brother thought it was a bit of a lark. He had agreed to transport Mickey. His girlfriend wouldn't be told until the time. I kissed Julia on the cheek. She blushed. Richard laughed. He gave her some more money and some chocolate. *Operation Mickey* was back on. I was still scared though.

The following Wednesday seemed appropriate. I tried to act normally, but I put on my Cub uniform a little earlier than usual. My Father's tools were hidden under the thick blue jersey. My pocket contained the 'subs' and a little extra. I gave my Mother a special hug just in case I 'didn't come back'. I met Geoff outside his gate and we sprinted up Wingfield Drive past the Cub hut. Richard and Terry were waiting. They both had balaclavas even though it wasn't that cold.

As the bus pulled away we looked down again at the pub. The pub sign was lit up, a couple of dim bulbs glowed over the windows, a single old street lamp shone on the road leading to the pub but there were no lights around the cage. Even the concrete lamp standards on the bridge didn't shine that far. The push chair was folded out. Richard pulled something from his pocket. He rubbed it on our cheeks.

'Burnt cork,' he said, 'Commandoes wear it to camouflage light skin.'

As before, we strolled down to the pub. The lights were on but nobody seemed to be about. It was only just gone six. I was trembling with excitement, or fear. Richard and Terry had torches. I wished that I had thought to bring mine.

''O'd me torch Geoff. Giz the screwdriver.'

I glanced around again. It was very dark by the shed. The bridge road was lit for traffic. I wanted to pee.

The screws came out fairly easily, but it still took fifteen minutes. I could hear Geoff breathing hard and Richard grunting.

Both torches were shone into the cage. Two wide eyes reflected the light,

'Right, let's get 'im. Got the lickle coat, Geoff?' Richard entered the cage. Mickey sprang away. Richard made another grab to no effect. 'Come in and shut the door. Keep the light on 'im, Tez.'

It was Terry who made contact with the monkey. Mickey jumped into his arms.

'Gotchya,' Terry said proudly. Then he shrieked.

'Wassermarra?' said Richard.

Terry was blubbing. 'He bit me. He bit my finger. It's bleedin'.'

Richard pulled Mickey from Terry and held him out, 'Put the coat on 'im. I've got 'im.'

I was shining Terry's torch. Geoff had the coat ready but wasn't making any move toward the monkey. Mickey was chattering, probably swearing. I wished that I was at home.

'Tip the bag out and giz it us,' commanded the leader in desperation.

Geoff held the now empty bag open. I put the torch under my arm and took hold of Mickey's legs. I guided the legs and tail into the bag. Richard crammed the rest of the monkey in. Between us we managed to contain the animal and pull the draw-string. Mickey's head poked out of the top. The bag writhed. Terry was sobbing. I really needed to pee now.

'Pick our stuff up, Chrisser.' said Richard, 'Away all boats!'

I grabbed at the fallen clothes, bottle and my tools. Geoff turned the pushchair, now with a rider under the blanket. He was still chattering and kicking. Terry staggered out still bleating. Richard pulled off his balaclava, 'Jesus! Yo'oright, Tez?'

'No,' wailed Terry, 'it hurts, an' it's bleedin' a lot.'

Gasping, we dashed onto Abbey Bridge. We needed to be on the other side to catch the bus back. It was obvious though that a bus ride was now out of the question. The pushchair could not be folded with its noisy wriggling contents. Terry was making an awful noise and dripping blood. Geoff and I were in uniform with blackened faces.

'We'll have to walk back,' the leader said.

'What time is it?' I asked Geoff.

'Five to seven,' he said mournfully.

We could not get back in time to look like we had just come from cubs. It was miles. Well, a mile and half. That was twice as far as Wollaton Park. I peed in the gutter. I was getting past caring. Geoff pulled out his handkerchief and wrapped it around Terry's damaged hand. Terry was quietly sobbing as we started the trek home. Richard guided the push chair. We had to almost run to keep up. A few cars and a couple of buses passed us but nobody was out walking. After twenty long minutes we reached Abbey Gates.

'You two tell y'mams y've been practising for a badge. That's why y'faces is black. Terry, tell y'mam yo' got bit by a dog.'

'What's going to happen to Mickey?' I asked as we pushed the monkey down Wingfield Drive. As we turned the corner onto Baslow Drive, Geoff peeled off through his gate with small clothes stuffed up his Cub jumper.

Richard said, 'Roger Green's got a nutch in his back garden. It's empty 'cos the rabbit died. We'll put 'im in there. Jus' for tonight.'

I didn't like the 'we' bit. It sounded like more commando stuff. All I wanted to do was go home. We turned the corner onto Anslow Avenue. Richard lifted Mickey up. I picked up the tools and the bottle, and collapsed the push chair for Terry. I wondered what he would say about having the pushchair and being wounded. I wondered what my parents would say. I felt sick. Terry peeled off down his close for his back door. Richard and I continued as far as Roger's house. I was nearly home. I could see Roger's back door from mine. Roger lived almost next door to Richard. We turned off down the alley way. Richard quietly opened the gate that served the front and back door. The kitchen curtains were closed, but, being cheap, there was sufficient light leaking onto the garden and the hutch. We tip toed up to the hutch.

"O'd still,' whispered Richard to the monkey. Mickey had been quite docile for the last ten minutes, but now he was wriggling again and baring his teeth.

The hutch had neither lock nor bolt. A wooden clothes peg was pushed between the staples.

'Are you going to let him out of the bag?'

Richard pulled the draw-string loose letting Mickey tumble into the hutch. I tossed in the bottle and shut the door quickly. Richard fitted the peg back.

'He's got nothing to eat.'

'I'll get summat. Get going.'

I didn't need any further persuasion. I slithered out of Roger's garden, leaving Richard to it.

On turning into our close I bumped into my Father.

'Ah, there you are. Where have you been? Do you know what time it is? I've been up to the Cubs, when you didn't come home. It was all shut up. Your mother's worried sick. She's sent me out to find you...'

'Sorry, Dad. I was playing with Geoff after Cubs. I forgot about the time. What time is it?'

'It's five to eight. You should have been home at ten past seven.'

When we got into the house, Mother looked delighted for a second or two.

'Whatever have you done to your face?'

I could hardly get to sleep. Anxiety got the better of me. They had believed my story, but I still got a lecture on behaving responsibly. I was anxious about Mickey. After all that trouble he was really no better off. I pictured him huddled in Roger's dismal hutch. I hoped Richard had got some food for him. I began to think of the police being called to the scene of the crime, and the man remembering us. I had awful dreams.

The morning was misty. Richard was at the end of the close. He looked solemn.

'He's gone. Mickeh's gone. I took him some things t'eat las' night. But this mornin' the 'utch was open and he was gone.'

'P'r'aps Mr Green saw him.'

'Well, I seen Roger this morning, an' he said nuffink about monkehs.'

'We'll have to find him. He'll starve to death.'

'Tez can't 'elp 'cos his mam took him off to the doctors with his finger. It's all swelled up.'

Geoff would be well on his way to school by then, and so should I.

'Let's pretend we're looking for a lost cat, if anybody asks. We need to look in every garden round here.'

Richard nodded and we began the search. I hoped that my mother was not looking out of the window. After ten minutes we had covered all the back gardens that joined Roger's. We ventured further calling 'Mickey' along the maze of back entries. When we had just about given up, I heard a cat growling. There was a tabby with its fur fluffed up growling at a monkey sat on rain barrel. Mickey was taking little notice of the cat, he was more interested in an apple core. The cat shot away as we approached. Mickey eyed us. Richard carefully slipped the duffle bag from his shoulder. He put his hand inside and produced a banana. I took the bag and Richard pulled back the banana skin. Mickey seemed very interested. Richard knelt down and slowly bit off the end of the banana. He held it out. Mickey sprang down towards the tempting fruit. He grasped it with his little hands and locked his teeth around it. At that moment Richard let go and made a grab. Mickey jumped but Richard had one back leg, and then two. He held the monkey upside down. 'Bag, quick!'

I thrust the open bag up over the monkey's head. He struggled, but Richard pushed him down. It was over very quickly. The monkey and the banana were in the bag.

We hung about at Richard's house until I could arrive home for lunch. Richard's parents were both at work and his brother was at secondary school. We decided it was too risky hanging onto Mickey much longer. It was Thursday morning and Julia's brother wouldn't be driving around until Saturday or more like Sunday. We fed and watered Mickey but didn't let more than his head out of the bag. I slid back home at twelve fifteen for my lunch. On the way 'back to school' in the afternoon, I met Geoff at the end of our close. He was with Terry.

'Hey up, Chris. What happened?'

I told them about the rabbit hutch, and searching for Mickey.

'Me mam was furious abaht the push chair. She thought somebody had nicked it. She dragged me off to Dr Briggs. He give me an injection. Said it was poisoned. What's Richard doin'?'

I told them that Richard and I thought it best to give Mickey to the PDSA, because the RSPCA shelter was miles away in Radford. We could walk to the PDSA as it was only in Dunkirk, just past the Lido. We couldn't wait for Julia's brother either. They nodded solemnly.

'Is Richard still at home?' asked Geoff.

We carried Mickey to the end of Woodside Road, climbed *'over tins'*, crossed the field to University Boulevard and walked the mile to Dunkirk. The PDSA was easy to find.

'What shall we say?' I said.

'We found him,' suggested Geoff.

'Yeah, that'll do,' said Richard, 'They know what to do with him.'

'D'y' think they'll send 'im back to the pub?' said Terry.

We all looked glum at the prospect.

We marched into the PDSA. It smelt of disinfectant. There was a lady in a white coat at the counter. 'Hello, boys what have you got there?'

Richard did the talking. It wasn't as good as usual. He sounded tired.

'Right, so you've found a monkey, and you want him looked after?'

We mumbled the affirmative. Terry fiddled with the bandage on his hand.

'Wait while I have a word with a colleague.'

She disappeared through a door behind her.

'Bet she's ringing the rozzers,' said Terry.

I thought about exiting quickly, leaving Mickey on the counter, but she returned with a man in a white coat. He looked at us keenly. 'You found the monkey?'

Richard blurted, 'No, not really, mester. Me Uncle Jack brought 'im back from Africa, but we don't know 'ow to look after 'im proper.' He sounded so sincere.

The man studied Richard and then said, 'Hmm, that's interesting because this sort of monkey comes from South America.'

'Could of bin South America,' Richard said sheepishly.

The man looked very serious, he nodded before saying,'You want him to go to a good home?'

'Yes, sir,' was our joint answer.

The man pulled Mickey from the bag. He knew how to hold him. He glanced at the woman and smiled. 'OK, we'll see that he has the best available. What's his name?'

'Mickey,' I said.

There was a report in the Evening Post at the weekend about the disappearance of a monkey from *The Three Wheatsheaves* public house in Lenton. A criminal gang, who specialised in taking exotic animals, was the chief suspect. My Father said he was glad that the monkey was out of that place and that he hoped the monkey was now having a better life. I was sure that he was. I thought it best not to say anything though.

Terry's finger got better. Sadly the scar faded. The 'dog' that bit him was not traced. His sister Glenys did not need the push chair for years. Roger sold the hutch. Richard reverted to being an amiable villain. Geoff and I planned constructing a box cart.

...and Mickey lived happily ever after.

Tanks for the Memory

Aunty Dorothy, Uncle Jim and little Clive came for a Sunday tea as usual. Little Clive was of no interest, as he was so young. It was usually Uncle Jim that had yarns to listen to. He was a travelling salesman who had many experiences. But that day it was what Aunty Dorothy had to say that caught my attention.

'Well, now our Clive's started school, I can go to work again. So I've got a little job.'

She paused to make sure that everyone was listening. My Mother was agog.

'Well, you see, I saw this advert in the Post. It said that they wanted a capable person to work in a canteen.'

My Father's eyes rolled.

'Where?'

'In Ruddington, at the Supply Depot. It's really handy because it's for the lunch time, and that means I'll be home for when our Clive gets out of school.'

'Isn't that the place where all the army stuff is dumped?'

'Yes, Ken, there's miles of it. So there's a team of blokes who want feeding.'

The words 'army stuff' caught my imagination. I was fascinated by the war that I had just missed. I had a collection of Dinky military vehicles. Sometimes I would see the real ones. It was thrilling to watch a group of tanks clattering along University Boulevard.

'They are *Comet* tanks going to Chilwell Ordnance depot for servicing. See they have their turrets turned to the rear.'

My Father seemed to know everything. Tony's father, Mr Wilmot, actually worked at Chilwell. He didn't drive tanks though, he drove a desk. My Father explained about the Ruddington Depot. He said that during the war there were piles of ammunition, but when peace came the army used the site for dumping unwanted equipment. Every now and again there was a sale. Fairground folks bought old army vehicles and painted them red and maroon.

Aunty Dorothy lived in a Council house on a new housing estate on the other side of the River Trent. Ruddington was only a short bus ride for her. When we visited it was two bus rides to cross the river. At that time there was only the Trent Bridge crossing for traffic, with two footbridges for local use. My Father didn't have a car, so the Ruddington depot might as well be on the moon.

Later in the week I recounted the story of the army dump with Geoff. I couldn't manage to get him to understand where it actually was.

'I've got a street map of Nottingham. It'll be on that.'

We spread the map open on Geoff's kitchen table. I hadn't seen such a thing before. It was fascinating finding our own Council estate and the nearby Wollaton Park. I found the vast Clifton estate where Aunty Dorothy lived. We saw the River Trent snaking through the bottom end of the map.

'We could go on our bikes: crossing on the Ha'penny Bridge.'

The so called Half-penny bridge was an ancient relic connecting Wilford village with the city. It was a toll bridge built by Lord Clifton for pedestrians. It cost a half penny to cross and a little more if goods were being carried.

'It's blinking miles.'

'Not really, look at the map scale.'

Geoff found a piece of string and cut it to the length of one mile as shown on the map legend. We stretched it along a proposed route and calculated that the distance was just about six miles. It would be the same for the return journey.

'Hey, look.' Geoff was suddenly excited and stabbing his finger at the river.

I examined the spot. There was a dotted line crossing over: it was labelled *'Barton Ferry'*. We traced a possible route from home through Beeston and on to Attenborough where a turning was actually named Barton Lane. The village of Barton-in-Fabis was on the other side of the river and not far from Ruddington. The supply depot was clearly marked.

It would be a great adventure, but, after the initial excitement had faded, it was agreed that parents would not be happy with a long cycle ride that included a river crossing.

'What if we say that we are going to Toton sidings train spotting?'

Toton sidings was a huge rail complex just beyond Attenborough. I had pestered my Father into cycling there once. We found a farm track that looked over the freight yards. I was happy but my Father was not keen to stay long.

'That would be fibbing.'

Geoff grinned and spread his arms, 'Only a little bit.'
'But going to Ruddington and back would take all day.'
'They know we are daft enough to sit watching trains for hours…'
It was possible.

In the school playground we discussed and planned the adventure.
'Hey, what yo' two planning? A bank robbery?'
Normally I would be careful of telling anything to Richard. He had a habit of trying to muscle in. This time I didn't mind because Richard didn't have a bike. His older brother, Alan, had a bike, but he wouldn't let is younger brother even touch it.
'What d'yo' wanna go there for?'
'To look at the army stuff close to. To see if there's anything to buy. Might be tanks.'
'Tanks! They woun't let yo' 'ave a tank. Where'd yo' keep it?'
'Not to buy. To photograph. I've got a Kodak 127.'
The Kodak Brownie 127 wasn't entirely mine. It was considered a family investment. It was to replace by Father's antique box-camera. My Mother wanted to take 'snaps' for the family album. I was allowed to use the camera… sensibly.
'I'll come wiv yo'.
'You haven't got a bike.'
Richard looked crest-fallen, but only for a moment.

Geoff and I carefully worked out the route. I wrote this route on the white side of a card rectangle that had separated layers of Weetabix (*Weetabix* was Geoff's nickname). The grey side was used for the return journey. Geoff copied his own set of instructions onto another piece of card. We also made lists of the necessary equipment. Geoff had binoculars. The hardest bit was to get parental blessing.
'Well, Bridget, he's got to grow up some time. He can't be tied to your apron strings forever. He knows how to ride properly in traffic. And he knows how to get to Toton. Geoff is a sensible lad too.'
She wasn't entirely convinced, but she did agree if I promised to be sensible, not to talk to 'funny men' and was back by tea time.

We chose a Saturday at the end of a sunny week. Everything was going to plan until Richard turned up wanting to know when the adventure was to start. He seemed very pleased with himself.

'Guess what? I've gorra bike now. It's Roger Green's, He's lendin' it for the day. Arh gin 'im half a dollar.'

Roger lived two doors from Richard. He was in the secondary school and wasn't inclined to play out on the street any more.

'An' guess what? Tez 'as gorra bike anall. It's his Glenys'.'

Terry's big sister Glenys was sixteen and keen on competition dancing. She was no longer interested in cycling. I was surprised that Terry would ride her bike. It was a girl's bike and it had been repainted pink.

'You'll need some kit as well.'

Geoff was still trying to dissuade Richard.

'We ain't goin' to Africa. We on'y need some sammies.'

Geoff had one last go, 'No mucking about?'

Richard pulled his hurt face and wagged it from side to side.

We really thought that Richard and Terry would miss the start, or tire quickly.

So, the adventure began at nine on a sunny Saturday. Richard and Terry were ready good and early. Geoff and I had haversacks full of stuff. The other two didn't seem to carrying much. Perhaps their lunches, pac-a- macs and tyre mending kit were in their saddle bags.

The first leg was easy as it was the same as going to school, and then on to Beeston. We turned left into Station Road to come out on Queen's Road, which was the Beeston bye-pass. We were soon into unknown territory, but it was straight-forward to Attenborough. With great delight we saw the left turn of Barton Lane. There had been little traffic, now there was none.

Geoff, who had a watch and was the time keeper, announced that we had done thirty-five minutes. Our narrow lane passed over a railway crossing. It was the line from Nottingham to Derby. On cue a passenger train rattled through. We waited for the lights to stop flashing before scampering over the rails. Beyond the crossing the lane became rural. There were no kerb stones but there were plenty of pot-holes. On our left were the great pools of deep water in the gravel pits: the very place where teenagers Keith and Graham had drowned.

We could smell the river before we saw it. The land was flat fields of grass. Ahead, to our right, was a single storey building. There was washing drying on the line. Beyond the house was the river. Our road petered out onto a wooden jetty. On the up-stream side of the jetty a boat was moored. A smaller row-boat was tied up on the other side of the jetty. Way across the river was Barton-in-Fabis. We could just make out red tiled roofs and brick chimneys. On the left loomed the great wooded mass of Clifton Grove. So far we had ridden four miles.

There was nobody about so Richard approached the front door. By the garden gate was a sign which said, 'Ferry crossing six pence per person one way. Animals by negotiation.' The sign looked old and it was listing heavily.

'Doesn't say anything about bikes, Chris.'

I began to feel uneasy.

Richard rapped on the door. A mature woman answered.

'You want to cross now? I'm not sure if Arthur is about.'

She turned and called for Arthur. A man came around the end of the house with a paint brush in his hand. We wore a flat cap and braces over his collar-less grey shirt. He looked at us and shook his head, but said, 'Ray will take you. Cost you six pence each and six pence a bike. Are you coming back?'

He disappeared and returned with a younger man. Ray seemed very friendly. I felt much relieved. He motioned us toward the larger boat.

'I think we can do it in one go. Two lads fo'r'd and two aft. I'll stack the bikes.'

There were wooden planks at the side of the jetty on different levels which made getting into the boat easier. Richard and Terry bagged the front seats. Geoff and I were happy with the back because we could see where we were going. Ray sat in the centre with two bikes stacked in front of him and two behind. The boat was pushed away from the jetty with an oar. Ray dipped both oars together, with the boat pointing up-stream. He had to work against the current which was not strong at this time of year.

The river smelt strongly of blocked drains. Hordes of gnats danced around. It was very exciting. It was cool out on the water.

Ray was facing Geoff and me, 'Where you to?'

He grinned when we explained, 'If you change your mind and want to cross back, you have to ring the bell.'

The crossing was shorter than I expected. Very soon the boat was heading for a replica jetty. A brass bell dangled from a metal post. The boat bumped gently against the foot planks. Ray stepped out and secured both ends. We scrambled out into the foreign territory. The ferry-man lifted up our bikes. We waved, and set off.

Barton-in-Fabis was a quiet village of a few farm labourers' cottages with a sprinkling of newer bungalows. We pedalled through and went out on New Road. We crossed a quiet main road, the A453, and followed Barton Lane again to a tee-junction. To the right was Gotham village. Our route was to the left in the Nottingham direction. After a mile Geoff spotted our next turn into the fairly new Clifton Council housing estate. It was vast and still being built. Farnborough Road took us to our next turn. The sign post pointed the way to Ruddington. We had covered three more miles from the ferry landing.

Terry looked worn out. He was not used to biking, and the sun was blazing.

'Cheer up Terry it's only another a mile now.'

Terry managed a grin.

We soon pedalled into Ruddington village. The Victoria pub signalled the turn to the right. There were little signs now that directed to the MOD Ordnance Disposal Depot.

The big double gates were shut and chained. A large notice warned of danger and penalty for trespass. In capitals it gave firm notice to keep out, and that the premises were patrolled. Next to the big gates there was a smaller pedestrian entrance with a small cabin. The cabin looked deserted, and that gate was locked too. The gates were joined to high chain-link fencing topped with rolls of barbed wire. A smaller sign, fastened to the gates, gave the date of the next auction.

'Urgh, arh fought we could gerrin.'

Terry was sprawled on the grass verge. I peered through the chain-link. Geoff said,

'Let's have lunch, it's about time.'

So, lunch packs were opened. I had cheese and tomato. Geoff had corned beef. We swapped a sandwich. Richard had door steps oozing raspberry jam. Terry opened his sandwiches and still looked puzzled.

'Hey, Tez, yer mam's gin yo' Kit-e-Kat.'

'No, Terry, Richard's joking. It's potted meat.'

The sandwiches were rapidly consumed and washed down with fizzy pop.

The chain-link fence obviously corralled the whole depot, but there was a service track running around too. We cycled along, but the view was obstructed by straggly bushes. After a couple of minutes the bushes ceased and we had a good uninterrupted view of the back ends of dozens of army three-ton trucks. Just a little further along there was a gap, and all sorts of vehicles could be seen. A line of motorbikes leaned over as though drunk. A small tracked vehicle painted white seemed out of place. Two sand coloured command vehicles stood together; as did the two tanks.

'Tanks!'

Geoff handed me his binoculars. The tanks came closer. Both were painted bronze-green but were much faded and chipped.

'They are *Comets*. They were right at the end of the war. We've got *Centurions* now. They are much better, so the *Comets* get dumped.'

'Are they for sale?'

Richard snorted, 'Yeah, Tez, but they will cost a load.'

'How much?'

'Dunno.'

I moved the view to the left. There were more soft-top trucks and cars. With the cars were some jeeps. A jeep would not cost as much as a tank. I wondered if one would still be there when I was old enough and had enough money.

I took three photos, but reckoned the targets were too far for my camera.

'Are we gonna ride all the way rahnd?'

Geoff advised us that it was time to head home.

'Is it a long way? Me legs ache an' I'm 'ungry.' Terry looked forlorn.

'Not going back the way we came. We're going back over the Toll Bridge.'

Terry looked puzzled.

This leg of the return journey was four miles but straightforward. It was necessary to ride single file on Wilford Road. We pedalled through Wilford village, where I had an uncle buried in the cemetery, and eventually saw the Trent again to our left. The river curled round in front of us. We passed the Ferry Inn and crossed the river using the little Toll Bridge. Nobody seemed to be collecting toll money. We turned left to head along the other side of the river with Clifton colliery and the six chimneys of the power station on our right. I had another uncle who worked there as a fitter.

Lenton Lane passed through the initial stages of the yet-to-be-built Clifton Bridge. We crossed over the railway lines again and turned left onto University Boulevard where there was a welcome cycle path. Terry brightened as he now recognised where he was. It was only a mile to the paddling pool. We felt like champions when we turned off Broadgate into Salthouse Lane. Within a minute we were back on our estate. It had been four miles from the Toll Bridge.

We were jubilant but exhausted. Terry could barely speak. Richard pulled a face and patted his bottom. We parted and I pushed my bike into the Close.

'Oh good, you're in time. Did you spot lots of trains?'

I made an affirmative noise and flopped into an arm chair. She gave me a glass of milk.

'Are you alright, Chick? You look tired.'

'Yes, well, we had a race coming back'

'Did you take any snaps of trains?'

'No, Mum, not really, they were too far away.'

I wondered how I was going to explain the photos of the tanks...

- The bike ride took place in 1956.
- Barton Ferry operated spasmodically by Arthur Tindall until the early 1960's.
- The A453 is now a very busy connection to Nottingham South Junction on the M1.
- Ruddington Ordnance Disposal site closed in 1958 and was converted into a public park.
- Nottingham Power station lost its six chimneys in the 1960's, to be replaced by one. The station was demolished altogether in 1981.
- Clifton Colliery closed in 1968
- Clifton Bridge was opened in 1958 and has subsequently been doubled in capacity.

The Treasurists

'Come on, now,' she said, 'it's not real.'

I knew that, but it was quite convincing. Somebody had gone to a lot of trouble to wrap shiny foil around all those discs. The beads were the plastic sort given away with breakfast cereal, but they had been sprayed exotic colours. The large royal brooches must have been fashioned from cardboard, but they looked like solid gold. All this stuff was spilling out of a chest as part of the window display.

I turned to go with my Mother. She was shopping for groceries. I was dreaming of treasure. To find treasure could make a person rich. Things normally beyond reach could be bought easily. The problem was in finding the treasure. It wasn't left around on street corners. Finding treasure involved a map, digging and usually adventure. We had all seen *Treasure Island* at the cinema. There was real treasure and well worth the dangerous adventure, apparently. I hadn't been on any dangerous adventures recently, so my treasure finds were of small value. I always made a point of sliding my fingers around the seat cushions on sofas. The treasure was in in the form of a sixpence or a three penny piece. If I trailed along, head down, with Mother, occasionally there was a small coin to be found. Was all the unfound treasure buried in the white sands of the Caribbean and well out of reach?

Later in the week I was at the Essoldo cinema with my Parents. There was a short on before the main noisy adventure film. This short suddenly became very interesting. An old man with a posh voice was talking to a group of younger enthusiasts. They were hovering around a hole in a field. It looked like a grave. The camera gave a close up of the old man's hands. He was showing what had been dug up. I heard the word 'treasure'. He was talking about digging up treasures from the past in our country. He said it was a gold bracelet from Saxon times. He said there would be more to find if we only knew where to look.

On the way home I asked my Father about where to find treasure. He told me that the best places were the sites of old battles or where really old buildings were.

'Were there any battles around here?'

'Maybe there was, but I've not heard of them.'

'Are there any really old buildings?'

'I suppose Wollaton Hall is the oldest. It was built in Queen Elizabeth 1's time.'

'What was here before the houses were built?'

'Just farm land.'

None of this sounded promising. If there was any treasure at Wollaton Hall, it would surely have been found by now. The place was so tidy.

Miss Timmins wasn't a real teacher. She was practising to be one. She did things with odd groups. At the end of the day she read a story to the whole class. It was *Five on Treasure Island.* There were no pirates but it got me thinking about treasure again. I chatted to Alan on the way home. I moaned about there being no possible treasure sites in our part of the world.

'What about the church?'

I knew he was a choir boy and his mother did the flowers, but I kept well away from St Bartholomew's. My Parents were not religious. Mother was sentimental, but Father was hostile.

'What about it?'

The church had been built about the same time as the housing estate. It even looked a bit like the Council houses. It was a big shoe box with a couple of pretty windows.

'The church is new, but it was built on the site of an old monastery.'

'How do you know?'

'It says so on the plaque near the door.'

I could almost taste the treasure.

Saturday morning was a good time to reconnoitre the place. I arranged to meet Geoff on the recreational ground right next to the church at 10 o'clock. There were some little kids playing on the swings and slide, Geoff was sitting on a bench.

'It's no good there's a wedding on.'

To prove the point a gaggle of excited people emerged. We could see through the bushes and the green painted metal railings. After a few minutes of photography the bride and groom ran the gauntlet of confetti to the waiting shiny black car with white ribbons. After a few more minutes the people began streaming away for the wedding breakfast. We walked past them.

There was heaps of confetti around the door way. We peeped in. The place seemed empty.

'Does it get locked?'

'Only at night. During the day it's open to the public. There's all sorts of stuff happening.'

'Like services?'

'Yeah. They have meetings too.'

I wondered how Geoff knew so much. Perhaps it was because his house was so close by, only a stone's throw away. We drifted in. There was nothing happening. I noticed the seats littered with hymn books and papers. At the far end was a big table with a huge bunch of flowers. Alan's mother had done it well. Behind the table were a couple of stained glass windows. Either side the windows were two doors. One of them opened and a man came out. He was wearing an ordinary grey suit. His shirt was black with a white collar and no tie.

'Hello boys. Are you with the wedding party?'

'No, Vicar,' said Geoff, 'We're just having a look round.'

'You interested in churches?'

'Well, yes. We've been learning about them at school,' lied Geoff.

'Good. I'd like to show you round, but I'm going to the wedding reception. Perhaps you could come back another time. How about on Sunday, say 4 o'clock. That's when Sunday school is finishing.'

'Yes, thanks.'

'Why did you have to say yes?

He grinned, 'It won't take long. There's not much to see.'

'Careful,' said my Father when I told him about what I was doing after Sunday lunch. 'They'll have you signed on. You'll end up in a white dress.'

'Now, Ken, let him go and have a look round. Alan's in the choir and he's nice boy.'

Alan was in the choir, but that didn't make him any different. He played football, collected Dinky toys and swore. Anyway he was in the choir mostly because he was paid.

I arrived at Geoff's front gate as he was coming out the house. We walked up to the church to arrive just as some children were emerging. I recognised a couple of 'goody-goodies'. They were the twins Christine and Valerie. They were exactly the same age as me. We started in the same infant class, but they became 'B' streamers. There was no correspondence. After a gap we ventured into the church. The vicar was talking to a big girl who was holding some junior bibles. I had one, Geoff had one. All school children had been issued with this edition of the New Testament to commemorate the coronation. My copy stayed unread. There were no pictures.

When the vicar saw us he smiled. The girl turned away to put the bibles into a cupboard.

'Hello, boys. Good to see you again. You are doing a project on churches, I believe?'

'Well, not exactly. We are making models of church buildings to go on display.'

It was a wonder that Geoff was not struck down by a lightning bolt for fibbing in church.

'This is rather a plain building, I'm afraid...'

'We are interested in what was here before.'

'Ah, the old Priory. There's not much left. Only a corner stone now.'

'Isn't there anything underneath?'

'Underneath the stone?'

'No, underneath the church.'

The vicar grinned and said. 'Come along, I'll show you around.'

I looked at Geoff. He looked at me and shrugged. We followed the vicar. He gave us a tour of the building. There wasn't much to see. He pointed out the contemporary chairs that stood in rows where wooden pews might have been. We looked at the two stained glass windows behind the altar. The altar was a plain table with wooden cross in the centre. On respective sides of the table were a pulpit and a piano. We followed him over to a door on the left of the altar. There was a small room where choir boys' robes hung on pegs. The room on the other side was like a small office with a desk and a filing cabinet.

It was all very disappointing. He took us to a door on the right at the back, which I had not noticed before. Inside the door was a small kitchen. At the end of the kitchen were two other doors.

'A toilet on the left, and the boiler for the heating on the right.'

We tried to look fascinated. He smiled again, 'The bell tower is false. The bells are rung by electric. They are on a timer.'

We trooped out into the main part of the church. I was wishing that we hadn't bothered. I could have been marshalling my toy soldiers at home. As we started for the door something caught my eye. Just in front of the altar the floor tiles looked odd. The church floor was made of hard orangey brown tiles. Here there was a section of tiles not quite in line. I caught Geoff's eye. His eyes followed mine down as we stepped over.

'Well thanks, Vicar,' said Geoff, 'that was very interesting.'

'Glad you came along. Are you by any chance interested in coming to Sunday school?'

We sat on the rec bench watching younger children being dragged away from the slide and swings.

'It's a trap door. I could see the metal edge.'

'There wasn't a ring though.'

'Which means it can't be used very often.'

'What do you reckon is underneath?'

'Dunno, praps some steps leading down to chests stuffed with treasure.'

We grinned at each other.

'Trouble is it'll be heavy. And we can't just waltz in and start pulling at it.'

I scuffed my shoe over a spent lolly pop stick. 'My Dad showed me how to get a man-hole-cover up with a spade.'

'And Sacko's mam has got the key to the church…'

The treasure under the church was practically ours. All that was necessary was to get Alan to 'borrow' the key from Mrs Saxton, and for me to smuggle my Dad's spade out of the shed. We decided to share the treasure with Alan, but only if he was in on the venture. We also decided that lifting the trap door might be hard work. So I suggested including Richard. Geoff pulled a face.

'He's strong alright, but…well, you know what he's like.'

I knew what he meant. Richard sailed close to the wind, but he was always resourceful.

The timing had to be right. The church had to be closed. It had to before dark. A Saturday seemed the best. Alan was persuaded to 'lend' us the key. Geoff had the idea to take it into Beeston after school and get a copy made. He had done this for his mother when she wanted another back door key. It cost a shilling, but that was considered an investment. Alan would get the real key back by tea time. Richard seemed delighted with the adventure and the prospect of acquiring treasure. His eyes gleamed.

We met on the benches near the swings on the rec at the allotted time.

'Urgh, what's he doing here?' said Geoff when Richard turned up with his side-kick Terry.

Richard explained that we needed a look-out. 'We might need these,' he said brandishing a couple of flash lights. He was resourceful.

I had the spade wrapped in a sack. Geoff had the shiny new key. We moved like a squad of commandoes towards the church.

We skulked at the door making sure that nobody was still inside or watching us. Geoff jiggled the key in the lock. 'It won't budge.'

'Let me have a go.' The lock responded to Richard's deft touch.

We pushed the door open and entered. Geoff thoughtfully closed the door. It was gloomy without the lights on. The trap door was lit with the light coming through the stained glass windows. Now I felt a bit scared. Richard knelt down. He traced the edge of the trap with his torch. He pulled out a penknife and worked it around the metal. 'OK, Chrisser.'

I placed the lip of the spade into the narrow gap. I waggled the spade. There was a brittle squeak and the lip sank a little deeper. I pulled the handle towards me. Another squeak.

'You gorrit.'

Richard pushed me aside and took over. He worked the blade deeper until he could put his strength on pushing the handle down.

'Yeah,' gasped Geoff as the trap lifted a fraction.

'O'd it wiv yer foot.'

Geoff kept the spade almost horizontal with his foot while Richard lay flat on the floor. He shone a light in from the side.

'There's a step. Get summat to wedge it open.'

We glanced around. There were no convenient spars of wood.

'This will do,' said Terry. He was holding the cross from the altar.

Before I could articulate an objection, Richard had the cross.

'Press down real hard.'

Geoff exerted himself. The trap moved slightly higher. It was enough for Richard to jam the cross into the gap.

'Right, Chrisser gerrold of this corner, an' Geoff gerrold of the other.'

Richard repositioned the spade so that the blade was touching the step. 'Pull!'

As we struggled to pull the trap further open, Richard levered the spade handle upwards.

'Tez gerra couple o' chairs, quick.'

Terry grabbed two chairs and placed them sideways to take the weight. It worked. The altar cross slipped off down into the darkness. Richard shone a torch after it. There were steps. I could see four.

'Right, now let's get the bogger open.'

Geoff and I pulled as Richard and Terry pushed. We managed to get the trap open and standing vertical. It seemed secure in that position. We were all gasping.

Geoff pulled the two chairs away. Both torches were shone into the depth. The steps went down into the darkness. Spiders scuttled away. It smelled awful, like the mud on the bank when the river was low. Nobody rushed down to retrieve the treasure.

'Hey, Tez, are yo' keepin' conk?'

Terry shuffled over to the church door.

Richard handed me his torch. 'You're the leader, Chrisser.' He grinned.

Carefully I began to descend. I was glad that Geoff was close behind with the other torch. I wondered what would happen if the trap fell back into place. It was quite cool. The steps were uneven pieces of sand stone. I shone the torch up. The church floor was supported by huge beams. The steps stopped at a level which would allow a grown-up to stand. We swung the torches around. Very small things scuttled from the intrusion of the light.

'Well, is there owt dahn there?'

'Don't look like it.'

'Plenty of spiders though.'

'Wait, look Geoff, there's a space.' My torch beam had detected a gap on the right towards the end of the bland hole we stood in. This space was cluttered with pieces of sandstone and broken beams.

'Shall we dig this stuff away?'

'Nah, don't seem worth the trouble. There's nothing here.'

There was a voice in the distance. It sounded like Terry. Richard called down into the void. He used a stage whisper, 'Terry's reckons somebody's coming. You'd best come back.'

As we turned, in something close to panic, my dancing torch beam caught a familiar shape where our shoes had scuffed up the dirt. Geoff was ahead of me. I bent to scoop up the disc shape.

Geoff stopped on the steps, 'The cross.'

I blinked as his torch beam dazzled me.

'There!'

But I couldn't see properly.

'There,' he said again, 'On your left.'

My vision returned and I saw where his torch was now aimed.

'Geoff, Chrisser, come on, quick.'

I stuffed the disc shape into my pocket and picked up the cross. I hoped it wasn't damaged.

We scrambled up the steps.

'Turn the bleddy lights off,' commanded Richard in a whisper.

We crouched near the trap with hearts beating heavily and ears straining. The church was even more gloomy now. I couldn't see Terry. I wondered if we had been seen, and the police had been sent for. Terry slithered out of the darkness.

'There's two on 'em,' he whispered, 'A bloke an' a woman. I seen 'em through the key 'ole.'

Terry had earned his 'share'. I glanced around trying to work out how to evade capture and escape through the door. Nothing happened. The door did not open, even though it was unlocked. Still nothing happened.

We couldn't just run off. The trap was still up, and the chairs and the cross were out of place.

Richard stood up. He tip-toed up the aisle and put his ear to the door. After a minute he carefully returned.

'It's a couple of teenagers. They're sparking in the church doorway.'

He looked at me, 'Are you sure there's no treasure dahn there?'

I shook my head. 'There's nothing, is there, Geoff?'

'No, just a load of old stones and bits.'

'Right, so let's tidy up. And then we can have some fun.'

Richard directed the careful lowering of the trap. It didn't quite fit back. So he sat down and put his heels to the proud edge. It made hardly a sound as it went home. Geoff replaced the cross on the altar. Terry and I put the chairs back, but we swapped them for two others further back because ours were slightly scuffed. All his was done very quietly.

We put our heads together.

'Them two fink nobody's here at this time. So we'll give 'em a bit of a scare. They won't be expectin' us to burst aht the door like maniacs.'

He surely was resourceful. Terry grinned. He was good at maniacs. Richard took back the torches. He gave one to Terry, who knew exactly what to do.

'Geoff, you got the key. Lock the door when they run off. Remember to scream when Arh tells you.'

We saluted and then followed Richard quietly to the door. He put his hand on the latch. He also switched on his torch. He shone the light up onto his face. Terry copied. They both looked ghastly. Richard nodded dramatically.

'Nah! –A-r-g-h-!'

He flung the door open. We burst through shrieking. Romeo and Juliet were frozen in an embrace, but only for a second. They bolted. Geoff closed and locked the door. We ran.

It was what I thought. It was a coin. When the gunge was scrubbed off it began to tell its tale. It was as big as an old penny piece, but it wasn't copper. Underneath the greenish brown coating it shone silver. There was no date or value. There were some words that I couldn't read.

'Where on Earth did you get this?'

I spun my Father a tale about finding it by the Tottle Brook where we played sometimes.

'It looks very old,' he said, after scrubbing it really clean, 'The writing could be Latin, though I'm no expert. And it looks like silver, real silver. It could be worth a fortune. We shall have to take it somewhere to be valued.'

The coin was taken into town. We visited a shop that specialised in stamps, medals and coins. The man was quite excited with it. He said that it was medieval, more than five hundred years old. When he offered a price that made my heart skip, my Father declined politely.

'You see, Chris, he's a dealer. If he is offering that amount he must think that he can sell it on for more. Perhaps twice as much. That's how he makes a living.'

'Where do we take it to, then?'

'The museum. They will have experts who can tell us all about it.'

'Will they buy it?'

'No, we will give it to the museum.'

The treasure was slipping away back into the silky sands of the Caribbean.

'Don't look so glum. You'll get your name in the *Evening Post*. It's part of the National Heritage.'

I had no idea what that was. All I could think of was how many toy soldiers could have been bought with what the man in the shop said.

I decided to give up on treasure hunting. It was far too hazardous. I decided to earn my fortune with honest labour. I would talk to Mr Leek at the newsagents, for when I was older.

Tom

On the way home at lunchtime I saw a van. It was worthy of interest because there was hardly ever any traffic on our street, and because it was a removal van. The big backdoors were open and folded back. Two men in overalls were fixing a ramp. As the van was parked outside the house where the Wards lived, I guessed the new people were moving in.

I was glad that the Wards had left. Mr Ward was a teacher but not at my school. There were two children. Deirdre was at secondary school. Her younger brother Julian was my age. I had tried to play with him but he was strange. He didn't seem to know how to play. He would snatch toys and push children. Once I saw him on a three wheeler bike. He was racing away from my house on my bike. Another time I spotted him stealing a Mars bar from the newsagent's counter. I told Mr Leek who quickly chased after him.

Richard said. 'Urgh, whaja snitch for?'

Julian was not included, and now he was gone. I hoped for someone nice.

After lunch, on the way back for the afternoon session, I noticed the two men standing smoking. The job wasn't finished. The van was gone, though, at twenty minutes past four when I walked home with Richard and Terry. We had been speculating who the new tenants of No 41 might be. There were no clues.

'New people in the Wards' old house.'

'Are there any kids?'

'Don't know, Chick. Why don't you go and knock on the door and ask?'

I wouldn't dare do anything such thing.

Terry said he had seen a kid on a bike.

'Yeah, what's he look like. An' how o'd 'is he?'

'Looks ord'nary. Bout ahr age.'

This seemed promising. I would hang around on the street. We might go bike rides together.

I wandered about at the end of our close. There was some movement at No. 41. A bike was being pushed out by a figure in a striped tee-shirt and khaki shorts. I moved up to make a casual meeting.

'Hello'

A head turned toward me. It had floppy mousey hair pulled to one side,

'Hi'

'My name's Chris. I live in the Close at No 25.'

'My name is Joe.'

Joe looked fine and spoke better than the barbarians on the street.

'Are you going for a ride?'

'Well, I was just going to ride around and see what there is.'

'I've got a bike. I can show you around. Have you been to the rec?'

'The rec?'

I ran home and pulled my bike out of the shed.

We cycled up the street and on to Baslow Drive. I pointed out the boy-scout hut and the church.

'This is the rec. There's bowling and a tennis court at the bottom end. And you can just see the top of the Essoldo cinema.'

There were a few children playing on the swings and slide. Mothers sat gossiping on the benches.

'Where did you come from?'

'We lived in a flat in Basford. But it was only two bedrooms and mummy is having a baby.'

I nodded as though all this was quite clear.

'If she has a boy we would need another bedroom.'

'Why?'

'Hah! Because I'm a girl.'

I stared at the grinning face. I suddenly felt stupid.

'A girl?'

This child was dressed as a boy and had a boy's hair-cut, and was named Joe.'

'Yes, I'm a girl. My name is really Joanne.'

'But you look like a boy.'

She grinned, 'Yes, I like boys' stuff. I like what boys do. I think girls are soppy playing with dolls.'

I studied Joanne. She was my height. It was only the clothes and haircut that made a difference. Girls wore dresses and had long hair. If the hair was bobbed it was parted on the right. Joanne's hair was parted on the left like a boy.

She ran her fingers through her hair and let it fall. The parting disappeared and a fringe covered her forehead.

I wasn't convinced.

'Mummy says that I have to wear a dress to school, but I can wear what I like at home.'

School.

'What school will you go to?'

'I think it's called Beeston Fields Junior.'

'That's my school.'

'We seen yo' wiv the new kid on yer bikes. What's he like?'

For once I was ahead of Richard.

'She's called Joe… and she's a girl.'

Richard and Terry gaped in disbelief, 'A gell?'

'Yeah she likes to do boys' stuff. Like running a train set or flinging stones or having adventures.'

Richard started to laugh, 'Neah. Yo're ayin' us on.'

'No, Joanne is a girl and she's coming to school on Monday.'

My street pals shook their heads and sniggered.

I guessed it was Joanne and her mother walking ahead of me. Her mother was quite big around the middle. Joanne wore a simple blue check school dress.

Richard and Terry caught me up. 'Hey, Chrisser, is that 'er?'

'Yeah. Her mum's having a baby.'

Terry sniggered.

Joe and her mother went straight to the school office while we hung around in the playground waiting for the bell.

Joe and her mother reappeared in my classroom. The school secretary spoke to Miss Hilton. The girls in the class were very interested. The boys were indifferent. Joanne was sat in the spare place next to Sandra Wilkins.

At playtime Joe moved away from the gaggle of girls who were skipping. She approached the end of the playground where the big boys played football. She was waved away. I thought she would go back to the skippers, but she joined the game. She took the ball and dribbled it about defying any boy to tackle her. Suddenly she was joined by another girl. Ann Banthorpe was calling for a pass. I knew

Ann was clever but I had no idea she could kick a ball. The footballing boys came to a standstill. The girls continued chipping the ball to each other. The skippers were watching now.

Richard pulled up beside me, 'Your new frien' is gunna gerra thumpin'.'

It didn't happen. The boy who owned the ball said something and pointed. The ball was passed to him and the girls joined opposing teams. They looked delighted. It was strange seeing two girls dashing about tackling top junior boys. I never played.

She caught me up on the way home. I was chatting to Gary King. He seemed put out that a girl would start talking to us. When Gary slipped away, Joe asked if she could see my train set. She had asked several times for a train set at home.

'Mum says it would be a waste of money because it's just a fad. Dad thinks it's funny that I want to do boy things. Do you want to do girl things?'

'Girl things? Like what?'

'Wear girls' clothes and do skipping.'

I laughed, 'No. I've got a dressing up box. But it's all army and pirates and...'

'Oh, great. Can I see your pirate stuff?'

She was really was quite different to the other girls on the street and at school, except for Ann Banthorpe. Ann had surprised me with her interest in football.

'Yeah, come round to my house after tea.'

'Who's coming?'

'Joe, the new kid in No 41.'

'What's he like?'

'She is a girl.'

'A girl?'

'Yeah. She wants a train set. And she likes playing football.'

My Mother looked perplexed. 'She's a tom-boy then.'

Joe was delighted with my Hornby Dublo train. It had to be taken out of the box and set up. She was eager and capable. She was equally delighted with my collection of toy weapons and the dressing up box.

'Do you go on adventures?'

'Well, sort of...'

I thought of the escapades that I'd been involved in. Some were dangerous and others illegal, perhaps. None of them involved girls, well, not directly.

'Where do you go? What do you do?' She was obviously thirsting for adventure.

'We could go *over tins*.'

As she had no concept of this, I explained about climbing the corrugated-iron fence into a wilderness with trees and a stream and no adults. It was agreed that we should go there after school on Friday. It was only a few minute from our street.

Before Friday there was Thursday. Thursday was games day. On Thursday afternoon Classes 3 and 4 came together. My teacher, Miss Hilton, took the girls for netball, or rounders, on the playground. The other teacher, Mrs Taylor, did art with Class 1. Mr Hall, from Class 1, did football on the field with the boys. Most of the boys enjoyed running, shouting and getting muddy. I hated it. The very keen boys had football boots with nogs on the sole. I wore a pair of old shoes. I felt sorry for the kids who had only plimsoles.

There were some school shirts but they were reserved for the top class match players. We were allowed to wear any team shirt. I didn't have one so I wore a white tee-shirt. I ran about trying to avoid the ball.

Just as the two classes were about to get changed and start collecting equipment, I witnessed Joe talking to Mr Hall.

'Certainly not. Boys play football. Girls do netball with Miss Hilton.'

Joe tried again.

'No. Stop being silly, Go and get changed for netball.'

Mr Hall turned his back on Joe. She slunk away.

The boys scurried off towards the field. It was chilly but the sun was trying. Mr Hall wore a navy track suit and had a huge silver whistle on a yellow team band around his neck. I would be in his class next year. And I was not looking forward to it. Two hefty boys picked teams. There were about fifteen each side. The whistle blew and the melee began. Most boys hadn't a clue about the rules, but Mr Hall had and he was quite strict. The whistle blew often.

Something made me look up to the steps onto the playground. There was a figure. Mr Hall saw the figure too.

'Come on, boy, you are late. Better join this team. They need some help.'

I recognised Joe. She was wearing football kit and had proper boots. She merged quickly into the rough and tumble. I wondered how long it would take Mr Hall to notice that the kid propelling the ball towards the goal posts was not a boy. The bored goalie was Terry. He was usually the goalie because he wasn't much good at the game. Now was his big chance. Joe the Juggernaut had flattened two boys who got in the way and was about to shoot. Her foot jerked out. The ball flew. Terry ducked, but it still hit him and bounced up. It hit the cross bar and dropped neatly into the net.

The scoring side shrieked with delight.

'Badcock, you should have stopped that ball. ~ Good shot, well done, boy.'

When the triumphant Joe was patted back to the centre of the field Mr Hall peered at her through his glasses.

'I haven't seen you before, are you a new boy?'

'Yes, sir.'

I wondered if all the other boys had been duped. Miss Hilton didn't seem to have noticed either that Joe wasn't at netball.

On Friday afternoon we came out of school together.

I had been asked earlier by the class matchmakers if I had a new girlfriend.

'No, I haven't got any girlfriend.'

'What about Julia Billington?'

'She's not my girlfriend. She's a friend.'

The matchmakers were disappointed.

Joe decided that if we were to scramble over fences and jump streams she should change out of her school dress.

Climbing the high metal fence was not a problem. She was delighted with the stream. I showed her where Richard had tried to leap across and missed. We chose a narrower section to leap. I showed her the special tree that I climbed and practised leaping from at increasing heights. Joanne had to do this.

'Geronimo!'

'Hey, yo."

Two boys were nearby. I recognised them as top juniors from our school. I didn't know their names, they were from the Beeston side. I sensed danger.

'Yeah, yo' wiv the floppy 'air. What's y'name?'

I glanced at Joe. I also noticed that there was nobody else around.

'Joe.'

'What's that short for?'

'Joanne.'

'You're the gell what pushed into the footy game.'

'That's right.'

'Nah yo're dressed like a boy. What are yo'? A boy or a gell?'

'A girl.'

I tried to choose between fighting and running, but neither seemed a good idea.

'Yo' look more like a boy, don't it?'

The second boy laughed, 'I fink we oughta fin' out f'sure.'

It dawned on me what they were planning to do.

'I don't think so.'

They grinned at me in contempt. 'Get lost curly.'

'Yeah, go on, run 'ome to y'mam.'

'OK, let's 'ay a look.'

The first boy stepped towards Joanne. I tensed, ready to dive at him, and yelled, 'Run!'

She didn't. Instead she pushed her right fist hard into his face.

'Ow.' His hands went up to his nose. It was bleeding.

She kicked her foot out and scored again.

'Argh.' His hands dropped down to his groin and he folded up.

The other boy looked like he'd been zapped with *Dan Dare's* paralysing pistol.

Joanne turned her attention to him. He lifted a flat palm.

'No, we was only kiddin'. Wou'n't really do nowt, 'onest Injun.'

She eased back slowly like a cat avoiding another.

The boy looked at me, and then tried to help his damaged companion.

'Joe, let's go.'

We walked away looking at the two would-be assailants. One was still on his knees moaning.

'Wow, how did you learn to fight like that?'

Joe grinned. 'Daddy was a paratrooper in the war. He says girls ought to know how to take care of themselves.'

'Weren't you scared?'

'Yeah, a bit. Were you?'

'Yes, very.'

'But you were going to bundle into him.'

I felt myself blushing, 'Yeah, well…'

'Thanks. Let's get some sweets from Woffington's. Have you got any money?'

Fortunately I always had.

'Hey-up, Chrisser. Arh 'eard yo' gorrinto a fight wiv Ding Dong Bell.'

'Who?'

'Dougie Bell. Yo' an' your gang jumped him *over tins*. Yo' gin 'im a right duffin'.'

Richard and Terry were impersonating Cheshire cats.

'No, I didn't touch Dougie Bell. I haven't got a gang either.'

'Well Ding Dong and his mate Stevie 'ave bin telling 'ow they was attacked by a curly-headed kid an' a *load* of uvvers.'

I told them the truth about the episode. Richard burst into laughter.

'The lickle liar. He made that up, him an' Stevie, 'cos they di'n't want us to know a gell done the duffin'. Would've liked to have seen that. Is she good?'

'Joanne was trained by her father. He was a paratrooper. She stopped Dougie with just one punch.'

'Bleddy 'ell. We'd better be careful Tez, not we?'

He was not joking.

Joanne and I went on cycle rides together. We dashed about in my back garden wearing cloaks and waving wooden swords. I had tea at her house, and eventually saw the new baby. Strangely she was quite happy cuddling it, and cooing over it. It was a boy named James. I was not impressed. Joanne also made friends with Lorraine who lived across the street. Lorraine had her own make-up set, and would never associate with boys. At school Joe still played football in the yard with Ann Banthorpe, but she joined the dance club too.

Joanne was turning into a real girl, and I didn't mind.

Wall of Death

'Nah y'afto jump.'
 I couldn't move. It was a long way down.

I didn't seem to notice the extra half an hour that the juniors did. By the time we emerged at four o'clock the infants were mostly gone. The conventional way back onto the Council estate was to turn right out of the school gates, walk a few yards to the cross roads and to turn left onto Wensor Avenue. These cross roads led to everywhere that I knew. Wallet Avenue led into another Council estate. Abbey Road was the route to Beeston where the toy shops lived.

Some juniors preferred a more dangerous route. Directly opposite the school gates there was a slender gap between the last house on Boundary Road and the Welfare. The Welfare was a brick building attached to the church which dominated the cross roads. Mothers and babies visited the Welfare to get *Ostermilk*, advice and have their babies checked. The slender gap had a brick wall to one side and iron railings to the other. The danger was in the thistles and nettles that grew happily, and the terror of being caught half way. To negotiate this gap it was best to cling to the railings and work one's toes along the lower bar. There was no real advantage to going home this way: it was just scary fun.

On the other side of the Welfare there was an even more scarey obstacle. The Welfare and the Church had been built on a slope. The entrance to the Welfare was on the level. The level pathway had been created by erecting a brick retaining wall to hold back the earth on the church side. The wall was quite long and as tall as my Father. Over time the retained earth had been eroded, so that now half the length of the wall was holding back nothing.

It was a scary attraction for juniors. Gary King, *Twilmop* and I had witnessed an older junior walk the wall. It was only one brick wide. The boy held his arms wide to keep his balance. He hesitated half way and dropped the short distance onto the scrubby slope.

'I'm going to do that. Arh 'bout yo' two?'
 Twilmop grinned and shook his head. He was never one for adventure.

I didn't want to commit myself, but I was reluctant to be labelled a scaredy-cat.

'After you, Gary.'

Gary took the bait. He walked up the concrete steps where the Welfare joined the church. The dare-devil got half way, stopped, wobbled and dropped out of sight like the older boy had done. He appeared very quickly round the end of the wall wearing a silly grin.

The welfare door opened and we moved away as a mother and pram came out.

A week later the wall claimed a victim. The chatter in the playground had advertised an attempt to walk the length of the wall and jump off the end. I didn't know anyone who had actually done that. It was one thing to balance along the wall, and something else to jump off the end where the ground was six feet down. It would have been very difficult to turn at the end and walk back. Walking backwards was inconceivable.

The latest dare-devil was Edward Wragg. He was at the bottom of the 'B' stream class. He had been egged-on to make the attempt, and saw success as the way to being a 'star'. About a dozen children gathered to watch. We watched him fall off. Edward had got two thirds the way before wobbling off. Unfortunately he fell onto the hard Welfare path. The screaming brought adults from the Welfare. The juniors backed off smartly onto Wensor Avenue.

'Looks like the poor lamb has broke his leg.'

'I'll ring for an ambulance.'

The women stood around comforting the moaning Edward. I waited long enough to see him loaded into a cream coloured Morris ambulance from the Beeston depot.

Sometimes at the end of morning assembly there were special instructions about such things as going straight home after school, not bringing bags of marbles to school and not throwing stones. Today it was declared foolish and dangerous to play around the Welfare building. Mr Reeves, the head teacher, gave special attention to the folly of walking on the wall. He cited the sad case of poor Edward who would be back at school soon with his leg plastered.

For a while the Welfare wall remained free of dare-devils. Nobody seemed to want to squeeze along the narrow gap either.

I had taken to walking home with two boys who lived on my street. Neither of these two had much in common with me apart from our addresses. Terry was in the 'B 'stream. Richard was a year older than me. Richard was a dare-devil.

'Let's ay a crack at walkin' on that lickle wall.'

'Mester Reeves to'd us to keep away.'

Richard laughed and patted Terry on the head.

'D'yo' ev' see o'd Reevy rahn the Welfare?'

Terry looked blank.

'C'mon. I'll ay a go. Ah can walk it, an' jump off the end. 'Seasy.'

I knew it wasn't easy. I also knew that it was something that had to be done before we got much older. The big boys didn't play around the Welfare.

After school we approached the wall from the conventional route. There were no mothers about and the door was closed.

'OK Tez yo' g' firs'.'

Terry was taken aback.

'Nah, ah don't wanna.'

'Yo' scared, Tez?'

'Yeah.'

'Ah 'bout yo' Chrisser?'

I shrugged.

'Looks like Richo 'll 'ave to do it all by 'is sen.'

Richard strode towards the Welfare door. He turned up the concrete steps and stood for a moment at the start. He began to walk carefully. The dare-devil stopped half way. I thought he had changed his mind or realised the danger. Not so, Richard began to clown about. He waved his arms and wriggled his body. I was amazed. He didn't seem to have any fear. The clowning ceased and Richard walked to the end of the wall. He looked down at us with a triumphant grin.

He dropped off the end. His knees folded as he hit the path. His hands touched the path and he sprang up beaming.

'Great, Richard,' we chorused.

When he suggested that Terry had a go now, Terry smiled and shook his head.

'Your turn, Chrisser, eh?'

I had watched Richard do it. He made it look easy. He hadn't broken his leg.

I mounted the steps and started out along the top of the wall. This I had tried previously but got only as to where there was still retained earth to land on. I edged past this point of no return and began to regret my action. It was very narrow. One foot had to be placed carefully in front of the other. My outstretched hands began to shake.

'C'mon, Chrisser, keep goin'.'

Slowly, very slowly, the end of the wall came closer.

'Nah y'afto jump.'

I couldn't move. It was a long way down. It would be impossible to turn around or step backwards. I started to feel dizzy.

Then I saw a group of people standing behind Richard and Terry. Mr Reeves was at the front of the group.

'I told you not to play in the Welfare.'

Standing next to Mr Reeves was my Father.

'What do you think your Mother will say?'

At my Father's side was a chubby old man in a red suit.

'No presents for naughty boys, ho-ho.'

Behind him was a man with a tea-towel on his head.

'You promised me that you would be good for ever and ever.'

A cream coloured ambulance pulled up at the back of the crowd. I jumped: or rather toppled. The ground came up very quickly. My chest almost hit my knees. My fingers hurt from hitting the path.

'Yo' did, it Chrisser.'

I staggered into my companions. The crowd had disappeared. There was no ambulance. My heart was pounding. I didn't feel jubilant: I felt sick.

'Yo' termorrer, Tez.'

'Nah, Ah ain't jumpin'.'

Terry had more courage than me to refuse, and more sense. It wasn't until we got to Manton Crescent that my heart stopped pounding and my breathing returned to normal.

There was no need to play around the Welfare anymore. There were plenty of other tasks to test us. Terry would prove himself. The poor lamb, Edward Wragg, fell out of a tree on his street. He died of a brain haemorrhage in hospital, whilst still a junior. He really was a slow learner.

Warrior's Way

One of my regrets as a child was that I had missed the war. The Second World War had finished, for most, a year before I was born. There were constant reminders of it. My Father told me tales of his military service. Many workers still had oddments of military kit as lunch bags. My Father wore his demob suit. Two German artillery cartridges now served as candle holders on the mantelpiece. Every week there seemed to be another inspirational war-time yarn at the Essoldo cinema. Boys re-fought battles with toy guns or small soldiers.

It seemed inevitable that I would become a soldier at some time in the future: my Father and my Grandfather had both served. I thought that it would be noble and right to be a warrior. History was littered with warriors who either had brilliant victories or valiant deaths. I was thrilled with the story of the Greek hero Leonidas valiantly holding back the Persian invaders, until he was overwhelmed at the battle of Thermopylae.

The body of the heroic warrior was usually given a befitting funeral. Or, like Sir John Moore at La Coruña: swiftly buried but later given a poetical epitaph.

That day I was on my own: all my associates seemed not available. So I set out to test myself. Usually I climbed *over tins* with companions. There was nobody else around. Butterflies jinked over the long grass. I tested myself by jumping the stream. There were places which were easy. There were places where the water was a little wider or the opposite bank was uneven. In the past I had witnessed Richard trying to prove himself at one of these spots. A flying leap had taken him clear of the water. His feet had made contact with the opposite high bank. The bank was not stable and it crumbled with his weight.

'Argh!'

Richard flailed his arms in vain and slid down into the wet.

Another test was to jump out of a tree. Successive jumps had to be higher. It was easy at first, but the third jump required more courage and the skill of bending the knees and rolling to the side when making contact with the ground. I hesitated at the fourth jump. It was daunting, but something had caught my attention. On the other side of the stream, where the bushes grew densely, there was a spiral of blue smoke.

I climbed down quickly and negotiated the stream. My plan was to investigate from the jungle side. The keen smell was wood smoke. Moving stealthily I came close enough to see the back of a seated figure. It looked like a burly man.

Over tins was a wild place just beyond our Council housing estate. Adventurous boys played there: occasionally an adult would walk a dog. This adult had no dog, and was busying himself with a small fire.

'Orright, boy, I heard you coming.'

The game was up. It felt like I should go back to the base and count aloud to a hundred. He didn't turn his head.'

'I saw you climbing the tree. Would you have something to eat with you?'

I wondered if he was one of those 'funny men' that my Mother had warned me against. I could simply slip away.

'Won't do you no harm, boy.'

I stood still.

'I'm brewing some tea, but unfortunately I ain't got no milk, or sugar…or tea.'

He laughed and turned sideways. Now I could see three twigs holding a tin can over a fire. He could see me and I could see him. He was an old man with straggly white hair below a bald head. Straggly white hair covered his cheeks and chin. Although it was a warm day, he was wearing a grubby top coat. It was open and revealing more layers beneath. He made a fist and held it to his eye like a telescope. I had seen my Mother do this to read small print.

'Are you a tramp?'

He snorted and tipped his head back.

'No, Sirrah, I am not. I… am a gentleman of the road.'

I took a few steps closer. He was really old: older than my Grandfather. His face was lined and marked. He wasn't burly. The extra clothes made him seem so. Everything he wore was ripped, scuffed and grubby. I paid special attention to his shoes. Tramps in comics always wore shoes with the soles flapping loose. His shoes were worn and shapeless with string replacing the laces.

'I can get you some tea.'

'And a bite of something, perhaps. A crust would do.'

This was a good excuse to depart.

'Yes, I'll come back soon. Will you still be here?'

He snorted again.

'I ain't rushing away, nowhere to go.'

There was always food in the house. I was sure that I could gather it without my Mother being involved.

I spooned some loose tea from the caddy into a redundant paper bag. I put it into my sandwich box along with two slices from the Wonderloaf, a small piece of cheese and an apple from the fruit bowl in the living room. It didn't look much so I added four biscuits from the biscuit tin. After a moment's deliberation, I took some dried fruits from the storage jars kept in the cupboard next to the fireplace. The dried fruits were for making Christmas cakes.

All this took only a few minutes. My mother was probably out shopping. I galloped off down the Close.

'Hey-up, where yo' off to in a tearin' 'urry?'

Richard and Terry were hanging around the lamp post at the beginning of the Close.

I wasn't too keen to tell them, but the desire to show off got the better of me.

'I'm taking some food to a poor old man.'

'Oo-er, Saint Chrisser. Who's that then?'

'He's a tramp. I found him *over tins*.'

I told them about the billy-can brew.

'What! Yo' talkin' to detty o'd men? Yo' want yer 'ead testin'.'

'He's just an old man down on his luck.'

'How'd yo' kno' he's not on the run, or an escaped maniac?'

'He looks scruffy, but he seems alright.'

'Right, we'll come wiv yo' an' mek sure it's OK, not we, Tez?'

'Argh.'

I wasn't too sure about returning with a gang. It might upset the tramp.

'You two wait here for a minute. You come when I whistle.'

He was still sitting there facing towards the stream. The little fire was still smouldering.

'Good lad.'

He was quickly examining the contents of the lunch box. The dried fruit disappeared swiftly. A small quantity of tea was dropped into the billy-can and a few more twigs were added to the fire. I explained about my friends. He nodded as he chewed. I whistle and watched Richard and Terry cross the stream.

'In here,' I called from the cover of the bushes.

Terry stood gawping, but Richard's eyes flicked about taking in everything. Now I noticed the bed-roll and kit-bag.

I introduced my chums and also myself. Richard prompted the tramp to give his name.

'James. Mr James to you. Once it was Corporal James.'

'Were yo' a sojer, then?'

'A long time ago.'

The billy-can started to steam. Mr James reached out to lift it from the fire and carefully decanted the brown liquid into a white enamel camping mug. He took a sip.

'Were you in the last war?'

'No. Too old for that. Too old for the Great War. I fought at Omdurman back in '98.'

He could see that we were puzzled.'

'Not heard of Omdurman? It's in the Sudan, in North Africa. There was a big battle there in 1898. We were fighting the Fuzzies.'

He took another sip of tea and started on a biscuit. The biscuit was eaten very carefully.

I was desperately trying to do the arithmetic. He must have been grown up to be in the army in 1898. So, if he was telling the truth, he must be very old.

'Did yo' kill any…Fuzzies?'

Mr James looked hard at Terry for a full minute.

'Oh, yes. I knocked a few of them down. It was them or us.'

'Were yo' scared?'

He took another sip of tea and screwed up his eyes as if trying hard to remember.

'Yeah, I was scared orright… before and after. There was no time to be scared when the fight was on.'

Terry seemed delighted with this tale. Richard was wearing a look of slight disbelief. To me it sounded like a story.

Mr James put his mug down and reached into his coat pocket. He pulled out a grubby handkerchief. It was opened to reveal a medal complete with ribbon.

'This one I kept. I lost most everything else. But I hung onto this. I'd made corporal in the Royal Warwickshire Regiment at just twenty one.'

He sipped more tea.

'I don't suppose you lads have got any smokes about you?'

I hadn't, but it didn't surprise me that Richard had a crumpled packet in jacket pocket.

Mr James' eyes lit up. A slightly bent cigarette was lit up.

'Ah, that's good. First I've had in a long while. Thank you…Richard.'

Richard beamed and claimed payment.

'What's your f'st name?'

The old man seemed to think for a while, 'Gerald.'

'Why are yo' a tramp?'

'Things don't always work out. I was married… twice. Both died. I had a job, several. Tried living with my sister, but that didn't work out. So I moved about. I drifted.'

'What yo' doin' 'ere?'

He sighed, 'Got to be somewhere.'

'We can bring you some more things tomorrow: if you are still here.'

'Yes, that would be nice. I'll still be here.'

'I'll get some more fags.'

'Where yo' gonna sleep, Mester?'

He patted the bed roll.

'Under the stars.'

On the way home Terry said that he wanted to be a tramp when he grew up. Richard said that he would be well suited. I suggested that we met at ten o'clock by the lamp. Nothing was said to my Parents about the tramp. My Mother would be horrified and my Father would be compelled 'to do something.' I did ask my Father about the Battle of Omdurman. He knew about General Gordon, the Mad Mahdi, General Kitchener, Young Winston Churchill and our lads standing up to thousands of blood thirsty Dervishes. It all seemed very exciting. Our lads must have been heroes. Corporal Gerald James must have been a hero too. He had the medal.

We met at the appointed time. Richard had a brand new packet of cigarettes which he most likely had liberated from one of his parents. Terry had smuggled out half a loaf and some sweets. I had filled my lunch box with a variety of foods.

'Are us gonna tek 'im stuff every day?'

'Don't fink so, Tez, tramps move abaht.'

'He might well have gone.'

We crossed the field towards the stream. There was no spiral of wood smoke. When we pushed through the bushes the place seemed deserted.

'He's gone.'

'Nah, 'e's still asleep, look.'

There was a bulky shape covered with a blanket.

'Mester James.'

'Wake up, Gerald. It's us.'

'Mester James.'

Nothing moved. We moved closer.

Richard stooped and lifted the edge of the blanket. The man still did not move. His eyes were closed and his faced was drained of colour. Richard shook Mr James, 'Wake up.'

We stood looking down for a minute.

'Arh fink 'e's dead.'

Terry gasped and stepped back.

'You sure, Richard?'

Richard stretched his hand out again and touched the pallid face.

'Urgh, 'e's co'd. He ain't movin' or brevin'. An' 'e looks dead white. He's dead.'

Terry squeaked. I stood and stared. I'd never seen a real live dead body before.

'He was a really old man. I worked it out, he was twenty one in 1898, so he was born in 1877. That would make him seventy nine.'

'Arh'll g'frough 'is pockets.'

'No. Richard. Respect the dead. He was a warrior, a hero.'

'Yeah, right. Arh woz only looking for owt that would tell uz abaht 'im...'

'We should tell some'dy.'

'Like who?'

Terry shrugged, 'Am'blance? Cops? A grown-up?'

Richard pulled a face, 'Yo' just' said 'e woz a warrior, a nero, Chrisser. We could gi'im a nero's send off.'

'What do you mean?'

'We could gi'im a nero's send-off like they do on the pictures.'

He looked expectantly at Terry and me.

'Y'know, like in that Viking film last week: the 'ero gets burned on a bomfire.'

Richard had had some weird ideas, but this was absurd.

'We can't just put him on a bonfire.'

'Why not? 'E ain't got no fam'ly.'
'What about his sister?'
'We don't know 'er name or where she lives or if she's still alive.'
'We can't just have a bonfire here. Somebody will see it.'
'That not matter cos it can be done quick.'
Again he was ahead of us.
'We put the body on a pile of wood, see. Then we slosh some petrol on… And woof.'
'I think we should tell the police. What do you think Terry?'
'Arh like bomb-fires.'
'See, Chrisser, Tez is in. We would be hon'ring an o'd sojer.'
This was painful. I knew what the sensible course should be. I was also intrigued with a noble gesture for a war hero.

We set to collecting anything that might burn. The best find was some disintegrating and abandoned wooden fencing. There was more usable stuff where people had dumped items over the tin wall. Luckily the weather had kept things dry.
'What about the petrol?'
Richard grinned, 'I'll get some t'night. Out of Pretty's wagon. I know 'ow to syphon.'
Mr Pretty parked his Bedford truck in the service alley behind the shop. Of course it would be stealing, but it was in a good cause. I declined to assist. Terry was more than happy to help.

I lay in bed unable to sleep worrying about what could go wrong and what the consequences would be. I thought about poor old Mr James lying out there in the dark. My dream was filled with flaming corpses rising up and chasing after me.

Richard had a can of petrol in a shopping bag. Terry had a bag of newspapers and a bunch of flowers. I had my doubts.
The corpse was where it was. I was willing him to stir, but he didn't.
'It's too near the bushes. They'll catch fire."
'OK, let's tek him furver back aht the bushes.'
Richard lifted the blanket. We took hold of the cloth he was lying on. After a few moments of tugging we realised that he was too heavy to move.
'We'll jus' have do it 'ere. Bring the stuff nex' t'im. We'll roll 'im onto it.'

We placed the bits of broken fence, fallen branches and other scraps alongside the body. Terry screwed up the newspapers and we inserted them in the funeral pyre. With some great effort we managed to heave the body into place. We covered the corpse with the ground sheet.

'What abaht the meggle?'

I didn't object this time to Richard dipping into Mr James' pockets. He fished out the medal, a few coins, a penknife and a wallet. The wallet contained nothing revealing, only a crumpled and faded photograph of a woman. There was nothing written on the reverse. Richard pocketed the coins and the knife. The wallet was returned to a pocket. The medal was placed on his chest. The kit bag contained nothing of any consequence.

Terry carefully placed the flowers on Mr James' chest too.

'Should we say something?'

'S'pose so. You say summat, Chrisser.'

'I don't know what to say.'

I was feeling numb and could barely breathe properly.

'Righto, let's gerron wiv it. Ay the matches, Tez, yo' like bomb-fires.'

'Attention!'

We stood tall and saluted the passing of a hero.

'Woof.'

It came from behind, 'Woof, woof, woof.'

A black and white Border Collie had us in its sights.

'Bob, Bob what have you found?'

The dog was joined by a man who appeared through the bushes. It was pointless running away: the dog would have easily rounded us up. Bob had moved over to Mr James and was sniffing his corpse. The man took in the scene.

'What's going on here, then?'

I was so relieved that the funeral had been halted, but my heart sank at the thought of all the explanation. Luckily Richard was adept at slipping out of sticky situations.

'We fink 'es dead, Mester. Could of died in the night. He's an o'd tramp we met yesterday. We brought 'im some stuff t'eat. He was alright yesterday, wa'n't 'e Chrisser?'

'Yes, his name is Mr James. He is very old: seventy nine. He was a war hero. He's got a medal.'

'You sure he's dead?'

The man stooped down and touched Mr James face.

'He's dead alright. The authorities need alerting. You wait here while I go to the phone box on the Boulevard. Don't touch anything.'

He turned and went back over the stream taking Bob with him.

'I'd best get rid on this.' Richard swiftly took the can of petrol away from the vicinity and parked it behind a tree. Terry did likewise with the bunch of flowers. We waited in trepidation for the authorities to turn up.

The man and his dog returned leading two constables. Not far behind them were a couple of ambulance men with a stretcher. The corpse was examined by a policeman and one of the ambulance men. We were questioned by the other policeman who took our names and addresses. Terry looked suicidal: he feared another visit by the law. Richard gabbled away about the poor old soldier. I just wanted it to end.

'Why's he lying on the pile of tat?'

'Mester James to'd us he was gonna build a shelter. 'E mustov c'lected all the stuff.'

The policeman held the medal close to his face and turned it slowly.

'Cpl Gerald James Royal Warwicks Regiment Omdurman 1898. It's his, or he nicked it.'

'Looks like he had a heart attack. He was old and not well cared for.'

'OK, take him away.'

The policemen had searched his pockets and found only the wallet. We had to recount the whole story for their notes.

'Well, off you go and tell your parents all about it.'

The warrior was lifted onto a stretcher and carried over the field to the waiting ambulance.

'Bleddy 'ell, 'ope the rozzers don't come knockin'. Don't matter we di'n't do nuffin', we'll still gerrit in the neck.'

'What are you going to do with the petrol?'

'Shove it back in o'd Pretty's wagon Arh s'pose. No good to us nah.'

Richard was wrong. A policeman did visit three households. I had prepared my Parents with most of the story. It was really just a courtesy call to let us know that no relatives could be traced and that Mr James would be buried in a pauper's grave. We were thanked for attempting to sustain him, but advised against talking to strangers.

'What happened to the medal?'

'It's been sent to the Regimental Museum.'

…That was disappointing.

Michael Terence
Publishing

www.mtp.agency

mtp.agency

@mtp_agency

Milton Keynes UK
Ingram Content Group UK Ltd.
UKHW031954281024
450365UK00009B/555